The Colonel

AND THE

Enchantress

THE ENCHANTRESSES BOOK FOUR

PAULLETT GOLDEN

Also by Paullett Golden

*This book is dedicated to all our service men
and women and their families, all of whom
fight battles even when the war ends.*

Praise for The Enchantresses

"The author adds a few extra ingredients to the romantic formula, with pleasing results. An engaging and unconventional love story."

— Kirkus Reviews

"The well-written prose is a delight, the author's voice compelling readers and drawing them into the story with an endearing, captivating plot and genuine, authentic settings. From the uncompromising social conventions of the era to the permissible attitudes and behaviors within each class, it's a first-class journey back in time."

— Reader Views

"[The Enchantresses] by Paullett Golden easily ranks as one of the best historical romances I have read in some time and I highly recommend it to fans of romance, history, and the regency era. Fabulous reading!"

—Sheri Hoyt *of Reader Views*

"It is an extremely well written novel with some sub-plots that add to the already intense main plot. The author Paullett Golden has a gift for creating memorable characters that have depth."

— Paige Lovitt of *Reader Views*

"What I loved about the author was her knowledge of the era! Her descriptions are fresh and rich. Her writing is strong and emotionally driven. An author to follow."

— *The Forfeit* author Shannon Gallagher

"Readers who enjoy a character driven romance will find this a story well worth reading. Paullett Golden is an author I will be following."

— *Roses R Blue Reviews*

"I would say this is a very well-written novel with engaging characters, a compelling story, a satisfactory resolution, and I am eagerly anticipating more from Ms. Golden."

— *Davis Editorials*

"With complex characters and a backstory with amazing depth, the story … is fantastic from start to finish."

— *Rebirth* author Ravin Tija Maurice

"Paullett Golden specializes in creating charmingly flawed characters and she did not disappoint in this latest enchantress novel."

— *Dream Come Review*

"...a modern sensibility about the theme of self-realization, and a fresh take on romance make the foundation of Golden's latest Georgian-era romance."

— *The Prairies Book Review*

"The novel is everything you could ever want from a story in this genre while also providing surprising and gratifying thematic depth."

— *Author Esquire*

"I thoroughly enjoyed meeting and getting to know all of the characters. Each character was fully developed, robust and very relatable."

— *Flippin' Pages Book Reviews*

"It is a story that just keeps giving and giving to the reader and I, for one, found it enchanting!"

— *The Genre Minx Book Reviews*

Newly Revised Edition

This book is a clean historical romance. There are references to kissing and innuendos to intimacy, but this is a closed-door romance.

The Colonel and The Enchantress was originally published in 2020 as a steamy historical romance but has been fully revised in this new edition as a clean read.

While the original version is still available in audiobook format and by request to the author, all digital and print versions available for purchase have been replaced by this new, clean edition.

If you enjoy reading this book and wish to share it with friends and family, refer with confidence that the version they purchase will be the clean edition. If in doubt, ensure this revision note appears before Chapter 1. I hope you'll enjoy reading the new edition, as this edit has been a labor of love and one I'm proud to share with all readers!

THE ENCHANTRESS FAMILY TREE

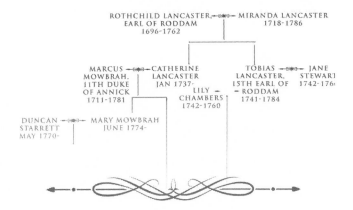

ROTHCHILD LANCASTER, ━━●━━ MIRANDA LANCASTER
EARL OF RODDAM 1718-1786
1696-1762

MARCUS ━━●━━ CATHERINE
MOWBRAH, LANCASTER
11TH DUKE JAN 1737-
OF ANNICK
1711-1781

LILY ━
CHAMBERS
1742-1760

TOBIAS ━━●━━ JANE
LANCASTER, STEWART
15TH EARL OF 1742-176·
━ RODDAM
1741-1784

DUNCAN ━━●━━ MARY MOWBRAH
STARRETT JUNE 1774-
MAY 1770-

Visit www.paullettgolden.com/the-enchantresses
to view the complete Enchantress Family Tree

Prologue

August 1790
Five years earlier

S tretching out his legs, Duncan Starrett lay across the picnic blanket, his forearm sinking into the dewy grass beneath. His eyes met those of his love's — wide, walnut brown, framed with black lashes against alabaster skin. For nearly a year he had loved her, yet one look still made his pulse race.

"I want to come with you," she said, brushing soft fingers against his cheek.

"I'll return before you notice I've gone; a decorated hero worthy of your hand."

She pleaded with her eyes.

"The battlefield is no place for you, Mary. How could I fight for Crown and country when worrying about your safety? Not that your family would ever consent for you to follow the drum."

"Oh, Duncan, let's elope! It would be so romantic." Wistful, Lady Mary clasped her hands, looked to the heavens, and fell back against the blanket with a sigh of youthful innocence.

Tree branches danced shadows on her features. His heartbeat quickened as he leaned over her, tracing her lips with his fingertips. Leaving her behind would be the most difficult task of his life. His Mary. His love.

"Dream of my return," he said. "We'll attend the best parties, dance until our feet blister, and ride into the sunset on our fastest horses. Once I return, I'll ask permission for your hand."

She combed her fingers through his hair, sending shivers from scalp to toes. Pulling him to her, she kissed him, a gentle pout pursed to his.

"We've lingered too long," he murmured, lost in the depths of her eyes. "Return home before they notice your absence."

1791

As an ensign in the Light Dragoons, Duncan saw more ballrooms than battlefields, easy to do when there were no battles. He craved the clash of swords and thunder of guns. After a childhood filled with his father's romantic war stories, Duncan longed to experience the scenes for himself: traversing impossible hills, meeting the enemy with sword drawn, wading through rivers, sleeping beneath the stars. In the quiet of the night, he brandished his sabre at the darkness, practicing his moves, striking a dashing pose.

1792

Lieutenant Starrett had yet to see war. Was this his route to heroism? Was he fated to return home an officer who had never drawn his sword?

Days turned to weeks, weeks to months, months to years.

The French were at war with themselves, launching a revolution against their monarchy. The British Army remained idle, waiting. Waiting for what? An opportune moment to fight? Duncan wanted to fight now. For too long he had waited for action. He recalled the promises made when his father purchased his first commission—the Crown would take advantage of France's weakness. When was this grand conquest, the coup to overthrow France? His blade was sharp, his gun was clean, and he was ready.

July 1793

Captain Starrett ached with desperation to prove himself.

And then, he found war. Or rather, war found him.

The daring! The glory! The action exhilarated him.

He roared into battle, a fierce foe, heart in his throat, body tingling with excitement tinged with fear. He fought for his life, for his country, for his father, for Mary. In this moment, he was *man*—raw power, passionate and invigorated, victory red.

He thought himself debonair, a real hero.

With the elation of battle pulsing through his veins, he wrote to Mary. He could not very well return after wielding his sword only once. He wanted more — thirsted, hungered for more. What was another couple of years after the three he spent waiting? It was not as though he would never return.

April 1794

Major Starrett dabbed the tender skin of his stomach with a wet cloth. The blade had come too close for comfort. Only now did he realize how close, as it had sliced through his waistcoat and grazed his skin. The more superficial, the more troubling. He winced with each stroke of the cloth.

However safe at camp he was, the apprehension of more bloodshed buzzed in his ears. The morning would see the fighting renewed. His limbs were clammy from the cold sweat all too familiar both post- and pre-battle. Tonight, he would dream of holding Mary, inhaling the aroma of her lavender-scented hair, savoring the feel of her velvet skin.

June 1794

He trudged with throbbing feet, overwrought muscles, and pounding head, disillusioned by war. Lost were his dreams in a sea of red, bathed in the glow of regimental coats mingled with blood. This was not heroic. This was not glamorous. This was a horror show of vacant stares and flashing steel. He was Charon, ferrying sons from their mothers and husbands from their wives. No longer did he crave the battlefield with its death and guilt.

And yet he still craved the valor, the camaraderie, the rhythm of the drums, the scent of victory, the sounds of gallantry.

August 1794

Atop his stallion Caesar, Lieutenant Colonel Starrett of the Light Dragoons led his men into battle. British, Dutch, and Austrian troops launched against the French, a proper invasion of a weakened and ruler-less country. With sabre at the ready, he leaned forward and squeezed his calves to the hot horseflesh, signaling his mount to charge. The formation was tight, mere inches between cavalry riders. A roar of power erupted as they broke through infantry lines, slashing an opening for the foot regiments.

There was no greater feeling than a horse beneath him, an inseverable bond between beast and man. Only his legs and weight signaled his horse's movements, for his hands wielded weapons of war rather than reins. His horse was an extension of himself.

Boxtel was a fierce and bloody battle, but Duncan was untouchable atop his stallion.

January 1795

Colonel Starrett shivered. More men had died from exposure than battle; a harsher winter they had not seen. With white clouds for breath, they prepared to defend the frozen waters of the Lower Rhine. The horses pawed the iced earth, ready. He stroked Caesar's neck, his hand trembling.

The enemy lined the opposite bank, muskets aimed, bayonets fixed.

Ignoring the smell of fear in the air, Duncan signaled his regiment with his sabre.

Time slowed. Seconds stretched to infinity between spur and charge. Duncan's attention funneled. He knew only the hoofbeats of his horse, the song of bullets, and his steady breath.

The cavalry hoofed alongside their field commander, an impenetrable wall of horse muscle and blades.

Convinced the Holy Spirit was on their side, the enemy marched across the frozen water.

Steel clanged and men cried as the dragoons broke the line at the riverbank.

A moment of victory before it all went wrong.

Another line crossed the river, muskets aimed, bayonets fixed. Another line behind them. And another. His regiment, decimated by the cold, chattered their teeth along the river's edge as they watched the endless onslaught of Frenchmen.

Retreat! The cry echoed through the ranks, the survivors running or fighting their way back to safety.

Duncan, one hand wielding his sabre, the other holstering his Elliot pattern pistol, nudged Caesar to about-face. Without further encouragement, the horse turned and retreated, the whole of the allied troops doing likewise.

His one thought: get the men to safety.

A slap to his lower back broke his focus. He looked to either side, expecting to see one of his men. Leaning forward to quicken the pace away from the river, he felt a tightening pressure along his spine, warming as it twisted, a fire poker sinking into his flesh then tugging.

The scorch spread, hot and wet.

As he straightened, slowing his mount, he felt winded, the air knocked out of his lungs. He panicked, struggling to breathe.

Before him, arms outstretched, hovered an ethereal Mary. His Mary. His ladylove. Even as he reached out to her, his head swam in a dizzying vortex. Their fingers touched as he slumped against Caesar's neck.

Chapter 1

August 1795

T he hedgerow in sight, Lady Mary Mowbrah lengthened her arms and loosened the reins. With a light seat and a forward lean, she urged Athena into a gallop.

The mare and rider rode as one, each an extension of the other. Their eyes focused beyond the hurdle. Their bodies relaxed, anticipating the pleasure of the jump. Athena vaulted into the air, hoofs soaring, and cleared the hedgerow. Gracefully, she landed on the other side before slowing to a canter.

Patting her mare's neck, Mary righted herself in the saddle, a laugh on her lips. There was no greater pleasure than a morning with Athena. They'd been together since Mary's seventeenth birthday four years ago, the horse a gift from her brother, the twelfth Duke of Annick.

For the return ride home to Lyonn Manor, Mary slowed to a trot, enjoying the weather, time to herself, and time with the thoroughbred.

Tomorrow, they might ride as far as the lake. It was Athena's favorite destination, but Mary found it difficult to avoid the assault of memories, what ifs, and could have beens each visit to the lake brought.

How could she be expected to go there without thinking of *him*? Ever since their first accidental meeting at the lake, the two had arranged trysts under the willow.

It would be five years this month since his father purchased his commission. Although he had written every few months during that time, she had not heard a word from him since before Christmas. Ten months? Perhaps not that long. It seemed a lifetime. She dared not question what his silence meant. Only on the fringes of her mind did she entertain the possibilities, never consciously. She could not, would not, think of that foreboding silence.

Two grooms waited for her in the stable yard. Slipping her gloved hand into a groom's proffered hand, she dismounted. It took little time for them to lead Athena into her stall and remove the sidesaddle.

For the next quarter hour, the grooms busied themselves elsewhere in the stables. Mary lingered at leisure. She took pleasure in rubbing down her horse. It was part of their time together, however unusual it might be for a duke's daughter to brush and cool her own horse.

With a final nuzzle to Athena's neck, the horse nickering gutturally in response, Mary headed to the house.

The butler awaited her approach. Not far behind him, a footman readied to relieve her of hat and gloves.

"Are they in the drawing room?" Mary enquired to the butler.

"Yes, m'lady," Mr. Hunter said. "Your brother wishes to have a word."

"Does he? About my nephew's latest accomplishment, no doubt. Tell him I'll see him at dinner." She turned to the stairs. "I desire a bath."

"Yes, m'lady." He bowed, giving no outward signs of surprise to her avoidance of the drawing room or her brother.

It was not that she was avoiding her family as much as that she wanted time to herself, especially after the unbidden thoughts of Duncan — thoughts she had tried not to think except for in the most guarded of moments. She would venture downstairs after a long, hot bath, a letter to her dear friend Arabella, and a nap.

Or so she thought. No sooner did she reach the top of the stairs than her brother caught up to her.

"Not so quick," Drake said. "This is one missive you won't want to miss."

He took the steps two at a time, brandishing a bit of parchment.

Turning, a hand on the railing, Mary quipped, "For your sake, I hope this is brief. I smell of horse and am eager to retire to my room."

Instead of answering, he leaned in and sniffed, his blue eyes twinkling with mischief. "To me, you don't smell any differently than normal."

She swatted his arm, then grinned. "Let me guess. Theo composed in perfect penmanship a treatise on the importance of play over studies?"

Drake knew she adored her nephew, and so he apprised her daily of two-year-old Theo's achievements. Although, given how much time she spent in the nursery, she was just as often the one sharing news.

"Not today." He laughed, flourishing the paper with a flick of his wrist. "This, little sister, is an invitation."

She waited, foot tapping, eyebrows raised.

"An invitation to take tea tomorrow with Colonel Sean Starrett and his family." He waggled his eyebrows.

The blood drained from her face.

She shivered, chilled to her toes.

However jovial her brother acted, she could not think of a rational reason for such an invitation. In all the years Duncan had been away, his father had not once issued an invitation. Her brother may have indulged Mary's childish infatuation with their neighbor, but the truth was that she was a duke's daughter, and Duncan was only the son of a colonel. Though blue blood ran through Starrett veins, the colonel was a youngest son, as was Duncan. The families did not share a close friendship.

Ten months without a word from Duncan, and now his father was inviting them for tea. Mary closed her eyes to fight a wave of nausea.

Swallowing, she asked, "Whatever for?"

She gripped the banister for strength. The thought of the colonel telling them over tea and biscuits what had become of his son was too much for her. Let Drake go alone and bring her the news in private.

Drake's expression sobered. "I'm a horse's arse for teasing, Mary. I should have approached this differently. Let me start again. He's *alive*, the letter says. Alive and home."

Mary pressed a fist to her mouth, stifling a sob.

"The colonel warns that his son is still recovering from an injury, but he is well and desires our company."

"An injury? What sort of injury? Why did he not write the invitation himself? How long has he been home? Why did he not write to say he was coming home?" Her ten months of fretting coupled with five years of waiting flooded her with emotion. She hungered for knowledge. *Oh, Duncan!*

Drake grasped her upper arm. "He's home. That's what matters."

Nodding, she squeezed shut wet eyes, reaching blindly for her brother's coat. Without hesitation, he pulled her into a reassuring embrace.

When he released her, his face returned to the jovial man she was accustomed to seeing.

"Now," he said, "shall I accept the invitation or tell the colonel you decided you'd rather accept one of the marriages Mother arranged?"

"Oh! Oh, you!" She could not help herself. She laughed. Even while rubbing the heel of her hand across her wet cheek, she laughed.

For the rest of the day, all she could think of was Duncan. He was alive. And he was home.

Colonel Duncan Starrett leaned against the hearth mantel, an arm propped against the marble, his chin resting against his fist. At any moment she would arrive. They would have half an hour in front of a curious audience to rekindle the six-year-old love affair that had kept him alive during his darkest moments of the Flanders Campaign.

He winced as his foot spasmed.

It would be the longest and shortest of half hours. He wanted an eternity with her, not thirty minutes. He wanted to pull her into his arms and tell her how much he had missed her and thought of her every second of every day. And yet he was unsure if he could sustain a smile for such a length of time. Already, exhaustion wore him thin.

Would she find him much changed? Though they had written throughout their time apart, did she still care for him?

He would not admit it when at war, but he had feared to read each letter, worried it would contain her admission that her mother was right—she must marry someone of her station. Part of that fear stemmed from the relief he worried he would feel. How wretched it was to think he would find relief in her marrying someone else. Duncan could not bear to lose her, but keeping her meant giving up his career or, worse, weighing her down with an invalid of a husband.

Running his fingers through his hair, he pounded a fist against his thigh, trying to stop the persistent spasm that worked from his spine through his thigh and down to his foot.

Eyes trained on the parlor door, he imagined how she would appear walking into the room. Vivacious. Bright eyed. Full of energy and life. She had only been sixteen when he last saw her. She was now one and twenty. Would he find her much changed? His heart thudded an anxious rhythm.

His father, Colonel Sean Starrett, stepped into the room, all five foot nothing of him, with his white hair, bushy brows, limp, and smile.

"Well, my boy, are you ready to win her heart anew?" his father asked, ambling to a chair by the hearth.

"This was your idea, not mine," Duncan mumbled.

With a hearty laugh, his father said, "Shall I send a footman to intercept His Grace and tell them to turn around?"

Duncan grunted and pushed himself from the mantel, his destination the chair. When his father made a quick move to stand and help him, Duncan shooed him, impatient. He was determined not to appear helpless or doddering in front of her. With slow and determined steps, he made it to the chair, only a slight stabbing pain from back to heel. He dared not sit. Once seated, he would need help rising, and that would not do for when she walked into the room. No, when she walked in, he would be on his feet. A man.

Posing in front of the chair, ready, hoping the wait would not be long, he said, "This is foolhardy. You should have written that I no longer wish to see her."

"And listen to my broken-hearted son sob over his breakfast every morning to have lost the love of his life?"

Duncan cast him a steely glare.

There was little in this world that would make him happier than seeing her again. But how did a war hardened soldier admit he feared the reunion?

Smoothing a hand over his slate blue coat, he tugged at the embroidered hem. How long it had been since he wore something other than his uniform he could not say. The clothes, newly tailored, fit to perfection, and yet they felt foreign.

He clasped his hands behind his back. Then unclasped and clasped again in the front. Releasing his hands, he hung them at his sides, rounding back his shoulders.

"Stop fidgeting, son," his father said.

The door opened, racing Duncan's pulse, but it was only his brother Quinn and his mother Georgina, ready to join for tea. They, too, were all smiles. In fact, Duncan was the only one not smiling. He gave his lips a twitch to see if he remembered how. It had been a long time indeed.

A footman stepped into the parlor before his mother had taken her seat. "The ducal coach has arrived."

Chapter 2

L ady Mary stepped out of her brother's carriage and took his arm. Though she had not been to Cois Greta Park in nearly five years, she did not look about her to see if aught had changed. Her eyes remained trained on the butler awaiting them at the front door.

She was not nervous.

She was petrified.

Stiff limbs moved her forward, her hand tense on Drake's sleeve. She summoned courage to face whatever awaited on the other side of the front door. Five years was an awfully long time.

Her heart in her throat and her chin held high, she followed the butler into the vestibule and down a short hall. Only vaguely was she aware of digging her nails into her brother's arm. When they reached the first door, the butler hesitated long enough for Mary to suck in a breath and brace herself.

"His Grace the Duke of Annick, and the Lady Mary Mowbrah," the butler announced, stepping aside for them to enter the parlor.

Bows and a curtsy greeted them. A flurry of activity occurred around her as people moved and talked, but she stayed rooted. She searched the faces, her breath short, her pulse racing.

And there he was.

Duncan in the flesh.

His lips curved into a smile as he stared back at her. Five years faded in that single glance. Her stomach fluttered to see the all too familiar smile, punctuated by the sensual cleft in his chin. For a moment that stretched into eternity, the two eyed each other, all else fading away with the lost years.

In a less than discreet sweep of her eyes, she took in his physique. Broad shoulders, wide chest, tapered waist, and masterful thighs replaced the boyish slenderness she recalled. Her fingers itched to touch him. Was he still ticklish around the soft sides of his stomach? His coffee brown hair was closely cropped, his cheeks smoothly shaven, his eyes alight with wonder. By some miracle, neither of them rushed forward to embrace each other, though her arms longed to wrap around his neck.

"Mary… Mary…" A voice repeated her name, but she could not make out whose or from where. "Mary, do be seated."

As though spoken from a distance, the voice of her brother interrupted her admiring. Turning, she realized Drake stood at her side, indicating a chair.

Reality intruded, abrupt and rude.

With a glance to the others in the room, she gave an acknowledging nod and sat on a comfortable cream-colored chair. The connection between her and Duncan may have been disrupted, but she was ever aware of his presence.

Before anyone could speak, the butler returned with a steady stream of footmen carrying various dishes and arranging them around the sizable table nestled in the center of the circle of chairs. There were enough plates of sweets and savories to keep them nibbling all afternoon. Mrs. Starrett served the tea as everyone chatted. Neither she nor Duncan spoke, though their eyes flitted to each other between the passing of tea saucers.

The more she glanced at him, the more she noticed little differences from the man she knew. How had she not seen them instantly?

His gentleman's complexion was now tanned with a tautness to his forehead. Shadows haunted the underside of his eyes. His nose, that once straight nose, was slightly crooked, as though it had been broken and poorly set. He looked older, more than what five years should have aged him. She had known him at first sight, and yet studying him, she hardly knew him at all, and what a curious thought that was.

Her observations did not diminish her attraction to him. On the contrary, they enhanced her physical awareness of him. The bridge of his nose added an aura of danger and mystique his youthful wholesomeness had not afforded. The width of his chest was at once formidable yet tantalizing. Mary's memory of his lithe softness was in stark contrast to the muscular soldier before her, and it made him all the more dashing.

"So you'll know now he's a colonel, like his dadaí," his father was saying when Mary made an effort to listen.

She looked up, startled. "A colonel?" A quick glance to her brother provoked a wink.

Duncan set down his teacup and saucer with a gentle but commanding motion. "I advanced in

December. Unlike my father, who bore his rank for
years, I only held it a handful of weeks before returning to England."

His voice was much like his movements, gentle
but commanding. The timbre had changed from the
voice of her memory. Somber now, less lighthearted.
But then, he had only spoken briefly.

So distracted by him, it took long moments for
his words to sink in. Had he returned to England so
long ago? And without a word to her?

Addressing Duncan, his father said, "But no less
noble, son."

"I don't doubt the confusion ahead of us." Duncan
squeezed his thigh, rubbing a hand against his
breeches. "Every social we attend will be the same."
In a high-pitched voice, he said, "'Allow me to intro-
duce Colonel Starrett. Oh, yes, and this is Colonel
Starrett, as well.' Then the conversation to follow.
'Colonel. Colonel. Yes, good to meet you Colonel and
Colonel.'" His smile widened as he joked.

Mary laughed along with the others. Duncan's
jests notably lightened the tension.

"I have devious plans to use this to my advantage.
Imagine attending a soiree uninvited only for the rumor
to get out that Colonel Starrett was at fault. All will
immediately think of my father rather than me." Duncan's good humor continued to set everyone at ease.

Before Mary could interject, the elder Colonel
Starrett, Duncan's father, turned to Drake.

"I hear you've a wee one now, but no thought
of the Starretts, eh? Not brought him around for us
to see, never mind you spent your youth here more
than home."

Drake chuckled. "I've been a neglectful neighbor, have I? I would blame my travels, for we've been out and about for concerts since I debuted my latest composition, but the truth is I'm a rotten neighbor. Theodore's his name, Marquess of Sutton. He's the most serious two-year-old you've ever met."

Mrs. Starrett chimed in, "Count yourself lucky. Though seven is no easy number, all my children tried to turn me an early grey. Into this and into that. Now I sit back and enjoy watching them wrangle their own herds."

"Ah, yes, how is everyone?" Drake asked.

"Well, let's see, Quinn here has three now, all under five, and all bringing chaos to the vicarage with their antics. Cian lives in London with his wife and son—he's a solicitor, you know. Briana is in her third confinement and doesn't live far, so we see her and the babes more than we see her sisters. You've not met my other three girls. They were married before we returned to England after Mr. Starrett left the army at last." She patted her husband's arm.

Mary only half listened. The conversation continued, polite and empty of substance. Her eyes were riveted on Duncan. She longed to ask questions, to know why he had not written of his return, to know about the injury, to know everything that had happened since they last parted. Yes, he had written over the years, but the letters were never prolific. How did one compare the written word to spoken poetry? After years of awaiting his return, the atrocities of polite conversation with family bound her.

His brother, the Reverend Quinn Starrett, rattled on about his children. Mary's attention faded in and out of the conversation, only skimming the surface enough to know if something important was said, anything about Duncan. Without discretion, she watched him.

With his every smile, her heart swelled. It was the same smile of old. The low chuckle was all too familiar, as well, one she had heard often beneath the willow, one that tickled her ear when he dipped his lips close to tease her.

He paid more attention to the conversation than she, or at least he seemed to. Only a few times did she catch his gaze, feeling no shame whatsoever to be caught so blatantly staring at him. Her eyes devoured him. If she thought him handsome before, she had no descriptor to do him justice now. Commanding. Devastating. Both came to mind, but even they were inadequate.

He spoke, then, responding to something she had not heard Drake say, diverting her attention back to the conversation.

"It was a lark, I tell you. If I could go back to battle tomorrow, I would. More fun than one can have in any ballroom," Duncan said, rubbing his hand once more against his breeches, long fingers gripping a strong thigh.

Unable to stop herself, she blurted her first words in the conversation. "If you've been in England all this time, why am I only now learning of your return?"

A hush descended. All eyes turned to Mary.

Duncan hoped she had not caught his grimace. What was he to say in answer? That he had arrived in England on a stretcher? That he had not wanted to alarm her? That he had spent months in London until he could safely ride in a carriage home? That he never wanted her to see him disabled or unable to stand on his own two feet?

There were no words with which to answer her question. He had hidden from her since arriving home, and that was the truth of it. His father called it convalescing. Duncan called a spade a spade. He had hidden from her.

With a deep breath, he plastered a smile. "I'm flattered by your concern for my well-being, Lady Mary."

His attempts to deflect failed. She returned his non-answer with a frown. All heads swiveled his direction. Bloody awkward.

Unspoken words wove midair, blanketing them.

His family knew how he felt about her. Her brother knew how they both felt. And yet never had there been a public understanding. At the time of his departure, he had been nothing more than the youngest son of another youngest son. Granted, his grandfather was a viscount, but that same man had five healthy sons, all of whom had hardy boys of their own. Nothing short of a plague would put him in line to inherit. Even in such an unlikely circumstance, he was a far cry from being of her station or an acceptable match. How was he to answer her question when his goal in leaving for the army had been to become worthy of her hand, and yet he had returned a broken man?

His father's voice unraveled the silence. "We are all honored by your concern, Lady Mary, and yours, Your Grace. This is not a subject for the ears of ladies.

Let us say, he's been convalescing. Now that he's recovered, we can give him a hero's welcome!"

Sean Starrett's laugh was met with smiles and nods except from Mary, who looked quite alarmed.

She set down her teacup, her hand shaking ever so slightly. "What happened?"

"Oh, nothing to be concerned about, milady," his father said. "He's fit as a fiddle now."

Her mouth tightened as she gave him her haughtiest and most commanding look. "I demand to know the truth."

"Mary —" the duke began with a tone of admonition, attempting to intervene. His efforts were met with an impatient flick of her wrist.

Duncan heaved a sigh. "I was shot."

Mary's hand covered her mouth, her eyes wide.

"The ball hit too near the spine to remain. When we evacuated to Bremen, the surgeons saw fit to remove it." He paused, watching her swallow, her eyes closing briefly before locking on his again. "They notified my father, who came straight away."

His father's jovial mood darkened. "Butchers, the lot of them. Butchers whose breath smelled of spirits. Arrived to find my boy living on gruel. They'd never faced the wrath of Colonel Sean Starrett, for they had the gall to tell me I could not take my son home since he would not survive the journey. Well, I said, I would rather take my chances than see him die surrounded by sawbones. And look at him now. Fit as a fiddle."

Duncan tried to lighten the mood by chuckling when he said, "And he's right. I am. There's a twinge now and then, but I've never been better."

"It's all to do with a mother's love," his mother Georgina said, smiling brightly as she refilled empty cups and plates.

He accepted his mother's offerings with little more than a glance, his eyes trained on Mary. The best word he could think of to describe her expression was troubled.

Digging deeply, he searched for a reason to smile. Everyone's smiles so far, his own included, had seemed artificial and tense, as though all were waiting to learn the two love birds no longer favored each other; or perhaps they were waiting for him to collapse from exhaustion and injury. He wanted to reassure her all was well.

Anchoring his emotions on a memory of her at sixteen, regaling him with a heartfelt story, he allowed that vision to fill him with a warmth he had not felt in years. Channeling that into his expression, he smiled.

Her affect relaxed, shoulders dropping a fraction of an inch, hands unclenching, and the corners of her mouth twitching into a returning grin that brightened her eyes and pinkened her cheeks. His body thrummed at the sight of her shy smile. Oh, what he would not do to get her alone, to capture her in his arms and tell her that memories of her had kept him alive. In an instant, the years faded, and it was only the two of them in the room, making eyes at each other.

She had not changed. And yet she had. She had become a woman. His recollections were of a pretty, slender girl, with long, coltish legs, a contagious laugh, and a rebellious streak. The person sitting across from him was a composed, handsome lady with curves he had no business admiring in present company. How had he ever left her?

As she had done to him when she first walked in, he did now, allowing his eyes to sweep over her and take in the coiffed black hair, the dark eyes with lashes long enough to fan against her still-porcelain skin, the Roman nose she had grown into since the last time he saw her, the arching neck that curved into a heart-stopping expanse of bare skin accentuated by a plunging neckline. Duncan barely noticed the mauve dress as his eyes moved over her. Good Lord but she had matured into a perfect lady.

With a sharp intake of breath, he met her eyes, knowing full well she would see the blatant ardor burning in his.

So enraptured, he forgot all discomfort, at least until his leg cramped, followed by a sharp pain lancing from his spine to his thigh. Tightening his smile, he clenched against the torment, refusing to allow her to see anything but a fit, whole man.

The call ended after more polite conversation, including the annual shooting party the duke and his duchess planned to host. Though it would not occur until late autumn, the duke extended a personal invitation for the Starrett family to attend.

Duncan hardly knew how a half hour had passed with so few words exchanged with Mary. But then, words were unnecessary when there was an invisible cord linking them. Surely, she had felt it too.

Chapter 3

T he steady sound of hoofs meeting earth and the sway of the beast between his thighs coupled to produce one of the finest mornings Duncan had experienced in ages. He had not been atop a horse since that ill-fated battle. Should a day come when he could not ride, he would as soon be dead.

Thankfully, life was good to him, for despite the hiccup of the surgery, all was righting itself — Caesar beneath him, Mary reunited with him, and his strength returning. Soon, he would be fit enough to return to his regiment.

"Feeling fiddle fine, brother?" Quinn asked, riding alongside Duncan.

"Quite fine, in fact. Concerned I'll tumble?" Duncan laughed at the absurdity of his own question.

"Not in the least. Your grin tells me you're a man on top of the world."

The two rode from Cois Greta Park to the village. The grand scheme was to pay a call to Quinn's family, after which Duncan would leave Quinn at the vicarage and return home on his own.

Earlier that morning, the proposition of such a scheme had raised a cacophony of disagreements. No one had thought him ready to ride, much less ride alone, save a shadowing groom. He was not a young boy, he reminded them. He was a man, an officer, a colonel, as a matter of fact, and if he could not challenge himself to so simple a task, there was nothing for him.

As though knowing today was a momentous day, the weather offered him a bright sun, a cool breeze, and the harmony of birdsong. With such beauty surrounding him, it was easy to ignore the pain in his back.

The closer they came to the village center, the more frequent were the stone cottages and white-washed buildings, each progressively closer to the next until they morphed into terraced homes and shops. Villagers gawked when they spotted Duncan, many waving. No doubt, his brother had spoken about him in sermons and visits, not to mention what his parents might have said to their friends. To them, Duncan was the returning hero.

Being conspicuous did not shock him so much as the village itself. Nothing had changed. A thousand lives he had lived. Here, time had stopped. All too familiar faces lined the road to greet him. They had not changed. Children were older, parents had a new wrinkle or two, but nothing had changed. Duncan Starrett, stepping back in time, he mused.

However refreshing that should have been, it disturbed him. He was not the same man as when he left, but he had little doubt they would expect him to be.

"Is that not the Duchess of Annick and Lady Mary?" Quinn asked, nodding in the direction of a sizable cottage.

Duncan's pulse raced at the sound of her name, his eyes surveying passersby. At first, he could not find her. He chuckled to himself, realizing he was searching figures and faces for the Mary of his memory, the wisp of a young girl rather than the grown woman. And there she was. His Mary. Her back was to him. She and her sister-in-law were paying farewell to a family. Waiting behind them were a footman and maid laden with baskets.

Without consulting his brother, he halted Caesar and swung his leg over, dismounting. Only when boots touched ground did pain stab from lower back to thighs. The sensation washed over him with such intensity, he feared he might collapse.

Teeth clenched and eyes closed, he gripped the saddle for support until the sensation subsided to a dull throb. *Accursed infernal wound.* Both his groom and his brother dismounted and approached, ready to help. Jerking his elbow away from Quinn's hand, he muttered unintelligible curses, desperate not to appear weak. An exhale later, he pivoted in Mary's direction, hoping she had not seen, or if she had, thought nothing of it.

They were mere feet away. Mary flashed a smile while the duchess eyed him with curiosity. He barely noticed the duchess, who, by all accounts, should attract more attention than Lady Mary. However, nothing could divert his attention. Oh, she was a vision of loveliness, his Mary, wearing a dress of canary yellow that shimmered a darker shade with her movements, mesmerizing him.

"Colonel Starrett! It *is* you! And Mr. Starrett, as well." Mary nodded to them both, giving only a

cursory glance to his brother, her eyes bright and
focused on Duncan.

He gave as dignified a bow as he could through
the rhythmic pulse at his spine. The tightness of his
jaw reminded him to unclench his teeth.

Polite greetings exchanged, the duchess made for
Quinn, leaving Duncan with Mary. Ah, he could not
have planned this better. It had been not but three
days since their reunion over tea but seeing her now
was like seeing her for the first time all over again.
He was as giddy as a schoolboy. However grumpy he
had been that his father had pushed him into seeing
her before he felt physically ready, he was happy to
have her back in his life.

When she reached her hand towards him, his
heart leapt, thinking she would touch him in front
of all, brand him as hers. Only when her slender wrist
extended past him in a sensual arch did he realize her
intention — to stroke Caesar.

"How handsome you are," Mary said.

Grinning, Duncan leaned in and asked in hushed
tones, "You still think so?"

The blush that spread across her high cheekbones
heightened the twinkle in her eyes.

"I was referring to the horse," she said coyly, peering at him from beneath long lashes.

Caesar's ears flicked as though he recognized her
compliment.

"And what is your name, you magnificent beast?"
she cooed, running a gloved hand down the stallion's
neck and shoulders.

"Lady Mary, allow me to introduce Caesar, my
dearest companion. Caesar, this is Lady Mary."

"Oh! So, *you're* Caesar! Yes, I've read all about you." Turning to Duncan, she said, "I didn't realize you could keep a warhorse."

"We're nigh inseparable, truth be told." He rubbed Caesar's muzzle, receiving a snort for his efforts.

Duncan glanced at his brother and the duchess, an idea forming. "Would you and your sister-in-law consider joining us for tea at the vicarage? Now that I have you in my sights, I'm loath to part too soon."

At his bold flirtation, her blush deepened.

Not for the first time, it struck him how much she had matured, the reddened cheeks the only outward sign of her pleasure, so unlike her youthful exuberance. The Mary of old would have reacted more dramatically with a feigned swoon or a fit of giggles.

She turned away from him to steal a private moment with her sister-in-law. Unable to control himself, he let his gaze fall to the arch of her neck where the alabaster skin, smooth as velvet and immanently kissable, was teased by black ringlets of her hair. Reining in his thoughts, he tore his eyes from her to look at Quinn. His brother eyed him over their heads, a raised brow his only expression. Duncan grimaced. Leave it to him to invite nobles to his brother's home without consulting him first, much less the lady of the house—Miranda would suffer vapors.

After conferring with the duchess and sending the footman and maid to finish calls on their behalf before meeting at the vicarage with the carriage, Mary returned to Duncan's side, unaware of Quinn's silent panic behind her.

The two pairs ambled through the village, Duncan and Quinn's grooms trailing behind with the horses.

Not so subtly, Duncan dragged his feet, eager to create a respectable but private distance between his brother and the duchess. He wanted nothing more than to have Mary to himself.

Once out of earshot, Mary said with a twitch of a smile that contradicted her words, "I'm most cross with you."

"With me? Why?" He eyed her askance.

Before she could answer, several villagers stopped them in greeting, showing deference not only to Lady Mary, but also to him, a reaction he was not used to.

When they passed, she continued, "I'm cross because you've been home all this time and not sent word. It wasn't even you who invited us to tea. After all this time, you didn't spare me a second thought."

"What nonsense." Duncan laughed. "After five years, what's a few months?"

"What's a few months?" Mary echoed. "What's a few months?" She stopped walking, her smile fading.

Running a hand through his hair, Duncan turned back to her. "Don't frown. In the darkest moments, I lived in hope of seeing your smile."

Her eyes widened. "Then...then why wait so long? Your father said you were convalescing, but that didn't inhibit your hand from writing."

Offering his arm, he nodded in the direction of the receding figures, not wanting to fall too far behind. She hesitated before accepting.

"You must know I would not have waited had it not been important," he said.

Expectant eyebrows raised for him to continue.

"Even now, I'm—" He swallowed, choosing his words carefully. "I'm not fully recovered."

Concern etched her features, but she said nothing.

"Not until recently could I stand on my own, much less walk. It's humbling to admit that. I dislike saying it aloud and to you, of all people."

"To me, of all people, you should be completely honest."

"Yes, well, not all things are for a lady's ears, and not all things are for an able-bodied officer to experience. I'll not have you see me in any fashion but my strongest. Even as we walk, I feel, how should I say, less than my best." The understatement of the century. The further they walked, the more intense became his affliction.

"If you're still in pain, why are you not resting? Oh, you foolish man. You always were too proud to listen to reason."

He laughed, all the discomfort in the world nothing in comparison to the pleasure of her company.

"Let's not talk of the past. I want to get to know the new you and for you to get to know the new me." He held a staying hand when she opened her mouth to argue. "Don't say we already know each other. We know who we used to be. I want to know you now, this breathtaking woman who barely resembles the young girl who stole my heart." When she worried her lip, he felt a jolt of alarm. "Forgive my impertinence, Mary, but it's been a long time since we last spoke, letters aside. Is there a special gentleman in your life? Anyone I should know about?"

She laughed. "What a preposterous question. Of course not."

"Then you've waited for me?"

Her hand on his arm tensed.

However selfish, he had hoped she would wait for him. The thought filled him with both elation and guilt, for he had not intended to leave the army so soon. Even now, he was impatient to return. Would she continue to wait for him when he went back? To his mind, she was his, and he suffered a burning jealousy at the thought of another man flirting with her, but for how much longer could he expect her to wait?

With a lift of her chin, she said, "I wait for no one. I've been busy with my own life, I'll have you know."

He lowered his head and whispered, "You've been busy becoming the most beautiful woman I've ever laid eyes on."

A pink tint blossomed across her chest and tendrilled up her neck. "You're a shameless flirt, Duncan Starrett."

"Only with you, my dear," he admitted. "Would my attentions be welcomed if I called on you?"

Handsomely composed, she glanced at him beneath sooty lashes. "There's only one way to find out."

With a sly smile, she hastened her steps to catch up to her sister-in-law, who slowed at the sight of the vicarage ahead.

Mrs. Miranda Starrett chattered about her children, her sewing group, the flower committee, and an endless stream of other topics, her attention riveted on Mary's sister-in-law Charlotte. Mary doubted the vicar's wife had ever taken tea with a duchess. Her talkativeness could be due to nerves, especially given she had no forewarning, but Mary thought it was excitement. She liked Miranda straight away.

Being here in the company of Duncan and his brother's family was like coming home. Mary found it difficult not to fantasize about a future with him. For as long as she could remember, she had wanted a large family, one with happy and boisterous children. She had wanted it while growing up, a household of siblings her own age; now she wanted it for herself, a dozen children of hers and Duncan's.

Mary wrapped her arms around the vicar's youngest daughter, of similar age to her nephew Theo.

"What's her name?" Mary asked, smiling at the knitted doll in the girl's hand.

"Briana, like auntie," said the girl, walking the doll along Mary's knee. "She's go to church."

A dimpled smile peeked up at Mary. Over the girl's head, Mary spied Duncan watching them with a devilish grin. Her heart pitter-pattered.

Was he thinking what she was thinking? Was he imagining their future together? Taking tea with the family, their own first child on her lap? It was not fool-hardy to dream. He had come home to her after all.

Seeing him now felt like a fantasy of its own. Any minute she would awaken to realize he was still on the continent. Yet no matter how many times she pinched herself, he remained seated across from her, making love to her with his eyes. Was it too soon to find a dark corner and kiss him? She had not felt those lips since she was sixteen. Did his kiss still feel the same?

"If she's bothering you, I can send her to the nurs-ery," Miranda Starrett said, a crease between her brows as she watched her daughter try to feed the doll a biscuit, the crumbs littering Mary's dress.

"It would break my heart if you did, Mrs. Starrett. Olivia is a darling." Mary ran her hand through the girl's silken curls.

"My sister-in-law will never leave now." Charlotte chortled. "She adores children. In fact, she spends more time in the nursery than the drawing room."

Setting his teacup in its saucer, the Reverend Starrett said, "In that case, you should call on us more often. We have three children who do nothing but cause trouble. Just yesterday, Sophie practiced writing her name. On the wall. In ink. With her bare hands."

"Quinn!" his wife shrieked. "Don't share embarrassing tales!" Turning to Charlotte, she said, "I assure you, I run a well-regimented household."

Charlotte leaned in and said *sotto voce*, "You fair better with three than I do with one. Theo found one of his father's compositions last week and decided it would make a grand pallet to paint with his fingers."

They laughed at the confession, no doubt imagining a duke's reaction to finding his heir destroying works of art. Mary laughed harder than the others since she had seen both the chaos and her brother's reaction. Drake had scooped his son onto his shoulders and galloped through the halls, claiming later that his son clearly had genius taste in music because even Theo recognized rubbish when he saw it. The next day, the manor had been filled with the sound of music as the duke composed a new piece inspired by Theodore's antics.

Just as quickly as Olivia had climbed onto Mary's lap, she climbed off, skipping over to Duncan and waving her doll at him until he lifted her onto his lap.

How shocking it must be for him to return after all these years and meet his nieces for the first time. What else had he missed? He had six older siblings, four of whom lived too far to have visited since his return. He must be returning to what seemed a different world, a world that had carried on without him.

"Our eldest," Mrs. Starrett was saying, "Emma, is just like her Grandmama Starrett, Scottish through and through."

"Much to the chagrin of Papa's family," the Reverend Starrett added. "My grandfather is a haughty British viscount, who married an Irish spitfire. I'll leave you to imagine the levity of family parties."

Mary glanced at Duncan as he turned his hand into a neighing horse for the doll to ride. To Mr. Starrett, she asked, "Do you see your uncles and grandparents often?"

"We don't," the vicar said. "The truth is the family is too large and spread across too many counties for us all to see each other often. The last party was nearly ten years ago. Such events were far more frequent when we followed the drum with Papa. Our little family, before Duncan was born, that is, traipsed after Papa from one campaign to the next, but between wars, we would return for the larger family holidays. By the time Papa left the army, my siblings had established families and lives of their own."

Mary studied Duncan, who was so entranced by his niece, he had not heard the conversation. She could relate in some small way to Duncan's childhood. He had been born twenty years after his eldest sibling. Mary was seventeen years younger than her brother, so she understood the separation of age between siblings, but unlike her, Duncan did have a sibling closer to his age, namely Mr. Quinn Starrett, a brother he had idolized growing up.

How wonderful it would be to get to know Duncan's family, to spend days taking tea with Mrs. Miranda Starrett, to watch their children grow up together. For the past few years, she had dared not dream; for she feared dreams would shatter with a single letter. Now, everything felt so easy, so right, all the pieces falling into place after an interminable delay. If his flirting earlier was any indication, he felt the same.

Mrs. Starrett stood, her eyes on Duncan and Olivia. "You can't stifle that yawn, sweetness. I saw it. Time to return to the nursery."

Olivia tucked her face in Duncan's coat, her whines muffled.

"Come now. Show our guests what a good girl you are."

"No' a goo' gir'. A big gir'," the girl protested, throwing her doll to the ground in protest. Arms crossed, bottom lip pouting, she choked a sob.

Mary recognized the beginning of a tantrum. Her nephew was far too serious for bad behavior. Even her cousin's eldest daughter was too sensible for tantrums. But her cousin's son, the heir to the Roddam earldom, was a holy terror when he did not get his way. She had rescued many an eardrum from his wails. It would seem he had a kindred spirit in little Olivia.

Without caring if she overstepped her boundaries as a guest, Mary made for the little girl's doll, picking it up and cradling it.

Smiling at Olivia, she whispered, "Briana is trying to nap. I think we should tuck her into the nursery where she can sleep in quiet. Would you like to rock her to sleep, or shall I?"

The girl stared at Mary, her clever child's mind trying to sort out if this was a trick. Deciding Mary was sincere, she climbed off her uncle's lap and took Mary's hand.

"Do carry on," Mary said to the others, heading for the drawing room door.

Mrs. Starrett and Charlotte started talking at once, animated voices remarking on Mary's way with children. Beneath their talk was an undertone of male mumbles. Before she had reached the door, Mr. Starrett spoke.

"You don't know your way around the house, Lady Mary. Allow my brother to show you to the nursery."

Smirking at their ploy, she turned just in time to catch sight of Mr. Starrett's hand on Duncan's arm as the latter rose from his chair. Brotherly affection, or had he needed help rising? She frowned. He was on her heels before she could ponder further.

It took mere minutes to settle Olivia in the nursery, her eyes held open only by obstinacy by the time they brought her to the nurse.

As soon as the door to the nursery closed, Mary began scheming how she could steal a few moments alone with Duncan before returning to the drawing room. He must have thought the same.

When they reached the end of the upstairs hall, Duncan grabbed her arm and pulled her into a room. Her first startled look about the place gave the impression it was a family parlor, but she hardly had a chance to find her bearings before she was pressed against the door, Duncan's hands grasping her arms, his face inches from hers.

She could feel his breath on her cheek, smell his cologne.

Beneath half-lidded eyes, he studied her. "I've not kissed you in half a decade," he said. "Since my return, we've seen each other only once, briefly at that. But all I can think of is kissing you. Would my attentions be unwelcomed?"

Her breath came in jagged succession. Shaking her head, she said, "Not unwelcomed. I've been thinking the same." Reaching up, she snaked a hand around his neck and pulled him to her.

Their lips met with a tentative touch, so unlike the frenzy she felt within her breast, the desperation to kiss him with five years' worth of pent-up passion. He brushed his lips against hers. Gentle. Inviting. An infusion of memory in a single touch.

Capturing her mouth with his, he leaned against her, the hard muscles of his shoulders flexing beneath her fingers, so unlike the softness she remembered from their youth. With a tea-flavored kiss, Mary's hand slipped behind Duncan's neck, wanting to pull him closer, wanting to entwine her fingers with his hair. Her hands itched to explore the planes of this new physique. He was Duncan, and yet he was an altogether different person. Harder, broader, fiercer.

They quitted the kiss as quickly as it began. Mary stood breathless from the exchange, her mouth hot and raw.

"I'm only stopping because we're in my brother's home." Duncan took a step back, his eyes trained on hers. "We're far too old for secret meetings under the willow, Mary, but I want to see you. I want to talk about all we've missed. I want—I want to kiss you in ways that will show you how much I've missed you. Shall I call on you in a few days? At Lyonn Manor? An official and open courtship?"

She could do nothing more than nod, her eyes wide, her fingertips touching her lips. The seconds of passion had left her bereft, her skin chilled by the distance between them. Mary pressed a hand to her abdomen, hoping to settle the butterflies.

"We can't linger long, but we should wait until my kiss isn't so obvious." He ran the back of his hand down her cheek before grasping her hand in his.

Bringing her hand to his lips, he kissed her knuckles, then her fingers, turning her hand over to kiss her palm. Everywhere he touched, she tingled.

Mary took a step forward, leaning into him as he had done to her. His grip on her hand tightened as her lips found his jaw. With a soft pucker, she kissed a trail down to his neck. The skin along his jaw, though closely shaved, was prickly with an early afternoon stubble, but his neck was smooth, the flesh hot. A curious pucker of her lips to his neck caused a sharp intake of breath that thrilled her to her toes. The same reaction as when they were young. A different Duncan, yet the same.

She leaned back to see his expression. "Only a few days," she said.

"Under the watchful eye of your brother, we'll have a respectable conversation."

She teased, "He can easily be distracted for a stolen moment." When she pursed her lips, she detected the subtle taste of salt.

"You're as misbehaved as ever, my wicked one." He pulled her to him in a chaste embrace, resting his chin against her temple. "I've missed you, Mary. Truly."

"And I, you," she said into his cravat.

When he released her, he stepped over to admire one of the wall paintings, his back to her.

Mind, body, and soul, she thrummed from his touch. She wished they could move past this part, past being in someone else's house, past reuniting and courting, and simply be together. *At last.* All her life she felt she was waiting, always waiting. She wanted to *live.* She was ready to break free and *live.*

"You're my niece's new favorite person," he said after a few moments of silence. "I hope she wasn't making a pest of herself. Do you really like children?"

"Yes, I do. I want to be the mother mine never was." She blanched at the confession. It was not quite how she meant to answer the question. But how did one say to a man not seen in five years that she wanted his children?

"You always did want a large family. I remember. Would you want them all to be yours, or would you consider adopting?"

She furrowed her brow. "Adopting? Whatever do you mean?"

"Well, you know, give home to children who might not have one. Illegitimate children or otherwise. Is that beyond the scope of a duke's daughter, or would you consider it?"

Chin raised, she said, "I'm inclined to be offended by that question. I'm not like my mother, you know. People can't help the nature of their birth, but they're still good people. I've never considered having children not of my own, though." After a moment's thought, she added, "No, that's not true. Most of the men Mother tossed at me over the years were widowers with children, except their children were usually older than me. Why are you asking me this?"

The first thought that sprang to mind was her cousin, the Baroness Collingwood, who oversaw an orphanage. Now that Duncan had returned from war, was he thinking of taking on a new project, something similar to Lady Collingwood's?

They had so much to talk about. Not for the first time, she felt him to be a stranger. As strong as their connection, there was a foreign air about him she did not recognize. Even his kiss, however titillating, was different. Did she wish for the Duncan of old, or did she prefer the new man?

"Let's talk more about this later, shall we? When we have more time? I think it's safe to return to the drawing room." He returned to her side, taking the liberty to kiss her temple before seeing her to the door.

Duncan shifted in the saddle for the tenth time in as many minutes. Caesar snorted his displeasure. The wound throbbed from the exertion of the day and the jostling of the ride. Even Duncan's feet tingled with numbness. He had pushed himself too hard today.

But what use was he to anyone from a convalescent bed? No, he needed to show his body who was in command. This was who he was and what he did, just as he had done in the army — he pushed himself with a determined, iron will against all odds.

Aside from the persistent pain, the day had been good. Better than good. There was a sense of wholeness when with Mary, as though all were right in the world. The trouble was, he did not know what to do about it. His heart spoke the same answer as it had when he was twenty — marry her. His head countered with a different answer.

There could be no doubt how his family felt. They were courting her with every opportunity, determined to see them matched. It had been the same before he left.

His father had pushed the relationship, encouraging their trysts. His father's attempts to matchmake had not been nefarious, as he was not greedily wanting Duncan to marry a duke's daughter. At the time, Lady Mary's mother ruled Lyonn Manor and would not accept Duncan as a suitor. In fact, the Dowager Duchess of Annick would accept no one as a suitor except aging nobles over forty years Mary's senior. Duncan's father knew their love to be true and wanted his son to marry, by any means necessary, in hopes it would force Duncan to stay grounded, a curiosity since his father had devoted his own life to war.

True, it had not been Duncan's intention to make a career on the battlefield. His only intention had been to make himself worthy of Mary's hand. But in doing so, he had found a place of belonging. He was respected. He was a leader. Purpose drove each day and each decision. Now that he was home, he felt restless, useless. Where did he fit? What purpose did he have?

His heart wanted to whisk Mary off her feet and marry her without delay. He still loved her. He had always loved her. He may not know the woman she had become, but that did not change his feelings. If anything, seeing her as a grown woman deepened his affection. It certainly deepened his desire. And yet what would he do once married? Leave her here while he went to war? Stay to become idle and drive them both insane?

He was not altogether sure she would even want him after learning of the man he had become. There was little doubt in his mind she still loved him just as he loved her, only she loved the boy of the past, not the man he was now. Would she still love him once she knew all he had done?

By habit, he slowed Caesar with a lean and squeeze of his knees rather than by the reins as they came up the drive of Cois Greta Park. And what a bonny sight to greet him! His mother stood at the front, all six feet of her, waving an arm in greeting. On her hip, perched a little boy with spindly arms and a toothy smile.

"He's begged for a ride since the moment you left," Georgina said when Duncan slowed to a stop.

A warm smile to his mother, he leaned to capture the three-year-old. Duncan winced through the pinch at his spine as he hoisted Bernard on the saddle.

Fighting a wave of dizziness, he asked, "Would you like to take the reins?"

With a squeal, the boy took the ribbons in hand, flicking them with abandon. Duncan chuckled, folding his hands over tiny fists. Never too early to teach horsemanship, he decided.

"Papa, make him go!" Bernard commanded. "Go, horsey!"

With a tap of Duncan's calves, the stallion set off, much to the delight of the boy.

Chapter 4

After threading the needle with purple for the peacock's tail, Mary turned back to her embroidery.

"It's all so tragic. Jilted at the altar," Charlotte said, rethreading her own embroidery needle. "The bride never showed. Rumors abound, but the truth of why remains a mystery."

"Poor Winston. He'll be forty soon, will he not? Hardly a respectable age for a bachelor." Mary admired the progress of the peacock tail. The green thread next, she decided.

"He brought it on himself. He loved his rakeish reputation too much to set up a nursery as a responsible gentleman should. What he needs is a woman who can teach him to love marriage more than gambling. He's coming for dinner later this week, you know, along with the Thompson sisters. Drake is determined to play matchmaker for his friend, though I told him it was a lost cause."

Mary leaned back, studying her screen. No, not the green. The gold. Definitely the gold. She swapped the purple thread for the gold for the finishing touches of the tail eyes.

"I was madly in love with him once," Mary admitted.

"With *Winston*?" Charlotte wrinkled her nose. "He's nearly twenty years your senior, and that's not mentioning his bad habits."

"Yes, well, I was all of twelve at the time. He was this magnificently mature man who called on my brother from time to time and always treated me as though I were a lady, not a child. And lest we forget, Mother disapproved him. How could I not fall hopelessly in love?" Mary smirked.

"Yes, I can see the appeal from the eyes of youth, but in all seriousness, Mary, that would have never worked out. He would have gambled away your dowry, dallied with every milkmaid in the county, and then gone grey before you reached your majority. Regardless, I do pity his plight. I earnestly believe he was in love with the girl."

Mary tutted.

Days with Charlotte were among her favorite. Only two years apart in age, they had become the best of friends after Mary's brother brought her home as his surprise wife. While no one would replace Arabella as Mary's best friend, there was room in her heart for more than one friend, and she did need someone close. It would be a most lonely life without Charlotte now that Arabella lived in Lancashire with her husband.

"What do you think of Duncan?" Mary asked, keeping her tone lighthearted, though her heart pounded a little faster to bring his name into conversation.

Out of the corner of her eye, she saw Charlotte's needle pause.

"I think he's as much in love with you as he ever was."

Mary dropped her needle.

"And I think he's devilishly handsome," Charlotte added, winking at Mary, who was retrieving her needle.

"It's the cleft in his chin. Oh, and his eyes. He has the dreamiest eyes." Mary sighed, recalling their shared moment in the vicarage parlor. Only just in time, she stopped herself from touching her lips in memory.

"No, I'm sure it's the military brawn. I don't believe I've ever seen a man quite so well-muscled."

"Charlotte!" Mary squawked.

"Now that he's returned, what are you going to do? Pick up where you left off? Torture him into a lengthy courtship? You must have a plan, Mary."

"I'm afraid I don't. Though I've dreamed of his return, I haven't *waited* for him. I made my own life. Now, what of my plans? We've not yet spoken of any of that. What do you think I should do?"

Of course, she *had* waited for him. There had been no other course of action for her but to wait. At fifteen, she had first fallen in love with him, with his passion for life, his flirtations, his maturity, all so juxtaposed to her own dull youth. There was no one for her but him. Her fear now was that they might not be as compatible as they once were. She had been a silly girl, and he had been a carefree boy.

It was only nerves, she told herself. It would take time for them to reach the point of comfort they once had. And they had all the time in the world together, a lifetime to explore their new selves.

Charlotte said, "I think you should punish him for staying away so long by making yourself irresistibly desirable while not letting him know how much you've missed him. It'll drive him wild and serve him right."

Mary smiled, feeling a little guilty that she had already foiled that plan.

"Let's start tomorrow. I'll help you choose the right dress for the occasion, something low-cut."

"Tomorrow?" Mary searched her memory for what could possibly happen tomorrow. He had mentioned calling in a few days, but it had not exactly been a few days yet. It had only been two.

"Oh, did I not mention?" Charlotte giggled. "I invited myself to tea with the Starretts. Drake isn't the only one who is determined to play matchmaker."

From the carriage window, Mary could see the house at the end of the winding driveway to Cois Greta Park. Though the Starrett home could not compete with Lyonn Manor's size or splendor, it was a sizable house of its own right—Palladian with a courtyard bounded by stables, charming Venetian windows and Doric columns, and two rivers that fed into a lake. *Their* lake. The lake that marked the boundary between the ducal estate and the Starrett home. The lake where she fell in love.

With the sun out and the air chilled with the promise of autumn, today presented perfect riding weather. How gauche to arrive in the ducal carriage, she thought. The homes were not far enough apart to warrant such extravagance. She would give her left arm to be riding Athena rather than being jostled about in a carriage. Alas, her sister-in-law preferred the carriage.

But that was not the entire motivation for taking the carriage, Charlotte had explained to her that morning. The point of the carriage was to ensure their dress and hair showed to advantage. It would not do, the duchess had said, for Mary to arrive in a militaristic riding habit, looking for all the world like a boy in regimentals. No, Mary needed to look coiffed and sensual, scented of lavender-water rather than horse sweat.

She tugged at the top of the dress.

"If you're going to fuss," Charlotte said, swatting at Mary's hand, "pull it lower rather than higher."

Tossing her gaze to the heavens, Mary tugged at it anyway. The dress made her bosom swell in indecent ways. If she made a concentrated effort not to breathe, she might survive the tea. What would his parents think? Seamless, peach satin plunged low to accentuate her proportions. The waist was higher than any of her other dresses, doing its own part at displaying her assets. She felt entirely underdressed. All morning, Charlotte had raved about how becoming the dress looked and how fortunate Mary was to have an admirable bosom to display. All Mary wanted was to don her riding habit.

The plan, according to Charlotte, was to ignore him while looking enchanting. Make him do all the work, she had advised. Make him believe he must act quickly or lose the chance.

"Aside from teasing glances," Charlotte had instructed over a cup of chocolate, "pretend you're not interested."

Mary had no intention of doing any such thing. Her plan was to find another parlor and kiss him until she was dizzy. Best laid plans were a far cry from reality.

The carriage came to a halt. Her pulse quickened. When her shoes met gravel, her palms began to sweat in her gloves. A lump formed in her throat.

She followed her sister-in-law and the butler to a modest garden terrace with an al fresco tea prepared. Mrs. Georgina Starrett, Colonel Sean Starrett, and Mr. Quinn Starrett were all in attendance alongside Duncan, just as they had been one week ago to the day. Mary was disappointed the vicar's wife had not joined them, but she ought not to care since her only purpose was to see Duncan. When she laid eyes on him standing by the table and looking powerful and virile, she burned with the memory of their kiss.

She thought she might die when his eyes swept over her. Was she blushing? Were her thoughts discernable? The urge to tug at the neckline to keep her bosom from rising with every breath forced her hands into fists. At this rate, she would be sitting on her hands before the end of tea.

Time slowed to a snail's pace as everyone exchanged pleasantries, Duncan and Mary sitting idle, catching each other's glances every few seconds.

How could she get him alone?

She could feign feeling vaporish from the outdoors and hope he insisted on showing her inside. Too contrived.

She could stand to take a better look at something in the distance — a particularly interesting sheep, perhaps — and pretend to turn her ankle so he would have to help her inside. Too obvious.

She was feeling so desperate by the end of fifteen minutes she almost blurted out that she needed an escort to the water closet.

Just when she was at her wit's end with all the talk of the coming autumn weather and the October shooting party, Duncan turned to her and asked louder than necessary, "Would you care to take a turn about the garden?"

Mrs. Georgina Starrett clasped her hands to her breast. "What a splendid idea. Do show her the view from the cherry orchard."

Mary eyed the land surrounding the house. The orchard was a fair distance but still within clear sight of the terrace with not a single place to hide from prying eyes. Blast.

When she stood, all at the table stood, except Duncan. He made a point of finishing his tea. Slowly. She turned to Charlotte with a comment, pretending not to notice his behavior — Charlotte would undoubtedly think him ill mannered, boorish, disrespectful even — but she watched him from her peripheral, her thoughts on his injury. Just as he had at the vicarage, Mr. Quinn Starrett aided his brother in standing, though this time, he put a fair bit more effort into it than she recalled from the other day. Duncan gripped the vicar's forearms as the latter pulled him to his feet.

The whole of it troubled her.

"Shall we?" he asked, walking up beside her.

To see his confident smile as he offered his arm removed all worries from her mind. Cheeks flushed, she left behind the family to accompany him.

They walked in silence until they reached the first row of cherry trees.

"You're stunning," he said, turning to her with brown eyes darkened by the shadows of tree limbs. "I thought I'd been shot again when you walked onto the terrace. I couldn't breathe for a full minute."

Mary met his gaze, feeling the heat of her blush spread up her neck and into her cheeks.

"If you're trying to flatter me, it won't work," she said in her haughtiest tone, knowing her flushed skin belied her pleasure. "I'm too wise to fall for a rogue's flirtation. You only want me for my dowry."

When he raised an eyebrow, she responded with a teasing smile, one he matched in return.

Were they not in full view of the terrace, she would wind her arms around his neck and sink her fingers knuckle-deep into his hair. She disliked having to hide her affection.

"Tell me about your come-out," he said, leading her through the orchard.

"I already have. I wrote to you about it."

"In a single sentence. Something along the lines of, 'I've suffered the come-out and survived to see another day.' I want to know more. I want to envision you as you once were, experiencing a London ball for the first time. I want to imagine that girl with her star-struck eyes becoming the mature woman I see today."

Touching a hand to her chest, Mary laughed. "That was nearly four years ago, Duncan. I've tried my best to forget it. I didn't want a come-out. I had you. I did enjoy the parties and dancing, though. All the same, it was a tedious year that my brother made me suffer only once. And before you ask, yes, I did receive proposals. Too many to count. Most of them Drake dismissed, but a few I had to suffer sitting through."

"Were you tempted?" Duncan paused to reach into a low-hanging branch for a handful of cherries.

"Not in the least, and you know it." She accepted one of the cherries and savored its sweetness.

"So, you did wait for me."

"Need I remind you that I do not need to wed. Ever. When my mother was head of the household, yes, but now that my brother runs the dukedom, no. I have my own wealth and am content with my freedom. Should I tire of living with my brother and sister-in-law, I could choose any one of several estates." There was an edge to her tone that surprised her. She had meant to tease, not sound defensive.

He stopped abruptly and leaned against a tree trunk, gripping his thigh and squeezing his eyes closed.

"I didn't mean that quite how it sounded," she said in haste, worried she had offended him or given him the impression she was not interested. "It's only, marriage is a choice for me, one I never thought to have under my mother's tyranny."

Duncan shook his head, grimacing, his hand massaging his thigh muscles. When she made to speak, he held a hand to silence her.

Mary covered her mouth with her hand when he dropped the cherries to grip the tree, bracing himself. His breath shallowed to a pant mingled with groans. She glanced back to the terrace, wondering if she should signal for help.

As though reading her mind, he growled through gritted teeth, "It'll pass."

He continued to rub and knead his leg, a sight full of contradictions given how fit and powerful his thighs were in the buckskin. Mary pulled her lips between her teeth, concerned.

His features softened with each passing moment. Whatever he had suffered appeared to lighten.

After a time, he leaned his head against the tree and chuckled. "I do apologize, Mary. How distressing for you and embarrassing for me. It comes and goes. It's nothing, really."

"It didn't look like nothing to me," she protested.

"It's a numbness. A tingling numbness that's accompanied by muscle cramping. It's nothing. Just a remnant of the wound that'll pass in time. I had hoped to spare you from seeing any residual effects by delaying our reunion, but here we are."

"I would rather be by your side while you heal than waiting in darkness thinking the worst."

He opened his eyes, his head still resting against the tree trunk, and looked at her. "Truly?"

She nodded.

Pushing himself against the tree, the corners of his lips lifting, he said, "I knew you waited for me."

Laughing, she took his arm for the remaining walk through the orchard. It was not lost on her that he squeezed his leg from time to time as they journeyed forth.

"What do you do with your time? Gossip with friends? Visit neighbors? Dance the night away?" he asked as they reached the edge of the orchard.

Mary looked out past the slope of the plateau, an admirable sight of a shallow valley, one of the rivers bubbling through it for a romantic vista.

"I'm the best horsewoman in the county. I don't say that with arrogance, only truth. Horses mean everything to me. I have plans to breed thoroughbreds. It might not be the most ladylike of endeavors, but I don't care. I have my own money and can do with it what I like."

"You're serious?" Duncan sounded more surprised than doubtful.

"I am. If you must know, I prefer the company of horses to most people, though if you're fortunate, you can be an exception."

He threw back his head and laughed.

As they turned back to walk the orchard towards the terrace, he moved his other hand to cover hers, hugging it between his forearm and palm.

"How did you break your nose?" she blurted out, not intending to start with what might be perceived as a rude question but wanting to know everything about him that had changed.

His laugh ended in a snort. "An ambitious rifleman at Tourcoing thought my nose should meet the butt of his rifle. It was a short-lived introduction, but one I'm not likely to forget. At the time, I was Captain of a foot regiment. That was the last time I fought on foot rather than from horseback. But let's not talk about war. Do you think my nose will come between us?"

Biting her bottom lip to keep from smiling, she said, "Only when I kiss you."

The deep rumble of his chuckle tickled her ears. "Well played."

"Don't laugh when I confess that though I found you handsome before, I think you all the more dashing now."

Her words understated her feelings. He had gone from innocent to roguish with a single broken nose. His muscular build contributed to her sentiments. How could it not? His height may be the same, an easy six feet or more, but his new physique accentuated that height, making him appear altogether taller, broader, and larger. There was something majestic about him, not unlike the stallion he rode.

He drew them to a stop at the edge of the orchard, as hesitant as she to return to the terrace so soon.

"Before I say what I'm going to say," he began, leaning against a tree again, "I need to know if your feelings for me have changed. Be honest, please. Don't play coy. Though I'm nothing more than the youngest son of a colonel, do you still feel as you once did? You aren't embarrassed by me or our differences in station?"

Mary clasped her hands at her waist, surprised by the turn in conversation. "I could never be embarrassed by you, Duncan. You needn't ask such a question. On the contrary, I'm proud of you. I wish you had never gone to war, and I wish you had not stayed away so long, but I'm proud of you."

"And what of my other question?"

She stared down at her hands, uncertain how to respond. "I'm not ready to answer that question. My feelings have not changed, and yet we both have."

"Fair enough." He cleared his throat and crossed his arms over his chest. "The thing is, Mary, my life circumstances have somewhat changed."

Brows furrowed, she frowned.

"A royal messenger arrived this morning."

Her eyes widened.

"You're looking at the newest baronet in the kingdom."

Mary shrieked and covered her face with her hands. When she peeked at him between her fingers, he smiled sheepishly.

Dragging her hands down to her bosom, she asked, "How? Why? Oh, Duncan!"

"That's Sir Duncan to you." His smile broadened, deepening the cleft. "Of all I did, it was the bluff I organized as lieutenant colonel that was most valued. It seemed nothing at the time. A defense tactic, nothing more. We were losing abominably and needed to bide time to recuperate. I bluffed the French into believing we were retreating. All the while, three of my companies were sneaking up at the rear. It really was nothing, but it would seem Crown and country think otherwise."

"Oh, Duncan," Mary repeated. "This is wonderful!"

"It's not without perks. I'm now the proud owner of Sidwell Hall in Durham. From what I gather, it's not large, but it does come with tenant farms and a moderate income. I'd like to ride out to see it next week. If I should invite my brother and his wife to join, would you come with us?"

With a bounce, Mary laughed. "Yes, yes, yes! Oh, yes!"

"From what I understand, it has a sizable stable block. Perhaps it would do for a future breeding farm?"

She was speechless; all she could do was gape.

He laughed at her silence. "We'll see, shall we? My parents will have shared the news with your sister-in-law by now. What they won't have mentioned is the invitation that accompanied the letter. It's in May, in

London, a celebration to honor the returned officers. I hope to attend with you at my side."

Tears stung her eyes as she nodded.

Her joy for his success faded when his smile tensed, and his jaw clenched.

"I need to return to the terrace," he said.

The walk was interrupted by continuous pauses wherein he clawed at one or both of his thighs. Mary felt helpless. He paced their steps until halfway to the terrace, when his brother approached and offered an arm of support. Though Duncan took his arm, he gave a subtle shake of his head, an unspoken communication passing between brothers but lost on Mary. She hated feeling so helpless.

Not long after they returned to the table to allow Duncan time to recover in a seated position, did Charlotte and Mary take their leave.

However concerned she was regarding Duncan's condition, it was difficult not to remain excited about his news, especially when Charlotte could talk of little else while the butler helped them into their traveling cloaks and bonnets. Mary divulged the invitation for May. After all, who else could she tell? And it was not as though Duncan would not ask for her hand before then or that she would deny his suit. It was simply a matter of time before all came to pass.

As they left the house and walked across the gravel to the waiting carriage, a young child not much older than Theodore ran out of the front door towards the carriage horses. A nurse bolted past the two ladies and launched herself at the boy.

"I wanter see horsey!" the boy exclaimed, trying to wriggle free of his nanny's grasp.

The nurse lifted him onto her hip. "I do apologize," she said, curtsying.

"What a little darling," Charlotte said, walking up to the pair. "And what's your name?"

The boy took one look at the two of them and hid his face against his nanny's dress.

Mary turned to Charlotte and said, "I didn't realize Mr. Cian Starrett had come from London. This must be his boy, though I had thought his son was older. Why didn't he join us for tea?"

The nurse interrupted before Charlotte could respond. "No, he's not come, milady. This is the young master's son."

Charlotte and Mary exchanged curious glances.

Charlotte spoke first. "And here I thought the Reverend Starrett's children were all girls. You're not a girl, though, are you, sweetie?"

The boy lifted his head long enough to shake it with vigor.

"Pardon me, Your Grace," the nanny said. "This is the young master's son, Colonel Starrett the younger. Brought him home from war, he did."

Mary's world crumbled.

However much she wanted to swoon to escape the moment, she was not the swooning type. Instead, the blood drained from her body, a chill shivering through her limbs. How she made it to the carriage, she could not say, but not a word was spoken for the return journey to Lyonn Manor.

Chapter 5

Brushing a curly lock from Bernard's forehead, Duncan bade him goodnight. The boy muttered unintelligible words, eyelids fluttering closed. He favored his mother, God rest her soul, with large, soulful eyes and brown curls.

It had been an awkward conversation to introduce the boy to his family, all knowing his origin. But without judgement, they accepted Bernard as one of their own. At some point, sooner rather than later, Duncan would need to introduce him to Mary. He was not at all certain that would go well. It was one thing to claim an illegitimate child was a person as any other and quite another to accept one as a son. He refused to hide the boy. He would raise Bernard in the open, a proud father, and curse anyone who said otherwise. Could Mary accept those terms? Could she raise another woman's child?

His bedroom suite was down a flight of stairs from the nursery. Gripping the rail with knuckle-white fists, he traversed the planes one steady step at a time. His feet were numb, and his legs prickled as though stuck by thousands of needles. The base of his spine had ached with a dull heat all afternoon, but the pain had evolved to a sharpness that stole his breath.

Even with the ball in his back, he had not felt this way. Pained, yes, but of a different nature. Post-surgery, the sensation had been less pronounced. He had been weak and sore rather than pained. All he could do now was hope this passed.

His valet saw to his evening care then retired for the night. Duncan took measured steps to his four-poster, a distance that stretched for miles. How the devil was he to proceed with courtship in this condition?

There was nothing for it. He would need to take a day or two to rest. Come the end of the week, he would be fit as a fiddle and ready to sweep Mary off her feet.

Ah, yes, he would invite her for a ride. Her brother was an avid horseman, so Duncan would call on them both with an invitation to ride. Some women enjoyed a promenade in a curricle. His woman would enjoy a vigorous ride across the countryside. She had always felt more at home in the saddle, as was how they first met at the lake, both out for a ride. He grimaced a smile at her confession of becoming a horse breeder. Whatever the conditions of the Sidwell Hall stables, he would make sure they were tip top, for her dream would come to fruition if it were the last thing he did.

It was a relief to know she would be taken care of when he returned to the regiment. He did not have to worry about leaving her in the care of his parents. No, she would have a house of their own and could set about achieving her dreams until he took leave between campaigns to be with her and their family.

With a grunt, he eased himself against the bed, careful not to put pressure on his lower back. It took three tries to lift his legs onto the bed. They felt heavy and unresponsive. A good night's sleep would relax his muscles. The riding earlier and the lengthy walk to and from the orchard had exhausted and over-worked him.

Snuffing the bedside candle, he turned onto his side, folded his arm beneath his pillow, and drifted into a dreamless sleep.

Eyelids shot open. Pitch black met dilated pupils.

Gripping a fistful of sheets, Duncan gritted his teeth. Was this a dream? Was he in hell? His skin tingled from a fine layer of sweat sheathing feverish flesh. This must be hell. This must be retribution for all the lives he had ferried to Hades.

A hot poker stabbed into his back, sending waves of heat lashing at his limbs. Nothing, he could see nothing. But he felt everything, every heartbeat, every breath, every twitch of muscle.

Before he could stop himself or realize this was reality and not the pits of hell, he cried out for mercy. *Please, God, forgive my sins, forgive my transgressions.* He screamed for salvation.

Tossing the blankets aside in a fiery fit, he launched himself out of bed, ready to run for safety. He landed with a *thunk* on the floor, his head collid-ing into the bedside table, his legs tangled in sheets. Like the hands of the undead, the sheets clung to his thighs, pulling him, weighing him down. His legs. He could not move his legs. He could not pull them free.

Swatting at the sheets, he cried out. Frantic. Desperate. He had to get out.

Footsteps in the distance clamored a crescendo. A door opened. The light from a myriad of candles blinded him. Shielding his eyes, he continued to cry out for forgiveness, for freedom, for home.

Strong arms embraced him.

"I've got you, son. Dadaí is here."

Duncan clung to his father, mumbling incoherent pleas to liberate his legs from the hands of French soldiers.

The soothing coos of his mother were heard somewhere nearby. More hands joined those of his father as Duncan was lifted full bodied onto the bed. As Duncan's eyes adjusted to the candlelight, he just made out the face of his valet before his father's came into focus.

"I can't feel my legs. I can't feel anything." Duncan clawed at his father's arms, trying to sit up.

"I've got you, son. I'm here." Sean repeated the mantra until Duncan calmed.

Mouth dry, eyes heavy, Duncan tried to focus on the voices around him. They eddied, swirling in a mist at the coffered canopy of his bed.

"I've given him enough laudanum to last the night," a voice said, reverberating inside Duncan's skull. "I'll return in the morning for an examination. We will need to bleed him at once for the fever."

Duncan moved his tongue to speak, but it held fast to his teeth, refusing to be so abused by the faculties of speech. *No more bleeding*, he pleaded into a thought cloud that he wished in the direction of the voice.

"He could require amputation," came the disembodied sound, ebbing in a tide of cyan. "I'll administer more laudanum on the morrow. There's a physician in Edinburgh who may be able to help. Keep the curtains closed."

Disjointed. Fragmented. Sounds the color of daffodils, cacophonous in the meadow of violins resonated.

Duncan struggled against the effects of the laudanum, the latter taking the form of a bilious French infantryman beckoning with an invitation to a ball. Relaxing, he rode the rip current into the pleasure dome.

Chapter 6

After another tasteless bite, Mary forfeited her attempts to eat dinner.

Nearly a week had passed since taking tea with the Starretts. Whatever promises Duncan made to call on her must have been forgotten, or more likely, he learned she met his son and was avoiding her.

He had not the courage to face her and admit his betrayal. All this time, she had waited for him while he was finding love elsewhere. Had he married the girl? Had he loved her? Had she been a camp follower who meant nothing but a way to slake his needs and overcome boredom? Mary was uncertain which was worse.

For the first couple of days after seeing the boy, she had suffered a range of emotions varying from denial to fury. By mid-week, she had convinced herself this was normal, and she was taking it too personally. All men had mistresses, did they not? Many of them had children by those mistresses. It had been five years, so could she really expect him to remain faithful during all that time? Men had different needs than women, after all. They might not be capable of loyalty. If his heart had remained chaste, would that not be enough?

By the end of the week, she accepted the situation, though she felt no better about it. Regardless of reason, what was done was done. She had two choices. She could confront him about it, demand an explanation, and try to understand the situation from his perspective so that they could move forward with their future. Or she could walk away.

This was the alternative she was not ready to consider seriously.

Six years she had devoted herself to their companionship. Six years was a long time to throw aside because of a single unmet expectation that had never been voiced. However serious she had been in telling him she did not have to marry, the future seemed bleak without the promise of their union.

For one and twenty years she had been alone. She never knew her father, he having had little involvement with her and passing when she was little older than a toddler. Her mother had no use for a daughter. Mary's brother had been at Oxford and then his Grand Tour while her nanny and governess raised her. Aside from Arabella, who had lived not far from Lyonn Manor and came from a family approved of by Mary's mother, she had experienced few interactions for the majority of her life. Charlotte was a dear friend now, and her brother was supportive and involved in ways he had never been before, but she was, essentially, alone.

Duncan offered a companionship that both pleased and excited her. His family was her ideal of what a family ought to be, of what she wanted to be part and create for herself. Could she have these things with another gentleman? Perhaps. But she had not lied to Duncan when she said she was not tempted by any of her suitors during her first

Season. Had her heart not belonged to Duncan, she may have taken them more seriously, but none of them gave her butterflies. None of them made her toes curl with a single glance. None of them took her passion for horses seriously. They only saw in her good lineage, social connection, and a lucrative dowry.

She could not, in good conscience, throw away happiness over a transgression.

What she would demand, though, would be his loyalty from this point forward. If he could not promise that, she would walk away. She wanted a life's companion, not a husband in name only.

With her mind decided, she should have a hearty appetite. Her stomach disagreed. However ready she was to make this work, Duncan must feel otherwise. The silence of the week spoke volumes.

"I've had quite enough of this behavior."

Mary's head snapped up, her cutlery clattering against the dish.

Her mother, Catherine Mowbrah, the Dowager Duchess of Annick, stared at her with eyes of coal.

Drake set down his own cutlery, dabbed at the corners of his mouth with his napkin, and said, "I'll not have you antagonize her, Mother. You only join us for dinner once a week, and I'd like it to be enjoyable. Tell us more about Lady Pennington's visit."

Undaunted, her mother said, "I've lost my appetite watching her poke at her food. Ladies do not poke food. I did not move into the dower house for my daughter to become a heathen."

Eyes narrowing, Mary said, "I am not a heathen. I am an adult who will poke my food if I wish."

"This is what happens to women who surpass the age of marriage. They become willful."

Charlotte tittered, making light of the situation. "Mary has always been independent. I find it an admirable trait most becoming of her. Mary, why don't you tell us your plans for the women's archery competition during the October shooting party?"

Before Mary could take the bait at turning the conversation, her mother harrumphed. "Independence is not an admirable trait. It's a trait that encourages a woman to associate with bumpkins."

Mary straightened her posture and lifted her chin.

In a commanding voice Mary rarely heard from her brother, Drake said, "I'll not have you speak ill of the Starretts in my household, Mother. They are of good stock and deserve our respect. If you so much as imply otherwise, I will have Mr. Hunter escort you back to the dower house."

Mother pursed her lips but remained silent.

The following morning, Mary sat in the conservatory with Charlotte. The morning light was perfect for her embroidering.

"Not *all* men stray," Charlotte said, nursing a cup of chocolate.

"I shouldn't ask this. I don't want to know the answer, but…" Mary stabbed at her silk. "Has Drake ever, you know, strayed?"

"Heavens no. He values his life." She giggled.

"What keeps him constant? Is it merely a matter of keeping him, um, satisfied?"

Mary's stomach was in her throat for asking a sordid and personal question, but she had no one else to ask. If she were to ensure Duncan's continued loyalty, she had to know how.

"Oh dear," her sister-in-law muttered. "Let me tell you something about your brother, though I can't say it helps your situation. Drake doesn't differentiate between emotional love and physical love. For him, physical love is a display of emotional love. He can't, you know, share himself with someone he doesn't love. And when he loves, it's soul deep."

"I'm the same. At least, I think I am. I have no interest in anyone outside my heart's desire." Mary knew she was blushing feverishly. "But all men aren't like that."

"No," Charlotte agreed. "All men aren't like that. I would venture to say most aim to keep the emotional and the physical separated. As many see it, emotional love means respecting a woman enough not to physically harass her, and so they take care of their needs elsewhere."

"I shouldn't expect him to remain loyal?"

"I would expect nothing less." Charlotte set her cup aside. "But what do *you* want?"

"I want loyalty."

"Right. Then why aren't you standing behind your convictions? You're ready to forgive him even when it goes against what you want."

"I know. But this is different."

Charlotte arched a brow.

"Well, it is. We had no official understanding. And he was away all that time."

"So?"

Mary sighed, setting her embroidery aside. "I at least want to understand his position. From there, we can set rules."

"And what about his son?"

The door from the house opened, interrupting them. Drake walked in, his face ashen, his expression grave.

Charlotte was on her feet and closing the distance before he spoke. "Where's Theo? What's wrong?"

Drake shook his head. "It's not Theo. Theo is in the nursery painting you a picture. I hope I didn't spoil the surprise." Blue eyes moved from Charlotte to Mary. "It's Duncan Starrett."

The foyer of Cois Greta Park was a wide, two-story gallery decorated with landscapes of the home and surrounding property. Mary stared, unseeing, at a painting of a river. Her brother's hand was tucked under her elbow.

Colonel Sean Starrett's letter to the duke had been brief and hastily scrawled. Two sentences.

Come quickly. He may not survive.

It was a missive she had expected to receive any day during the long stretch of his absent years. Never had she anticipated reading those lines after his safe return. They had so little time together. Three afternoons, half an hour each. All three had been shared with family looking on and little opportunity to talk.

She wanted to rail at Fate. She wanted to cry until her soul was drained of feeling. She was too numb to do either.

Mr. Starrett stepped into the vestibule, his cheeks gaunt, his eyes red and sunken.

In the moments it took him to walk across the space, eternity stretched, and Mary's breath seized.

"He's sedated," the colonel said. "I wanted him conscious for your call, but the strain was too much to bear. Thank you both for coming."

"What's happened?" Drake asked, tightening his grip on Mary's elbow as though he expected her to swoon.

"Don't know. He woke in a fevered delirium, unable to move or feel his legs. I can only blame those butchers." Mr. Sean Starrett rubbed his eyes and pinched the bridge of his nose with thumb and forefinger.

A glance to Mary, Drake asked, "What's being done for him?"

"We sent for the best, a physician all the way from Edinburgh. I'm at my wit's end, I tell you. He has no more answers than the local leech. All the way from Edinburgh to close the curtains, bleed my boy, and keep him fed with soup so thin it wouldn't nourish a dog. I don't know what to do. If I send the physician away, what will happen?"

Forgetting himself, he grasped the duke's arm and choked a sob.

They waited for Mr. Starrett to collect himself, and then followed him upstairs.

Once outside Duncan's chamber door, he turned bloodshot eyes to Mary and said, "This is no place for a lady. You should wait out here. You're coming means the world to us, and I can convey any messages you have when he's conscious."

Mary blinked, aghast. "Bar me from the room if you'd like, but it won't keep me from going in to see him."

"He's in no condition to be seen by a lady. We—we're afraid to move him, you see."

"You underestimate me, Mr. Starrett. Lead the way."

Too exhausted to argue, he acquiesced with a nod and opened the door.

Fingers steepled against her lips, Mary followed the two men into the room.

Darkness greeted her. A sweltering room of black. As her eyes tried to adjust to the wane light of a single candle, she struggled to breathe. The room was oppressive. Heavily brocaded curtains covered all windows, shutting out both light and air circulation. The smell of death hung in the air, causing her to fan her fingers over her nose and mouth.

Mrs. Georgina Starrett sat at the bedside, needlework in her lap. Mary focused on Duncan's mother, afraid to look at the bed.

The woman set her work on the table and walked over, pulling a startled Mary into her arms. "You can take my seat," she said, releasing Mary and indicating the chair.

Glancing at her brother, who nodded, Mary walked to the bedside. She sat, smoothed out her dress, clasped her hands, and kept her eyes trained on the edge of the bed, steeling herself to look up.

Time suspended as she followed the covers upwards, catching sight of a bare arm exposed. Her heart raced. Closing her eyes, she took a deep breath. The hammering of her pulse in her ears did little to still her nerves. She clenched her fists.

When she opened her eyes, she looked straight at Duncan.

There were no words to express her shock.

He looked…normal.

His chest rose and fell in slumber, a wondrous sight given it marked him alive and well, despite the room resembling a tomb. Even with him in such a vulnerable state, her breath caught at the sight of him. He lay in a laudanum-induced sleep, his chest bare above the covers. A dusting of dark hair covered his chest all the way to the hollow of his throat. Across the expanse of skin, scars decorated the muscles, the tell-tale signs of a soldier who met with bayonets, swords, and bullets. His flesh glistened in the candlelight with a layer of sweat. His expression was relaxed, his eyes closed with long lashes dark against his skin, and a week's worth of beard on his cheeks. Why had no one shaved him? Why were they keeping him drugged? He was not even dressed. The Duncan she knew would not want to be bedridden and forced to sleep. He would not want stubble on his cheek.

Further inspection of him revealed the numerous wounds on his forearm from the scarificator. She covered her mouth and closed her eyes, ill at the thought of him being bled. Barbarous.

Mary did not care how unseemly it was for her to see his bare chest, for her to sit at his bedside, or for her to touch him. She forgot her week of anger and resentment at his betrayal. All she knew was this was Duncan, and he needed her. She clasped his limp hand in hers and laced their fingers.

Looking up to the figures gathered at the end of the bed, she demanded, "Why is nothing being done for him?"

Mrs. Starrett stepped forward, her hands resting on the foot of the four-poster. "We're doing all we can. That's my boy, Lady Mary, my baby boy. We're doing all the physician tells us to do."

"To the devil with the physician," Mary cursed, shocking those in the room. "Nothing's being done except draining him of life. Why is he being given laudanum? I'm sure he wouldn't want that."

This time, Mr. Starrett spoke, his arm around his wife's waist. "You don't understand. He's suffering. When he wakes, he's delirious. We're doing what we can, my lady."

"We can't leave him like this, drugged and bled. We must do something," she protested, feeling increasingly frantic at her helplessness.

She did not doubt his parents were doing everything they could and feeling as helpless as she, but lashing out seemed the only course of action to ease her distress.

Her brother cleared his throat. "If I may, I'd like to bring a medical expert of my own."

All eyes turned to Drake.

"My cousin is something of a genius when it comes to medical needs," he said.

Mary stared in confusion. There were no physicians in their family. The only cousins she knew of were the Earl of Roddam and his sister the Lady Collingwood.

Drake continued, "She and her family are visiting her brother for a few months, not but fifteen miles from here. I could bring her as early as this afternoon or as late as tomorrow."

Mr. Starrett rubbed a hand to his chin. "*She*? It's against the Crown for a woman to practice medicine."

"Ah, yes, well, she's not a physician. She's a midwife, actually, a former midwife at that, but you'll not meet a keener medical mind."

"See here, I'll not have an unqualified woman looking to my son," the colonel argued.

"I understand your concern," Drake said, calm to the colonel's increasing agitation. "The way I see it, you can continue to trust the butchers, or you can trust me. If I'm mistaken, and she can't help, what was the harm?"

Mrs. Starrett leaned in to whisper to her husband.

After a brief exchange of lips to ears, Mr. Starrett crossed his arms over his chest and said, "I'll be present for the examination or she doesn't see him."

Early the next morning, Lilith Hobbs, Baroness Collingwood, accompanied her two cousins through drizzling rain to Cois Greta Park. Her spine was straight, her lips pursed, and her attire plain — a medical professional calling on a client.

Mary did not know her cousin Lilith well. Though Lilith's brother Sebastian Lancaster, the Earl of Roddam, had spent a good deal of time at Lyonn Manor over the years, Mary had met Lilith for the first time barely four years ago. The previous earl had sent his daughter to an orphanage when she was quite young. Mary was not surprised given how her own mother treated her. Women did not contribute to the family, Mary had always been told. They were a drain on the finances and a burden until married. It was any wonder she had not ended up in an orphanage, as well.

Mary had not been present when Drake rode to the castle to enquire if the baroness could assist. As unlikely as it seemed that a former midwife could do anything in favor of a soldier with a war wound, Mary did not deceive herself in believing there was hope beyond Lilith. One physician was like any other. Perhaps a woman's perspective was what Duncan needed.

They arrived at the house just as the heavens opened to turn the drizzle into a downpour. Rushing inside, they took a moment to compose themselves under the ministrations of the butler and the watchful gaze of Mr. Starrett, who eyed Lilith with narrowed lids and a frown. That he would even allow a woman to examine his son, much less an unqualified one, showed his desperation to help Duncan.

To everyone's surprise, Lilith marched straight to Mr. Starrett without waiting to be introduced and held out her hand like a man. The colonel stared at it in hesitation before resigning to shake it.

"How do you do, Colonel Starrett? Let's dispense with the formalities and social delicacies befitting our stations and talk business. From this point forward, you will refer to me as Lilith. I feel this a necessity because I'm about to become very familiar with your son's body."

The colonel blanched and flicked a horrified look at Drake.

"As I'm sure you already know, I have no formal medical training as a physician, such is the plight of my sex, but I do have a great deal of experience with anatomy and physiology. I believe your son may be beyond the realm of my expertise, but I'm here to do what I can. Please, take me to him."

Another glance to the duke, and Mr. Starrett led them upstairs. The room was exactly as it had been the day before. The only difference in Duncan's appearance that Mary could ascertain was new marks on his forearm from bloodletting. A wave of nausea threatened. Her brother tucked her arm under his and patted her hand.

"There can be no doubt," Lilith said, hands on her hips, "that a physician has been here." She scoffed and strode to the first set of curtains, yanking them aside to fill the room with the leaden light of a rainy sky.

"What are you doing?" Mrs. Starrett stammered, rising from the bedside. Her voice was pinched, her tone panicked.

"If you expect me to examine him, I can't very well do it in the dark, now can I? These curtains are to remain open from this point forward. Darkness will not save your son. I will be most cross if I arrive here tomorrow to find them closed again."

"Tomorrow?" Mrs. Starrett walked around the bed, watching in horror as Lilith went from one window to the next, flinging open curtains.

"I may not be able to help him, but you've brought me here to do what I can." Looking about the brightened room, her eyes fell on the sleeping

figure. "If he has a valet, please send for him. I'll
need his help in moving Mr. Duncan Starrett during
the examination."

Simultaneously, Mrs. Starrett and Mary spoke.

"Move him? But you can't move him!" Mrs. Starrett cried.

"Colonel Sir Duncan Starrett, not mister,"
Mary said.

Lilith looked from one to the other then over to Mr.
Starrett. "I need everyone to leave the room except
the valet. I'd like to do my examination now."

"I'm not leaving," Mr. Starrett answered, his arms
crossed, his brows furrowed. "And I don't like the
sound of you moving him. We've taken great pains
not to disturb him."

Smoothing her hands down her dress, she took a
moment to breathe before saying, "You may stay, but
if you say one word during my assessment without
first being asked a question, I'll have you removed.
Now, if you please, fetch the valet."

Mr. Starrett glowered at the duke before snorting
his displeasure and walking to the dressing room to
ring for the valet. Before the fellow arrived, everyone
single-filed out of the room.

Mrs. Starrett looked from Mary to Drake and said,
"I hope she knows what she's doing."

Not knowing how long the process would take,
the trio made for the upstairs parlor and called for a
tea tray, though no one did more than take a few nibbles. Mary certainly could not eat a bite. Her nerves
were frayed.

Drake attempted conversation. Mrs. Starrett
answered in monosyllabic witticism. Mary did not

answer at all. How could anyone talk at a time like this?

The mantel clock ticked the progress of time, but Mary was unaware of how much time passed. Well over a half hour. Perhaps not a full hour. The tea was cold, the treats forgotten.

The parlor door finally opened to a frowning Lilith and a silent colonel. All in the room stood.

Lilith held her hands to her side, palms out. "I'm a former midwife, not a physician," she said.

They waited for more.

When she heaved a sigh, Drake circled his hands in the air to prompt her to continue.

"I've found something. I don't know what it is or if it's the cause of his paralysis. It is *not* at the site of his surgery, though it is within inches of the scar. On his lower back, in line with his spine, is a concerning swelling. There is light bruising, but it is the swelling that is troubling. I believe, in my unqualified opinion, that whatever is causing the swelling is compressing his spine, thus numbing and paralyzing his lower extremities."

Mary pressed her hand to her chest. "So, you can heal him?"

Lilith's frown deepened. "I don't know what's wrong to do the healing."

"But you said—"

"I said my hypothesis based on a brief observation, nothing more. I would like to invite my personal physician from Hampshire. He oversees our foundling hospital and is the only physician I have ever trusted. It could take up to two weeks for him to arrive, but if I send for him, he will come."

"What are we supposed to do until then?" Mrs. Starrett asked, not looking the least comforted.

"Feed him real food, bathe him, and shave him."

Incredulous, Mary wanted to laugh. Was this to be their saving grace? She did not wish to doubt her cousin, but this was madness.

"I will come every morning for one hour," Lilith said. "I would offer more time, but my son is only six months and needs me on hand. There will be no more gruel, but instead meaty dishes. I want to speak with him, but I believe you might be right to administer the laudanum until my physician arrives. I've left instructions with his valet to prepare a bath and shave him. I don't care if it takes ten men to carry him and five to bathe him, it will be done. How do you think he feels to wake each day to find himself in such a state? Be gentle when moving him, but I believe it's safe to do so."

Chapter 7

The sound of green was a clashing cymbal, blue a resonating B-flat. Hoofs against the clashing cymbal of meadow grass shaded hues. With each hoofbeat, purple puffs of smoke rose, mingling into a muddy grey clock face.

Duncan slowed Caesar to signal to his companion, his arm arcing in a ray of tangerine. Joining Duncan, his companion grinned, the sound like clinking glass.

He was back with his regiment, some of his closest companions riding alongside him, camaraderie renewed. It was a day such as this that fueled his love for the army. This day embodied his passion — a respected leader, surrounded by familiar and trusted faces, riding across the countryside, seeing the sights, feeling the earth beneath his horse's hoofs. Without questioning why she was present, for it made perfect sense in paradise, he was pleased to find Mary riding with him, dressed in a riding habit that looked remarkably like that of his lieutenant colonel.

He never wanted to leave. He never wanted to return home. Here, there was no pain, only his men, the countryside, and his love, all together in a sea of symphonic color and hued sound. Even the air was visible, an undulating azure.

Mary sat sideways on the horse, as though seated in a chair, a peculiar expression on a haloed face. Angel wings, gossamer, shown behind a wreath of candlelight.

He heard them before he saw them — snarling, gnashing, ripping, the stench of death in their wake. A glance down and he saw, where his horse had been, not the purple of hoofs or the cymbal of grass, but the faces of soulless soldiers clinging, climbing, grappling at his lifeless legs. Bound by sheets, he thrashed, pleading for mercy. All he could do was wait to be devoured.

In a moment of lucidity, he recognized the effects of laudanum wearing off. A nightmare was coming, horrors he could not face. *Oh, sweet Angel of Mercy, I cannot face it.* He begged, he thrashed, he cajoled until a liquid the sound of red and color of a creaking door met his lips, and he was back in the meadow with Caesar beneath him, Mary riding at his side, his men singing in chorus.

From her horse, Mary reached a hand to clasp his and did not let go, a lifeline.

A voice broke through the clouds, deafening.

"Turn him onto his front. Gentle. Yes, that's it."

Duncan had been lounging by the river, Mary playing the harp, his men grazing with the horses, when the voice interrupted. All in his meadow looked to the clouds, aware of the intruder.

"After the clot is drained, movement and feeling should be restored," said the man in the sky.

Clot? Movement? Feeling? Duncan rose from the riverside, cupped his hands, and shouted up to the man, a sound not unlike a groan, though he articulated his words with the eloquence of a king.

The response was not directed to him.

"How much did he drink? He's coming to," the voice said.

Who? Who was coming? Duncan brandished his sword, readying for battle. This was his paradise and no one else's. He signaled for Mary to get behind him. The river overflowed from the edges of the bank, bubbling and churning, lapping at Duncan's feet, a tickle of cold water against his soles.

Tossing his sword aside, the voice forgotten, he splashed in the water, enthralled by the sensation of grass, rocks, and waves under foot. He twirled his love into a merry dance.

Morning sun slanted across Duncan's face, a cool breeze tickling his cheeks. He opened his eyes to see the coffered wood canopy of his four-poster. He dared not move.

A chill shivered through him. Clammy skin prickled into gooseflesh. Disoriented in time and space, afraid to discover if this was a dream or reality and which version of dream or reality he would face, he closed his eyes again.

His name was Duncan Sean Freeman Starrett. His rank was Colonel. He was a baronet.

There were no demons, no dead soldiers, no meadow, no talking clouds.

This must be reality. If true, then had he dreamed the whole of it, or was his worst nightmare about to be confirmed?

Fear gripped him with a stranglehold on his heart. He gulped desperate breaths of autumn air wafting in from the open window.

It could have all been a dream. All could be well. Just a wriggle of the toes could confirm it was all a dream. He could not bring himself to do it. Never had he been so afraid of anything. In this moment, reality was suspended. If he could hold onto this moment forever, he would. In this moment, he did not have to face the truth.

The truth that his life was over.

Living was not done from a bed. What of Bernard? He could not raise the boy from a bed. What of Mary? He could not marry her from a bed. What of his new home? He could not run an estate from a bed. What of his regiment? He could not lead them from a bed.

His mind rifled through everything in life that brought him pleasure—Caesar, riding, his family, dancing, Mary, swimming, an endless list that required the use of his legs.

A sob ripped through his throat, then another. Covering his face with his arm, he wept, his body racked with convulsive heaves until nausea swept over him. He rolled onto his elbow and wretched over the side of the bed.

Hours later, Georgina sat in the chair at his bedside, watching her son take it all in. All Duncan wanted was to be alone.

His forearm itched at the memory of the bloodletting.

His stomach cramped.

He was agitated, impatient.

Three weeks. The meaning of her words did not fully process. He had been in bed, trapped in a laudanum dream, for three weeks.

Bernard had not seen him in all this time. The boy was upset, wanting to know where Papa was. The most humiliating part was learning Mary had called on the family every day and seen him in this state. That was worse, even, than the mortification that he had been carried to a tub, bathed, and shaved by footmen and his valet during this time, not to mention other indignities. There were flashes of memories, some bits of lucidity when he recalled being in a bath, recalled Mary's hand holding his, recalled being fed by a woman who looked remarkably like Mary only older. He had not the wherewithal during any of those times to realize he was not still dreaming.

Propped against the headboard, a pillow serving as a barrier against the cold wood, he strangled the fabric of his nightshirt, his legs stretched before him, limp and motionless.

"The physician is speaking with your father," his mother said. "He'll come soon to discuss the surgery. He's optimistic."

Duncan did not respond. His eyes fixed on the outline of his feet beneath the covers. He felt nothing from the hips down. Dead, lifeless extremities.

"I know this is a lot to take in, son, but we're here for you. We'll see this through." She reached into her apron pocket and pulled out a card. "I thought this might cheer you, give you something to look forward to."

When he did not take it from her outstretched hand, she set it on the edge of the bed. Not a glance, he spared it.

"I'll give you some time before the physician comes. Is there anything I can fetch on your behalf? Anything you need?"

He could have laughed if he were not so despondent. Instead, he shook his head. She studied him in silence, then leaned over to kiss his forehead before stepping out of the room.

He stared at the outlines of his legs beneath the sheets. Long, strong, muscular. The legs of a cavalry officer. The legs of a warrior.

Picking up the card, he turned it over to see the royal invitation for the May ball, the celebration of the returned officers. Crumpling it, he hurled it across the room.

Chapter 8

By the time the chamber door opened, and a smartly dressed, middle-aged man entered, Duncan had explored his physical state. He was cleanly shaven and recently bathed, but weak and nauseated. Scabs had formed on his forearm where the lancet, or whatever the leech had used, had pierced his skin for bleeding. His legs were, as he suspected, immobile and devoid of feeling. The future as he knew it was over.

The fellow gave a bow upon entering, a woman following close behind him. Duncan fisted the sheets in startled confusion to see the woman. For a moment, he thought it was Mary. Only, this woman was older, perhaps mid to late thirties. It took him several long seconds to convince himself he was not having a residual laudanum hallucination.

The two women shared the same black hair, dark eyes, Roman nose, and tall height. The immediate distinction was the physique. This woman was pear-shaped rather than hourglass, beautiful in her own way, but not Mary. Her breasts were smaller and her hips wider. Smile lines framed her mouth where Mary's skin wore the smoothness of youth. Aside from the resemblance to Mary, there was something familiar about the woman he could not readily identify.

"I take this as a compliment of my success to see you sitting aright," said the man, fussing with his cravat.

Duncan scowled. "And you are…?"

"Dr. Knowlton. I see our previous meetings were not memorable. I assume you remember Lilith, at least?" He waved a hand to the woman.

Duncan shook his head.

"Yes, well, at least the laudanum days are behind us. As I said, I'm Dr. Knowlton. I saw to your treatment and will be staying for another week. My companion is Lady Collingwood. She saw fit to send for me, and rightly so."

Duncan's gaze moved from one to the other. Lady Collingwood stepped forward and put her hands on the foot of his four-poster, an intimate action for a woman he had never met.

"Please, call me Lilith. I'm the Duke of Annick's cousin and have come on his behest. Though you don't recall, I have visited every day for two weeks. We have spoken on numerous occasions. I realize you were not entirely lucid during those conversations."

All he could do was continue to shake his head, feeling like an imposter in his own body, a traveling soul who found his way into another man's shell.

The physician approached the bedside, taking a seat where Georgina had been not long before. "I'd like for us to talk about your treatment."

Duncan curled his lips. "No more bloodletting. And no more surgeries. Stay away from me."

Instead of appearing offended, the man smiled, crossing one leg over the other. "I'm not a surgeon, leech, or apothecary, Sir Duncan. I'm a doctor. I do not bleed my patients, nor do I saw off limbs. I'm the youngest son of an earl, educated at Oxford, and had the great honor of working with Domenico Cotugno in Italy before settling in Hampshire to help Lord and Lady Collingwood with their hospital. You're a rarity, my good man. Only twice have I seen a case like yours, both while working with Cotugno."

"I don't understand."

Duncan continued to look between the two of them, feeling exposed and uncomfortable. They were strangers standing in his bedroom, clearly familiar with him, while he sat trapped in his bed, wearing nothing but a nightshirt and without the faintest clue who they were aside from the informal introductions.

"You had a clotting of blood compressing your spine. Had I not studied with Cotugno, I would have been at a loss. God appears to have smiled on you, good sir. I have already drained and removed the clot. The swelling at your lower back is gone, though there will remain bruising for another week or longer. I'm surprised you haven't walked out of the room already. Have you tried?"

Incredulous and alarmed, he pulled the covers more tightly around him. Was this some kind of cruel joke? He was not going to be walking anywhere ever again. The horror of knowing they had performed a bloodletting operation while he was drugged was bad enough, but to be taunted about his condition was going too far.

"You need to leave. Now." Duncan growled through bared teeth.

The doctor had the courtesy to look chagrined. Lady Collingwood was another matter. She walked to the other side of the bed, sat on the edge—Good Lord!—and reached a hand to take his. He stared at it, balling his fingers into fists.

"Lady Mary and I have spent a good deal of time together and with you over the past two weeks, Sir Duncan. I've come to know you as a strong and determined man, as well as an intellectual. She tells me of your love for riding and your enthusiasm for your new baronetcy. I know it's difficult to trust strangers, but I'd like you to consider me a friend. Will you give me a chance to help you, as a friend?"

Her hand remained suspended, reaching out to him. Looking from it to her and back, he knew not what to do. If Mary trusted her, he wanted to, also. Slipping his hand into hers, he nodded.

Dr. Knowlton clapped his hands and stood. "Now, tell me, do you feel any pain?"

"No," Duncan said. "I don't feel *anything*."

As soon as he spoke the words, it hit him. He felt no pain. For the first time in six months, he was free of pain. No throbbing. No stabbing. No pain at the base of his spine.

"Feeling in your extremities should return, as should your ability to move. Small steps, literally and figuratively, my good man." The doctor leaned over the bed and held his hand a foot above Duncan's shin. "Lift your leg to my hand."

Oh, this was the outside of enough. Grinding his teeth and squeezing Lady Collingwood's hand a touch too tightly, he questioned, "If I can't move my legs, then how the devil am I supposed to lift it that high?"

"Will power. Now, lift." Dr. Knowlton raised his brows expectantly, his hand held steady.

Throwing back the covers and hoping Lady Collingwood would not be shocked to see bare legs below the edge of the nightshirt, Duncan concentrated on the doctor's hand and willed his leg to move. Nothing happened. How he could lift a leg he could not feel was beyond his comprehension. He grunted in frustration. The doctor did not move his hand, simply waited patiently.

Minutes passed of Duncan glowering at the hand, willing his leg to lift.

"This isn't working."

Dr. Knowlton lowered his hand until it was barely two inches above Duncan's leg. He nodded.

Duncan strained until his head throbbed.

Lady Collingwood interrupted, "I think Sir Duncan is tired, Frederick. Shall we try again tomorrow?"

The doctor hesitated, not in the least agreeing with her, but he withdrew his hand. Duncan covered his humiliation with the covers.

"We'll have a tray brought up with a hearty meal," Lady Collingwood said, "and an herbal tea. I've mixed the herbs myself, so drink the tea in its entirety. It'll help regenerate your strength. I believe you'll enjoy the meal. It's my husband's favorite recipe, and I've shared it with your cook."

The two bade their farewells at last and left Duncan in peace.

He let his head fall back against the headboard. This was hopeless.

The blush of the rose petal looked remarkably realistic, Mary thought as her fingertips caressed the silk thread.

Steadily, over the past two weeks, she had been working on hem embroidery for dresses to surprise the orphans in Lilith's orphanage. How delighted they would be to have their overseer return with an armful of gifts. For the boys, she had collected books from the Annick library to use for their lessons. The image of their excited faces swelled Mary's heart. Kindness aside, finding and crafting gifts for them busied her mind.

It was difficult to think straight while worrying over Duncan's condition. As much as she loved her rides with Athena, there were only so many times one could ride in a day. She had no wish to exhaust her horse just to forget her own troubles. Archery took up at least an hour of her time each day as she prepared for the October party and the archery competitions she would host, but a weapon in trembling hands, given the current emotional straits, was a dangerous thing.

The door to the parlor opened, startling Mary and Mrs. Starrett. Eyes wide, breath hitched in anticipation, Mary looked up as Lilith joined them. Her cousin's brows were creased, a tight smile on her lips. Mrs. Starrett set her book aside and leaned forward. Having seen Lilith's expression and reading the worst in it, Mary looked to her embroidery. With careful precision, she tied off the thread and tucked away her work.

"Well?" Mrs. Starrett asked, her voice full of hope.

"It's a process," Lilith answered. "Recovery may take some time, but he's through the worst of it."

Mrs. Starrett sat up straighter, gripping the arms of the chair. "The doctor said he would be able to walk today."

"Not precisely." Lilith's tone was as soft as the silken thread. "He *hoped* your son would be able to walk today."

Duncan's mother heaved herself against the chairback. "It didn't work."

"On the contrary. It did. The pain is gone, as is the swelling. The clot is no longer compressing the spine. After seeing a similar case in Italy, Dr. Knowlton was hopeful this would be nothing short of miraculous. Your son *is* better, Mrs. Starrett. We both have faith he will regain sensation and mobility. It is a matter of time and effort."

Mrs. Starrett did not respond. As silence lingered, Mary imagined Duncan in his room, alone, angry, possibly scared. She should be there with him, not sitting in a parlor.

Lilith reached out to Mrs. Starrett, covering the mother's hand with her own. "He's in shock. He needs your hope and optimism. The only way he will walk out of that room is with determination and sheer will. In his current mood, that might not be possible. You must be his strength."

Still holding the woman's hand, Lilith pulled out a handkerchief for Mrs. Starrett, whose cheeks were streaked with tears.

"May I see him?" Mary braved.

With a subtle but unmistakable cringe, Lilith said, "While that's for Mrs. Starrett to decide, I wouldn't advise it. Not yet."

"But I can talk to him. If he knows I'm here, surely that will lift his spirits." Mary was desperate to tell him she did not care about his condition. It changed nothing, not really.

"You must understand. He's in shock. He feels emasculated. You, I'm afraid to say, are the last person he needs to see right now, and I say that with tenderness."

After wiping her face with the handkerchief, Mrs. Starrett said, "I'm inclined to agree, Mary, love. I am in your debt for all you've done for my boy. Let's talk in a few days, shall we? Just the two of us."

The words hurt. Mary understood, truly, but the words still hurt. Her place was by his side. After all she had done, she was being pushed away. From their perspective, she was not part of the family. She was the concerned neighbor and friend, nothing more.

Mary did not care that there was no formal under-standing. As often as she had come to the house over the past two weeks, and as many times as she sat at his bedside, regardless that it was always with a chaperone, the whole of the county would assume they were betrothed by now. Servants talked. Servants talked to their families, to each other, to the servants of other houses, and to their employers. Employers then talked to each other. If there was a person in Northum-berland who did not know by now of his condition or of her bedside vigil, she would be shocked.

As far as she was concerned, Duncan and she were bound for life. If not, she had compromised her reputation and her heart for nothing.

The carriage ride back to Lyonn Manor began in silence.

What was there to say? The farther she moved away from Cois Greta Park, the more melancholy she felt. Would they tell him she had been there every day? Would he know she still cared? If she thought she felt helpless before, it was nothing to now.

"You understand, don't you, Mary?" Lilith asked.

"Yes, of course." Her words were brusque and dismissive.

Lilith gave a reassuring smile. "That is to say, not at all?"

Uncertain how to respond, Mary turned back to the window to watch the rolling hills pass.

Over the past two weeks, she had the opportunity to get to know her cousin. Lilith was a likable woman — direct and honest. Mary could not recall meeting anyone quite like her. Even Lilith's son was a treasure, one of the happiest children Mary had ever met. He smiled and laughed at everything and never cried. It was love at first sight when Lilith brought him with her on several visits, giving the Mowbrah family a chance to spend time with him. With a head of dark brown curls and the greenest eyes Mary had ever seen, Benjamin would one day be a heartbreaker.

Much to Mary's surprise, Lilith spent an hour of each of her visits at the dower house, conversing with Mary's mother. Why anyone would want to voluntarily spend time with that harridan was beyond her understanding. She declined to accompany Lilith. Each time, Lilith took Benjamin with her, as if Catherine would want to spend time with a six-month-old baby. As far as Mary knew, her mother hated children.

Lilith laid a hand on Mary's knee. "I know you want to be at his side, but he does not want or need a nursemaid. With you there, he would feel more helpless than supported. He's a man, Mary. He must do this on his own."

Mary insisted, "I wouldn't be a nursemaid. I would encourage him."

"You are the most instinctively mothering woman I know. I mean that as a compliment. At the present time, he does not need mothering. He needs a swift kick to his buttocks to get him out of bed."

She disagreed. What she felt he needed was her loving support. With her at his bedside, she could encourage him with plans for his new home and his future. Oh! And the May ball. That would be something to look forward to. Though they each loved dancing, they had never danced with each other. How wonderful of a motivator that would be!

"Have you thought about what you want?" Lilith asked.

Brows knit in confusion, Mary turned to Lilith. "What do you mean, what I want? I want Duncan to return to his normal life. Maybe it's too much to assume we'll marry, but it is something I hope for."

"How shall I say this?" Lilith sighed. "Duncan's life will not return to normal. There's a chance he could never walk again. That isn't something I would say to his mother, but it is something I'll say to you. There's a chance he could never regain feeling and never walk. That's the future he's facing, Mary. If he does regain mobility, and perhaps feeling too, and Dr. Knowlton firmly believes he will, his life will always be shadowed by this ordeal and the possibility of it happening again, given the weakness in his lower spine caused by the malady."

"What are you saying?"

"I'm saying you need to think about what you want and if Duncan can offer it, assuming he's willing to offer it. Just promise me you'll think on this." Lilith patted Mary's knee.

Mary turned back to the window, the world outside a blur.

Chapter 9

It was not the laudanum he craved so much as the paradise it offered, a reality he could never have. Never again would he and Mary sit by the lake, dance, or ride side by side. In a single night's horror, his dreams had shattered.

However ill he was over the next few days, and however much he wanted to return to that paradise rather than face reality, he refused to drink a single drop. It had not been his choice to use laudanum to dull his pain, but it certainly was his choice now not to use it. Thankfully, there was no physical pain for him to dull other than a lingering nausea and chill.

Dr. Knowlton visited every three hours, every day, prompting Duncan to lift his legs to reach the physician's hand. A hopeless effort. Duncan was to the point of telling the physician not to return. The man frustrated him with his arrogant optimism. The physician was of the opinion that Duncan could not move his legs because he was not willing to move them. It was the single most asinine thing Duncan had ever heard in his life. Did the man not realize that if Duncan could move his legs, he would? He did not *want* to be bedridden. He did not *want* to rely on his valet and footmen for even the most personal of matters. It was humiliating and degrading.

The daily effort of trying to move legs that would not move was straining. As far as he was concerned, his life was over. He would never be able to walk again. A hollowness settled in the pit of his stomach. Aside from the visits from the doctor and his family, he spent his time staring at the open window, unseeing, focusing on the hollowness.

When his chamber door opened, he did not look up.

Wood floorboards creaked, the sound of the steps muffled by the rug. The chair at his bedside dragged across the threads.

There were not many moments in life as humiliating as receiving a caller while trapped in bed. He had encountered the more humiliating moments this week, to be sure, but it was one thing to be unmanned in front of servants and quite another to be seen as weak by his family. He was not a weak man. He had led battalions into war, faced his enemy with bared teeth, proven his prowess with a sword time and again. He was anything but weak. And yet here he lay, vulnerable.

"Nothing will improve if you refuse to get out of bed," his brother said, nonchalant.

Duncan turned his head. Quinn raised his brows and drummed fingers on his knee.

"Oh, pardon me. Did I forget to stand in greeting? How discourteous. Leave the room and come back in so I may rise and bow in reverence."

Duncan immediately regretted the rudeness of his words.

His family had been nothing but encouraging. He valued their company, love, and support. Regardless, his speech became sharper with each conversation, his patience worn thin. He wanted them to visit, but at the same time, he wanted them to leave him alone. His brashness was winning the war.

Quinn did not flinch. "I have a proposition. I want you to take tea with us every afternoon. In the parlor."

"And how do you suggest I do that? Shall I fling myself over the side of the bed and crawl on my forearms?"

"Aw, brother, your acerbic tongue has not gone sweet. Your valet will dress you. The footmen will aid in your transport. And you'll take tea with us in the parlor."

"I'll agree to it if you agree to be dressed while horizontal and then carried about the house as an invalid. What do you say? Is it a deal?" Duncan's sarcasm thickened.

Quinn scooted the chair closer. "'And he said unto me, my grace is sufficient for thee: for my strength is made perfect in weakness. Most gladly therefore will I rather glory in my infirmities, that the power of Christ may rest upon me.'"

Duncan scoffed. "If you've come to spout sermons, leave."

"'Be strong and of a good courage. He it is that doth go before thee; he will be with thee, he will not fail thee, neither forsake thee: fear not, neither be dismayed.'"

Turning away, Duncan returned to his philosophical study of the open window.

"Will you at least see Bernard?" Quinn implored. "He asks after you every day. Mama says he cries himself to sleep because you don't read him a story.

If you can't do something for yourself, do something for him. You're turning into the most selfish man of my acquaintance."

"Selfish?" Duncan jerked his head to face his brother. Pushing himself into a seated position, he glowered. "I hardly call my condition selfish. I didn't ask for this to happen."

"No, but you're allowing this to dominate your life. You've become a right grump who is thinking only of himself. Not everything is about you, Duncan. Yes, it's humiliating. Yes, it's frustrating. But staying here pouting is selfish. There is a little boy out there who depends on you and a young lady who is head over ears in love with you, not to mention the tenants of the baronetcy who depend on the baronet for their employment and are eager to meet you."

Duncan threw up his hands in a gesture of helplessness. "What can I offer any of them? I'm a broken man."

"'Count it all joy when ye fall into divers temptations; knowing this, that the trying of your faith worketh patience. But let patience have her perfect work, that ye may be perfect and entire, wanting nothing.'"

"If God cared a whit about me, I wouldn't be in this condition. Now, get out." He pointed his brother to the door.

Quinn sighed and stood. When he reached the door, he paused. "We expect you for tea tomorrow. Bernard will be there waiting. If you disappoint that boy, I will come in here and personally show you the wrath of God."

That same afternoon brought another caller.

It began with a knock and entrance by his mother. She marched into his dressing room to summon the valet without a word of acknowledgement to her son. Duncan set aside the book he had been reading, though reading implied an active participation, when in truth, his gaze had been trained on the same passage for the past half hour.

With hands on hips and chin held high, she said, "You have twenty minutes to dress before your guests arrive." Her voice boomed, authoritative — the voice of a mother of seven, of a woman who had spent twenty years following the drum with her husband.

"What guests?" Duncan questioned, not at all liking the direction the day had taken.

The valet stepped into the room, awaiting orders.

"The first of your guests for the week. Starting tomorrow, you'll be receiving callers."

"What the devil is going on?" His ire churned his stomach, rising in a burning fury.

"You are a sought-after man, son. Half the village want to come and offer their good wishes. They all know, it would seem, that something has befallen you. You're their returning hero, Duncan. You'll not deprive them of the opportunity to show they care."

"Yes, I will," Duncan insisted. "I don't want to see anyone. I'm in no state to see anyone. If they knew my condition, they wouldn't want to see me, either."

"I don't care what you want, young man. These people have watched you grow up, respect and admire the man you've become, and idolize you as a hero. You will see them. You will be kind."

"Oh, this is quite enough, Mama. I'm anything but a hero. Just look at me! I'm nothing."

Georgina nodded to his valet. "Peter has already set aside a handsome ensemble for you to receive your guests. Is that not so?" The piercing look she gave the valet would have sent the most war-hardened soldier to his knees. "If my son balks, you have my permission to flog him."

On that, she turned heel and left.

Duncan gaped at the closed door. What sort of life was this? Since when was a man of five and twenty bullied by his own mother? He was a colonel for crying in a laudanum bottle! He was a baronet!

Tossing aside the covers, he signaled to his valet. "Well, get on with it. Neither of us wants to be flogged."

"Right, sir," his valet said with a bow.

No more than twenty minutes later, Duncan was dressed in silk breeches, matching green coat and waistcoat, a simply knotted cravat, and clocked stockings. He was as tidy as a man could be with only twenty minutes to dress. The stubble on his cheek made him feel unclean, though. Normally, he was meticulous about his appearance, but since waking to this new reality, he found it difficult to care.

Two footmen had aided the valet in moving him to the snug in the front corner of the room. If his mother wanted him to receive guests in the parlor or drawing room, she would have to give him more notice.

Duncan picked non-existent lint from his sleeve, annoyed. He did *not* want to see anyone.

At precisely twenty after — his mother's punctuality at its finest — a knock sounded.

"Enter," he barked.

Why anyone bothered to knock was beyond him. They had been barging in all week.

The door opened to the face of Mary's cousin, Lady Collingwood, or Lilith as she insisted on being called. She stepped inside, a surprised expression to find him seated by the open window.

"Excuse my rudeness for not standing," he said, waving a hand to one of the empty seats across from him.

She hovered by the door, her hand on the frame, one foot in the room. "I thought for a moment you had good news to share."

"Alas, my lady, no." He enunciated the last word.

With a knowing smile, she stepped aside, opening the door wide behind her. "I've brought someone to cheer your spirits."

He frowned, not at all interested in seeing Dr. Knowlton again today. Nothing was more disheartening than that man's outreached hand, ever expectant.

Only, it was not Dr. Knowlton who stepped into the room.

His heart thrummed a Scottish reel when Mary walked in, tentative, eyes a hopeful shade of walnut brown, a half-smile on her lips. Duncan swallowed against a maelstrom of emotions.

She was the apple in Eden, a sinful delight he could not have. Gooseflesh rose on his arms as he flushed with hot pleasure in the coolness of the room. Her luscious figure was framed in a cream dress with high waist and low neckline, her pale bosom swelling and falling with each breath. There was some sort of woman's work on the hem of the dress and sleeves, but he hardly noticed when there was such a person as she to capture his attention. Her hair ringleted around her oval face, the darkness of the tresses emphasizing the pearl of her skin.

All he wanted was to embrace her and set his lips to hers.

As the memory of their recent kiss teased him, he felt a warring anger. How dare they allow her to come here. She was the mirage of water to a parched man. Never could they be together. He could not even bed her, much less be the man she needed. Mary was a vibrant flame. A woman who spent her mornings riding at full pelt had no business being with a man who could not walk.

"What are you doing here?" he asked in way of a greeting as the two ladies entered the room, leaving the door ajar.

Mary's half-smile slipped. "I should think that's obvious, don't you?"

Lady Collingwood hovered behind Mary. Clearly the cousin was here only as a chaperone.

"You shouldn't be here," he said, sinking his fingers into the arms of the chair. "There's nothing for you here."

Mary's chin raised half an inch. "I'm here to tell you that no matter what happens, I'm by your side. Together, we can get through this."

Duncan heaved a sigh, glaring at the rug before looking back to Mary. "There's nothing to get through. I'm sorry if you've waited for me all these years only to meet a broken man, but take it as a blessing. This is your chance for freedom. We're not married. We're not even betrothed. We're in no way promised to each other. You need to leave and not return."

Though her chin wobbled and her eyes narrowed, her shoulders straightened. "Say what you like to me, I'm not leaving. I know your heart. You're frightened and angry about what's happened. You're lashing out."

"What do you know about me? Your loyalty is to a fresh-faced boy naïve enough to think he can touch the sun and steal the moon. I'm not that boy anymore. I'm not even a soldier. I'm an invalid. I'm useless. I have nothing to offer you, Mary, not even friendship. Get out, and don't come back." His voice rose in anger.

"Do you think so little of yourself?"

"You're coming is nothing short of cruel, dangling something I cannot have."

Mary studied him, searching his eyes. "But I'm here. Can't you see that? I'm here. I want to help you. Think of all the things we can accomplish together once we have you walking again. Dr. Knowlton believes in you, and so do I."

"The sooner you face reality, the better," he snapped. "How do you think this would work between us? Shall I court you from a chair? Wax poetic about the river we can't walk beside? You can't come to my bedchamber every few days to talk about the weather. Have you thought about what marriage to me would be like? We couldn't even have children. Has that occurred to you? You'd be a glorified nursemaid."

Hugging her arms, she said, "This isn't you. The Duncan I know would fight to get out of the chair.

He wouldn't let this come between his dreams or between us."

Slamming a fist on the side table, he accused, his voice venomous, "Do you think I want to marry a duke's daughter? I would always be your inferior. People like you don't marry youngest sons of military men. You would grow to resent me, just as I would regret marrying above my station. I can never be the man you want me to be. Please, Mary, leave. I don't want to see you again."

Knuckles white as she gripped her upper arms, she said, "You're right. You can never be the man I want because the man I want is courageous. You're nothing more than a cold-hearted coward. You can go to the devil, *Sir* Duncan."

Singeing his skin with her words, she about-faced and walked out, taking her cousin with her.

His heart wept. He fought the urge to cry out for her, to wail that he needed her more than he needed air to breathe. Rational thought convinced him he had done the right thing. He had saved her from a life of misery. This was for the best.

Chapter 10

Dark clouds loomed in the distance. Mary leaned against the window frame in the upstairs parlor of Cois Greta Park.

They had all heard the argument. When she walked into the room with Lilith, his parents and brother were waiting, identical looks of pity on each face. They likely all expected her to cry into a handkerchief. Behind her eyes was the welling heat and tension of unshed tears, but she refused to cry over *that man*.

That man was not Duncan. The eyes were muted, the expression menacing, the words cruel. Duncan would never have said such things to her. Whoever that man was, she wanted nothing to do with him.

"He's not in his right mind," Colonel Sean Starrett said. "Being in a room for so long does funny things to a man."

The family conversed behind her. She could feel their eyes on her, watching for when she would turn into a watering pot.

"The villagers calling on him will help," Mr. Quinn Starrett said. "He needs to see we all support him."

Mrs. Starrett voiced her agreement. "We need to remind him of all the things he enjoys. Bring his horse below his window so he can look out on it. Nothing more encouraging than that, I say."

The colonel added, "When my leg met a blade, laming me, I thought life was at an end. Over twenty years I had served Crown and country. What was I to do? Just as I did, the boy needs encouragement."

"Making plans for the future is the way of it," his mother said. "We should make plans for the celebration ball in May. He needs to ready his dancing legs."

As they talked, Mary's mind worked. Part of her wanted to run. She did not want to be burdened with *that man*. But as they spoke, and as the clouds rolled closer, blotting out the sun that had heretofore shined on Cois Greta Park, she realized something.

The whole time Duncan had looked at her, it was as though he were the sun, watching from behind the storm, *that man* the cloud. A protective barrier? A guardian? Duncan pushed her away because he was scared. Perhaps this was wishful thinking. Or perhaps it was truth. She had no way to know if she was making the most significant mistake of her life. But in her heart, if she focused on the Duncan she had loved for so long, she knew that now, more than ever, he needed her.

"No." Mary turned from the window, curious faces looking back at her. "I disagree. The last thing he wants is to look to the future. He is focusing only on *now*, and so should we."

"That's no use," Mrs. Starrett said. "He needs to think to the future and all the things he'll be able to do once he's walking again. That'll encourage him to try harder during Dr. Knowlton's calls. The doctor leaves in two days. Duncan must try harder."

"Don't you see?" Mary walked over and perched on the edge of the chair next to Lilith. "All he sees is that he'll never walk again. For all we know, it's true. The more we focus on his future, the more upset he will become. We must meet him where he is. The present."

His father rubbed his chin. "What do you propose?"

Mary thought for a moment, then asked, "What can we do to convince him there is a life to be lived even if he never walks again?"

"I don't want this talk of him not walking again," Mrs. Starrett protested. She removed from the chair and began to pace in front of the hearth. "I won't hear of it. And I don't want him to think of it."

"Please, Mrs. Starrett. We're not resigning ourselves to the condition," Mary said. "We're only trying to help him see that he has choices beyond walking or being bedridden. He sees only those two choices at present. We need to help him see this condition is not the end of all things."

Lilith scooted to the end of her chair. "What about a Bath chair? It would aid in his mobility. I could send for one. From time to time, we have such supplies made for the hospital."

The colonel frowned. "That impossibly heavy contraption they use to move the infirm to the pump rooms in Bath?"

"I would recommend one of those for outdoors," Lilith explained. "It would be too large and too heavy for inside, but should he wish to visit the garden or the stables, it would aid in his transport and give a sense of independence. For inside, there's the smaller and lighter wicker version that could be pushed from room to room and carried up and down the stairs."

"Yes, this is it," Mary said, excited about this new direction. "He needs a modicum of independence. And a focus, not of the future but of the present. We all know how much he hates being idle, so what if he had something to do? Something that helped him feel useful and in command."

Mr. Quinn Starrett turned to his father. "Does the baronetcy have a steward? He could be sent for. Duncan could learn the accounts."

The conversation gained momentum, enough for Mrs. Starrett to seem moderately convinced by the time Mary and Lilith took their leave.

Before Mary climbed into the carriage, Mrs. Starrett took her aside to embrace her and invite her to pay another call soon. However much Mary wanted to show Duncan she would not be pushed away, she did not think it good form to continue to show up uninvited. Instead, she asked Mrs. Starrett to pay her a call at Lyonn Manor. At least for the time.

The parting struck a chord in Mary. She had made the right choice. She knew it. Duncan may doubt they could have a family together, but did he not realize that his entire family would be hers, the family she had always wanted? And what of the little boy? It was not the boy's fault he was born of sin. The boy needed a mother as much as she wanted a family. Such a thought pained her since his birth marked a betrayal she had not forgiven, but it was a reality she had to face if she was determined to remain in Duncan's life.

For how long he sat with his head in his hands, Duncan could not say. He had been in that position since Mary's departure. His words echoed in his head, tormenting him. There was no way to recall the ugliness. How could he explain he wanted her to stay but did not want to ruin her life?

The sound of the door opening stirred him from his stupor. The last thing he wanted was more harassment. If his family heard the disagreement, he would never hear the end of it. The sun rose and set on Mary as far as his parents were concerned.

"Papa?" A tiny voice cracked from the doorway.

Duncan's head jerked up, shocked to see Bernard holding the door handle, half his body hidden behind the frame.

"I'm sorry," said the barely audible whisper from the door.

"Come here." Duncan gestured to the boy. "Why are you sorry?"

"You're angry with me." He had not moved from the door.

"Oh, Bernard, I'm not angry with you. You're an angel. Come sit with me." He held out his arms wide.

Bernard shuffled over, his eyes downcast. When he stopped next to the chair, Duncan wrapped his arms around the thin waist and hauled his son onto his lap. However disconcerting it was that he could not feel the weight against his thighs, it felt reassuring for the boy to be there. Duncan leaned Bernard's head to his chest and rested his own head on the unruly curls. He was all the boy had in this

world. How selfish he had been. Curse his brother
for being right.

"You're angry or you'd read to me," the child said,
tugging at the buttons of Duncan's waistcoat.

"It's not that I didn't want to. I've been ill."

"You don't look ill. Are you better?"

"Getting better, yes. Where's your nurse?" Duncan
eyed the door, curious what a three-year-old was
doing roaming the halls alone, not to mention
descending the stairs from the nursery on his own.

"She fell t'sleep. I sneaked. Are you angry now?"

"Nothing you do could anger me. How about you
bring the book to me and we read in here?" Duncan
ruffled the curls.

"Now?"

"Well, I suppose we can. We can do it every night,
as well. Won't you feel like a big boy reading in Papa's
room," Duncan said with a chuckle.

Goodness. It was the first time he had chuckled
since the night to end all nights. His eyes burned to
think how good it felt to laugh.

"Don't move." Bernard jumped off his lap and
raced out of the room.

Duncan almost laughed again at the command
not to move, but the irony was too harsh for a joke.
And what a louse he was. A selfish louse. This whole
time feeling sorry for himself when another soul
depended on him. His brother would never let him
live down being right.

While alone in the room, he concentrated on wiggling his toes. It was something he had not tried. In
fact, he had put no effort into moving except the
times when Dr. Knowlton visited. The spinal drain

or whatever the doctor had done was supposed to be a magical cure, but it had not worked from Duncan's perspective, however confident the doctor was. But what if Duncan was wrong? What if it had worked and he had been too distraught to find out?

Closing his eyes, he concentrated on his toes, willing them to move.

His eyes flew open, his heart racing.

If he could not feel his toes, how would he know if they were moving inside the shoes? They could be moving, and he would not know it. The thought was elating.

Leaning over, he pulled off both shoes and tossed them aside. Eyes trained on the stockings, he tried again.

Nothing.

He pounded a fist on the table.

It was not for himself he tried again. It was for Bernard. He changed his tactic. His goal was to lift the whole foot. Staring at the stocking, he focused on the hinging of his ankle, pleading it to move.

Footsteps pounded on the floor outside as Bernard raced down the hall and back into the room, book waving in his hand.

Duncan held out his arms to catch the launched cannonball that was Bernard. His efforts would have to continue later.

After nearly an hour of reading to Bernard, who never once tired, Duncan stopped only when interrupted. The nurse came to fetch him, looking harried and chagrined to find him in Duncan's bedroom, pestering the young master. With promises to return at bedtime, the boy followed his nurse.

The self-pity must end, he decided. If he could not do it for himself, he must do it for Bernard. His brother had said as much. It took the boy himself to shake Duncan into the realization.

The trouble was, he was uncertain how to go about life without the use of his legs. The goal was to walk again, and ideally with returned sensation. But what if that was not an option? Life was going to carry on without him either way, so he had to sort out a plan. He was a military leader who specialized in strategizing. The baronetcy was an accolade for organizing a notable coup. If he could plan war tactics, surely, he could plan life from a chair.

That was not to say he would give up on mobility. For the past week, he had not even tried, already having lost hope. Failure in movement could not bring him any lower. What was there to lose by trying?

If the doctor did not have such confidence. If the pain had not been removed by the doctor's ministrations. If he did not want it so badly. Well, he might have a different outlook on his plight in any of those cases. But the doctor was so arrogant in his belief that mobility *and* sensation would return, it did seem foolhardy to believe otherwise, despite the evidence to the contrary. The object — some sort of clotting of blood, the doctor had explained — that had compressed his spine had been drained and removed, and now there should be nothing to prohibit his lower extremities from returning to normal.

Unless permanent damage had occurred.

But if so, the doctor would have doubts, would he not?

Duncan looked down at his legs, still deceptively strong. Lifting them with his hands, one at a time, he stretched them out to see their length before him. With renewed spirit, he focused his attention on lifting his right leg. It had always been his leading leg. However strange it must look for a gentleman to sit staring at his lap, he was hard at work, willing his leg to move.

At times, when marching across the continent, their destination had seemed impossible to reach. They had entire countries to traverse by foot. If they had focused on the end goal, they would have given up. Instead, they had given themselves end-of-day goals, one short distance at a time. When realizing they only had to cross a hill, everything seemed manageable. That was what he needed: one goal at a time. His goal would not be to walk or to ride or to dance. His first goal would be to move one leg a fraction of an inch. From there, he could consider making a new goal, but for now one mission at a time.

And so, he stared at his leg, moving—or at least attempting to—for all he was worth, though outwardly nothing happened.

The door to the bedchamber opened once again, this time with more gusto. Did no one knock anymore?

"Duncan Sean Freeman Starrett. I am quite finished with your sullenness." His mother marched into the room, hands on hips, her fiery mane frizzing beneath her cap.

She was a formidable force, his mother. Not just because of her intimidating height, but also her approach to opposition. Judging from her fierce scowl, she expected opposition.

Duncan held up a hand to speak, but she refused to be interrupted.

"It has been five days since the good doctor worked his miracle," she said. "According to him, you should be training every three hours, every day. And what have you done? Lie in bed feeling sorry for yourself. I won't have it. Not in my household. If you want to wallow, do it elsewhere."

Stunned, he stared wide-eyed at his mother.

She continued before he could take a breath to speak. "I did not raise my children to be wallowers, woah-is-meing as the day is long. So, you can't walk. Boo hoodley hoo. How do you think your father felt when he took a sword to his leg in battle? Did he wallow all day? No. He limped along, refusing to let it stop him."

Abashed, Duncan held up his hand again. "Mama, I unde—"

"You, sir, have a little boy whose world revolves around you. Have you given a thought to him?"

"Yes, Mama, and in fact—"

"You've a young lady so in love with you she's compromised her reputation by coming here nearly every day. Don't think that's not been noticed. If the two of you didn't have an understanding before, you had better have one now. I'll not see her heartbroken or ruined because of your selfishness. And that's what it is. Selfishness."

Frowning, he tried again to interject. "Mama. Really. This is quite—"

"I tell you now, Starretts do not give up. We'll be sending for a Bath chair, but if you disobey the doctor's orders, I'll set it afire below your window. Don't think I won't do it."

Well then.

Crossing her arms, she jutted out her chin, daring him to rebut her.

He waited.

Silence stretched.

"Have you nothing to say for yourself?" she asked at last.

How he kept from laughing, he would never know. "You've a convincing argument, Mama. Consider me persuaded."

Georgina puckered her lips and narrowed her eyes, the crease between her brows deepening. "Prove it." With that, she marched out of the room and shut the door behind her none too gently.

Only when her footsteps receded down the hallway did he laugh.

Chapter 11

"'Tck 'tck, walk on," Mary said to Athena.

They had been to the lake, she and Athena. It had been the perfect morning for such an excursion—autumn breeze, warm sun, clear skies, all in contrast to the evening's storm.

The lake brought an onslaught of nostalgia and memories of Duncan as he had once been. Was it only those memories to which she clung? A future could not be built on memories alone, and yet any thought of walking away brought panic. She would not have the past five years be waited for nought.

Everyone had unsolicited advice for her. Lilith had been first with her encouragement to consider what Duncan had to offer and if it was what Mary wanted from life. Charlotte had been next with more questions than recommendations, namely how Mary felt about him and if it was Duncan or the memory she was in love with. It had been Charlotte's questions that sent Mary to the lake in hopes of finding answers.

Arabella had written to advise Mary to reconsider, for five years was not a lengthy loss when one considered a lifetime with a virtual stranger who could not give her children. She was of the firm opinion Mary should look elsewhere. Conversely, Drake wanted her to follow her heart, and just as when she was sixteen, he offered to do whatever he could to help her reach her destination.

Even Winston had offered his thoughts during one of his dinner visits. He inspired her with an impassioned speech about remaining loyal, for there was not enough loyalty in this world. Though he said it in a cheerful fashion, she could hear his own heartbreak in the words.

Surely, the love she and Duncan had shared ran deeper than a childish infatuation. The least the two could do was find out. If there was no substance aside from memories, they could both walk away, but backing out now was out of the question.

Since setting out that morning, she could think of little else except how to help him. The intention of visiting the lake had been to search for answers to their relationship, but her mind would not cooperate. It whirled with strategies to make Duncan's life manageable until he could walk again, as well as in the event he did not regain the use of his legs.

The priority, in her opinion, was getting him back on his horse.

The situation stymied her. He loved riding as much as she, if not more so. He was a Light Dragoon, after all. Their greatest mutual love had always been riding together, be it galloping, jumping, or merely trotting. How could he survive without time atop his horse?

Her best idea was a mounting platform. At first, it could be used to help the footmen hoist him onto the saddle, assuming he was not too proud. Once he regained mobility, such a platform could help ease the distance to the saddle until he was back to full form. If they could build a ramp up to the platform, he could access it with his Bath chair, allowing for even more independence both before and after recovery.

Such a construction would be fast and easy to erect. The trouble was that his pride might get in the way. Of course, it was altogether possible he would not want to ride without the full use of his legs or even be able to ride in such a state, but Mary doubted both. The Duncan of old would not have allowed anything to keep him from getting on a horse.

For the ride back to Lyonn Manor, she explored possibilities for the mounting platform and mulled over her proposition of the idea to his family. Not only was it an unusual idea, but they might not support his getting on a horse in his condition.

She took her time returning home, in no hurry to stop her ride or to end her plotting too soon. There was no other way she knew to help Duncan than to strategize.

Some time later, after having refreshed and changed, she sat with her nephew Theodore in the nursery. Only by moments had she missed Charlotte, the nurse had explained. The duchess had visited with her son for nearly an hour before returning to her duties. Mary was relieved to have missed her. Not that she did not want to see Charlotte, but she wanted time to reflect without more probing.

As much as she tried to engage Theo in a game of spillikins, he insisted it was time to write. The boy, in all his somber seriousness, was determined to have his name written in perfect penmanship by the end of the day. The ruffled auburn hair with its unruly tufts was incongruous with his sober nature. Head bent over his desk, tip of his tongue angling out of the corner of his mouth, he worked the quill across the parchment.

Mary sat behind him, observing with words of encouragement. Though she concentrated on his letters, her mind wandered. What of Duncan's little boy? Could he write his name yet? Was he playful and outgoing like the Reverend Starrett's children? Serious like Theo? A little hellion like the Earl of Roddam's son? Or maybe he was shy like the earl's daughter? Perhaps he was eternally happy like Lilith's son? Nearly a month had passed since she had seen Duncan's boy, and she knew no more about him than that one meeting.

She dared not bring up the subject to the Starretts. Such a topic was not for polite conversation. However much the implication behind his existence pained Mary, she longed to meet the boy and get to know him. She could not even recall if the nurse had spoken his name. Did he miss his mother? Oh, she could not possibly think of that. If she thought of that, it would be her undoing.

The nursery door opened to a footman.

"Pardon me, my lady. Her Grace has summoned you to the dower house," he said with a bow.

Oh, fiddlesticks.

If her mother wished to see her, it must not be good. Never did her mother summon Mary for conversation. Only when the dowager duchess wished to reprimand Mary on some account or inform her of some new decree, did she summon her daughter.

Snarling with a mental arsenal of vulgar words, she kissed the top of her nephew's head and left the nursery to face the hangman's noose.

Her lady's maid was not the least perturbed by Mary's request to change into a warm walking dress after so recently changing out of her riding habit into an at-home dress. The lady's maid knew at once the dowager duchess must have summoned her daughter. No one defied Her Grace's expectations for perfect decorum and proper fashion. Well, no one except Mary. All Mary had done was defy her mother throughout the years. Today, though, she was hardly in the mood for an argument.

Go in. Face the beast. Get out. Cause not a stir that could instigate a lengthy visit.

As she walked with her maid across the estate to the dower house, she fretted. With her mind on the little boy, all she could do was worry her mother had somehow found out about him. That would be the end of days. For the disapproved young man to have an illegitimate child living with him, well, that would be enough to warrant a public cut direct from Her Grace.

The butler, Mr. Taylor, opened the door with a dour expression. He had been with Catherine Mowbrah since she first married the duke. Mary was not sorry when he moved with her, along with a personally selected set of staff. The man was stern and humorless, just like Mary's mother.

With a perpetual scowl, the butler saw her to her mother's sitting room near the back garden before departing with Mary's lady's maid on his heels.

"If it isn't my ruined daughter," said the voice in steely austerity.

"Lovely exchanging pleasantries with you, too, Mother."

Mary took the seat across from the dowager duchess, leaning against the chairback in an unladylike slouch she knew would annoy her. Catherine took her daughter's measure with a quick glance and narrowed eyes.

The afternoon sun filled the room with warm and welcoming light, shadowed only by the neighboring trees and their lingering autumn leaves. Tall casement windows lined one wall, overlooking the tree-spotted lawn out to the arboured entrance of a walled rose garden. Peeking through the iron gate were Catherine's prized China roses. If only her mother could be as pleasant as the view.

Returning her mother's haughty expression, Mary arched an eyebrow.

"You are a spoiled girl with no respect for yourself, your family, or the rules by which we live," Catherine said.

"I hardly call ignoring me during childhood, then trying to pawn me off on aged nobles before I reached my sixteenth birthday *spoiling* me, nor do I consider refusing to be pawned a lack of respect." Mary tilted her chin, her hands folded in her lap.

"You're spiteful," her mother responded.

"Speaking when spoken to is not considered spiteful, Mother. Now, did I come for you to accuse me of my ruin, or shall we ring for tea and discuss this marvelous weather we're having today?"

Ignoring Mary's quip, Catherine said, "You've ruined yourself with that boy. I'm ashamed to call you my daughter."

"Oh, so you know about our trysts and our love-making until dusk?"

Catherine's eyes widened, her eyebrows lifting into her hairline. "How *dare* you, you insolent child."

"Was that not the ruin to which you referred?"

"I'll not listen to such vulgarity. I've shown you nothing but kindness and done my part in trying to see you settled; yet these words are how you thank me. You slash at my heart with filthy lies. Don't think I don't know every step you take. Don't think I didn't have you followed on your so-called trysts. Don't think he wouldn't have come to collect his reward had you succumbed to his seduction. You're a fool."

With a tight-lipped smile, Mary asked, "Then to what sort of ruin do you refer?"

"You know very well. You've paraded yourself to and from that house bearing our coat of arms. You've entered that boy's bedchamber time and again, bold as brass. Your behavior is disgraceful. I would expect this impropriety from his family, but not from you."

"He's been ill, Mother, unconscious during the visits. Each time I've had a chaperone present. Not a compromising situation, is it? But then, so what if it is? I suppose we'll be forced to marry," she said the last with a smirk.

"I could never allow such a union. He is nothing in our world, the youngest son to another youngest son. His grandfather may be a viscount, but his blood is polluted, mixed with that of heathens. He hasn't even the courtesy, respect, or wherewithal to formally court you or seek your family's permission to do so. Now he has even less to recommend him. He—"

"He didn't ask your permission because he knew your answer."

"Don't interrupt me." Her black eyes pinned Mary to the chair. "Now, I ask you, what sort of a man arranges trysts with a fifteen-year-old girl rather than publicly court her? Not an honorable man. What sort of a man abandons the girl he claims to love to play soldier? Not an honorable man."

"He—"

Holding up her hand to silence Mary, Catherine said, "Before you attempt to throw at me his baronetcy, know that I'm aware of it, but such an accolade does not an honorable man make. I forbid you from seeing him again."

Mary sat up, spine straight, shoulders back. "You cannot forbid me from doing anything. I've reached my majority. Before you threaten to toss me out on my ear, know that I answer to no one except the Duke of Annick. And I have his full support."

"You disgrace this family."

"From my estimation, you're the only person with qualms. You wouldn't care if I fell in love with a prince. All you care about is my obedience to wed someone of your choosing."

Overlapping voices rose in crescendo as each spoke at the same time, determined to be heard.

"You've made it clear I must renew my efforts to find you a suitable spouse," Catherine said. "The pool will have decreased given your advanced age, but we can assuredly do better than a disabled baronet."

"Has it ever occurred to you that I am not solely the daughter of a duke?" Mary asked, talking over her mother. "Has it occurred to you that I am a person? That I have dreams and hopes and fears of my own?"

Catherine's voice trumpeted over Mary's. "There is no place for dreams, hopes, and fears for women of our station. There is only duty."

"You've never even tried to know me," Mary said, her words drowning out her mother's. "You've never had a single conversation *with* me."

"Silence!" Catherine commanded, pounding a fist into her palm.

A hush blanketed the room. Mary observed her mother's lips trembling with anger.

"Our time is at an end. I have more pressing engagements," Catherine said at last.

Dr. Knowlton's departure marked a milestone in Duncan's progress. Nothing physical changed, but Duncan accepted the responsibility that he and he alone must make a change in his life. He had to accept his circumstances while simultaneously focusing on improvement.

The villagers called on him, two and three at a time, filling the afternoon calling hours. Day after day, they filed in, an inspiration. A few cast such pitying looks that he ground his teeth until they left. Others could not quite meet his eyes, as though his condition made them uncomfortable. The majority, however, were supportive and loving. It was the local blacksmith who took on construction of the Bath chairs, starting on the indoor chair first. He took pride in this project and hoped to have it to the family by the end of the week.

However much Duncan had dreaded the calls from neighbors, their visits cheered him in ways he had never expected. There was such an outpouring of love that he did not dare disappoint them by wallowing in self-pity and returning to his bed.

An hour each evening was reserved for Bernard's bedtime reading. Duncan heartily despised not being able to carry the sleeping boy to the nursery, but his Papa took great pleasure in the task on Duncan's behalf. The evenings were not the only time spent with the boy. Throughout the day, Duncan thought of excuses to send for Bernard. A quick joke he wanted to tell before he forgot it. A game he wanted to play. A part of a book he needed Bernard to read to him. Anything to spend more time with his son. It was with him that Duncan felt the most alive, the most positive about the future.

Today marked the day the steward from Sidwell Hall would arrive. Though not familiar with estate accounts, letting tenant farms, or any such practices, he was eager to learn. He caught himself rubbing his hands together in anticipation. Foremost on his mind, though it realistically should be the last thing on his mind, were the stables. He wanted to know the conditions of the stables, the size, and if the setup was sufficient for a stud farm. Something he did not know that he would need to enquire from Mary was what she hoped to breed. Hunters? Draft? Thoroughbreds? Had she already told him thoroughbreds? He could not recall.

There were more reasons not to pursue a courtship with Mary than he could list on a single piece of parchment, but he would not give up on their future together. Given his last words to her had been unfor-givably harsh, she may never want to see him again. His family felt otherwise.

Three hours before the steward was set to arrive, he called a family meeting. His sister-in-law, Miranda, was able to attend with Quinn, their children settled in the nursery with Bernard.

Miranda smiled encouragement. His mother wor-ried her bottom lip. His father's brows wrinkled with concern. Quinn leaned forward with an expectant half-smile.

"I've called you to the table," Duncan said, "to say that I love each of you, but I don't want to be a burden."

A rush of overlapping words assaulted his ears as everyone talked at once, all misinterpreting his meaning. Both hands raised, palms out, he bowed his head to request silence.

"What I mean to say is, I don't want anyone to feel they have to nurse me. Having all of you cater to my needs, entertain me, and suffer my foul moods is not a situation I want us to find ourselves…again. After speaking with Quinn yesterday, I've come to the decision that I must be as independent as possible. I want to focus on what I can do, not what I can't do. If I know I'm going to be a burden, I can't…I can't live like that."

This time, no one spoke. Quinn gave a nod, lean-ing back in his chair. Everyone else sat motionless.

"Be honest, please," Duncan said. "If there's a remote chance I'll be a burden, I will remove myself to Sidwell Hall as soon as the steward arrives. I don't wish to stay if I'm a blight."

His father spoke first, his bushy brows knitted. "We all want to see the hall, and we want you to see it soon. But not yet. We're in this together, son. You could never be a burden. Whatever you want, we support. Just know we're here for you."

Georgina reached a hand across the table, clasping Duncan's. "Don't you leave me until I'm ready. I say now, I'm not ready."

Duncan was not sure if he was relieved or disappointed. He did not want to burden them, but neither was he ready to do any of this on his own. Waking each day in a strange, family-less home while he was still coming to terms with his situation sounded nothing short of a nightmare. But he would not burden them. They had their own lives to live.

Duncan cast a smile around the table. "I'm sorry for being a selfish nit. This is about all of you as much as it is about me."

"Truth is, we need you," Miranda said, her smile holding steady. "You're an integral part of this family. For too long, you've been away. Now that we have you back, we're not letting go."

His eyes feeling warm and wet, he glanced at his brother, who nodded again, emboldening Duncan to voice what he had been thinking all day.

"In that case, here goes." He exhaled a deep breath. "I've set goals, milestones, really. You'll think me mad but hear me out. My first milestone, something I'll need considerable help with, is to mount Caesar."

As he suspected, the room erupted with noise, protests volleyed. He waited for them to say their piece.

When the room grew quiet again, he said, "Whether or not I regain the use of my legs, I need to be able to ride. The stablemaster is the best choice for helping me into the saddle. He's the strongest servant we have, as far as I'm aware. I'm not saying this will be easy, but I want on my horse. I can't sit here day in and day out, not even with occupation."

Georgina launched into a tirade of what ifs that all ended in certain death. Miranda joined the naysaying. Sean rubbed his chin, staring at the table.

Not until his father cleared his throat did the objections quiet. "I've not mentioned this, but it seems a good time to do so. I've a letter from the Duke of Annick with plans for a mounting platform."

The chatter started up again, everyone questioning at once.

He continued, "The idea, says His Grace, came from Lady Mary." He cast a knowing glance at Duncan. "The platform, according to the plans, would ramp on one side and step up on the other to meet a plateau in the middle. This would make for an easy mount with the aid of grooms."

Duncan's heart pounded at the mention of Mary's name. He could hardly hide his excitement that she had been thinking of him rather than fuming in anger or rejection. Leave it to Mary to know what to do. If he could not swallow his elation, he would end up grinning like an idiot before his family.

"Handrails," Duncan said. "It needs handrails."

His father quizzed him with a stare.

"With the right handrails, I could hoist myself onto the saddle." When his mother huffed, he chuckled. "You underestimate my strength."

At his wink, she rolled her eyes.

Each day followed the same rigorous regimen. At dawn, Duncan awoke and rang for his valet Peter, who, with the help of a footman, moved Duncan to the middle of the room. Once alone again, Duncan undertook a series of exercises lasting approximately two hours.

The workout began with triceps dips off the side of a table. Then came bicep curls with a set of dumbbells one of the grooms found for him. Shoulder presses next. The abdominal crunches required extra effort to keep his legs steady, namely tying his feet to the legs of the table. Push-ups were next, which occurred in two rounds, one set on the floor and the other set with his legs planked on the table. The most awkward exercise, which left his forearms sore, was the arm crawl from one side of the room to the other. While not the most attractive of movements, it was invigorating, not to mention strengthening. He followed this with a series of practical workouts, such as attempting to lift himself into a chair without tipping over either the chair or himself.

Fitness was not new to him. As an officer, he had pushed his men to stay fit, providing himself as an example. They fenced, boxed, played cricket and bowls, lifted weights, and did chin lifts and muscle-ups on tree branches before chopping said branches into firewood. When the opportunity presented itself, they swam.

Regardless of what the future brought to his legs, he would continue his regimen. Never again would he feel weak or helpless.

Only when sweat dripped from his brow did he stop his morning workout and call for Peter. Depending on the day and circumstances, Peter would prepare a bath or bring the basin stand for Duncan to refresh and clean before a close shave, followed by the dreaded dressing—Duncan's least favorite part of the day. Next came the punctual arrival of his morning meal. Such a time as this made him all the more excited for the Bath chair to arrive, for it would enable him to join his family for the breaking of their fast.

The longest part of the day began with two footmen carrying him to the parlor at the end of the hallway. This would be his second to least favorite part of the day, being carried. It was unmanning. It was also a necessity until the chair arrived. Once situated near the hearth, his feet propped on a footstool, he spent hours with other people.

His family came first, eager to share with him stories from the village, letters from his siblings, or the progress of the mounting platform. The Sidwell Hall steward took his family's place shortly after. The man, a slight fellow with heavily pomaded hair and spectacles, had agreed to stay as a guest for several days before returning to the hall.

Duncan met with him every day, poring over the accounts, learning the tenant farmer names and specialties, visualizing the layout of the land, and asking endless questions. Rather than seem perturbed, the steward was excited by Duncan's interest. The previous owner had loved the land and people as though he had built it all with his bare hands. These were big shoes to fill. Duncan had no idea what he was doing. With the help of Mr. McLarren, Duncan saw a rhythm to the place. Even the farming techniques used, which he knew nothing about until the steward explained them, seemed logical. There was a clear strategy employed not much different in craftsmanship than his attack and defense plans. If he could lead a regiment, he could run an estate.

Once the steward departed to do whatever it was he did as a guest at Cois Greta Park, the villagers arrived to call on Duncan, a new set each day, none staying beyond a half hour, most a polite fifteen minutes. By the end of the afternoon, he was exhausted and stiff from sitting in the same chair for hours. It was not yet time to move, though.

The nurse brought in Bernard for game time. The two played pantomimes, name games, counting games, color games, animal noise games, and any other game Duncan could invent to entertain the boy until they were both in tears of laughter. Only when Bernard returned to the nursery did Duncan have the opportunity to move.

The same two footmen carried him from parlor back to bedchamber where he ate a hearty dinner and read a book. This was also his time to plan the potential stud farm. His steward had brought all the information he had on the stables and grooms, data Duncan studied at length, putting quill to paper as to what else would be needed to make Mary's dream come true. He had little to recommend himself at the present, but by Jove, he could make this dream come true.

Each evening came to a close with a second visit from Bernard for their reading time. Duncan read until the boy could no longer open his eyes, at which time the nurse, the boy's grandpapa, or sometimes his grandmama would carry him back to the nursery.

This was the time when Duncan propped himself against the headboard and, by the light of a single bedside candle, focused on moving his legs. He stared at one leg at a time, willing it to lift, cajoling a toe to wiggle, begging a foot to flex. Nothing happened, but he kept at it each night until the candle snuffed out. At times, he would swear he felt a tickle at the base of his foot. Other times, he was positive he saw a twitch of muscle. But then, his eyes were tired, his body exhausted, and the lighting poor.

Chapter 12

An arm over his eyes, he groaned to wake from a lucid dream. Mary had been straddling him, head back in a cry of passion. If only he could have another hour to sleep. What he would not give to return to that vision and explore the myriad expressions of Mary being pleasured.

With a harrumph, he propped himself on his elbows. The room had already been prepared for morning. A mug of coffee sat on his nightstand. A low fire glowed in the hearth to combat the autumn chill. The curtains had been pulled from the windows, letting in a grey glow.

Three days of intermittent rain had dampened his hope to try the completed mounting platform. Surely, it would not rain again today.

Today!

He shot upright, alert. Today, Mr. Swansbourne was bringing the indoor wheeled chair. The missive from the day before said he could deliver it at one. A whole morning to wait! Duncan had plotted all night that regardless of rain, snow, or shine, his first adventure in the indoor chair would be to have it wheeled outdoors to the mounting platform. He champed at the bit to get on his horse.

Gulping the now lukewarm coffee, he tossed aside the bedding, pulled his legs over the edge, and called for Peter. Today was the day! Oh, today was the day. He looked back to his bed with a modicum of longing to return to his dream, and then faced forward to reality.

He launched himself into his morning workout with vigor. So help him, he would get on his horse from the chair without the aid of the stablemaster. After a renewing scrub and a meaty meal, he was ready to take on the world. Not wanting the chair to be brought upstairs just to be brought back downstairs, he had two footmen take him to the drawing room. It was the first time he had been brought downstairs, and he could not say he liked the experience of being carried down; if he let it bother him, though, he would not go far and certainly not back on his horse. He could have, he supposed, worked his way down the stairs himself, but he dared not think of the condition of his clothes after such a feat.

His parents joined him, as anxious for the chair as he, though they avoided any mention of his mounting Caesar. They passed the time with a game of cards, eyes flitting to the door. No one concentrated on the game. Even when his mother laid down the wrong card, no one noticed.

A noise from the front stilled their hands. All eyes turned to the door. A squeak and a whisper. Footfalls and shuffles. A hushed commotion approached the drawing room. Exchanging glances, Georgina and Sean stood. Duncan tossed down his cards.

When the butler opened the door, nothing at first seemed amiss. He stepped inside to usher in Quinn and Miranda, both of whom were grinning. Rather than close the door behind him, the butler unlatched the connecting double door and opened it wide. A crowd stood waiting, eyes twinkling, hands raised in prayer. Half of the village filed into the drawing room, followed by Mr. Swansbourne and a mammoth wicker and iron chair rolled by two wheels at its side and a small wheel to the back.

Duncan was unsure what to look at first. His brother winked at him. His mother sobbed into her handkerchief. His father greeted everyone. The townspeople filled the room, all looking between him and the chair expectantly.

The chair was a glorious work of craftsmanship and looked as comfortable as a wheeled chair could look. Given its size, he questioned how much larger the outdoor Bath chair would be, for how could it be larger than this? This chair had a tall wicker back to allow for resting his head, handles in the back for pushing, wheels as tall as the arm rests, and even a leg rest to the front.

Mr. Swansbourne approached, as though to lift Duncan and carry him to the chair. Waving the man to lean closer, Duncan said for his ears only, "Bring it around to sit parallel with my chair. I'll get into it myself, though I'll need you to hold it steady."

The butler and a footman moved the card table on Duncan's command while Mr. Swansbourne wheeled over the chair.

Eyeing the eager crowd, Duncan said, "Thank you for accompanying our Mr. Swansbourne. It means the world to have you here in support of this momentous occasion. With any luck, I can join you at church soon."

A round of applause erupted, encouraging Duncan further. Never would he have dreamt of having an audience. He had assumed today would be a quiet family affair, and his attempts to get into the chair his own private fumble, not for the eyes of the world. The surprise was not unwanted. In fact, he felt the hot sting of tears to see such an outpouring of love from his fellow parishioners.

The wheeled chair was saddled next to his drawing room chair, the blacksmith at the helm, holding it steady.

The only thing worse than making a fool of oneself was doing it in front of a crowd. Duncan took three deep breaths to steady his nerves. *Do not fall*, he chanted to himself. Gripping the arms of the drawing room chair, he heaved himself up until he could shift his weight onto one arm, praying he did not topple the chair. As many times as he had practiced this in his bedchamber, he had never tried with a drawing room chair, much less a chair on wheels. Firmly seated on the coupled arm of each chair, he lifted his legs one at a time with a hook grip behind his knees until he moved them from one chair to the next, then hoisted himself into the wicker chair, sinking into the bowed seat with relief.

This was met with another round of applause. When Duncan looked up, he caught sight of two young ladies giggling and batting eyelashes at him. He could fathom nothing less attractive than a grown man having to climb into a chair, but there they were, flirting from across the room.

It was not for another half hour before the villagers left. They all wanted to see the chair wheeled around the room and gossip about the autumn fête.

Another half hour later, he cajoled his father into arranging for Caesar to be brought around to the mounting platform. Today was the day. Nothing would stop him.

Mud caked the wheels, delaying Duncan's plans every few feet as his father and a footman worked to clean the chair. It was designed for indoors, not out, and the wet earth did not help matters, but he refused to wait for the second chair to be constructed. He had waited long enough.

A darkness shrouded the stable yard, clouds threatening more rain. The weather should know better than to battle two Colonel Starretts, for Duncan and Sean both would wage war if so much as a single drop fell. Ignoring the sky as best he could, Duncan focused his stare on the mounting platform, a strange but glorious sight. Caesar waited, flanked by two grooms. The sight of the horse, the build of anticipation to ride, and the sense of normality this moment inspired had Duncan's pulse racing.

Sean wheeled his son up the ramp, stopping only when they reached Caesar's side. At the sight of the chair, or perhaps the sense of his master's anxiousness, Caesar snorted, pawed, and pranced. The grooms' attempts to hold him steady sent Caesar into a panic.

Within moments, anticipation turned to fear for those in the stable yard as the stallion reared onto his hind legs, fighting to free himself from the grooms. Georgina screeched and demanded her husband move Duncan off the platform. Thunder rippled through the air.

"Release him," Duncan commanded, his voice low and calm but no less authoritative.

The two words, however softly spoken, were enough to silence the commotion. At once, the grooms stepped away from the warhorse.

Motioning his father to move him closer, Duncan spoke to his horse, keeping his voice low and calm. "Happy tidings, stranger. I hope you've not been rusticating all this time. It feels like a year since our last ride. What do you say we give it a go today?"

As he spoke, the horse calmed, shimmying closer to the mount. Reaching over the chair, Duncan stroked Caesar's neck, continuing to talk to him.

Sean leaned down to his son. "This is enough for one day. You can try to mount tomorrow."

"No," Duncan said. "I'll mount today or never. Hold the chair still, please."

"This is too fast, son," Sean insisted. "Tomorrow we can have you lifted onto the saddle."

Ignoring his father's protests, Duncan pushed himself out of the chair using the arm rests and grasped the handrails on the platform. His father grunted his disapproval as he grappled to hold the chair steady. Georgina let out another screech. At least Quinn and Miranda had left with the crowd, or his attempts would be accompanied by a duet of women rather than one.

Caesar began to prance but not before Duncan hauled himself onto the saddle, his legs dangling to one side. He chuckled, imagining this was what it must be like to ride side-saddle. With one hand braced on the handrail, he used the other to lift his left leg over Caesar, straddling the horse as he had done for so many years.

For an endless age, he sat in the saddle, accustoming himself to the position. It was unnerving;

he could not feel Caesar between his thighs. He felt wobbly and could not secure his feet into the stirrups. How the devil was he to ride if he could not feel anything?

Nodding to a groom, he said, "Tie my feet into the stirrups."

Without hesitation, the groom fetched two short ropes to secure the feet.

The tension in the yard was palpable. A quick glance at his mother reminded him not to look at her again until he dismounted. Her hands covered her mouth, her eyes wide.

Well, he was mounted. Now what? To the devil with it, he thought, and squeezed his legs to launch into a gallop.

There was an awkward moment of him leaning forward instinctively, only to realize Caesar had not moved. Duncan cursed. Of course, Caesar did not move. Duncan's legs had not responded to the command. Heaving a sigh, Duncan loosened the reins. The horse hesitated, unused to rein commands, for cavalry rarely used the reins, not when they needed to wield weapons in each hand, but then Caesar stepped forward once, then again, and again until they were off at a walk.

As foolish as he might have felt to be walking a horse about the stable yard like a novice rider rather than a cavalry officer, he recognized no other emotion than exhilaration. He was *walking*. Yes, it was Caesar's legs and not his own, but he was walking again. Horse and rider connecting as one flesh, Caesar was his legs. It was the single most freeing moment of his life.

With a further release of the reins, Duncan signaled the stallion into a trot, a movement that had Duncan bouncing in the saddle more than he was accustomed to since his seat was neither light nor lifted. Flashing his father a speaking glance, he moved into canter, leaving the stable yard behind him to the horrified gasps and exclamations of his mother.

There was no pain in his lower back as with the last time he rode, although, granted, he did have feeling in his legs at the time. However unsettling the lack of sensation was, he was elated to have the ground moving beneath him on his own terms and the feel of his torso responding to the ride. The horse's gait, the rhythm of the hoofbeats, and the motion, all thrummed through his torso, engaging his muscles. He could not recall feeling so alive.

Crisp air kissed his cheeks. The smell of rain filled his nostrils though drops did not yet fall. Hoofbeats sang a symphony. The taste of freedom was sweet to his tongue.

Not wanting to risk his luck, he circled back to the yard after barely fifteen minutes, slowing Caesar to a trot. As the house came into view again, he flinched at a tingling in his right thigh. It stopped as quickly as it started. His imagination, he rationalized. A reverberation from the ride, perhaps. But there it was again, a tingling, a stabbing of a thousand scarificators, a tickle that extended to the base of his foot. He kicked out, expecting his leg to move, but it ignored the command, limp as ever. And yet he was not mistaken. This was not his imagination. The feeling abated once again, his leg a dead weight by the time he reached the platform where his father waited with the chair.

"Twice a day," he said in greeting to his father. "I want to ride twice a day."

His mother rushed over to the platform as Duncan patted Caesar's neck, moved his leg to the other side, and hoisted himself up and over into the chair. For the muddy return to the house, he listened to his mother rant and scold about reckless behavior. All the while, he wore a dazed smile, unable to concentrate on anything except the memory of renewed sensation.

Mary crumpled the letter and tossed it aside. She did not like the word *no*, and she especially did not like the word when accompanied by a lack of alternatives.

Weeks ago, she had written to the new proprietor of Tattersalls, Mr. Edmund Tattersall, to enquire about the purchase of a stud, along with several other questions she needed answered if she was to see her dream of a horse breeding farm to fruition. A point on which she had hoped for advice was if she should auction the horses bred or if she should make her farm a private breeding establishment.

While she recalled her brother speaking most highly of Mr. Richard Tattersall and that he had, in fact, procured most of his horses directly from the man, she thought the apple had fallen far from the tree. As Tattersall's son made a point to tell her in the letter, he would not now nor ever do business with a woman, but should her husband wish to send enquiries…well.

The man needed to brush up on the peerage and their children and siblings if he did not know who she was, and he needed to learn more progressive business habits considering it was always Mowbrah women who ran the estates and conducted family business. Everyone knew that. This new man doubled his insults, first with a slight to her sex and then to her marital status. Only if married, and only if her husband did the correspondence, would he converse. Well, *harrumph*.

She had been in the mopes for days now, and this letter did little to lift her mood. The manor seemed a prison, isolating, with so little interaction with the outside world. What could she do? When she went to town and was treated with the deference befitting her station — bowing, scraping, and carrying on — taking tea with the villagers felt like something akin to torture. No one was genuine. Except Mrs. Miranda Starrett. There seemed a genuine woman. It took a great deal of self-discipline not to call on the vicar's wife. While Mary only wanted the company, her visit could be misconstrued as a way to gather information about Duncan.

Yes, Mary had her own brother, sister-in-law, and nephew — not to mention her mother, who hardly counted in such matters — but they had each other as a family, and she was nothing more than the unmarried sister.

A few days prior had been one of the happiest she had known in some time with guests in abundance, all visiting for the day since it was Lilith's last week in Northumberland, her family eager to make haste to Devonshire before winter weather made the roads impassable. Lilith, her husband Baron Collingwood, her son Benjamin, her mother-in-law the Dowager

Lady Collingwood, and even her dog Jasper, had come to spend the day, accompanied by Mary's cousin, the Earl of Roddam, his wife, and their two children. Even Charlotte's father Mr. Trethow was in attendance.

Of the guests, Mary saw Mr. Trethow most often since he lived not far from the manor, having recently moved from Cornwall to be near his grandchildren. She enjoyed Mr. Trethow's visits to the manor. He danced attention on them all, and though she was of no relation, he made a point to carve out time to talk with her about horsemanship, running a business, and the like, all topics most men would shirk in the presence of a lady. In Mary's perfect world, this was the kind of father she would have.

Duncan's father was not unlike Mr. Trethow. What must it have been like to be raised by such a doting father — or by any father at all, for that matter?

When the family stayed at the manor, they distracted Mary from her melancholy. It was during these times that it was easiest to fantasize her perfect life, surrounded by a large family with a multitude of children. Once they had left, though, the echo of her footsteps in the halls was enough to drive her to Bedlam.

She laid her forehead on her escritoire. There seemed only one course of action for each of her problems. Regarding the horse farm, she would need to stomach her pride and speak with her brother. He would be able to set up something with the snap of his fingers. That was hardly the point; she had wanted this to be of her own making, or dared she think it, of her and Duncan's. Regarding her solitude, she would need to call on the vicar's wife, regardless what the woman thought of Mary's visit. She wanted a friend, and there was only one way to go about it.

A knock on the door interrupted her plotting.

Mr. Hunter stepped into the room, a letter in his hand. Not until the butler bowed out did she open it.

Only of you I thought when all was lost.
Your eyes of love brightened the darkest times.
Your hand held mine, ethereal bliss, through frost
And death, armor against enemies mine.
Our future I beheld on horseback high,
A union blessed with happiness. Until
I see you next, I dream of walnut eyes.
Your lips I kissed with promise to fulfill.
But then I was a horse's arse, and said
Words I ought not, spoken in haste, untrue.
Though I may be a lesser man, I dread
A life without eternal love from you.
Unless you wish to read a sonnet still,
Our lake you'll be on morrow ten at will.

Mary read his lines several times over, uncertain if she should laugh or cry. A poet he was not, but that he penned an apology sonnet meant the world to her. Complexing, however, was his request to meet at their lake in the morning. Her heart pounded at what that could mean. Had the miracle occurred at last? Could he walk again?

At precisely ten the next day, Lady Mary rested against the trunk of the willow tree, Athena grazing a few feet away. Fiddling with the buttons on her riding habit and adjusting her bonnet for the nth time, she eyed the horizon for some sign of Duncan. Time ticked.

She had taken special care with her curls knowing she would see him. A sizable azure ribbon tied her hair at the nape of her neck, ringlets spilling down her back. Her habit was one of her favorites with cobalt camblet embroidered in gold. Though she had not seen Duncan in his regimentals, she had fashioned this ensemble from his descriptions. Such a choice seemed silly now, but at the time she had thought it a way to connect them from afar. Today, she honored his struggle by wearing his colors.

Regardless how many times she had come to the lake without an escort, she brought a groom on this day. It was a last-minute decision but one that helped her feel more secure, namely in case something happened to Duncan. Not knowing Duncan's condition was distressing. The groom kept a respectable distance only just within eyesight.

A brisk breeze shivered through her despite the warm layers. Circling a finger around a button, she squinted against the sun, waiting.

Just when she was ready to give up, she heard the thunder of hoofs. On her feet and alert, she watched. The rumble increased, its rhythmic pulse in time with her heartbeat.

Over the hill crested her hero at last. He was magnificent, a powerhouse of masculinity, riding at full tilt on Caesar. She pressed her gloves to her mouth to see him, such a different view from the chamber bound, scruffy, and angry man she had last encountered. He slowed his stallion as he drew closer. Curious, her eyes fell first to his legs. Muscular thighs gripped the horse, housed in form-fitting buckskins tucked into boots so shiny they reflected the world around them. When she looked into his face, she only just stopped herself from licking her lips. His hair was windblown, his cheeks freshly shaven, his smile broad.

He came to a halt within arm's reach.

"I take it I've not upset you beyond forgiveness with my inanity?" he asked, his gaze sweeping over her.

"I knew you would come to your senses." She stroked Caesar's neck, another glance to his legs.

"Have I surprised you?" He ran a hand down his horse's neck until he caressed her knuckles.

"The understatement of the year. Am I to know your secret, or shall you keep me in suspense?"

"Alas, there's nothing to tell. Your mounting platform, coupled with the blacksmith's chair, has helped me accomplish this, but if you've not noticed, my lower half is secured to the horse. I still cannot walk, Mary."

She heaved a sigh, noticing for the first time the ropes tying his boots to the stirrups. The news was not as disheartening as it might have been. He was, after all, riding his horse. The Duncan she had last encountered was a man determined to be bedridden, and yet here was the Duncan she knew, the colonel to whom her heart belonged. That was heartening news indeed.

"I can't linger," he said, Caesar prancing away from her. "I only just managed to escape the escort of my brother and my groom. Thank you, Mary. Thank you for coming."

"You invited me, didn't you?" She reached a hand to him.

Taking her hand, he leaned with caution just low enough to kiss the air above her knuckles and said, "My mother will invite you to tea any day now. Unless you want me to wax poetic with more terribly penned sonnets, I suggest you accept. And if you arrive looking half as fetching as you do today, I'll tell you about the tingle I feel in my thigh."

With those enticing words, he winked and turned to canter in the opposite direction, leaving her to wave to his blurry silhouette.

Not but two days later, she received the invitation from Mrs. Georgina Starrett. Tucked inside the letter was another sonnet.

To tea you are invited, love of mine.
The clouds will part. The sun will shine, divine.
The stars envy your beauty, dear; the moon
Moves waves as you move me, tidal typhoon.
Together, we shall ride at dusk and dawn
For all eternity. To you, I'm drawn;
For you, I yearn; for us, I burn; to you
I'm pledged. One word from you, and I'll pursue.
Be not alarmed by clouds of leaden grey.
Alongside you, I'll walk with faith; I pray.
Should you begin to doubt sincerity,
Hark now my words of true fidelity.
With each new day, my will grows strong, to be
The man you long to see. But first, some tea.

Mary's smile lingered through the evening and next morning and still tugged at the corners of her lips when she rode to Cois Greta Park the next day, a groom in tow.

It was not at all the thing to call on neighbors via horse rather than carriage seeing as how she would now smell more like horse than lavender-scented soap and since she would be in her riding habit rather than a visiting dress, but that did not stop her. Such trivialities never stopped her.

The first ten minutes of her visit sped by in a blur. There was little she could concentrate on aside from Duncan. She did admire his new wheeled chair and heard tales of the outdoor Bath chair Mr. Swansbourne was constructing, and Mrs. Georgina Starrett did ask after Mary's family, among other things; Mary hoped her answers were appropriate, but she could not say with any clarity how or even that she replied to anything said. All her attention remained focused on the gentleman seated across from her. His legs were propped on a footstool, feet crossed, a fine ensemble of emerald silk hugging his frame, an elbow hoisted on the chair arm, a coy smile playing at his lips.

So distracted was she that she missed whatever Colonel Sean Starrett said that preceded he and his wife moving to the window to talk together. Their departure was so unexpected, though she was sure they gave a good excuse for it, that she sat straighter and looked about as though waking from a dream.

Duncan adjusted his seat, leaning forward with a broadening smile. "Alone at last."

"Yes, I had noticed. Not at all obvious, are they?" Mary smoothed the skirt of her habit with fidgety hands.

"To my disappointment, they'll not leave us in the room alone. At least we can converse somewhat privately."

"I don't see why they can't leave the room," she said, reaching for a biscuit. Invited to tea, yet she had not eaten a single bite. "What do they expect you to do? Regain full use of your legs for the sole purpose of ravishing me?"

Duncan threw his head back in laughter, drawing the curious glances of his parents.

After a hasty sample, she added, "My mother, for one, is positive I've been somehow compromised by visiting your bedchamber. The fact that you were unconscious and ill makes no never mind to her. I suppose she assumes I took advantage of you, as I would do."

Another bark of laughter had his parents turning with raised brows and smirks.

Continuing to chuckle, he studied her, his eyes glinting. Under such scrutiny, she could do little except blush, thankful to be wearing a high-collared habit rather than another of Charlotte's low-bodice recommendations.

"Before we say anything more, let me begin with this. I don't deserve your forgiveness," he said, his smile slipping into a more somber expression. "I spoke out of turn the day you called. After all you had done, I lashed out. I can't apologize enough."

"Yes, well, you were a bit of a grump. But here I am, and here you are, and that's now behind us." With a last nibble of the biscuit, she added, "If you do it again, however, I warn you, I'll pour scalding water on your head and leave hay in your bed."

Though he laughed, his features remained serious. "Let's not beat about the bush today. My parents won't stand aside forever. I don't know how to proceed, Mary. I would like to continue my plans to court you, but as you well know, I have little to offer and don't know if I ever will. You could be looking at a future pushing me about in a wheeled chair. If you would rather draw a line now and remain as friends, I'll understand. You need only say the word."

Ah, the conversation had come to this so soon? She had not expected such forthright speech on their first meeting. But then, why should she not have expected it? They had always spoken openly with each other.

"You must understand," she said, folding her hands in her lap. "I'm more than a duke's daughter. I need you to see me as more than that. Though the words were said when you were less than your best, there was truth to them. You said you would always feel my inferior. If that's the case, then we should not proceed. If that's all you see me as, there's really no point, is there? I'm a woman with hopes and dreams that go well beyond the aspirations of the sixteen-year-old girl you left behind. If this is to go anywhere, you must see *me*. In my eyes, this has nought to do with your injury."

Duncan ran a hand through his hair, frowning. "We hardly know each other anymore. Are we clinging too much to the past, do you think?"

"I do. But I'll not have the last five years lived in vain. What we once had is enough for me to want to proceed, to fight for what we could have been. At least then, we'll know. If we learn there's not enough to sustain a future, we can walk away, but at least we'll know."

Nodding, he said, "Always sensible." Eyes trained on the arm of his chair, he picked at the embroidery on the hem of his sleeve. "The only time I thought of you as the daughter of a duke was when I planned to ask your mother for your hand and knew it would be foolhardy to do so. It was memories of *you* and our future together, not memories of a duke's daughter that kept me alive in the darkest moments of war. Granted, the future didn't contain this." He swept a hand over his legs. "Would I not be a burden to you?"

"Only if you pouted in bed for the remainder of eternity. You're no good to me in bed."

The corners of his lips inched upwards. In a lowered voice he asked, "Is that a challenge? I'll remember you said that."

With a groan, she covered her eyes with her hand to conceal her embarrassment.

"There is another matter we need to discuss, Mary. It could very well change your mind on whether we should proceed. I can't delay this any longer, and the fact that it's been delayed this long is only because of the injury."

She peeked at him through parted fingers.

His brown eyes trained on her, he continued, "There's someone I want you to meet. Not today, but soon. I *need* this meeting to happen. I realize you might not accept the person I plan to introduce to you, but I feel it's important that you do or at least understand my stance on the situation. Not many women would be understanding or accepting. You're unlike any woman I know, though, and that gives me hope."

Her breath hitched. Lowering her hands to her lap, she strangled the tips of her gloves. Of all the topics, this was the last she would have assumed to arise over tea, much less with his parents still in the room, however distant they stood. She knew, of course, exactly which topic he planned to broach. Or she thought she knew.

Clearing her throat, she said, "Yes, I know all about the little boy."

He sat upright, startled. For a moment he could do nothing but stare.

At length he settled against the chairback, propping an elbow on the arm and resting his cheek against his forefinger. "You know about Bernard?"

"As it happens, I do. There's no need for a lengthy preamble or explanation. I understand perfectly and can say we're acquainted. I met him and his nurse not too long ago, though I didn't know his name until now." She rather liked his name, however much she resented there was a child not hers to have a name.

"It's a relief, if I'm honest, that you already know. Though I'm sorry not to have been there for the introductions. If it makes you in any way uncomfortable, his nurse can raise him, and you needn't be involved, but I do need you to know I plan to raise him as my son. I know it's too much to hope you'll accept him, much less want to be a mother to him, but oh, Mary, I do hope."

At least he was being honest. Most men would hide their by-blows, see the children as a disgrace. In some way, despite his betrayal, she admired him for accepting responsibility and not leaving the child in an orphanage, or worse. She could not, however, answer his hope. Could there ever be a time when she would look at the boy and not see what his existence meant?

When she spoke, her voice trembled. "I don't know, Duncan. The most I can promise is that I'll try. I assume he's illegitimate?" The last word strained from her lips.

These were details she did not want to know, but she could not stop herself from asking. The thought of him marrying while on the continent…she shuddered, feeling ill.

"Yes, there's no doubt about that." He laughed, as though telling a joke. "I know such people aren't acknowledged by society, but I'll not have him ashamed of his origin. He's a great boy, Mary. I can't wait for you to meet him. He has a way with horses, too."

To see the look in his eyes when talking about the boy nearly broke her heart. He may never have another child. She may never have one of her own. Together, they may never have one. And there he sat, a twinkle of pride in his eyes over a boy that was not of their union.

She stifled her sob and asked more questions she did not want the answer to. "Do you — do you miss his mother?"

Brows crinkled, he eyed her quizzically. "I hardly knew her. She was one of the camp followers."

"Hardly knew —" Mary bristled.

What a wretched thing to say! How foul! How, how roguish!

"I'm not so naïve that I don't know about camp followers," she said, "but to say you hardly knew her is, well, is the outside of cruel."

"I meant no disrespect to her, believe me. She wasn't what you think. A camp follower, yes, but camp followers aren't what I think you think they are. We're a community, and everyone has a role. The women who follow us are supportive, help treat wounds, do the laundry, cook the meals, and other tasks. The children that travel with us are especially fortunate because they're raised by the whole of the community, everyone looking after each other. I imagine this is how my siblings grew up when following the drum with Papa. As an officer, I had few dealings with the followers, though. I spoke with her only a handful of times."

"Enough times, it seems," Mary muttered.

She did not want to turn this into an argument, but he had caught her off guard.

"I do beg your pardon," he said. "Even had I never met her, I would still pursue this course. The boy needs a father, and he took to me right away. What else could I do but take him with me?"

"Did she have no say in it, then?" Mary's words were sharp as steel. This was not at all going how she had rehearsed.

"She died of a fever, Mary. We endured a harsh winter that took many men, as well as women. It's a miracle Bernard survived, but he's a resilient chap." Leaning forward, he added, "I'm not blind; I can see you're not happy about this. Just because I want to raise him doesn't mean you have to be involved. I had hoped, well, never mind. Let's talk about something else, then, shall we?"

"How can I be happy about it? I'm not saying I won't be open minded. I'm here, aren't I? Even after meeting him, I'm here. But no, I'm not happy about it. He is the symbol of your betrayal, and I'll not forget that easily. It is difficult enough to know you could not wait for me, but to have the evidence everyday reminding me…" Her words trailed off.

"Wait." He held up his hands to keep her from interrupting. "Are we having two different conversations? Devil take it, I believe we are. Oh, Mary. Oh, my darling Mary. You said you met him and the nurse and needed no further explanation. I thought you knew. I thought something was said. I — oh, for heaven's sake. Bernard is not my child, Mary. I have *never* been unfaithful to you. I've never so much as thought about being unfaithful. My day rises and sets on you. Bernard is not mine, but I fully intend to raise him as my own son, and all I could think of while convalescing in London was us raising him together."

Before he finished, Mary had already pulled out a handkerchief and began to sob noisily into the linen and lace. Out of the corner of teary eyes, she saw him wave away his parents as they approached, concerned.

"Bernard is the son of one of the camp followers, a young girl named Eleanor. There's no way to say delicately that the father could be any one of a handful of soldiers, but before her death, one of the fellows had taken a shine to her and the boy, a young ensign named Philip. They intended to marry after the campaign. Life had other plans. We lost her to fever and Philip to a skirmish on the border of France. Bernard had no one. He had taken to me, and I to him, and what could I do? I know he's illegitimate, but I don't give a fig. He's my son, and that's all there is to it."

Though her sobs softened, Mary's tears continued to rain rivers down her cheeks. There were no words to express her relief. And the boy — that poor boy!

"Mary?" The softness of his voice caressed her as gentle as a touch.

Looking up to see him reaching a hand to her, she nodded, wiped her eyes, and clasped his hand in hers.

"I have never been nor ever will be unfaithful to you." He rubbed a thumb over her knuckles. "My only concern was raising an illegitimate child as my own. I worried you would object."

"No," she said, squeezing his hand. "No, I don't object. I wholeheartedly do not object. And I want to meet him, though not today. I might frighten him in this state."

Duncan dazzled her with a smile.

It was not until she was halfway home that she realized they had not once spoken of his condition. She had half a mind to turn around and demand a full report. Knowing she would join them all for dinner in another two days kept her riding home. After meeting Bernard, she would demand to hear about the tingle in his thigh he alluded to the day prior. What a tease not to tell her!

Chapter 13

Duncan, comfortably seated in his wheeled chair, made his best impression of an elephant trumpeting.

"Elephant!" Bernard shrieked. Leaping onto Duncan's lap, he said, "My turn! Roar, roar, roar!" Hands turned to paws, fingers to claws, and teeth to gnashing fangs for the full effect.

"Hmm. Let me think." Duncan tapped a finger to his chin.

"Roar!" Bernard bounced on Duncan's legs.

"A tiger?"

"No! A lion!" Jumping off his papa's lap, the boy pounced around the room in imitation of a lion.

"Oh, yes. I see the difference now between a lion and tiger. How could I have made such a mistake?" There was nothing else to do but laugh.

As Bernard rounded the room, the drawing room door opened to the butler's sober expression, the corners of the man's mouth twitching in telling contradiction.

"The carriage approaches, sir. Shall I show her in directly?"

"Yes, Lowand, straight away. Do send for my mother, as well."

"Already done, sir." He left with a bow.

Before the door clicked closed, Bernard came neighing at Duncan, galloping his way back across the room.

"Not at all fair," Duncan said. "It was your turn to guess."

"What am I? What am I?" The neighing continued until Bernard launched himself onto Duncan's lap again.

"If I guess, then you must have two turns after this." More neighing was his answer. "Only a true horseman could make such a convincing likeness. You must be a horse."

"Yes! Yes!" Bernard shrieked his delight.

The door opened once more to the smiling face of Georgina.

"Grandmama! I'm a horsey horseman!" the boy exclaimed, once more climbing down from Duncan's lap to gallop to Georgina.

Duncan beamed at the boy.

Eyeing one of the drawing room chairs, he was tempted to transfer to something more suitable for Mary's visit before dinner, but the wheeled chair was so comfortable, he was reluctant to leave it. It would be far easier, anyway, to remain in the chair, ready to be wheeled into the dining room once Quinn and Miranda arrived.

Georgina pulled the boy into her arms and carried him to the hearth by Duncan. "I thought he was learning his capitals today."

"It was a losing battle, Mama, I tell you. Every country had an animal sound rather than a capital. I conceded after being told the capital of Denmark sounded remarkably like a bird of prey."

"Why don't you take him for a ride tomorrow?" She attempted to smooth Bernard's riotous curls.

"I think I shall. A trot about the yard will do him some good."

Mr. Lowand opened the door once more, stepping into the room this time. "The Lady Mary Mowbrah."

A woman of noble bearing and birth sauntered into the drawing room, her dinner dress regal, her expression haughty. Duncan's lips curved in a smile. He was not yet accustomed to seeing her like this, in such contrast to the young girl of his memory, but each time he saw her, the woman she had become imprinted. How the devil could he be so fortunate? She was perfection.

Though his mother released Bernard to give a curtsy, and Duncan gave a seated bow, the formalities did not last long before Mary's smile illuminated the room. Georgina approached Mary with arms wide. Bernard had quite a different reaction. He took one look at the newcomer and ran behind Duncan's chair, but not before Mary had glimpsed his mad dash, careening her neck to see where he was hiding.

Duncan winked at her. "Come out, Bernard," he said. "There's someone who wants to meet you."

Silence answered him.

Mary approached with Georgina on one arm, her other arm hidden behind her back. They took their seats facing Duncan and the hidden boy. From behind her back, Mary pulled a wooden horse on wheels with a waxed rope attached. It caught Duncan so by surprise, he chuckled.

"Are you as fond as I am of the game horse and hound, Sir Duncan?" she asked, twirling the rope in her hand.

Duncan arched an eyebrow. "Horse and hound?"

"Yes, you see, this is the horse, and I'm the hound. Wherever I lead, the horse follows."

She stood, set the wooden horse on the floor, and bent low to reach the rope. With a most unladylike bark and bay, she pranced around the seating area, pulling the horse behind her.

Duncan was in tears. Try as he might to stifle his laughter, he could not. His sides hurt from the effort. His mother was not immune either, as she was red in the face from trying to hold back her laughter.

At length, Georgina stood and said, "I do believe hounds hunt in packs. May I join your pack?"

Mary woofed in response, continuing her journey about the room. Soon in step with Lady Mary, Georgina's hound-howl bayed in unison. If Duncan made it out of the room without splitting the sides of his waistcoat, he would be shocked. Of all the ways he had envisioned the first meeting between Mary and Bernard, this had never factored in as a possibility. What would aristocratic society think to see this sight?

Lo and behold, from around Duncan's chair, out stepped Bernard. His hands gripped the wheeled chair, knuckles white, but his eyes were wide with fascination. He watched his grandmama and the stranger walk in tandem about the room with a horse in tow. He took another step forward. Then another.

Mary paused, cocked her head to one side, and asked, "Would you like to be a hound and join our pack?"

Bernard shook his head. "I want to be a hunter."

Another step forward, and he raised an imaginary rifle.

It would seem the whole room was in on the game except Duncan. Initiating the hunt, Duncan made his best bugle trumpet, and off the hounds went, the horse following, and the hunter romping at the rear, ready to catch his fox.

The game was still afoot when Miranda and Quinn arrived, entering the drawing room with mouths agape.

"Should I have brought the girls here instead of to the nursery?" Miranda asked, looking from the madness to Quinn.

Bernard stopped in his tracks to hear that the girls were in the nursery. Looking from the door to Mary and back again, Bernard finally walked up to Mary and offered his hand. She took it without hesitation.

Leading her to Quinn, Bernard said, "This is my new friend." He looked back to her and asked, "Are you my friend?"

"I would love to be your friend. Only, I don't know your name, master hunter," Mary said.

When he glanced to his papa, Duncan said, "Lady Mary, allow me to introduce to you my son Bernard. Bernard, this is Lady Mary."

The boy's eyes widened. "Do I call you lady?"

"Mary will do. Now, would you like to show your new horse to your cousins, or shall I keep him here?"

"He's mine?" A face of wonder peered around her to the wheeled horse.

Nodding, Mary fetched the horse, handing it to Bernard to carry to the nursery. With a shy mumble of gratitude, Bernard and his horse raced out of the room, eager to share his toy and stories of his new friend.

As though the past quarter of an hour had not occurred, Mary straightened her shoulders and greeted Miranda and Quinn with all the noble pomp one might expect. Shortly thereafter, a footman arrived with the butler to announce dinner and to wheel Duncan into the dining room.

That evening, while propped against his headboard, Duncan admired the vision of Mary from dinner. Though he rarely paid attention to women's fashion, he could not help but pay attention when she had been so enchanting.

Her ebony hair, worn high with ringlets bound in an interlacing bit of white ribbon, had contrasted against her dinner dress of white sarsnet. His gaze had been drawn to her bosom, not because he was a lustful man, but because it was a low bodice edged with silver lace and fastened down the center with rosettes of pearls that trailed all the way to the lower hem. The dress ended with a vee mid-shin, a satin petticoat worn beneath and reaching to her slippers.

Only to reach for his wine did he look away from her. The animation of her features, the natural red of her lips, the flush of her cheeks, all captivated him.

The dinner conversation focused on the sensations of Duncan's lower extremities during his twice daily rides. Each ride produced the same results. And each dismount returned him to his original, senseless state. The table was abuzz with conversation after Duncan shared the news. He had yet to tell anyone aside from Mary in the brief tease by the lake, though he had been bursting to tell everyone. The delay, he reasoned, was to determine if the stir was by chance or something more. Given it occurred repeatedly, it promised to be something more.

Hope ignited, he worked longer and harder to move his feet or lift his legs. It was a nightly ritual that never yielded results.

Until tonight.

Glaring at bare legs stretched across his bedsheets, the covers flung to one side, he concentrated on wiggling a toe, flexing a foot, lifting a leg, something, anything. Attempts to replicate the sensations he experienced on horseback failed. He could not say what it was about the movement of the horse, but the gait, position, or maybe the rhythm awakened dormant feelings. All he could do from his bed was try to move the unmovable.

When it happened, he nearly missed it. The flick of the toe was so minute he thought it might be a blur in his vision or a trick of the candlelight, a shadow guttering. There was no mistaking the movement by the fifth time. He could feel nothing. With eyes closed, he would never know his toe was moving. With eyes open, he could see clearly his toe moving on his command.

Once it started, it would not stop. Every time he moved his toe, it responded. It mocked him, as if he had never *not* been able to move it. Up, down, up, down. He curled the big toe, his other toes joining the chorus by the end of a half hour. Only his right foot, though, never the left.

The tick of the clock chiming eleven kept him from whooping with joy and calling all in the house to witness the miracle. Who could sleep at a time like this? What if he fell asleep and woke to an unresponsive foot?

He kept at it until the shadows were long and his eyes were propped open only by optimism. By the time he slumped onto his pillow from exhaustion, he had twitched his foot into a semblance of a flex. Such a feat was worthy of sleep.

When morning light woke him, he flung back his covers, furious at having slept well past dawn. In his final thoughts before sleep took him, he had sworn to wake early. And here it was, late into the day, his coffee cold, the fire low, and the sun rising steadily higher. Cursing, he propped himself against his headboard, just as he had done the night before, and tossed back the frigid beverage. With a grimace, he stared at his feet.

Three deep breaths. Make that four deep breaths. He held the fifth breath and gave his toe a wiggle.

HA!

It moved on command.

A night's sleep had not diminished his progress. A madman's grin on his face, he waved his toes and flexed his right foot. His left taunted him. The big toe on the left foot gave a stuttering flutter every third try. Nothing else on the left responded. His right, however, was more responsive with each try. Feeling gutsy, he moved his legs over to the side of the bed.

Fighting gravity, he attempted to lift the right leg. Only an inch it gave, but it gave an inch. It moved one whole inch! He kept at it, commanding his right leg to lift and then his left. The right remained steady, moving an inch. The left hung limp. Not wanting to embarrass himself in front of, well, himself, he should not be tempted to try to stand, but he was feeling inexplicably grand. How could he *not* try to stand? No, a toe wiggle did not mean his legs could hold his weight, but he could not stop himself from wanting to try.

Inching further over the edge of the bed, he watched his feet until they met the floor. It was not the easiest of tasks, for without being able to feel the floor or straighten his left foot, he was unsure if his entire foot was touching the floor or if it was positioned well enough to hold weight. His right foot was easier to position, though he could not feel the floor against the sole. When he felt confident enough about the positioning, he grasped high on the bedpost and pulled himself up until his legs were as straight as they could be with him gripping a column, his right leg bearing most of his weight. With a gentle push, he righted himself and released the post.

For nearly two full seconds, his legs held him, the muscles engaging, and then he crumpled to the floor, his left foot giving under the pressure. Picking at the rug threads, he propped himself on an elbow and grinned again. Two seconds.

From his horizontal position, he aimed to bend his right knee and even flex his leg muscles. Neither happened, but his foot continued to respond to every command. Heaving himself up by the edge of the four-poster, he climbed back onto the bed. Legs dangling over the side once again, he kicked out his right leg, the movement sluggish, but there, and the distance a solid inch and a half if he had to wager a guess.

The aftertaste of the coffee had turned to a bitter, stale flavor by the time he was ready to ring for Peter and resume the day as normal. For at least an hour he had worked, likely longer.

Before calling for his valet, he positioned his feet against the rug for what seemed the hundredth time and pulled himself up with the bedpost. Each time had been steadier. Each time had been longer. This time, he held onto the column and stood.

He concentrated on how the rest of his body felt in the stance, how his torso engaged, how his hips were positioned.

Understanding how he needed to balance himself was vital. There could be no doubt his leg muscles were working, or else his legs would not hold his weight as they were doing now. Their contractions seemed intermittent and untrustworthy, disconnected in some way from his commands. And yet they were working. He was fascinated.

Delaying the call for his valet for just a moment longer, he attempted to take a step forward. His right leg inched upwards and forward, dragging his foot beneath and behind it, and — blast! He could not lift the leg enough to straighten the foot. Grasping the post to keep himself from falling, he looked down to his foot, trying to turn the ankle to straighten his sole to the rug.

His arms shook from the strain of holding himself upright for so long. By the time he had his foot straight enough to put weight on it again, his upper body burned. He released his hold on the column by ruled measure, not wanting to put too much weight and twist his ankle. He simply could not tell if his foot was positioned correctly. Not being able to feel the floor was unnerving.

At last, he was standing again, his legs holding his weight. Perhaps attempting to take steps should wait until after more practice with lifting, flexing, and the like.

And then he realized the sticky wicket he had put himself in. The bell pull was by the bed table, at least four steps away. Bollocks! He had three choices: climb back onto the bed to scoot his way to the bell pull, attempt walking again and hope he did not collapse, or shout for Peter and hope the man was in the dressing room and not downstairs. After a look down to his legs, standing proud, and a wipe of the sweat from his brow, he opted for the latter.

As luck would have it, the man came dashing into the room, expecting the worst.

When the valet saw Duncan standing on his own two feet, hands on hips, nightshirt damp with sweat, and a fool's grin on his lips, Peter gaped.

The remainder of the day proceeded much as every day, aside from the fuss his mother made to hear his progress, and aside from the grin that would not fade. Oh, yes, and lest he forget, the arrival of the outdoor Bath chair.

Mr. Swansbourne had worked himself ragged to get the chair to him a week ahead of schedule. Such work was not taken for granted, for Duncan was well under the impression such a chair took a great deal of time and an exorbitant amount of money. Had Mr. Swansbourne not been acquainted with the family, and had the villagers not seen Duncan as a war hero, it would have likely taken months for the chair to arrive. As it happened, it only took just over a week.

One look at it and Duncan was more motivated than ever to walk again. He was not ungrateful. It was exquisite craftsmanship, far and away more impressive than his wicker chair, but it was enormously large, too heavy to lift if needed, and not easy for him to maneuver in or out of it without assistance.

The Bath chair was mostly iron with a seat to the back, two wheels to the sides, one wheel in the front, two handles in the back for pushing, and one curved rod for the rider to steer. The exciting aspect was that he could guide the direction of the chair with the steering rod, which he could not do with his indoor wheeled chair. But the massiveness of the thing was daunting. He was unsure it would even fit on the mounting platform, and heaven help the person pushing him up the ramp.

In the chair's defense, or more in Mr. Swansbourne's defense, the seat was well cushioned for comfort, more akin to a carriage seat than what he would have expected. There was even a retractable canopy to shield the rider from sun or foul weather.

Duncan made a show of having himself wheeled about the gardens. The chair rode smoothly and did not slip on gravel or stick in mud as his indoor one was wont to do. He could see its uses, certainly, but he did not care to use it unless he had to. After all, how was he to climb onto Caesar with any finesse from this contraption? For the first trial, he had the indoor chair carried to the platform so he could transfer from one chair to the other to be then wheeled up the platform in his wicker chair. It was all too cumbersome. He was grateful, but having tasted the elixir of life, he wanted his freedom.

The one joy was when Bernard thought it would be grand to go for a ride in the Bath chair with his papa. Around the garden they went, Sean pushing them rather than a footman, making the excuse that he wanted to spend time with his boys.

By dinner, Duncan could not wait to get back into his room and work on his movement. He was a man obsessed. His conversation was limited to grunts, and he nearly shoveled his food. The sight of his bedchamber some time later was a welcomed sight indeed. Burning down another candle until it guttered, he worked at lifting one leg and then the next, his left leg responding a hair more than it had that morning. Had it truly only been last night when he had moved his right toe for the first time? It was all happening so quickly! From nothing to *this*!

Before the candle snuffed itself, Duncan had removed from his bed to attempt walking again, having no more success than that morning, but nothing stopped him from trying.

Two days later, the first week of October, he rode out to meet Mary at the lake.

His progress was notable but slow. He could lift both legs against gravity, rotate both ankles, and stand for nearly thirty seconds before the muscles shook and gave. All attempts to walk had failed in the same way as his first tries. Without being able to feel the ground or lock and bend his knees at will, walking was an unachievable task, but given all he had accomplished in only two days, he remained optimistic, fueled by each new goal reached.

After lengthy deliberation, he decided not to tell Mary until he could show her. If he could make enough progress to stand before her as a man, then he could reveal the surprise. In the back of his mind, Duncan also worried that telling her too soon could raise her hopes for nothing, but that was not a thought he wished to entertain in the light of such recent success. He was hesitant, even, to pen a letter to Dr. Knowlton this soon. Just a little more progress.

Guiding Caesar with reins, not yet brave enough to try signaling with his legs given how delayed their responses, he slowed to a trot, the lake in sight. His groom accompanied at a respectable distance. From beyond a dip in the terrain, Duncan spotted Mary, looking splendid even from afar, her groom following at an increasingly slower pace, likely having seen Duncan approaching. He sighed. Gone were the days of their unchaperoned, clandestine meetings. Though to say such a meeting as this met the standards of propriety would be laughable.

Like the lovesick fool he was, he smiled as she slowed to a walk.

Athena, he recalled her horse being named. The mare was a thoroughbred beauty, sleek chocolate with a distinct white star on her forehead. She was quite the contrast to his pearl Andalusian. Patting Caesar's neck, he paused near the willow. He burrowed into his greatcoat, the breeze frosty.

Mary returned his smile, pulling up alongside him. She wore the same habit as last time, its style surprisingly similar to his regimentals, though she looked far more attractive than any Light Dragoon he had ever met. A vague memory tickled his conscience. Had she not worn this same habit in one of his laudanum dreams? Try as he might, he could not form a complete image of the hallucination. There was only a fuzzy recollection of her riding alongside him in a military uniform not unlike this riding habit. Curious.

"Shall we ride?" she asked without additional greeting.

"Let's."

Not another word was spoken before she cantered away from him, looking back only long enough to laugh before signaling Athena into a gallop. Though Caesar aimed to keep up, before long, Athena ran circles about them. Saucy minx.

Duncan slowed to a trot, Mary slowing to ride alongside him.

"Is your lower half tingling?" she asked.

Askance, he cast her a seductive smile and waggled his eyebrows. "Always when I see you."

"Naughty!" She swatted at his sleeve, her half-lidded gaze belying her pleasure.

They fell into easy conversation, much like old times. It began with a discussion of her pastimes, including embroidery, which surprised him since he recalled her love of archery. To think of her doing needlework was a side of her he had never known or considered, a new dimension. The conversation turned to each of their favorite sweets and savories. And finally, to poetry, her appreciation of his poorly penned sonnets the opener.

"How can you favor that dried windbag Donne?" he asked, incredulous.

"Dried windbag! Have we read the same works? I ask you, how is 'The Flea' not a work of art?"

"Anything about a flea is not art," he protested.

She laughed. "As good of a confession as any for not having read it. Have you actually read Donne? I believe you have some studying to do before we can be friends. 'The Flea,' I'll have you know, is a naughty little poem about coupling, a persuasion to couple. I would recommend you read it to brush up on your rusty flirtations."

He flinched dramatically. "Harsh words, my lady. First you accuse me of ignorance, if not outright illiteracy, and then you insult my prowess with romance. You may not realize this, but I'm considered the catch of the village. Girls were swooning to see my flexing pectorals when I first tried the new chair. Even as an invalid, they want me."

"Try as you might to flirt through jealousy, it will not tempt me. What are the desires of villagers to a noble? A keen mind is what I desire. Someone who will recite witty rhymes from horseback."

Clearing his throat he said, "'For God's sake hold your tongue, and let me love, Or chide my palsy, or my gout, My five grey hairs, or ruined fortune flout, With wealth your state, your mind with arts improve, Take you a course, get you a place, Observe his honor, or his grace, Or the king's real, or his stamped face

Contemplate; what you will, approve, So you will let me love!'"

"Oh, bravo. So, you *do* know Donne, or at least one stanza. You've yet to woo me, but you're closing in."

"Accuse me of being all brawn and little brain if you will, but I have a verse or two stored for your wooing pleasure," he said, tapping his forehead.

"What I really want is a skilled horseman. Prove yourself, Sir Duncan!"

He studied her for a moment, trying to devise a plan of action. Caesar was a warhorse, after all, not a racehorse. Jumping hurdles was the first idea that sprang to mind, but he was not at all confident that was the best course of action in his present state.

Ah, he had it.

Curling his forefinger for her to come hither, he said, "A little closer, my dear, for I've a secret to share."

She obeyed, none the wiser.

As she leaned towards him, Athena flanking Caesar, Duncan reached over and unseated Mary. He wrapped strong arms about her waist and hoisted her off her horse and onto his with little more than a grunt. She squealed and tried to flog him with her riding crop. Undaunted, he pulled her sidewise to nestle between his legs, and held her steady with one arm, while the other cupped her cheek to pull her lips to his.

As soon as their lips met, her crop went limp. She leaned against him, wrapping her arms around his neck. Her lips were as he remembered — full, welcoming, yielding. Teasing the seam, he slipped in to tangle his tongue with hers in a fierce battle of wills. Caesar pranced beneath him. When he released her lips and gazed down, his heart pounded to see the ardor in her eyes.

"Skilled enough?" he asked, tracing her bottom lip with his thumb.

"I, oh, yes, quite. Oh my." She stared at him, dazed.

"With that proven, let's get you back to your horse before Caesar boots us both off."

Blinking the stars from her eyes, she glanced around, as though only now recalling she was not atop her own horse. Athena remained flanked, her only signs of annoyance a pawing of the ground, punctuated with a snort.

"Shall I lift you back on the saddle?" He offered.

"No, thank you. That sounds as startling as being lifted off in the first place. I'll mount Athena myself, thank you very much."

"Oh, ho ho, this I must see. I didn't think a woman *could* mount a side-saddle without assistance," he teased.

"Watch me."

Challenge accepted, she slid off Caesar, hoisted her skirt in a flirty way that revealed a hint of stockings above her half-boots, hiked her foot into the stirrup, and in one leap, spun herself backwards onto the saddle where she could hitch her leg over the top head. Sorting out her skirts, she made herself comfortable, smirking at Duncan the whole time.

"Tell me you don't do that in front of anyone but me." Duncan was still staring at the skirt where the glimpse of leg had teased him.

"Wouldn't you feel charmed if I concurred?" With a wink, she turned Athena around to head back to the lake.

Chapter 14

D uncan stared at his prone legs, a fresh candle at his bedside, a manuscript of Lord Rochester's poetry open on the sheets. In many ways, it had been a perfect day. First, the progress with his legs. And then Mary. The feel of her in his arms had thrummed his blood for the rest of the afternoon. Had he been unencumbered, had there not been grooms nearby, had life played fair, he would have tossed his greatcoat to the ground, dismounted his horse with Mary cradled in his arms, laid her on the greatcoat, and taken her in a moment of uninhibited passion. In truth, likely not, for he would never preempt their vows, but he liked to know he *could* if he wanted. Alas, he could not even if so desired, for although she had been pressed to him in the saddle, he had felt nothing. What sort of man was he? Rather than weep, he thought it best to prepare for their marriage in the only way he knew how.

Now, when he was supposed to be working his legs, he was instead fantasizing her lips and how her body would form to his on their wedding night. The lewd poetry was intended to enhance his fantasies.

There was nothing more vulgar than Lord Rochester's verses. They had circulated through the camps, helping officers more easily recall their beloved back home. This eve, however, it did not work.

Sneering, he glanced down to the poem he had been reading.

Naked she lay, clasped in my longing arms,
I filled with love, and she all over charms;
Both equally inspired with eager fire,
Melting through kindness, flaming in desire.
With arms, legs, lips close clinging to embrace

He looked away from the page midline. He could not get past the references to liquid raptures without feeling ill. Regardless of Mary's curves, of his desire, of his mental readiness, his body refused to respond. *He* had been ready for love the moment her lips touched his. The rest of him lay silent. Even now, despite his best efforts, nothing happened. He supposed it did not matter if something did, considering he could not feel anything below the hips anyway, but some sign of life would be encouraging.

Here he was wanting to court and then marry her, but he could not bed her, never offer her children. What sort of marriage was that? Yes, he could think of a dozen other ways to pleasure her, but in the end, he could not consummate the marriage properly, never give her a home with a dozen babes.

With a flick of his wrist, he tossed the pages off the bed in a flurry of paper, growling in anger as they fluttered down, littering the bedchamber floor. A rhythmic knocking filled the room as he beat the back of his skull against the headboard. Useless, useless, useless.

Snuffing the candle, he slipped into a dreamless slip, not bothering to work on his legs. After all, what was the point?

By the time he awoke, he felt refreshed and far from morose. He even smiled to realize he was awake at dawn, the coffee at his table steaming hot and fresh. Pushing himself to a seated position, he surveyed the room to see the pages neatly stacked on the low table in the snug. Chagrined, he wondered if whoever had picked them up had read the words.

The coffee, black and searing, remained cradled in his hands as he flexed his legs. He experimented while he sipped. There was far more movement than yesterday. Both right and left legs lifted against gravity, bent at the knee, and rotated on command. Every move was sluggish. Every move half his desired goal. But everything was moving.

Gulping the rest of the liquid and returning the cup to the table, he scooted off the bed to practice standing, just as he had done the day before. Curious, he tried to stand up on his own from a seated position.

Hands against the bed, his soles met the floor. With one deep breath, he pushed himself from the bedding, expecting to rise to his feet. Alas, it all went wrong. His knees bent rather than straightened and collapsed beneath him, bringing him to the floor with a *thunk* and a curse.

Undaunted, he climbed back onto the bed and used the bedpost this time, as he had done before. It was easy work. Easier than yesterday. He pulled himself into an upright stance by grasping the post, holding his weight with his upper body. Steadily, he positioned his feet and released his hold. His legs held. When he attempted to sit back against the bed, his knees bent at an awkward angle, crumpling him against the sheets, at least a soft landing this time.

He practiced for well over an hour, testing himself time and again, his aim to rise and sit on his own. All efforts failed. But pulling himself up became smoother and easier, and each time the legs held his weight. Steps were another problem.

Both of his legs lifted on command, even if the movements were measured. He could not, however, walk forward or balance without a hand to the bedpost. The motions were jerky, his hips thrusting with each step, as if the legs refused to move of their own volition. Progress was progress, so who was he to complain? The true accomplishment of the morning was in taking three steps forward, all while holding onto the post. He wagered he could have made it further if his legs had not begun to shake and if he had something else to reach for past the edge of the bed.

By that evening, he was at it again. This time, the room was ready for him. He had requested tables, chairs, anything sturdy, be lined from the bedpost to the far window. His room looked somewhat like a child's nursery game, he mused. As long as it worked, who cared? All evening, he practiced cruising. With a hand gripping, steadying, and even taking some of the weight at times, he could move one leg forward and then another. This could hardly be called walking, but he was unsure what else to call it. It was not something he wished to do in front of another person, not yet at least, but it was closer to walking than he had dreamt possible.

One pivoting hip after the other, his legs dragged forward, trembling after three steps, then five steps, then ten steps. The more he worked, the longer he could walk before his legs gave in.

By the next morning, he was exhausted from a sleepless night of practicing, but ready to go again.

He cruised from his bed to the window and back. The trouble was, in addition to having to hold on to something to help steady himself, he also had to look down to watch his feet move. Without being able to feel when foot touched floor, he had no way of knowing if his ankles were straight or if he had even made contact with the floor. If he misjudged its proximity, the result was a hard stomp or an equally hard fall.

The more memorable occasions of these disasters occurred within the same roundtrip. Duncan looked up to reach for a chair only to think his foot had made contact when it had not. Vaulting forward with a crack of his elbow against the chair leg, he learned not to take his eyes off his feet. Unfortunately, he forgot this lesson moments later when reaching for the bedpost. He stomped too hard on the floor, sending a jolt reverberating through his body.

How the devil was he to make use of his progress if he could not walk without looking down and could not walk without bracing against something?

By that night, one part of the problem resolved. His legs could hold his weight and move forward without his gripping an object for balance. Staring at his feet, he took one mindful step after another, walking from bedpost to window and back.

He was walking.

"Peter!" he cried to the dressing room, hoping the valet had not yet retired. It had been less than half an hour since the valet had readied Duncan for bed.

The valet rushed in, ready to assist.

"Peter," Duncan repeated. "Watch."

With a shaky step, he moved his right leg forward, and then his left. After five such steps, he looked up to his valet.

"Well done, Sir Duncan. Well done!"

"Wait there. I'll come to you."

Duncan was still smiling at his valet when he took his next step. He realized his mistake immediately. With a cry, he careened to the floor, his ankle turning under.

Peter was at his side in seconds, checking the ankle. "Does it hurt, sir?"

Despite the anger and humiliation he felt, he barked a laugh. "Of all the things I feel, pain is not one of them. No, Peter, I cannot feel my ankle to know if it's damaged or not. I suppose if I attempt to put weight on it and it angles again, we'll know it's in need of a physician's touch."

Nodding, the valet leaned into Duncan, wrapping an arm about his master's back while Duncan supported himself on Peter's shoulders. With a heave, Peter helped Duncan back to his feet, bearing the brunt of the weight until Duncan could test the ankle.

There was no pain, but there was a distinct wobble when he attempted to lean on the leg.

"I believe I've turned it. This is my punishment for boasting. To the bed, please."

A rough night he spent fretting about his ankle.

To the dower house she went. Again. Summoned to see her mother an hour before she was set to leave for tea with Mrs. Starrett did not bode well. Mary was already dressed in a warm visiting dress, braced for the chilly carriage ride to the park, her hair turbaned, her cheeks rouged, her hands muffed. On her schedule before the tea was not a talk with her mother.

Bundled in a fur-lined pelisse, she nevertheless shivered her way to the dower house, crunchy leaves underfoot. Each day was colder than the one before it. Except for a few sunny hours that warmed the air, it had been grey skies for days.

As soon as she stepped into the house, she knew it was bad news. However passive was Mr. Taylor's perpetual scowl, she could detect a tell-tale smirk at the corners of his mouth. The drawing room was a true blow.

Her mother stood by the window, leaning heavily against a gold-handled cane. What caught Mary's attention was not her mother but the table in the center, prepared for tea. Oh dear.

"Join me," Catherine commanded, approaching one of three seats arranged at the table. "Sit."

Mary remained standing. "However appreciative I am for such fare, I'm afraid I have other plans."

"Nonsense. You have plans here. Sit." She waved a hand to one of the empty chairs.

Still not moving, Mary said, "I'm to take tea with Mrs. Starrett in less than an hour. I really can't stay, nor do I wish to spoil my appetite."

"You'll stay and take tea with my guest and me. That woman will make do without you."

"She's not *that woman*. She's Mrs. Georgina Starrett, and I happen to admire her. Had you invited me in advance, I could have arranged my schedule to take tea with you both. As it happens, you did not think enough of me to consult my schedule."

Catherine pinned her daughter with a piercing stare. "There you're quite wrong. Mr. Taylor consulted your schedule and learned this afternoon would be a perfect time for a rearrangement of poor choices. You will be taking tea here with the Duke of Wiggins and me. He will be arriving shortly. He was delayed, I'm afraid, or he would have been here to greet you." Her mother's eyes roamed over Mary's visiting dress and grimaced. "Not what I would have liked to see you wear to meet His Grace, but it'll do."

"Wiggins?" Mary repeated, incredulous. "Don't think you'll trap me in one of your matchmaking schemes. I'll not be party to this. If you want to take tea with the Duke of Wiggins, you can do so alone. And next time you see fit to alter my schedule on my behalf, *don't*."

So angry was she, her head throbbed with an oncoming migraine.

Before her mother could say another word, Mary bolted from the room. When she reached the entry hall, she spotted an approaching carriage, the Wiggins ducal crest emblazoned on the side. Blast! Mary about-faced and made for the conservatory to escape out a back door.

Only when she stepped outside did she realize her coat and muff were still in the vestibule. Double blast!

Not even a biting chill could induce her to return inside and risk coming face-to-face with His Grace. She had never met the duke, nor did she want to.

By the time she reached the manor, her teeth chattered, and her skin was aflame with pink gooseflesh. She shook herself back to her bedchamber and rang for her lady's maid. New shoes, a new pelisse and muff, a hot brick, and a cup of chocolate were in order before the carriage was called around to take her to Cois Greta Park.

The chill was bone deep by the time she joined Mrs. Starrett for tea. Nothing seemed to warm her. At least she was not sniveling or sneezing like an old maid.

Only the two of them met in the drawing room. It was Mrs. Starrett's special treat, she said, both for herself and for Mary. Mrs. Starrett was fast becoming one of Mary's favorite people. For nearly a half hour, they talked about the grandchildren, especially those Mary had not met, the viscount and viscountess who happened to be Mrs. Starrett's father- and mother-in-law, and other familial topics.

How different life would have been with such a mother. As with her most recent visit, Mary was greeted with a hug from her hostess. *A hug*. Not once had her own mother ever hugged her.

Looking back, she could not recall her mother ever touching her, not once. Surely it had happened at some point. Or perhaps not. As far as she knew, she had a wet nurse. The years went by with a governess to care for her and little interaction with her mother aside from dinner or tea when she was old enough to join the adults rather than stay in the nursery. Growing up, all she had wanted was to be loved, a lap to climb onto, arms to hold her, a kiss to the brow, some sort of physical affection, something tangible she could feel and understand.

As Mrs. Starrett carried on about life following the drum. Mary's attention faded, her fingers on her lips in memory of Duncan's kiss, his display of physical affection.

The warm blush that spread through her chilled limbs recalled the memory of the first physical love between she had witnessed between a man and a woman—far more intimate than a hug or kiss; it was a kind of intimacy she had never known possible. Rather than be frightened or repulsed, she had been curious, she who had never even been hugged.

At the age of eleven, she had stolen into the kitchen after dark to fetch carrots for the horses. Sneaking through the kitchen garden, she ran to the stables. She only made it to the first horse before she heard a commotion in one of the rear stalls. With the groaning and grunting and carrying on, she had assumed someone had fallen and been injured.

Inching her way to the stall, careful not to make noise lest she be caught and punished, she spied the felled groom, only it was not quite an injury she witnessed. One of the grooms was tupping a maid. At the time, she had no words or concept for the sort of hug he gave the maid. She was uncertain she would want to be hugged like that, but she had craved physical touch ever since, yearning for someone to hold her and love her.

Glancing to the drawing room door, she wondered where Duncan was and if there was a way to sneak a greeting while she was here. He could be out riding, she supposed. Twice a day he rode, once in the morning and once in the afternoon. Dreadful bad luck if such were the case, though if not, she was unsure how she would escape Mrs. Starrett's delightful company in search of a secret kiss.

"Shall we visit the nursery to see Bernard?" Mrs. Starrett asked, pulling Mary back to the present. "He asks about you every day. Wants to know when his new friend is coming to play."

"What a lovely invitation. Yes, I would be honored to see Bernard. I hope it was not too bold of me to bring him a toy the other day."

"He loves it! We are so grateful for your kindness." Georgina reached a hand to touch Mary's arm.

Mary stared at the hand. A simple touch with a world of meaning.

"I'm pleased he likes it. My nephew is far too serious for toys. He would much rather pore over his studies. He's two going on twenty. What does a two-year-old *study*, I ask you? His mind is sharp, and his desire to learn keen, but really, what's the point without a little fun? Thrice now he has thwarted my efforts to play by insisting he has to practice writing his name. All my gifts and games are wasted on him. I assure you, Bernard won't be the only one enjoying playtime."

The two laughed, Mrs. Starrett leading the way to the door.

They made it as far as the fifth step on the main stairs before the butler approached.

He bowed to Mary with apologies for intruding before turning to Mrs. Starrett to say, "You're needed in the kitchen."

"The kitchen? Now? I'm sure it can wait. We're off to see my grandson," she protested.

"Cook insists it's urgent, or I would not disturb you."

"Well…" Mrs. Starrett looked towards the top of the stairs, then to Mary. "I would hate for him not to see you." She wrung her hands.

Mary said, "You see to the kitchen, and I'll see to Bernard. It's perfectly understandable."

Her shoulders relaxed as she patted Mary's arm, thanked her, and followed the butler.

Mary climbed the stairs to the second floor and turned on the landing to ascend to the third when she heard a little boy's squeal of laughter coming from the hall. Retracing her steps, she followed the sound to the parlor.

Without thinking she might be interrupting, she opened the door and stepped inside.

At first she was unobserved, giving her a moment to witness some sort of game of charades between Bernard and Duncan. Bernard was hunched over, limping and growling, with an occasional break in acting to prompt his father to guess. Duncan was seated in a parlor chair. Had it not been for the wheeled chair pushed into the corner, no one would imagine he was anything but a cavalry colonel.

When she realized Bernard and Duncan were the only two people in the room, she made to bow out.

"Mary!" the boy screeched before she had one foot over the threshold.

Running at her, he dove into her petticoat, wrapping spindly arms around her legs.

"Oof!" Mary said, taken quite by surprise.

"Tut tut," Duncan intoned. "That's no way to greet a lady. Take a step back and try that again, young man."

Looking up at her, his arms still grasping her legs, Bernard grinned from ear to ear, ignoring his papa. "Have you come to play?"

"Indeed, I have, but only with a good boy who obeys his father. Are you a good boy?"

With an enthusiastic nod, Bernard stepped back and sketched the sloppiest bow Mary had seen in her life. When she nodded in acknowledgement, he leapt back into her skirt, resuming his hold on her legs.

"Yes, well, I suppose that will do. Come, let us sit with Papa."

Taking his hand in hers, she escorted him over to Duncan.

Duncan had his turn to bow to her from his seat. "Did you lull my mother to sleep by reciting Donne?"

"Don't you dare insult Donne or my ability to charm an audience," Mary scolded. "She was called to the kitchen with an emergency."

He winked and looked to Bernard. "Tell Mary five capitals you learned today."

"But I wanter play." The lower lip protruded. "Not fair. My friend's here."

Duncan cringed. "I swear it's not all play around here."

"I believe Bernard and my nephew could learn a great deal from each other. One is far too serious and the other not nearly serious enough. Should we trade for a week, do you think?"

"I wouldn't trade him for the world," Duncan said with a playful pinch to Bernard's arm.

"And what a big boy you are to be down here without your nurse," Mary said.

The boy's eyes widened. "Mrs. Eloise!"

With those words, he bolted from the room, closing the door none too gently.

"What did I say?" She stared at the door, concerned she had lost her new friend.

Duncan cleared his throat. "Well, you see, a certain big boy sneaked away from the nursery when his nanny fell asleep. It happens more often than I care to admit."

"I wouldn't chide him too terribly. He is, after all, sneaking away to spend time with you."

Propping his elbow on the arm of the chair, he said, "I hadn't thought of it that way, but you're quite right. Does this mean you find me a bad influence?"

Mary blushed when she said, "On the contrary, I find you to be a model father."

She stared down at her hands, in full realization of what she was implying. Given his condition, she did not misapprehend that there was a real possibility they would never have children together. Though not of their union, adopted children would receive as much love and care. She need only look to his affection for Bernard for proof. This seemed a topic they should discuss. Her mother would be appalled.

Looking back to Duncan to realize he was studying her with a curious expression, she asked, "Does he ever talk about his mother?"

Duncan frowned. "No. At least not to me. As I mentioned before, he was raised as part of a community with most of the women acting as his mother, as they did with all the children. He would have still been well-aware of her as his mother, but I wonder if it was enough to miss her. I don't know."

"And what of you? How did he come to call you Papa?"

Chuckling, he said, "He proposed to me, actually. Of all the men, he favored me, even before his mother's death. I didn't see much of him after her death. I assume Philip spent time with him, but their deaths were only weeks apart. Less than a week after Philip passed, Bernard sneaked into my tent and proposed. With all the maturity of an adult, he said to me, 'A boy needs a papa. I choose you. Will you be my papa?' I couldn't tell you where he got such a notion, but I would wager to guess it was either from his mother or Philip to accustom him to the idea of having Philip as a father. And so, here we are."

"What a brave boy to ask you. Do you suppose no one else would have taken him had you said no?"

"I honestly couldn't say, Mary. It's possible. I wouldn't have said no in any case. I had already planned to approach him with a proposal of my own, if we're being honest about the matter. I was torn with how it might affect our chances. I spent more than one sleepless night over the situation, wondering if choosing him meant the end of us or if by choosing us it would mean an orphanage or the streets for him. I had even written a letter to you not only about him but about my promotion to colonel, but it was never sent, not with the forthcoming battle at the Rhine, not with the injury."

She imagined for a moment how she might have received the letter. There was no way to guess her reaction to his having adopted or wanting to adopt an illegitimate child. She would like to think she would have accepted the boy without question, even without the misunderstanding. But she could not honestly say.

The feel of his hand touching her arm startled her. Her eyes first went to his fingertips as they ran the length of her forearm from wrist to elbow. She shivered in response, a warm shiver of delight. Old calluses made his fingertips rough to the touch, but his hands were well-manicured with clipped, half-moon nails. For his return pass, he used those nails rather than his fingertips to trail back down her forearm with a light tickle.

"Has it escaped you that we're alone?" he asked, his voice husky.

She gave a studious examination of the room, slow, steady, thorough, exaggerating her peering around furniture. "It would seem so. Whatever do you plan to do about it?"

His smile could only be described as wicked. "I plan to discern if we're—how shall I say this—a good *fit*."

Her eyes widened as his fingertips caressed her arm again, making another circuit to her elbow and back down.

Swallowing against the lump in her throat, she said, "What should I do?"

Even with her imagination running amok, she had not the foggiest what he intended. They were, after all, in the family parlor, one door away from discovery.

"Let's start with your affirmation that you can run an estate."

Brows drawn in, she said, "I beg your pardon. Can I—can I what?"

"You listed for me what you want in a man. I believe you said something about a witty and well-read man who is also a good horseman. A short list, but it's something I can work with. You, however, don't know what would be a good, er, *fit* for me. Now, I ask you, can you run an estate?"

His eyebrows waggled.

She laughed at his silliness. This was the Duncan she remembered. Although he looked differently with muscles and steely glare, this was most certainly the Duncan she fell in love with as a young girl.

Gathering her wits about her and calming her laughter, she cleared her throat, looked at him from down her nose, and said in her best daughter-of-the-Duke-of-Annick voice, "You dare to question if *I* can oversee an estate? You, a mere peasant?" She scoffed. "Since birth, I've been raised to serve as mistress to even a royal estate. One more word from you, sirrah, and I shall call the guards."

Barely had she said the final three words before she dissolved into laughter.

His expression smoldered. "But can you select the month's menu to appeal to the hearty appetite of a colonel?"

Still giggling, she asked, "Will meat and potatoes do?"

"I wasn't referring to food."

Her smile faded until she tugged at her bottom lip with her teeth. *Oh my.*

And then she did what she suspected was the last thing he would have expected or intended. She stood from her chair, took one step in front of his, and climbed onto his lap, her legs perpendicular to his, her bottom tucked against his side, and her arms around his neck.

With bosom pressed to his chest, lips inches from his ear, she asked, "Do you still tingle when you ride?"

His hands wrapped about her hips. "Mmm. Yes. Twice a day, I feel alive."

"Even more alive than when I do this?" She peppered kisses along the curve of his face.

"Perhaps there's one exception." Running a hand from her hip up her back, he palmed her head and pulled her to meet him, his lips slanting over hers.

As the kiss deepened and lengthened, she felt lightheaded and giddy. This was what she wanted — to be touched. Be it hands held, lips puckered, arms embraced, or simply fingertips to bare arm, she wanted to be held.

Following a mutual sigh of contentment, he drew back, his eyes sweeping over her.

"You should leave," he said.

Surprised, she asked, "Am I hurting you?" She looked down to his legs, embarrassed she had not thought of his comfort.

Darkened eyes stared back at her, half-lidded, lingering on her lips. "You are weightless, my love. But at some point, my mother will come looking for you, and I'm not sure you want her to see you like this."

If her cheeks had not felt heated before, they did now, aflame with embarrassment. Reluctant, but not wanting Mrs. Starrett to think her disrespectful or wanton, Mary climbed off Duncan's lap. With a farewell kiss to his cheek, she saw herself out of the room.

At the break of dawn, Duncan awoke with a start. His torso was drenched with sweat, his skin afire. Tossing aside the covers, he breathed in the chilly autumn air, hoping it would cool his desire. He had been dreaming of Mary again. In the dream, he had been seated in the wheeled chair, she astride. Try as he might to unbutton his fall flap in the dream, the buttons snagged, leading to a frustrated struggle before he awoke.

The dream should have readied him for love — except for one important factor. With a quick check, he confirmed his plight. Still no evidence of function. Turning over, he pummeled his fists into his pillow. How could he ever think of marrying Mary when so unmanned?

He moved to the edge of the bed, eyeing his ankle. It was red but could bear his weight. Even the swelling had decreased. It did not appear to be sprained, as verified by one of the grooms Peter had brought in the day before. Duncan had not wanted to tell his father or have a physician sent for, so he was grateful to both Peter and the groom. Although the groom was not a medical expert of any kind when it came to humans, it would seem he was correct.

Relieved though he was, Duncan did not take chances. He focused on his usual regimen of upper body exercises rather than his walking practices to allow for more healing time.

Once washed and dressed, he climbed into the wheeled chair and had a footman wheel him to the morning room, always an inconvenience when it came to having to carry the chair down the stairs, but well-worth the effort so Duncan could enjoy a sense of normality by breaking his fast with his family in the morning room. However many times they offered to have breakfast in the upstairs parlor, he refused. He would not be an invalid forever, he told them.

The selection at the sideboard was all his favorites. Cook was spoiling him. When he reached his place at the table, his mail waited in a neat stack next to his plate. The first letter was from his steward, Mr. McLarren, with the Sidwell Hall news. Such letters always invited a smile. That he was a baronet with an estate never ceased to amaze him. He really must plan a trip soon, but so help him he would walk through the front door during the first visit.

The second letter bore the seal of Major-General Andrew Pierce, Earl of Langley. Duncan's breath caught in his throat. This had to be an enquiry of when he would be fit to return to service. He could think of no other reason to receive a letter.

Why, why, why did this have to come now? He was not ready. Time. Time was what he needed. He wanted to return, did he not? But he needed time. First, he had to see if he could heal well enough to return. And then there was Mary.

Tucking the second letter in his coat to read later, he instead read the first letter aloud so his parents could enjoy hearing about Sidwell Hall. Mr. McLarren had specific orders to keep Duncan abreast not only of the hall, but of the people. He wanted to keep up with the comings and goings of the neighbors and workers so that when he met them all, he would know their lives.

After breaking his fast, he withdrew to the drawing room, eager to pen a letter to Dr. Knowlton on his progress before his morning ride with Caesar. While progress was not quite where he wanted it to be before he revealed the news to his family, it was miraculous enough to share the news with the good doctor.

Seated in his wheeled chair at the escritoire, his hand followed the quill as it danced across the page, line after line depicting his exercises, his assisted walking, and his standing without aid. Though he mentioned the sensations while riding, he also confessed to a lack of feeling once dismounted, and thus the need to look down when taking so much as a single step. With luck, the physician would write back with a suggestion Duncan had not considered.

Mid-sentence, an idea formed.

Returning the quill to its holder, he pushed himself away from the desk. Ready or not, his ankle would have to go to work.

Careful, anxious, both hands gripping the arms of the chair until his knuckles whitened, he pushed himself up. His legs straightened. His ankle bore his weight. For a moment, he simply stood upright.

Then, closing his eyes, he shifted his weight from one leg to the other, not enough to lift a foot off the ground, but enough to test the feel of one leg bearing weight versus the other.

He concentrated on his hips. Though he felt nothing below the hips, he could feel the hips themselves. What he wanted to test was if there was a noticeable difference in how the weight-bearing hip felt to the non-weight-bearing. Back and forth he swayed.

Yes, there was a difference. It was slight. Imperceptible to someone not paying attention, but there was a difference. He could feel each foot pressed to the floor through the hip.

Eyes open, he took a tentative step forward, watching his foot to ensure it contacted the floor. As it moved heel to ball on the floor, he focused on how the hip felt in the movement. The hip moved up, creating the sensation of contraction.

Rocking back onto his right foot, he lifted his left leg off the floor then heel-to-ball stepped on it once more. Still on the left foot, he stepped forward and back countless times, memorizing the feel of his hip at the moment of contact and moment of release. And then the other foot with a focus on the other hip.

Before attempting to walk with eyes closed, he tried a few more moves. He feigned a step forward with a foot hover, as though he missed contact with the floor. Stomping his foot, as though the floor were closer than he anticipated, his attention narrowed to the feel of the hip's reaction to the movement. He tried stepping side to side, backwards, at an angle, and of course, forward.

Not entirely confident yet, he rolled each foot from heel to ball and back several more times, marched in place, balanced on the balls of his feet, lifting and lowering, all while concentrating on the feel of the hips. He balanced on the heels, and after that bit of fun, he tried swinging each leg forward as if to take a step, trying to gauge by feel alone how far his leg might be swinging. There was nothing pleasant about taking a step too wide or too narrow, after all.

To the hearth and back seemed a reasonable goal.

He stared down at his feet as he had been doing, but his focus remained on the feel of the hips. As he took one step after another, he thought about what his pelvis was doing—remaining level but tilting and twisting ever so slightly with each step. A series of intentional missteps helped gauge the inappropriate hip and pelvis reactions. He tried forcing a knee buckle and hyperextension, as well as dragging his toe and slapping his foot—both problems he suffered nearly every time he tried walking without looking.

Finally, he was ready to test his theory.

Thinking a silent prayer that he did not sprain the ankle this time, he closed his eyes and took a step. It was not a brave step. It was a gauged step, one in which he felt for the floor with the hip, the leg lowering inch by inch until he could feel the upwards shift, tilt, and contraction in the hip. Following that step came another. He moved one foot after the other in measured time, slow-motion walking to the hearth with eyes closed. While his feet could not feel the floor beneath them, his hips told him everything he needed to know. Holding a hand out in front of him, he waited to open his eyes until he felt the cold marble of the mantel under his palm.

He had walked across the room without looking down.

A run through the fields might not be his next move, but by Jove, he had walked across a room unassisted. With eyes open but refusing to look down at his feet, he walked back to the escritoire, taking great care with his steps and focusing on nothing but his hips. It would not do to lose his concentration or move sloppily. At this point, he doubted he could walk confidently enough to fool anyone, much less walk and talk at the same time, but he did not see why he could not achieve those goals with more practice. If he could only regain sensation, he would be back to normal.

Seated again, he returned to his letter to Dr. Knowlton, striking through the last few sentences and adding in what he had just accomplished.

One evening to practice this so he could walk with a little more speed and confidence, and he would reveal all to his parents. Did he want to reveal this to Mary now or later? He did not see why he should wait. It did not seem false hope when he was able to achieve so much now. Yes, it was time to show Mary.

Good heavens. It had not even been a full week since he stood for the first time. Five days. In five days, he had gone from standing to walking. Miraculous. There seemed little in this world he could not accomplish!

After sanding the ink and addressing and sealing the letter, he set it in the mail bin for Mr. Lowand. A new goal was in order. By Sunday, he would make it to church and back.

He reached for the bell pull, then recalled the letter in his coat pocket. In seconds, he broke the seal, unfolded it, and began to read. Before a full minute passed, he ripped the letter in half, ripped it again, then crumpled it in his fist and hurled it across the room to the fire, missing by less than a foot. His frustration unsatisfied, he pounded a fist against the desk.

Now hereby discharged.

Chapter 15

The needle moved in and out of the silk, shaping the blue thread into a bird. Stilling the needle, Mary pulled her shawl more tightly around her shoulders.

A rustle of paper distracted her attention.

Settled at her brother's feet lay Theodore, prone on his stomach, stockinged feet saluting the air, pages covered in the dark lines of charcoal spread before him. Theo sat up and held out a page for his father.

"My son's an artist," Drake declared between puffs of his cheroot.

Theo shook his head and pointed to the drawing. "Head's too big."

Squinting, Drake stared at the paper. He tilted his head, his brows furrowing. When satisfied with his examination, he leaned back and said, "Looks brilliant to me."

Theo harrumphed and waved the paper for Mary to see.

She set the embroidery in her lap to study the artistry. Two well-proportioned, charcoal figures stared back at her. So carefully sketched were they, she would never have guessed this drawn by a toddler. Mind, the bodies were square, the hair nothing more than lines, and the smiles a lopsided and sideways letter D, but it was nevertheless quite good. She saw nothing alarming about the sizes of the heads.

Her nephew looked up at her with expectant eyes.

Pointing, she said, "You're right, of course. The head on the left is too big."

Satisfied that she agreed with him when his father was clearly too daft to see the discrepancy, Theo nodded and returned to work, his tongue inching to the corner of his mouth as charcoal met paper once more.

Mary had only just slipped the needle into silk to finish the bird's breast when the parlor door opened to a breathy wind of chatter.

"I thought Mama Catherine would never relent. On she talked about who I should have invited to the foxhunt and shooting party and who I shouldn't have. If I hear one more sigh of exasperation, I'll scream." Charlotte bustled into the room with her cockatoo perched on her arm.

"Why you insist on consulting her is beyond my comprehension," Mary said to her sister-in-law.

"I value her opinion. She may seem abrasive, but she means well."

Mary mumbled to herself, "My mother never means well. She's a crusty bat."

Returning the cockatoo to his tree, Charlotte stepped over to kiss the top of her son's head and her husband's temple. She wrinkled her nose. "Don't smoke that filthy thing in the parlor, darling." With a sweep of her hand, she stole the cheroot from his grasp and smothered it into a silver ashtray. "Has no one taught you it's poor etiquette to smoke in front of ladies?"

Drake sputtered in protest. "But, but how else am I to relax after a long day of being a duke?"

When she leaned over to whisper into his ear, he chuckled throatily. Mary's cheeks heated. Head bowed, she focused her attention on her embroidery, curious to think what she might have whispered to Duncan in a similar situation.

As though reading Mary's thoughts of Duncan, Charlotte said as soon as she took a seat, "If one more bouquet arrives, we'll run out of space in the parlor."

Not that Mary had forgotten, given the multitude of flower bouquets decorating the room, but she surveyed the room, nonetheless, admiring the lavished attention from Duncan. An array of reds, pinks, and blues adorned every surface and tabletop. At least three times per day for several days, a messenger from Cois Greta Park brought a bouquet or five for Mary's pleasure, each accompanied by a one to two-line verse penned for her eyes only. How his mother's hothouse had any flowers remaining was anyone's guess.

"It is kind of him," was all Mary could say, her memory lingering on her most recent visit and their intimate moment.

Drake barked a laugh. "Kind? No, this is an ardent suitor preparing to propose. I expect him to call on me any day." Tapping a forefinger to his lips, he said, "I've not decided if I'll turn him away the first time or not."

Charlotte gasped. "You wouldn't!"

Drake grinned in reply.

Mary glanced between them, not at all comfortable with the turn in conversation. "You're being silly. He's in no condition to call on anyone. And why would he propose now when we need first to become better acquainted after the long separation?"

"Better acquainted?" Drake scoffed. "Nonsense. I'm a man; thus, I know how men think. He'll want to secure the betrothal and move into the hall. The Starretts, though good people, are likely driving the poor man insane."

"You forget his affliction," Mary defended. "He'll be in no rush while he's chairbound."

Returning to her work, she ignored her brother's chuckle and insistence of knowing a man's mind better than she. Propose indeed. Fiddlesticks. She knew Duncan better than anyone, and he would not want to marry until he could either walk or come to terms with the permanency of his condition.

Not that she would mind if he proposed sooner rather than later. The sooner she had freedom from her mother and the sooner she had her own home, the better. There was a world of accomplishments singing for her, all to the tune of marriage. With the right marriage, she would be set free.

"Tell me," her brother said, "were you intentionally aggravating Mother at dinner or do you really want to breed horses?"

She looked up at Drake, needle poised above silk. "I'm in earnest. That does not mean I wasn't also antagonizing her, but yes, I do want a stud farm."

"Why am I only hearing about this now?" He slapped his leg and leaned forward, all that was enthusiastic. "This shall be a grand adventure! I can have a stud and mare in your possession before the month is out. We rarely use the rear stables anymore. Why not have those for your own purposes? Are you thinking thoroughbreds? I'll send a letter to my man straight away."

Waving her needle, she said, "Oh, please don't. Not yet at least. It may come to that, but I would like to do this on my own."

Drake frowned. "You don't want my help?"

"It's not that I don't. But this is my dream, and as such, I want a hand in fulfilling it, not have my brother do it for me. What part do I play if you do all the work on my behalf?"

"I see," he said, his tone implying he did not at all see her rationale. "In that case, send a letter to Tattersall's son, request whatever you'd like, and have him charge me. You have carte blanche, of course."

Pursing her lips at the mention of Mr. Edmund Tattersall, she said, "Thank you. I will consider the offer, and I may come to you with questions, but for now, I'm handling everything myself."

Or rather, she was handling nothing, as empty handed now as she had been from the start. Perhaps she was being too stubborn. It would be so easy for Drake to take care of the details.

"Does a certain colonel know of your ungenteel pursuits?" Drake asked. "I should think if he got wind of this, he would request the return of his flowers to send to someone staid."

Mary laughed so heartily, the cockatoo joined in, both parties receiving a scowl from Theodore, his concentration on the art broken. Charlotte chided her husband but soon joined in the mirth. The thought of Duncan being under the impression that Mary was of a gentle constitution was too absurd not to laugh.

"'A man's heart deviseth his way: but the Lord directeth his steps,'" Quinn was saying, his horse in step with Duncan's.

"For once, we're in agreement." Duncan loosened the reins to prompt Caesar to quicken his pace ahead of Quinn.

Though he did not yet confess to his brother, he was leading them to the lake. Some things could not be dissuaded, and so, it was in everyone's best interest not to broach the subject until necessary.

"I thought you wanted to return to service?" Quinn's horse trotted to catch up.

"I did. I do. It doesn't make it the right choice."

"If you see God's plan is greater than your own, why the initial hostility?"

Duncan delayed answering, transfixed by the feel of his calves rubbing against his boots with each flex. If he could find a way to live atop Caesar, he would. Each ride brought new sensations, even a tenderness along his inner thighs so pronounced he could almost feel Caesar's movements, almost discern the heat from the horseflesh. Would he ever regain feeling when dismounted?

"I'm angrier the decision was taken from me than I am to be medically discharged. I can't say if I would have chosen to return. It's likely I wouldn't have; but I wanted that to be my choice. What am I to do now? I'm a leader, Quinn, a natural born leader, and now I've nothing to lead. I'll throw myself into running the estate, I suppose."

He did look forward to his estate. It was not the type of leadership he craved, but he would do the best he could. The hall was, after all, a symbol of his military skill.

Quinn continued to keep pace as Duncan attempted to gain ground again. "And you've not told Lady Mary yet?"

"Not about either, no. I want to tell her while standing on my own two feet and able to walk to her. I want her to see the miracle. I've not resolved how to tell her about the letter, however. Does she need to know? She can assume I sold out."

"Don't ask Miranda. She'll rain fire and brimstone about lying. If there's one thing I've learned in my years of marriage, it's never to lie, even by omission. Women are curious creatures. They always know when you lie."

Another spur with Quinn on his heels, Duncan said, "Right, then. Tell her, I must. May her relief outweigh her perceptiveness. It would do no good for her to think I'd rather be in the Army than by her side. I wouldn't, of course. If I could have both, I would, but never could I put her at risk, not when I know what life in the camp is like. That's no place for a lady."

"Not to change the subject, but is there a reason you're determined to outpace me? And for that matter, why are we going in the direction of Lyonn Manor rather than home?" Quinn searched the rolling fields for clues.

"Only one way to find out, brother." With those words, Duncan moved Caesar into a canter.

The weather was far too cold for what he had in mind, but nothing would deter him. Once decided, he was determined. Cresting the hill to the west of the lake, he slowed, relishing the final moments of lower body sensations before he was to try the impossible.

Quinn caught up to him just as the lake came into view. "The lake? Why would you want to come here?"

Duncan did not answer.

Once at the bank, he halted, eyeing the terrain for a safe place to dismount. He needed flat ground without worry of roots, mud, or debris.

He must be mad. Not once had he attempted to dismount using his legs. It had not been a full week since first walking and only a few days since learning that the pressure and gait of the hips could guide him. Even with daily walking practice, he relied on the indoor and outdoor chairs to move about the park. The little walking he did was reserved for the drawing room, parlor, and bedchamber. And yet today, a hefty distance from the park, with only his brother present, he wanted to attempt the impossible.

As Quinn approached, Duncan said, "I need you to stand behind me in case I fall."

He did not look back to see his brother's expression, but he heard the hiss of a sharp intake.

"Tell me you're not about to—"

Before Quinn could finish the sentence, Duncan swung his leg around, praying his muscles worked. His brother scrambled off his horse. Not that Duncan noticed. He was too busy memorizing the feel of his legs as they supported his weight and did all he commanded. In slow-motion he moved, delaying the inevitable loss of feeling to come.

The moment both boots met earth, tingling abated, and a numbness settled into his flesh. Alas.

Turning to Quinn, he said, "Well? How'd I do?"

"You're mad! What if you had slipped? What if a leg gave out? What if you missed the ground? I have visions of ten different ways you could have been trampled or met with a broken neck." Quinn crossed his arms, his face pink with anger.

"And I thought you'd be impressed." As he spoke the words, he began to disrobe.

His brother stared, wide eyed. Looking from water to Duncan and back, Quinn finally said, "Oh no, no, no, you're not going to do what I think you're going to do. Dismounting was one thing. You'll catch your death!"

"No need for melodrama. We used to swim in far colder temperatures, as you'll recall."

"When you were ten and when I should have had more sense. What's the meaning of this? You can barely walk. What makes you think you can swim? Now I'm going to have to go in to save you from drowning. Blast it, man!" Quinn peeled off his great-coat, coat, and waistcoat, tugging at his boots.

Duncan did not wait for him. In tentative strides, he approached the bank. While he normally would have dived in, he was not at all sure he could propel his body in such a fashion, at least not yet. Instead, he stepped forward and tipped into the lake, smacking the water with his side.

He knew two things simultaneously. The water was an icy nightmare, and his legs seized on impact. His first reaction was to panic. Arms whipping the water around him, he struggled to kick out, but his legs were lead, pulling him to the bottom of the lake.

Once the initial shock of the cold passed, he schooled himself to relax. Arcing his arms in wide half-circles, he scooped the water away and inward. In seconds, he resurfaced, his arms keeping him afloat, and tread water.

"Ahh ha ha! Woo!" He screamed with a teeth-chattering laugh.

Quinn, he saw, was readying himself to dive. Hands clasped overhead, the vicar cut the water with barely a sound. In seconds, he surfaced a fair distance from Duncan and screamed a stream of curses.

"Why are we freezing to death?" Quinn demanded, his teeth chattering.

"Admit it. It's not *that* cold. If the lake isn't frozen, it hardly counts as cold."

Duncan peered into the water every few seconds to see if his legs were working. Their limpness after accomplishing so much was both alarming and frightening, but as he calmed, so it seemed his body did also.

His legs began to respond to his commands. To say he was relieved was an understatement. He may be able to tread water with arms alone, but it had been no less disturbing to have to prove it.

"Are you intentionally avoiding my question?" his brother asked.

"I'm distracted, eh? It's not like you must concentrate to stay afloat. I, on the other hand, do. Although, I do have one advantage over you—I can't feel the cold from waist down. Go on, envy me. I know you're jealous but thinking of five verses to punish yourself for it."

"Har har. Are we quite finished? I suppose you haven't thought about the wet ride back." Quinn buoyed, slicking back the hair that matted to his face. "We'll be lucky not to freeze on the way home."

Ignoring him, Duncan propelled himself through the water. He could not feel his legs to know if they kicked, but given the speed and success of his swim, he assumed they did. A few times, the swim slowed, and he felt as though he dragged his lower limbs behind him, but just as soon as it happened, his body seemed to right itself.

When he surfaced after several laps, he said to Quinn, who bobbed in the water, "I have no way to exercise or strengthen my legs, at least not until I'm more confident with their reliability. Swimming seems a perfect solution, does it not? Today was a test. Now that I've done it, I want to swim once a day until it's too cold to do so."

"It's already too cold, you imbecile."

"You've become stodgy in your old age. Has Miranda ever told you?" Duncan baptized the vicar with a mighty splash.

As his brother made to return the favor, Duncan dived into the water, pumping his legs, a freeing experience since he was not worried about falling or tripping or making a fool of himself while swimming.

Burrowing into the blanket, Duncan wrapped his trembling hands around a cup of tea, warming limbs inside and out after the vigorous workout. However long it had taken him to dry and warm, the swim had been worth it. He felt renewed. The onset of winter would cramp his recovery, but he would make the best use of autumn while he had the chance. Every day that it did not rain, he would ride and swim, anything to exercise his legs and revel in the feel of returned sensation, regardless of how dull and intermittent.

The peculiar part of the day, he thought as he watched the flames lick the logs in the fireplace, had occurred ten minutes into his swim, moments before he returned to the bank. His right knee sensed an icy coldness. His imagination? Possibly. But he would swear on his brother's bible that he had, for a brief moment, felt the water against his knee.

That evening he drifted to sleep with the fantasy of normality. Everything was happening just as Dr. Knowlton promised, though not as quickly or as suddenly as the physician had expected. Soon Duncan would be back to his old self as though nothing had happened. Never would he take for granted the ability to walk, feel, or love.

That evening, sleep overtook him as he imagined a return to sensation, the celebration his wedding night with Mary. He envisioned her voluptuous curves, her eyes dark with desire for her husband, his name a moan of promise on her lips.

He jerked awake. A fierce wind howled, the sound not unlike a moan, the patter of rain a mimicry of the rhythmic thumping the headboard in his dream. Groaning, he turned on his side, wanting nothing more than to return to his illusions.

He could not immediately will himself back to sleep. The fire had long ago died to ember glow, leaving the room chilly. Nestling further into the bedding, he pulled his knees to his chest. He thrummed with longing. His upper body, that was. As usual, he felt nothing below, but the rest of him pulsed from the dream. *Come, sleep*, he coaxed. *Return me to my lady. This is my only opportunity to love her as a man.*

If he thought the knee incident had been peculiar, it was nothing to what happened next. Duncan tucked a hand between his knees to warm his fingers. When his forearm brushed against the unexpected, he tossed off the covers and sat up in haste.

Breath held, fingers stretched, he reached for himself.

By Jupiter! He wanted to cheer into the night. For days, for weeks, for however long, he had not even been able to will himself to attention, a serious barrier to his matrimonial pursuits. And now, in a single moment, his future shifted.

The frustration in the elation stemmed from the realization that he remained void of feeling, regardless of being ready for love. Much like with his regaining of mobility, albeit by slow measure, the muscle was responding but without nerve sensation.

Well, devil take it. What good did this do him if he could not feel anything?

Lying back, he pulled the bedding to his chin, burying himself into the warmth. With frustration waring against elation, it was a long time before he could find sleep again.

However freeing it felt to walk, it was far more fatiguing than Duncan would wish. When walking, his full concentration had to be centered on the feel of his hips. In time, he should become accustomed to the movement, but given it had been only a week, progress was slow.

Everything acted as an impediment to success. The grass was slippery, the gravel loose, the steps uneven. The wheeled chairs were his dearest friends throughout each day, but he could not reside in them forever — if he did not practice even the most arduous of tasks, he would never succeed. What he wanted, but would not voice, was to awaken to the return of his full range of motion and sensation. He might celebrate with a run should that happen.

His goal of making it to church was delayed for another week. As much as he wanted to go, he did not want to go without Mary on his arm, nor did he want the villagers to see him walking before Mary did. And so, he found himself on this fine day on the doorstep of Lyonn Manor, having handed his card to the butler.

Caesar would be disappointed to learn Duncan had taken the carriage instead of riding him, but on such a day as this, he could not arrive smelling like a horse.

He realized only after giving his card that he needed to order new cards. These did not reflect his baronetcy, though that hardly mattered when the duke knew, but it was still something he ought to do. Tonight, he could send a note to Mr. McLarren; how important it felt to have one's own man of business.

Duncan fiddled with his cravat and tugged at his shirt points. They felt too tall, too starched, and too tight.

Never had he been to the manor. Intimidating was putting it mildly. It was a palace. How she must have laughed when she first saw Cois Greta Park. And how would Sidwell Hall compare to this? He could not imagine the hall being large, likely not even of equitable size to his parent's home. And she still claimed to want him after living *here*? Humbling.

Tapping his heeled shoes, he watched in fascination how the narrowed tips of sky blue lifted and lowered with each tap, just as they should, just as though he were normal and healed.

When the door opened, Duncan's pulse raced, his heart pounding against his ribcage. He could scarce hear for the sound of trepidation in his ears.

"Follow me, sir," said the man.

They spent only enough time in the entry hall for Duncan's coat, hat, and gloves to be removed and disappear around a corner. The entry was the size of his bedchamber. Busts on pedestals stared at him, judging. He tried not to gape.

The butler led him around a curved, grand staircase, into an oval hall, and through a door into a study. The duke's study. Duncan swallowed.

Shoulders back, head high, he marched into the room, stopping only when he spotted the Duke of Annick seated behind a desk, scratching with a quill across parchment. Was it too late to run? Did he dare try to run? Knowing his luck, he would trip on the rug. Though the butler announced him and closed the door, the duke did not look up to acknowledge Duncan. The quill worked. Duncan gulped.

The wait was interminable. Staring at the top of His Grace's pomaded, black hair and watching the ringed fingers strangling the feather did not ease the tension. Duncan glanced at the clock on the mantel, the second hand ticking a death toll to the moment of

judgment. Tugging at the hem of his coat, he chewed
on the inside of his cheek.

Tick tock.

Scratch scribble.

At last, with a flourish, the duke signed the letter,
returned the quill to its stand, and sanded the ink.
Only then did he look up. When his eyes met Duncan's, his eyebrows rose high on his forehead, one
corner of his mouth inching into a grin.

"Well, what do we have here?" The duke looked
Duncan up and down, a lingering stare at his feet. "I
expected Mr. Hunter to wheel you in. Standing and
walking again, I see." Lacing his fingers, he rested
his palms against the back of his head, leaning into
the chairback.

"A new development that is not without difficulties," Duncan said, still standing, anxious he had not
yet been asked to sit.

"Not a miraculous recovery, then?"

"Depends on your definition of both miraculous
and recovery. Early this week, I regained movement
but not feeling, and the movement is not entirely
reliable, though I will not begrudge my progress."
Duncan shifted his weight from one leg to the other,
mostly to assure himself both legs worked.

"Does my sister know? Ah, never mind. If she
knew, she would have told me. And so, you come
to me today to share the good news and discuss the
weather, I assume. Please, have a seat."

His Grace waved a hand to the chair across the
desk. Why Duncan had thought they might share a
coze by the fire, he had no idea. He would take what he
could get. In a few steps, he was to the chair and seated.

The duke's smile turned to a smug grin, though what there was to be smug about, Duncan could not say.

"Cheroot?" he asked, opening a drawer.

"No, but thank you, Your Grace."

Closing the drawer without grabbing one for himself, the duke said, "We've been neighbors for years, old boy. I should think it time you call me Annick. Did you know your father taught me to shoot when I was younger?"

Duncan shook his head, stopped, then nodded. "He's not mentioned it in years. I had forgotten, but yes, now you mention it, it was a point he brought up at many dinners, a point of pride."

"I spent more time there than in my own home. That was a long time ago, certainly when you were still in the nursery." Annick unhooked his fingers and leaned forward to the desk, propping his chin on his fist. "Despite my mother's disapproval, I've always been fond of your family. You come from good stock. But then, aren't you supposed to be the one convincing me of that fact?"

Taken aback, Duncan frowned. "You know why I'm here?"

"It's written in the droplets of sweat beading down your temple, old boy."

Embarrassed, Duncan pulled out a handkerchief to dab his forehead. It was frigid outside, and here he was, sweating like a laborer.

"Right, well, best to it, then." Duncan twisted the handkerchief between his fingers. "I'm here to ask for your sister's hand."

Annick studied him before asking, "Do you know what I do to fortune hunters?"

Duncan shook his head, clenching the linen. Not the answer he had hoped to hear. Of all the adversaries he had faced in battle, knowing it was their life or his, he had never felt this nervous.

"I snap my fingers and watch them disappear," the duke said cryptically.

"I've no interest in her dowry, Your Grace." Duncan dabbed his brow again. "Put it in a trust only she controls. She'll want pin money, of course. I've a pension from the Army, and now the income of the baronetcy. My pocket is modest, but not empty. I ask for her hand because I've loved her since I first laid eyes on her."

Annick assessed him in silence.

Tick tock.

Gulp.

Annick slapped the desk and laughed. Duncan nearly jumped out of the chair.

"Took you long enough to ask. Although, I admit, had you asked me six or even five years ago, I would have thought you a scoundrel, but you've proven yourself a steady and determined match. I couldn't think of a finer fellow for my sister or better in-laws for me. Shall we talk details first, or would you prefer I have her brought to the drawing room?"

It took nearly an hour for the two men to work up a contract. Duncan was not prepared for the assets Mary would bring to a marriage. This was all beyond his experience and bookkeeping skills. A long conversation ensued on what to do with the dowry because Annick saw no reason Duncan should not have it, but Duncan wanted there to be no question of him seeking her fortune and insisted it be placed in a trust instead. The discussion was contentious, Annick thinking him needlessly hardheaded.

At last, with all decided, Annick rang for the butler and walked Duncan to the study door.

The duke caught Duncan's hand in his, his smile gone, his twinkling eyes turned to steel.

Gripping Duncan's hand until the rings cut into his flesh, Annick said, "I have agreed to allow you to ask for her. Should she choose to marry you for love rather than to marry a duke as is fitting of her station, know every moment of your life what a prize you have married. If for one second you forget and she comes to me in tears, I'll make you wish you had never been born." As quickly as his expression altered, it reverted, the duke laughing as he pulled Duncan into a one-armed hug. "Welcome to the family. Or should I say, good luck with the proposal?"

He winked, pushing Duncan out of the doorway to follow the butler to the drawing room.

A married woman. In three weeks, she would be a married woman, free of her mother, free of Lyonn Manor, free. Finally, she would know love's touch with an endless stream of kisses, hugs, and, oh, *and*.

Had she known what was to happen when Mr. Hunter said there was a special caller for her in the Red Drawing Room, she would have danced down the stairs, pirouetted across the hall, and leapt into her lover's arms. It had all come as a shock. She knew something was amiss when the butler said the formal Red Drawing Room rather than the cozier Blue, or even the parlor, but for a heart-pounding moment she worried her mother had arranged a bit of trickery.

She closed her eyes to better remember, although it would be an occasion she would not soon forget.

When the drawing room door opened, she beheld an empty room. Confused, she turned back to Mr. Hunter only to find the door closed behind him. Was this a child's game? Something her nephew had planned? No, he was not the playful type. Turning back, she surveyed the room, at first scanning past the gentleman leaning against the hearth mantel. How she had missed him, she could never say, but once she saw him, she could not unsee him.

Never had she expected to find Colonel Sir Duncan Starrett standing in the Red Drawing Room. Not just in her home but *standing*.

His eyes locked with hers.

Ever the gracious hostess, she could not move or speak. Struck dumb, was she, by this vision. It hit her what he was doing here just as suddenly as she had spotted him in the seemingly empty room. Her brother might have granted them far more leniency than what was accustomed of an unmarried lady and a gentleman, but he would only leave them alone in a room, least of all in his own home, for one purpose.

A wave of dizziness swept over her. *Don't swoon*, she told herself.

Finding her voice, she said, "How pleasant you should call on me, Sir Duncan. Do, please, be seated."

She waved to the chairs surrounding the fireplace. He bowed, his eyes never leaving hers, and strode to her rather than sitting.

Her breath caught in her throat as he prowled to her. He stopped within arm's reach and took her hand in his, raising it. Turning it over, he pressed her palm to puckered lips. A warm thrill trembled through her at the touch.

"Let's skip the pleasantries. Mary, my love, will you do me the honor of walking life's trials with me, of standing by my side, of wheeling through tribulations should I be in a chair? Will you be my wife?"

Her heart beat so erratically, she was positive she would faint. What happened to them getting to know each other? What happened to his inability to move his legs? What happened to his lack of sensation? What about Bernard?

Throwing rational thought and gentility aside, she threw her arms around his neck and peppered his face with kisses.

"You know I will," she said, leaning back to take in his flushed cheeks, broad smile, and bright eyes.

An errant strand of coffee-colored hair dropped over his forehead. She swept it back, running her fingers over his brow, tracing his sideburn down to his mouth, touching a lazy fingertip to the cleft in his chin. Without awaiting an invitation, she hugged him and met his lips with an open mouth. He sucked in a breath and pulled her more tightly to him. Though his lips embraced hers with the hunger of a starving man, his kiss lightened as quickly as it had begun.

Duncan's arms loosened as he took a step back to admire her. His eyes roamed her face with tenderness. With another step back, he took her hands in his and pulled her to the nearest set of chairs, urging her to sit. She did not want to sit. She wanted to resume kissing, to feel his arms about her, that physical touch for which she had longed all her life. It was not to be had. With a sigh, she sat, draping an elbow over the arm of the chair.

Looking him over, she could not imagine him confined to a chair and could not reconcile this image with the one she had seen nearly two months prior, an invalid trapped in a laudanum-induced sleep, his skin feverish, his body helpless and unresponsive. Now, he looked like a colonel, strong and commanding, not quite like the slender and jovial boy she had loved so long ago, but more appealing as the man she now wanted to marry.

Duncan sandwiched Mary's hand between his. He smiled, the corners of his eyes crinkling.

"Would you believe me if I said that I worried you would say no?" he asked.

"Why ever would I say no?"

"A host of reasons. One look at this house made my knees knock. I couldn't imagine you wanting to live in any humble home of mine after growing up in a palace. And there's my condition to consider. And that we agreed to court first and become acquainted all over again. And Bernard. And all the old concerns of my station. And—"

She covered his mouth with a finger. "Hush. You've asked. I've answered."

Nodding, he kissed her finger before moving it to join her other hand, wedged between his. "I couldn't wait another day for life to begin. I want to embark on our new life now. We'll be able to spend more time together as a betrothed couple. No more waiting for my mother to invite you to tea and hoping we'll have a moment's privacy under watchful gazes."

"Most importantly, I can kiss you whenever I want," she said.

"Yes, that too." He chuckled. "What of your mother? Should I worry she'll have my parent's house set to fire?"

Mary giggled. "Hardly. At worse, she'll have you hanged at dawn."

"Oh, is that all?" He ran a hand across the back of his neck.

"Don't worry about my mother; I'll handle her. Enough distraction, though. Are you going to keep me in suspense?" Mary nodded to his legs — enticingly muscled in tailored, silk breeches.

"It's a miracle, is it not? I'm not recovered, but by each day, I'm improved. Other than when riding, I have not regained sensation, but I do have use of my legs now. There are times when I'm unsteady, times when they're slow to respond, but after daily practice, I believe I can fool most. How'd I look? Were you convinced? Did I walk to you as a normal man?"

His expression held such intense conviction, she giggled again. "Not at all like a normal man."

Crestfallen, his gaze dropped to the floor.

She said, squeezing his hand, "You swaggered like a colonel who knew he was about to get the girl."

Duncan swung his eyes back to her, the corners crinkling once more. "If we should marry immediately after the banns are read, that will give me three more weeks to practice. With faith, I could have sensation by then. I could be normal by then." Under his breath, he said, "By God's grace, I hope so."

"I'm here even if you find yourself back in the wheeled chair. I'll wheel you into the church myself if I must." She had meant the words to be encouraging, but he frowned in response, drifting into thought.

When he looked up again, he said, "You should know that my father wrote to the Army of my circumstance. He meant well, of course, but I've been discharged for medical reasons and will not be returning. You're stuck with me, I'm afraid."

"Oh, but that's wonderful news, Duncan! Now you won't have the weight on your shoulders of selling your commission. Knowing you, you would have felt guilty, thinking you had abandoned your men, or some such rubbish. Now it's been taken care of, neat and tidy."

"Yes, I suppose so."

His answer was spoken so softly, she wondered if he was as happy about the news as he ought to be. Surely, he had not wanted to return to service. The thought strangled her breath.

"Before your brother interrupts us, and I must admit, I'm surprised he's left us alone for this long, I have an important question to ask."

She pulled her hands from his to grip the arms of her chair.

"What type of horses are you hoping to breed?" he asked.

The question was so unusual, she laughed. "What type of horses? Of all the questions, I hadn't expected that one. To be honest, I don't know. Thoroughbreds? I don't even know if I want to breed them for auction or by request. It's a point of frustration, I admit. Why do you ask?"

"If I tell you, it won't be a surprise. Only, I need to know the breed. Think on it?"

She puckered her lips in thought. "What about warhorses?"

He raised his brows. "Are you trying to stud my horse?"

Blushing, she said, "Now that you mention it…"

"Caesar would be ecstatic. Let me think on the possibilities. I'll say nothing more now lest I ruin your wedding present."

Chapter 16

The carriage swayed its way into the village. On the horizon rose a sun that promised a day of good weather. Mrs. Starrett and Mary sat together facing Colonel Sean Starrett and Duncan, whose backs were to the horses. Bernard, in his Sunday best, perched on his papa's lap.

Duncan had shared with Mary his grand plan to walk all the way to the church for his first appearance since that fated evening, but given his fatiguing struggle to walk without feeling, he listened to reason and accompanied the family in the carriage.

When the horses halted, Mary reached a hand to cover his. He returned a nervous smile before offering to hand her down the steps.

She saw the crowd before he did.

Duncan's eyes were riveted on her descension, none the wiser. With a flick of her head and a nudge to his arm, she enticed him to turn around. A double queue led to the church door, the Reverend Quinn Starrett standing at the entrance in his vestments. All the village, or so it appeared, were gathered to greet Duncan for his walk into church. Back rigid, jaw clenched, hands furling and unfurling into fists, he stared at the crowd, all of whom waited for him to promenade and be the first to enter.

At Mrs. Starrett's coaxing, Bernard took her hand so Duncan could walk the aisle unencumbered.

With chin high, Mary placed a hand on her betrothed's arm, tugging him forward with a gentle squeeze. It was the inducement he needed. Relaxing his shoulders, he took one step forward, and then another. His gait smoothed with each step, Mary hugging his arm with her fingers.

Applause rippled through the crowd as he approached his brother.

"Welcome back," the vicar said, holding out a hand to shake Duncan's.

They made their way to the first pew, the closest to the pulpit. After Bernard scrambled in ungentlemanly enthusiasm to wedge between her and Duncan as they took their seats, Mary looked around her. She had never been in the village church before. The family only ever attended the private chapel, the estate clergyman crafting sermons befitting the dowager duchess's preferences. It was strange and exciting to be sharing her Sunday with so many people.

She reached an inconspicuous hand to touch Duncan's only to find her fingers wrapped around the thin arm of Bernard. He smiled up at her, legs kicking air, grabbing her hand with his cold palm. Goodness. For a moment, in her awe of the present situation, she had forgotten about him. His hand remained in hers as the vicar stepped into the pulpit.

His opening words were the reading of the banns. Mary glanced at Duncan as the words wove through the church. He winked back at her. These words made it real. There was no turning back, no second thoughts, no fire-breathing mother who could smote them asunder.

"I publish the banns of marriage between Lady Mary Mowbrah of the Mowbrahs of Annick and Colonel Sir Duncan Starrett of the Starretts of Norham. This is the first time of asking. If any of you know cause or just impediment why these two persons should not be joined together in Holy Matrimony, ye are to declare it."

A murmur, followed by a hush, swept through the congregation. Although today was the first official time of asking and announcement of the betrothal, everyone already knew. How people knew was beyond Mary's understanding, but everyone knew. They knew even before the two walked to the church arm in arm. All the same, Mary held her breath, a dreadful vision of her mother breaking down the door of the church to declare her just impediment. But what would the dowager duchess say? That she would not have her daughter marry a commoner? That would not bode well for Catherine's popularity nor local reception. Only when the vicar proceeded to the sermon did Mary release her breath.

Her mother had made a point not to speak to her at dinner. How her mother had found out about the engagement, she did not know, but likely Drake had told her to save Mary the trouble. All through dinner, that once-a-week dinner in which her mother graced them with her presence, Catherine had talked as though Mary were not at the table, as though she were invisible, absent, or dead. That was perfectly acceptable to Mary. If she never had to deal with her mother again, life would be as it should be. It was, after all, one of the perks of marriage.

The voice of the vicar slipped through her thoughts, his tone filled with a genuine praise she had never heard from the estate clergyman.

"'Rejoicing in hope; patient in tribulation; continuing instant in prayer,' Romans 12:12 points us to the miracle of faith, faith that has, as Colossians 1:11 reminds us, strengthened the weak 'with all might, according to his glorious power, unto all patience and longsuffering with joyfulness.'"

The Reverend Starrett held a hand towards Duncan, though his eyes surveyed the church. His voice lowered, as if sharing a secret, before rising again in triumph. "'Blessed is the man that endureth temptation: for when he is tried, he shall receive the crown of life, which the Lord hath promised to them that love him,' James 1:12. Before you today, you see a miracle. 'And God wrought special miracles by the hands of' Dr. Knowlton, physician. My brother, our returned hero who fought for Crown and country, walks before us, renewed of strength, rewarded with love. Should faith ever falter, look inward to our flock, for the touched walk amongst us, reminders of God's love and charity."

Tears stung Mary's eyes. So moved was she by the vicar's words, she released Bernard's hand to fish out her handkerchief. Her watery gaze found Duncan's when she looked up. His stare was stony, his jaw ticking with tension. She nudged Bernard to take his hand. Though the boy did, Duncan did not seem to notice. His hand took the tiny one in his as though by instinct, his expression shielded.

Was he moved, as well, but fought to show it? Was he angry his brother spoke of the condition so openly? She could not read him. She had always been able to read him. One look and she would always know his thoughts and feelings, and yet now, she hardly knew the man sitting one tiny person away from her. And she would be married to this man in three short weeks.

She bit her bottom lip, eyes watering anew but for a different reason this time. All her dreams were coming true at last, so how foolish to cry, but of a sudden, she was overcome with the weight of it all. They had spoken so little since his return. She knew nothing of this man. Did anything of the old Duncan remain? Oh, and there was motherhood of Bernard to consider, a new life in a new place somewhere in Durham, a move away from family with only him and Bernard, though it had been his family she had fallen in love with. It was all overwhelming. On the happiest Sunday of her life, she felt a conflicting loss of self.

It was a good thing the vicar preached more about miracles for there was hardly a dry eye in the church, making her likeness to a watering pot one of many.

By the time they walked out of the church, Mary had recovered herself, as bright eyed and refreshed as when she first walked in. No one could say she did not have a noble constitution.

Everyone crowded outside, eager to speak with Duncan, to welcome him back, ask about his baronetcy, ask about his recovery, a few asking about the betrothal and if they would have the wedding here. Duncan's affect had changed, she noticed. He was all smiles. Clasping hands, the corners of his eyes crinkling, an aura about him that commanded everyone's attention, he spoke to each and every person.

She hardly knew this version of him either, though she liked it better than the man she had seen in church. The Duncan she knew had been a flirtatious jokester, always ready for a laugh, always wanting to break a rule or two with her. Together, they were daring and adventurous. They rode against the wind, swam in petticoats and breeches, played pranks on the grooms, kissed until they panted. Would she ever see that Duncan again? Did she want to? She was not the same person any more than he was, but *that* had been the man she loved.

Ah, blast this wretched onslaught of melancholy on a happy day! Breaking into a fierce smile, she rounded the crowd with Mrs. Georgina Starrett and Mrs. Miranda Starrett, accepting congratulations, Bernard dawdling alongside her since he refused to leave his new friend's side.

By the time she returned to the carriage, she was in good spirits. The people treated her in unexpected ways, differently from normal. No, that was not quite right. They still afforded her the deference of her station, but they were far more welcoming than they had ever been. Rather than treating her as the austere daughter of a duke, they treated her almost as though she were one of them. Almost. They were not obviously intimidated or knee-scraping, at least. All the times she visited with her sister-in-law with charity baskets and conversation, she had been met with blushes and blusters.

Maybe, in time, they would see her. Really see *her*. No one had ever really seen her. No one except the old Duncan, that was. No one but he had seen past her parentage. Maybe she had a chance to be seen if on Duncan's arm.

"Did you enjoy the sermon?" Mrs. Starrett asked as the carriage jolted on its way.

Mary did not answer at first, thinking mother asked son.

Mrs. Starrett touched her arm.

Turning a smile to her hostess, Mary said, "Oh yes, very much so. I've never heard such impassioned words on a Sunday."

"No? Goodness me, why ever not?"

"The only sermons I've heard are those from the Annick clergyman. Mother sends him notes on what he's to compose. Attendance is just the family in the private chapel, of course, and we rarely meet every Sunday anyway."

Duncan looked at her over Bernard's head. "What do you mean by rarely?"

"Let's just say my mother isn't the God-loving sort. We hold chapel once a month at most."

"I didn't know you weren't devout," Duncan said, staring at her with a frown.

"It's nothing like that, only I've not had the opportunity to attend church regularly. It would not have been the thing to drag my maid to the village church every Sunday, after all." She said this with a laugh, not seeing cause for concern. "I enjoyed today. I wonder what the church is like near Sidwell Hall."

Colonel Sean Starrett clapped his hands. "There's a trip we must make, my boy. Say the word, and we'll make ready."

"Soon," Duncan said, his voice soft.

They fell silent for the remaining drive. It had been an emotional Sunday for Duncan, no doubt. She need not examine his countenance for clues to his mood, for though he wore a dour expression, she knew not his mind.

Waving to Bernard, whose head popped out of the receding carriage window, Mary stood in the drive of Lyonn Manor. She watched them navigate the circle drive and onward, loath to part with the sight of the vehicle, wishing she could carry on to Cois Greta Park with them rather than return to her own home. Her hand lowered only when the dot disappeared around a corner.

Ready to relieve her of coat, bonnet, and gloves, Mr. Hunter waited at the door. As did her mother.

Schooling her features not to give away her alarm, Mary stepped into the entry hall. The butler busied himself with her items. If he hurried, maybe she could make a dash for the stairs before her mother spoke.

"Your absence from chapel was noted."

Blast.

The butler scuttled off with her belongings one moment too late.

"I hadn't thought you would notice," Mary said, her chin raising in defense, or arguably, in defiance.

"Into the parlor. Now." Without awaiting a response, Catherine tapped her cane into the Gray Parlor.

Mary sighed. It had been an unusual morning, and she would have preferred to retire to her bedchamber for a brief respite and an opportunity to mull things over. Following on her mother's heels, her shoulders back and spine straight, she clasped her hands at her waist and waited. When the door clicked closed by the unseen hand of a footman, Catherine turned to face her daughter, her eyes narrowed, her lips set.

"Why were you not in chapel?"

"I went to the village church instead, as guests of the Starretts."

Nostrils flared. "*We* do not attend the village church. I forbid you to go again."

Mary laced her fingers then unlaced them, steepling her fingertips and looking to heaven. "Soon, Mother, I'll be a married woman. You cannot forbid me to do anything."

"You're not married yet. I'll not have your head filled with nonsense. Country vicars are all the same. They'll have you under God's thumb in a fortnight, all with teachings that a man controls you, using religion to justify his actions."

Mary gave a hollow laugh. "What are you talking about? No one is trying to control me except you. What actions?"

"Men use religion to control women, to make submissive, sniveling servants of them. I can be thankful, at least, that boy is not Catholic, but you must not be swayed by the church's manipulations."

One look at her mother's expression revealed her distress. Mary could not imagine what would have her mother in such a state or speaking such nonsense. The woman's face was pale, the hand on her cane trembling. Never had Catherine been a religious woman, as far as Mary knew, but she could not say why. The monthly sermons were short, obligatory, and guided by the dowager duchess' requests, as they had been for as long as Mary could remember.

"No one is trying to control me," Mary said. "The Reverend Quinn Starrett is a God-loving man who spoke today of miracles and faith. I hardly call that manipulation."

"God-loving, you say? God is not loving. God is a puppeteer, an orchestrator of sorrow. I was raised by the right hand of God and taught to fear Him. And fear I did. Where was this loving God when my feet bled from a caning? Where was God's love when my fingers were battered and bruised? Where was God when I had to crawl up flights of stairs with a broken leg? I can count more brutality than you have days in your life, all done in the name of God, all brought on my head through righteous condemnation of my misdeeds — spine not straight enough, tempo not steady enough, plate not clean enough. You know nothing of this world or the evils of men."

As Catherine railed, her voice shaking, Mary sank into a chair, unable to hold herself upright under the weight of the words. They had never spoken like this, not as mother and daughter, not as friends, not as loved ones. They certainly never spoke of Catherine's childhood or beliefs. Mary's mother was a mystery to her. And here, unraveling before her, was a woman with a terrifying past, revealed for Mary's horror by the simple act of attending church with her betrothed.

Mary was unsure how to feel as her mother continued to besmirch religion, blaming it for the abuse she had all too clearly suffered. Did Mary feel sympathy? Did the past humanize Catherine? Did it explain why she did not love her children as she ought? Mary was overcome with emotion—but she did not know what emotion—a maelstrom of confusion, pain, heartache, and yes, sympathy. Her heart bled for the girl her mother once was.

But why say all this now? Because Mary had attended church?

The sudden silence shook Mary.

A hand to her heart, she looked back to her mother. "I didn't know."

Catherine scoffed but said nothing, leaning heavily against her cane.

"It was not God's hand that did that, Mother, but the devil's. If you wish, you could come with me next Sunday and listen to the vicar's words for yourself. He speaks of love, not vengeance. I enjoyed the sermon today. I intend to return. I think you should come."

That was the last thing Mary wanted, but what more could she say? Her mother was a stranger to her, a stranger with a haunted past she knew nothing about. There were no words of comfort Mary could offer, no questions she wanted answers to.

"You're a defiant and willful gel," Catherine said. "You have no respect for me, but it is of my own making. I never should have left you to your own devices. I should have taught you how to think." She waved a dismissive hand. "Do what you will. You're already betrothed to the boy despite my warnings. Pray to your loving God your husband never resents your superiority in station, for then he'll aim to dominate you. And what will you do then, when God abandons you to the hand of man?"

Mary stared at her lap, lips pursed. How easily her mother made it to go from one emotion to the opposite.

"On that account, you can rest assured. He's not like that."

"Don't be naïve. He is accustomed to commanding men and being obeyed. What makes a woman different?"

The question was rhetorical. With a sigh, Mary stood.

"The Reverend Starrett will be conducting the marriage ceremony. We'll wed in the village church. I hope you'll attend, but I don't expect it. You may not be happy with my choices, but they are mine to make."

Her mother sank into a chair, covering her eyes with a hand. Uncertain what to do, Mary took a step forward towards her mother.

"Leave me," her mother said in response.

And so, Mary left.

Mary lay awake, eyes focused on the curtained window, her mind whirling with her mother's words. Nothing her mother said about Duncan surprised her. No one would be good enough for a duke's daughter except a duke, it would seem. The whirlpool of thoughts centered on her mother's words of abuse, all in the name of religion.

The image of a beaten girl contrasted with the woman Mary knew, for Catherine was an impenetrable force; no weak or submissive woman resided in that figure. Mary wanted desperately to feel sorry for her mother, but how difficult that was when the mother she knew was cold and unloving, critical of all Mary did, and dissatisfied by everything.

Both her cousin Lilith and her cousin Sebastian's wife got along well with Catherine. Even Charlotte favored her now, though their relationship had been rocky in the first few months. What did they all see in Catherine that Mary did not? The dowager duchess must treat them differently; but why? What was wrong with Mary that Catherine hated her so? After being so abused, it seemed unusual that Catherine would not dote on her children to make up for her own childhood.

All Mary had ever wanted was her mother's love. It was too late now, but some acknowledgment would be appreciated, some nod of pride or affection or acceptance. Something. Anything.

Chapter 17

T he guests arrived the following week. Not wedding guests, but rather the Duke and Duchess of Annick's house guests for the annual foxhunt and shooting party. For a week, guests took advantage of the hospitality, lavish dinners, and land, all in pursuit of pleasure. A musical soiree was planned, rather than a grand ball, to end the party.

The guests consisted mostly of Drake's friends and their wives, along with a few friends of Charlotte's and their husbands. For the unattached, there were an equal number of ladies to gentlemen, the former hoping to land the latter before the end of the week. Duncan was not among the guests. Drake did invite him for the shooting party and the soiree, though he had asked Mary in advance if he ought, for he had been concerned with Duncan's ability to walk. Well, of course, he should be invited, Mary had insisted. It would be up to Duncan to decide if he felt comfortable attending.

Through the week, Mary arranged rides with the women since none of them wanted to join the hunt. A pity since Mary enjoyed riding to hounds. She suspected the women cried off because they were not skilled with the ribbons. It took a fine horsewoman to join the hunt, after all. And so, she played nanny to the tittering and sniveling ladies, never mind that most of them were older than her. On sedate rides they went, and in archery tournaments, they competed. Most of the ladies only wanted to participate if the men could watch, but they agreed, after persuasion, to practice while the gentlemen were distracted by the hunt.

More than once per day, Mary thought about her future and how it would look. She could not imagine foxhunts or shooting parties at Sidwell Hall. Every year, she looked forward to this, and yet this year seemed lackluster without Duncan by her side to share it. Perhaps they could find their own annual tradition that would be equally as enjoyable. They could, of course, attend the party at Lyonn Manor every year, but the crowd was not Duncan's type.

Was that disloyal to say? Aside from a few heirs and a handful of second sons, those in attendance were titled. Duncan had little in common with these people. On the contrary, they had always been *her* people, but she would not be sorry to see the back of them, for none of them cared one whit about her or her interests. The feeling was mutual.

Nevertheless, the days leading up to seeing her betrothed were exhausting, but fun. Most of the guests were the same each year, and so she knew them, for better or worse. Among the numbers was her brother's childhood friend, Mr. Winston Everleigh, eldest son of Viscount Rutherford. His presence made for a happy occasion as she adored him, despite his age, gambling, and rakish reputation.

His mood was somber this year, and she could not help but recall Charlotte's *on dit* about him having been left at the altar. All the same, she wondered how many bedchambers he visited over the course of the week. Oh, that was terribly unladylike for her to wonder, but she still did. She was not as naïve as most young girls. With an older brother who had been a rake in his youth, not to mention having older beaux when she was a budding girl, she knew a thing or two about the lives of men and the behaviors of rogues at parties.

The one guest she was not thrilled to see was the Earl of Altonwey. He was one of the attending bachelors, quite the matrimonial prize. Newly inherited, he had not too long ago served, having sold his commission on news of his father's death. It was all awkward, really, for Lord Altonwey's father had been one of her suitors, as arranged by her mother.

It was rare that she had met the children of her suitors, but as it happened, she had met this one. The previous earl had danced attention on her, by her mother's invitation, at a party not unlike this one. She had been perhaps seventeen at the time. The earl brought both his sons to the party, thinking they would enjoy the hunt. And so, both sons knew of the earl's addresses to Mary, making the situation wholly awkward since the sons were older than she, the earl being distastefully aged — not that such a fact was unusual with the men her mother chose. Given their past, she was not keen on seeing the son, especially since he waggled his eyebrows at her far too often. He gave her the shivers.

Nevertheless, she was sorry to hear that the earl had died. As much as she disliked the man for his flirtation in her youth, she would not have wished him ill.

What a curious thought, though—had she married him, she would now be a widowed countess. She would have married and been widowed all in the time it took Duncan to go to war and return. Such a curious thought. In the back of her mind, she wondered if that had been her mother's design all along, for all the men she arranged for Mary to meet were aged. But no, she would not rationalize her mother's actions. Nothing her mother did was in her best interest.

On the whole, the week was one part enjoyable and one part tedious. She would far prefer to be with Duncan, riding neck or nothing, but as sister to the host and hostess, she was duty bound to entertain. She did not see Duncan until the day of the shooting party, and even then, she did not have a chance to speak with him until the soiree.

Duncan trained the shotgun at the sky, steadying his breath until his target flew into sight. It felt good to have a weapon in hand again. Although he never used a shotgun in battle and typically wielded a sabre rather than a pistol or rifle, the sounds and smells of the shooting party brought back a wave of nostalgia. If he closed his eyes, he could almost imagine he was on the battlefield again.

"Colonel Starrett!" a fellow officer called to him.

Duncan lowered the firearm. "Major." He gave a curt nod, turning back to the field.

"Of all the people here, I never expected to see you. How the devil have I missed seeing you all week?"

It took slow minutes for him to realize reality. He was not on the battlefield. He was in a field on the duke's lands, shooting pheasants with Annick's guests. Brows furrowed, he looked back to Major Brumley. Memory superimposed reality. Shaking his head, he looked again. Brumley was still there, making his way to Duncan.

"Colonel! Capital to see you again." Brumley approached, smiling, a hand held out, happy to reunite with a friend.

Inch by inch, Duncan's face broke into a smile of his own. "Charles? Is that really you? I've not seen you since Boxtel."

He took the man's hand in his, leaning closer to hear what he had to say over the volley of shots.

"I sold out. You didn't know? Old man went toe up, left me the title and all that. Between the battle-field and an estate, there's not much contest, is there? Not Brumley. Altonwey, Earl of. I'll excuse you from kissing my boots seeing as how you were once my superior." The man guffawed, slapping Duncan's arm in good humor. "Heard you took a bullet. You look right enough."

"It's been a long journey. I had expected to be back in the field by now, but life had other plans. I'm not in your ranks, Charles, but I've been granted a bar-onetcy. Sir Duncan. How do you like that?"

Charles slapped Duncan's arm again. "Capital, capital."

Letting the group move ahead of them, they slowed their pace to share memories of old times. The day, which had been good so far, improved by the minute with renewed friendship, reminding Duncan of what he had enjoyed about service. *This.* This was one of the aspects of the Army he loved and missed, the camaraderie.

Initially, Duncan had been nervous about the shooting party. Excited, certainly, but also anxious his legs were not ready. Over the week, sensation had teased into his hips, but no lower aside from when riding and now when swimming. His gait smoothed with practice. He believed he could fool onlookers into thinking he walked as a normal man rather than as an injured man who used the pressure against his hips to know if his feet met earth.

To his annoyance, through all the practice he did in preparation for the shooting party, he could think of little but Mary enjoying the party, surrounded by eligible men vying for her attention. Paranoia. Ridiculous paranoia.

He imagined her enjoying the guests so much she would change her mind about marrying him, choose some titled chap who could keep her in the life she was accustomed. The party was an ill-timed reminder of the life she would leave behind to become his wife. Ridiculous worries, indeed, considering that in all the years he was away, she still preferred him to those of her world. But jealousy rarely saw reason.

Realizing he knew no one in the shooting party except his future brother-in-law did not help ease his discomfort. A friend at his side was just what he needed. He could not wait to introduce Charles to Mary and vice versa. Rather than tell his friend of his betrothal, he decided to wait until the opportune moment he could announce it with the lady present.

If he could steal Charles away for an evening, he would like to invite him to dinner, though dinner at Cois Greta Park might not be on the menu for a newly minted earl. Although he and Duncan had not exactly been friends, they had trusted each other in battle as only soldiers could do. Once upon a time, the major had been a fierce fighter, one of those men who took pleasure in the bloodlust, a frightening foe, but an excellent man to have on one's side during battle.

For the remainder of the day, they hunted side by side as they once had on the battlefield.

The Duke of Annick raised his glass. "It is with great pleasure that I announce Her Grace is expecting our second child! To all you romantics in the room, know my wife is in good company, for her sister and my cousin, the Earl and Countess of Roddam, that is, are expecting their third at the same time."

Duncan raised his glass to toast alongside the other guests, hearing only half of what Annick said since his attention was otherwise engaged. His gaze locked on Mary, standing on the opposite side of the room, talking with a group of ladies. They had spoken before and after the musicale, but only briefly. She was obligated to circulate, she had said.

He made a point to stand in a corner of the drawing room and not move, this not being his scene. The curious part was nearly every person in attendance had sought him out for one reason or another, some hearing from Charles of his heroism on the battlefield, some hearing from Annick he was Mary's betrothed, and others wanting an introduction for no obvious reason he could discern.

The women were the most peculiar aspect of the evening. Everywhere he looked, female eyelashes batted. More than once, he cast a puzzled glance at his person, wondering if they could see something he could not that would warrant such flirtation. As far as he knew, he was outranked by all, a commoner amongst peers of the realm. And yet there were those fluttering lashes everywhere he looked.

With each round his eyes made, they landed on Mary for suspended seconds, and each time she caught his gaze he saw no fluttering lashes, but instead a coy smile from the woman he felt held the secrets of the world, or at least to him. He pushed himself off the wall, his destination Mary.

Before he could take a single step forward, a woman appeared at his side. She was one of those who had asked to be introduced to him, or so Charles had winked to him afterwards. In her early thirties, or thereabouts, married to one of the toffs in attendance, the one without a chin, if he recalled correctly. For the life of him, he could not immediately remember her name. Not that he cared. She was an attractive woman, he supposed, though she could not hold a candle to Mary — strawberry ringlets, charcoaled eyelashes, rouged cheeks, full lips also rouged, slight of frame, and with a dangerously plunging décolletage that made Duncan cough to wonder what might happen if she breathed too deeply.

"Colonel Starrett," she said on a wisp of air.

As she slithered next to him, her shoulder rubbed against his arm. Her attention was on him, but her body faced the room. When he turned to look at her, all he could see was the top of her head and the heaving bosom below it. Intentional positioning, then? He suspected so. Smirking at her wasted wiles, he turned back to the room.

"My lady," he said.

"Letty, please. My friends call me Letty. And we're destined to become good friends."

"Are we? I hadn't realized there was a fortune teller in our midst." He caught Mary's glance across the room and winked. She arched a brow, her judgement sweeping over dear Letty.

The woman tittered. "And a sense of humor, too. My my. You are a perfect package." Lowering her voice to nought but a whisper, she said, "I'm staying in the green room, third floor. Come to me tonight."

Had he been in any other setting, he might have sputtered, coughed, or laughed. As it was, his jaw hardened, and his expression blanked.

"And your husband?"

That tinkling titter again. She sent a cold shiver down his spine.

"He would never enter my bedchamber at a party."

"And my betrothed?"

"My lips are discreet. She'll never know. What you need is someone who appreciates a man such as yourself. Allow me to appreciate you."

This was rich. He could not wait to tell Mary. Surely, she would be as amused by this as he. Such propositions were not new to him, though he had never experienced them in quite this setting or while being affianced. The officers' wives during his time in service were notorious for browsing. For whatever reason, they always targeted him first. Until they learned better, of course.

"I take it Lord Altonwey has put in a good word for me?"

"Let's say your reputation on the battlefield precedes you. Not that I need enticement. One look at you tells me everything I need to know. The green room. Tonight."

Just as she made to slip away, he said, "Oh, Letty, my dear. You should know that until a week or so ago, I was in a wheeled chair. Full disclosure is best in these circumstances, don't you think?"

She turned back to look at him. Gaze roaming over his figure, she frowned, and then broke into a laugh that sounded none too different from breaking glass.

"That humor again! You are a living doll."

"Not a jest, my lady. I've only recently begun to walk again. It's not without its challenges, but full recovery is on the horizon. If I'm feeling fatigued this evening, I'll need to make use of the wheeled chair. Shall I have a footman wheel me to the green room, then?"

The look of horror on her face was one Duncan would have painted if he had the skill.

Her head swiveled. "My mistake."

With a quick glance about her, she left him alone in the corner. All he could do was smile at her receding back. What a louse. If this was a glimpse of Mary's world, it was no wonder she was so willing to join him in his.

The smirk lingered until he felt a slap to his shoulder.

"My good man. Gratitude is in order. I witnessed your conquest, and of course, you have me to thank." Charles's wine sloshed in its glass.

"Do I? You failed to mention my injury and recent recovery. She was none too eager for a liaison once she heard about the wheeled chair."

"Good Lord. You didn't mention that, did you? Why the deuce would you say that? No one wants a cripple. Listen to me, now; I've ploughed the field for you. There's not a woman in this room who does not know of your heroism, not that you need the help. Women swoon over muscles, take it from me." The man guffawed.

"I've done you a favor, then, for you'll have more ladies for yourself."

It was funny how memories worked. Duncan recalled with fondness the campfire camaraderie. As the former Major Brumley spoke, the clearer his memory became of just what conversation had been over the campfire, and how the only aspect about it he had enjoyed was the close bond of soldiers after a day evading death. He had never enjoyed the conversation, had he? Disenchanting.

It was not in this moment that he would be thankful for life's perplexing turn of events. That would come later upon reflection. But he did feel an inexplicable relief that life had barred him from returning to duty. With an aching yearning, all he wanted was Mary at his side, Bernard in hand, and a stable full of horses.

She saw Duncan first, making his way around the perimeter of the Red Drawing Room. She wondered if he had any idea how much attention he was

garnering this evening. Aside from the obvious overtures of Lady Carrol, she thought he did not. Though
he was not a peer of the realm, all eyes were on him,
especially the female eyes. He was magnificent.

While all the other men wore padding, Duncan's
physique was very much his own. He wore silk of
dark wine, the shoulders tailored to hug his powerful frame, the waist tapered to emphasize narrowed
hips, the breeches snug and fitted to his legs, every
sinew seemingly visible to the naked eye. His dark
hair was slicked back, his cologne light but enticing,
his expression smoldering. She licked her lips at his
approach.

The gaggle of ladies around her simpered.

"Ladies," he said.

His bow caused a collective sigh.

He turned, then, to the gentleman beside him,
"Allow me to introduce one of my former fellow officers. And this is my betrothed, Lady Mary."

As the girls nearly swooned around her, she
nodded to his companion, only realizing in alarm
when Duncan spoke his name that it was the Earl of
Altonwey. The earl took her in with a look as lecher-
ous as his father's. She felt undressed, exposed, dirty.
Yes, she recalled his father quite clearly now, as well
as the sons. Shuddering, she allowed, albeit begrudg-
ingly, the man to bow over her hand.

"We're acquainted," he said, blue eyes probing
hers, "but I'll never turn down an introduction to
such a vixen."

Mary bristled. How dare he say something so
vulgar. Before she could respond with a reprimand,
albeit lighthearted given the audience, he spoke again.

"You dastardly dog, Duncan! Betrothed to Unattainable Lady Mary. You know how to pull military rank when you want something, don't you?" He slapped Duncan on the shoulder before turning to the ladies. "We served together; I'll have you know. I was but a humble Major Brumley then, heir to the earldom."

The ladies tightened ranks, spying a new conquest. Lucky for them, this one was available, eligible, and all-too-clearly willing, though Mary doubted he had marriage in mind.

He continued his monologue, an arm resting on Duncan's shoulders, although Duncan stood at least a foot taller. "We were not the type to sit back and shout orders. No, we were the first to lead the charge, swords drawn, determined to be heroes. Colonel Starrett, here, always came out the victor, a real hero, and dare I say a hero with the ladies, as well."

Duncan cleared his throat and said, "I appreciate your vote of confidence, but I must refute the charge. The men who served with me were the true heroes."

"Modest, too!" the earl said to his avid audience. "The only other man on the field half as brave, myself excluded, of course, was Lieutenant Colonel Wesley. He fought with ferocity at Boxtel, though in a line infantry regiment while we were on horseback. I know a man with a fine military career ahead when I see one, and I knew when I saw Wesley and Starrett both, they would be heroes of whom we would tell tales for decades to come. There is no place in this world for such men except the battlefield."

The earl carried on, entertaining the ladies with exaggerations of daring, or at least Mary assumed they were exaggerations as the depiction entailed a caped crusader defeating enemies with a single glare. All the while, she observed Duncan's expression harden, much like it had during the church sermon. Though the earl was crass, she could not see fault with his words. They cast Duncan in the very best light, and in doing so, made himself look all the better, not only for fighting at the colonel's side, but for bragging about someone other than himself. Sly, but it was working wonders on the ladies.

A voice behind her interrupted the conversation. "A few of us are set for the billiard room. Care to join?"

Mary turned to find Winston standing behind her, a tired smile trained on her before including Duncan in his invitation. The present party misunderstood, and all clamored their delight at being invited to such an exotic place as the billiard room. So much for being rid of Lord Altonwey's company. Winston looked as thrilled as she.

Leaving the soiree behind where they would doubtless not be missed, Mary and Duncan paired, slowing their pace behind Winston and the earl, both of whom were surrounded by the fawning women. Up ahead of them were a few gentlemen, friends of Winston's, also heading upstairs.

When they were far enough behind not to be overheard, Duncan said, "I'm not a hero, you should know."

Well, that was not how she expected to start the conversation.

"You look heroic to me. You're *walking*, need I remind you. How many men at this silly party could do the same in a similar situation?"

"That's not what I mean," he protested. "I'm not a war hero. War is not about heroism. It's men like

Charles who warp the whole of it for accolades. It's about survival. By his definition, is the enemy any less heroic? They, too, want to bring home pride and honor, just as all soldiers do. We're all equals on the field, fighting for survival, not for glory. I went in wanting the glory, Mary. I wanted to impress you and your family. I learned quickly the error of such thinking. Only young pups think that way."

Mary touched his arm. "People need heroes. They need someone to believe in. The Crown believes you to be a hero, or the baronetcy would not have been awarded. I believe you to be a hero, even if for different reasons. You may not feel heroic, but you *are*."

He grunted, staring daggers at the group ahead of them, making their way through the gallery with brief pauses to point at paintings.

"It's a wonder anyone makes it out alive. Did I ever tell you of my captain when I was an ensign? Nothing more than a twelve-year-old boy. He's fortunate we didn't see a battle. It's better than the captain who still needed a wet nurse, but not by much. I rose in ranks because I needed to. I was not going to be led by children."

"And what a hero you were to the soldiers you led. No more of this talk about not being a hero. Now, I want to talk about a far more serious matter while we have this moment alone."

He glanced at her sidelong.

"I've heard whisperings from the guests that you are the handsomest man in attendance. How smug am I?"

When Mary looked him over with a flirty smirk, he said, "Let's find out."

As the group ahead of them turned the corner to follow the stairs to the billiard room, Duncan latched an arm around her waist and spun her into a room at the foot of the stairs. He closed and locked the door behind him, pulling her against his chest.

The room was dark except the low glow of a fire in the far corner, readied in case guests wanted to make use of the room. She knew them to be in the stag parlor. Palms flat against the embroidery of his waist-coat, Mary slipped her hands beneath his coat until she found the hem of the waistcoat. Inching under it, as well, she smoothed her hands over the linen shirt until she could lace her hands at his back.

He leaned in to kiss her. Their lips met in a fevered embrace. His hands cupped her cheeks, sinking his fingers into her hair. He deepened the kiss.

With a sharp intake of breath, he held her away from him before releasing her, freeing strands of her hair in the process. She stared at his shadowed sil-houette in confusion.

"My God, Mary." He breathed the words in an exhale. "I can feel you."

She laughed, leaning towards him in hopes of resuming their embrace. "Of course you can."

"No, you don't understand. I can *feel*."

Oh.

Oh.

Grasping her shoulders, he spun Mary so her back was against the wood paneling. His lips moved to her neck, peppering kisses against her skin.

Voices in the gallery beyond stilled them both.

The volume of voices increased, approaching the parlor.

Silently, Duncan released Mary and stepped back. Mary, in turn, released her hold about his waist and made her own retreat. As the voices drew closer, Mary adjusted her dress and walked in the semi-darkness to the table where she knew a candelabra stood. With deft hands, she freed a candle, took it to the fireplace to ignite, and lit each candle in turn. The voices paused to talk outside the door as Mary remedied her fallen hair in a mirror. She did not look at Duncan but suspected he was adjusting his own clothing.

The handle on the door jiggled.

Mary nearly leapt out of her shoes. She leaned against the table, ready to face the intruders. The handle jiggled again. Locked.

In short steps, the voices receded, moving down the gallery and up the stairs to the billiard room. Not until silence engulfed them did she breathe.

With a shaky laugh, she looked to Duncan, who leaned against the wall, arms crossed over his chest.

"That was the closest I ever want to come to scandal," Mary said. "Now, let's talk for a moment before we join the group. We don't want our absence noted, but neither do we want our guilt branded on our cheeks."

"Wise." Duncan looked at her from half-lidded eyes.

"Let's begin from the end and work our way backwards. You said you could *feel*?"

A low chuckle tickled her ears. "Only in, er, certain parts. Not the best topic if we're trying to recover before leaving."

"Oh. I see. Yes, good point. How about Lady Carrol? Would that douse you with cold water?"

His brows knit. "Who?"

"The trollop who was showing you her bosom."

"Ah. Letty. I'm to wheel myself to the green room for an evening tryst. Third floor. Footman optional."

Mary laughed. "I can't leave you unattended, can I? Women are throwing themselves at you."

"Jealous?"

"Should I be?" She looked at him from beneath half-lowered lids, a grin on her lips.

"Fortunately for you, they're not much competition," he teased. "Most are already married, so not looking to shackle themselves with someone beneath their station. They have something, shall we say, *different* in mind for me."

"Oh, I know. The party is annual, after all. There is no mystery to me what happens behind closed doors, though I daresay, most of the unmarried ladies would be shocked to learn the truth." She batted her eyelashes, exaggerating the effort for his amusement. "I wish you were staying here this week. I might have something *different* in mind for you, as well."

Rather than calling her out for the flirtatious fib, Duncan coughed a laugh instead, uncrossing his arms and propping a hand to the wall. "We're trying to leave, remember? No more teasing. New topic. You know Altonwey?"

She frowned. "If there's one name that will curdle my insides, it's his. I can't believe you're friends with the man."

"Not as such. We shared a brief battle or two, nothing more. One of the many fellow officers I met in my short career. Why the dislike?"

"His father was one of the suitors my mother arranged. I'm positive I wrote to you about him, but there were so many, it's difficult to recall who made it into the letters and who didn't. This lecher brought his sons with him, both of whom were as interested in me as their father. If that doesn't tell you all you need to know, nothing will."

"Indeed, it does." Duncan shuddered. "He was a good man, as far as I can remember. Brutal on the field, though. There's a fine line between fighting for Crown and country and enjoying the kill."

"Right, well, enough of that. How do I look? Is it safe to leave? Am I still flushed?"

"You're ravishing, my love, but I believe your cheeks are a safe enough color for us to return. Shall we?"

The game was enormous fun, Mary thought. When they arrived in the billiard room, the men were playing while the ladies admired and giggled. Mary rolled her eyes at their silliness and challenged Winston to a game. After their initial shock, the ladies decided if Mary could play, so could they, initiating a game of ladies versus gentlemen.

A few of the enterprising men took it upon themselves to teach the women how to hold the cue. Naïve chits.

Mary moved about the table with skill, paying little attention to those around her other than to flash a haughty boast to make everyone laugh. Part way through the game, she looked up to find Duncan leaning against a pillar some distance away. Casting him a questioning look, he shook off her concern.

Near her, Winston lit a cigar, the ladies about him coughing and fanning their faces. "Oh, I'm terribly sorry. Is this offensive?" he asked, blowing a cloud their way.

He passed cigars around the room for the other gentlemen to join, effectively eliminating the women from the room.

Lord Altonwey leered. "Aren't you going to follow the ladies to safety?"

Mary narrowed her eyes. "If you think I'm not accustomed to cigar smoke, you've forgotten who my brother is."

She lingered with the gentlemen a tad longer, at least to finish the game. Before leaving to make her way back to the drawing room, she paused by Duncan's pillar, her brows raised, her eyes saying she would not take another dismissal as an answer.

"It's nothing," he said. "Just fatigue. Left leg is shaky, if you must know. Go on. I'll stay here, rest my legs for a time, and make a new friend or two." When she hesitated, he growled. "I don't want a nursemaid, Mary. Go."

Chastised, she bade her farewell to the group and followed the stairs down and into the gallery, leaving only because she did not want to embarrass him by fussing over him. Men and their pride. Granted, he had done a considerable amount of walking today, and so soon after his recovery. She hoped he had not overworked himself. The last thing he needed was a setback. He had come too far to be back in the wheeled chair.

Halfway through the gallery, she about-faced and walked back to the closed door of the stag parlor, resting a hand to the woodgrain. Biting her lip in memory, she opened the door and slipped inside.

The room was as they had left it. The fire burned low still, the candelabra's candles snuffed. But if she closed her eyes, she could recall the feel of his lips on hers. Soon, she would be a married woman and know what it was to be held and loved.

And he said he could *feel*! She was not fully aware of what he meant by that statement or what it was he could not feel before, but she did understand he lacked sensation in his legs. Did that also mean…oh, she was uncertain. Naiveté was not exclusive to the ladies in the billiard room. She pressed cold hands to hot cheeks.

The week's wait to see him had been worth it. Each time she saw him, the more she longed to be with him. If there had been any doubt, the party nullified it, for though she enjoyed this life, she desired more being *known* as her own person. With Duncan, she would know that love.

A rustle at the door stole her attention. Mary pivoted, her heart in her throat, expecting to see Duncan leaning against the doorframe.

Her fingers curled into her palms.

Lord Altonwey stood where Duncan ought. "Your betrothed appears to be indisposed."

Mary raised her chin. "Is there something you need? Shall I ring for a footman?"

"Only here for friendly conversation, my lady. One foot in the door, one foot out, nothing improper." His eyes swept over her, his body blocking the exit. "How might I please you, Lady Mary?"

Her eyes widened and her teeth clenched. "I beg your pardon."

"We both know your preferred sort of man, and it's not a commoner. For someone like you, the colonel is a bit of fun, not for marrying. I, on the other hand…" His voice trailed off. One corner of his mouth lifted in a mock smile.

"My relationship with my betrothed is none of your concern."

He took one step forward.

She took two steps back.

"I wish to make it my concern. We all know you've been angling for years for a peer, the more powerful the better. A stream of suitors flowing in and out of Lyonn Manor, and yet no one has suited you, not even my father. Not many in England were as powerful as he. What do you want, Lady Mary? What do you want from Colonel Starrett that, say, I could not offer?"

"You?" She stared, her expression blank.

"Marriage to me would be advantageous to us both, would it not? And I wouldn't begrudge you a bit of fun if you wished to keep the colonel as a pet."

Her face contorted into a sneer, but her voice remained steady. "I beg you not to interfere with my life. You know nothing of me. I find this conversation offensive and wish to return to the drawing room."

He took another step forward.

She took another two steps back, bumping into a leather chair. Bracing herself against its back, she lifted her chin higher, looking down her nose at him, refusing to be cowed.

"Mary?" A commanding voice asked from the doorway.

Duncan saw red, fury pumping through his veins.

He had not heard much of the conversation, but what little he did hear infuriated him. Was this what his old friend thought of him? Was this what they all thought of him? Some commoner who was good for nothing but the battlefield and a bit of fun?

And there stood Mary, clearly discomposed, her hands trembling against the back of the chair, her eyes darting to the door. To anyone else, she looked a strong woman in control of the situation. To him, she was a woman cornered, antagonized by unwanted advances of an arrogant swell.

However much legal trouble he might face in laying hands on a peer of the realm, he was prepared to plant a facer if need be, or worse. His body readied for battle.

Charles turned to face the door, as surprised to see Duncan as Duncan had been to hear their voices carrying through the hall as he reached the gallery.

As Charles's brows drew together, he let out a mighty howl, then hissed. "You little hussy," the earl cursed through gritted teeth.

Duncan looked to Mary just in time to see her stomp on the man's foot, for the second time, apparently.

"If you ever speak disparagingly against my betrothed again," Mary said, her heel grinding into the man's foot, "you'll face more than my wrath. Oh, and your proposal is declined."

She walked around him to the doorway. Duncan stepped aside so she could pass.

Nodding to her, he said, "I'll be but a moment, my love," and shut the door behind him.

He folded his arms over his chest, not convinced he would not punch the man. Charles hobbled to one of the leather chairs and sat, nursing his foot.

Duncan broke the silence. "Your title aside, give me one reason I should not take you outside and beat you."

His companion laughed. "As a good friend, I've tested the sincerity of your bride. You should thank me. Her loyalty did not waver, though I had not yet added my charm to be certain."

"Ah, yes, I can see the logic of a good friend cornering one's betrothed." Duncan's fists remained clenched.

"Even you must admit it's peculiar. Everyone wonders. She's the Unattainable Lady Mary, after all. And whatever your merits, you're crippled now with not the brightest of futures outside the battlefield. People wonder. The duke is a powerful ally and has the ear of the prince. She has a dowry that would save half the *haut ton* from debt. And yet she chose *you*? You were a grand soldier, old chap, but this match is preposterous."

Duncan said, "I believe my beloved voiced it well when she told you that you know nothing of her. I valued your friendship for the years you served, Charles. I entrusted you with my life many times over. From this point forward, however, I beg you not to come near Lady Mary. Crippled though I may be, I will rain pain as you've never felt. You know what I'm capable of, in or out of a wheeled chair."

With a steely glare, he left Charles to his own devices, closing the door with a soft click behind him.

Chapter 18

The earl's words echoed in Duncan's head all the way to the church. Would marriage clip Mary's wings? Was he doing her a disservice by shackling her to him?

It was an unlikely match. It always had been. As youths, they had not cared. As adults, they clung to their youthful ideals. Perhaps they both should have faced reality and let each other go, she to marry someone of her station, he to do the same.

He could not even promise the wedding night would be successful. Sensation had flowed into his thighs the day of the soiree and thrummed through his pelvis until he thought he would be back to normal by the end of the day. Alas, it had stopped just above his knees.

His lower legs remained without feeling, but by Jove, he could feel the important bits necessary for a wedding night. But would it last? He worried at any moment he would lose sensation and function, or a leg might give out from beneath him, or any other myriad of concerns.

None of his worries kept him from the church. He stood at the altar, his father to one side of him, his brother in front, waiting for his bride on their wedding day.

Nervousness clenched his stomach. He had not checked since he arrived, but he suspected half the village waited outside to celebrate. Inside the church, it was immediate family only, a quiet ceremony. Bernard sat with his cousins in the first pew. Duncan wondered how much of today Bernard understood, for despite a long talk between men, the boy continued to ask if his new friend would be staying with them for long.

A noise from behind him stirred his pulse. He turned just in time to see the church door closing. Disappointment.

The Duchess of Annick, with her son the Marquess of Sutton, looked about her, then granted a smile and took her seat next to his family. The wait began anew. Quinn cleared his throat, thumbing the Book of Common Prayer in his hand.

The door opened and closed again with an echoing *thunk*. When he turned this time, his stomach somersaulted. Elation!

His bride stood mere pews away.

Mary, on her brother's arm, halted Duncan's breath. In a dress of blue with silver embroidery and elbow-length sleeves that ended in laced cuffs to her wrists, she stole his heart. Raven hair coiffed in an array of curls and a bandeau of pearls interwoven with some sort of tiny white flowers. Two pink ovals dotted her cheeks, but he knew them to be genuine spots of color and not rouged. As she walked the nave, the pink darkened her neck until disappearing into the fichu covering her chest.

Could this be happening? After all these years, was he really marrying her? Life stretched before him, a life full of promise and enticing mystery. From this moment forward, he would do all he could to ensure she never regretted marrying him.

When Quinn began to speak, Mary waved a panicked hand, "Wait. No, not yet. Please, just a few more minutes."

Duncan heard a buzzing in his ears, his heart pounding erratically. Was she having second thoughts? Afraid of what he might see in her expression, he rested a hand on the hilt of his sword, imbuing himself with strength.

"Mary?" he asked, his voice cracking.

Her teeth tugged at her bottom lip. "My mother's not here. I—I don't want to begin without her."

He frowned but nodded.

And so, they waited.

And waited.

Not until her chin wobbled did Duncan nod to Quinn to begin again. His heart broke when a tear rolled down her cheek, but there was nought he could do. Why did she care if her mother attended? The woman did not approve of the marriage. Duncan could have told Mary the dowager duchess would not attend, and yet Mary had all too clearly hoped she would.

"'Dearly beloved, we are gathered together here in the sight of God,'" Quinn began.

As the vicar continued, Duncan took Mary's hand in his. She gave him a quick smile, her eyes red-rimmed but no less beautiful.

"'It was ordained for the procreation of children, to be brought up in the fear and nurture of the Lord, and to the praise of his holy Name,'" Quinn continued.

Mary gave a sniff, but as her chin raised higher and the vicar moved further into the ceremony, her tears dried.

"'I require and charge you both, as ye will answer at the dreadful day of judgement when the secrets of all hearts shall be disclosed, that if either of you know any impediment, why ye may not be lawfully—'"

His words cut off as the door opened and closed with a gust of cold air.

Stepping to the back set of pews, a gold-handled cane in her hand, was the Dowager Duchess of Annick. A dour butler hovered behind her. Duncan stared in stunned silence; everyone did. Nobody breathed.

He turned full bodied to face her, waiting for her words of censure, her argument why they should not be married. Though he did not glare, he let his eyes challenge her. She responded by straightening to her full height and looking down her nose at him, an interesting experience since she was across the nave from him. Had it not been his wedding day, and had he not before faced his enemy in battle, he would have cowered in his boots. The dowager duchess was a sight to behold. As regal as a queen and just as austere.

On the bright side, if this was any indication to how Mary would age, he was to be one lucky man indeed, for the lady, though likely in her late fifties, was remarkably handsome with minimal grey lacing her black hair. When she did nothing but stare back at him, he raised his brows.

"Well?" she questioned. "Carry on." With a smack of her cane to the stone floor, she took a seat in the last pew.

He glanced at Mary as he turned back to his brother. Her eyes rimmed with red anew, brimming with tears that had yet to fall. Taking her hand in his once more, he nodded to Quinn to resume.

He heard little of the ceremony after that except the words he had to repeat. All his attention focused on Mary. He was aware of her every motion and could feel the warmth of her hand in his, even through their gloves. At times, their eyes met, and those pink spots returned to her cheeks. By the end of the ceremony, her neck was blotched with red. Had his skin shown beneath his regimentals, she would have been reassured he was just as flushed with happiness.

In precious moments, they were signing the register, husband and wife until death did them part.

He was correct, of course, about the villagers. As soon as the couple stepped out of the church, they were showered with an assortment of hothouse flower petals, bits of bread and biscuits, and he dared not ask what else. If the whole of the village were not there to see them, he would be surprised.

The ducal carriage, courtesy of the duke, awaited to escort them to Cois Greta Park for the wedding breakfast. Before handing Mary up the steps, he wrapped an arm about her waist and for all the world to see, planted a chaste kiss that was not without flair. He dipped her, lifted her, then turned to bow to the applauding crowd, the duke himself whistling.

Without a backward glance, they climbed into the carriage, renewing their embrace as soon as the door closed behind them.

A late morning frost silvered the lawn, a romantic sight from the double Venetian windows of the dining room at Cois Greta Park. The children had other plans for the view. Dotting the landscape, children ran to and fro, a well-bundled Bernard among them, frolicking with the vicar's daughters and other village little ones.

This.

This was Mary's ideal — a house full of family, friends, and children, voices raised to hear over the commotion, the clamoring of footfalls as little feet ran in and out again, laughter filling the air. Knowing she was flushed with happiness, she glanced at Duncan between bites. It was all going to be perfect. She could sense it.

The wedding breakfast was in full swing. Most of the villagers attended, as did Mary's cousin and family — the Earl and Countess of Roddam, their two children, and the countess' father. A few neighbors stopped in, those either close to the Starretts or curious about the couple. Not all neighbors lingered once they realized guests ranged from the duke to the local blacksmith. Mary had not a care in the world for what anyone thought.

She was not even bothered that her mother declined to attend the breakfast. What mattered was Catherine came to the wedding. Why it should matter, Mary could not put into words, but it had mattered. Oh, how it had mattered.

Mrs. Georgina Starrett was regaling neighbors and Charlotte with a tale from Duncan's youth of him hiding eggs on carriage seats. Colonel Sean Starrett was bowled over in laughter alongside several villagers and Mary's brother, who laughed just as exuberantly. Mr. Quinn Starrett was whispering into his wife's ear something that made her blush. All the guests smiled and cut up gaily.

It was all so different from the dinners she had recently suffered. Nasal intones, elongated vowels, straight spines, hushed voices, monosyllabic laughs, the ever-present ennui, and if the memory continued, she would spoil her fun.

What was missing was Duncan's other siblings, none of whom dared travel so far this close to the winter months, though they sent their congratulations. Mary's cousin Lilith and her family also sent their congratulations, hoping to see the couple in London during the Season if they chose to accompany the family. The party was also missing Mary's dearest friend Arabella, who gave as her excuse the possibility of being with child. How happy Mary was for her if true. And how disappointing if Arabella conjured an untruth because she disapproved of Mary's choice.

Mrs. Miranda Starrett, the vicar's wife, looked to Mary. "The girls will miss Bernard. They've been so happy to have a cousin with whom to play. If he's lonely in that great big house, send him to stay for a few days."

Mary looked to Duncan before saying, "Such a generous offer. May I extend the same to your girls. I hope it's not presumptuous to speak on behalf of Duncan, but I believe we would both be happy to have them any time and for any length."

Duncan, who sat next to her, reached for her hand, lacing their fingers. "Yes, please, you're all welcome at any time. As it happens, Mr. McLarren, the steward, has two boys of his own. A few years older, granted. If he's to be believed, the two are looking forward to making Bernard's acquaintance. With any luck, our boy will have two new friends before the week ends."

Mrs. Miranda Starrett clasped her hands to her bosom. "How lovely! I do hope he likes them."

"You'll meet them tomorrow," Mary said. "That is, if we make good time to Durham."

She was relieved Duncan's family would be coming to Sidwell Hall for the first visit. They would stay for a week before returning home, leaving the couple to start life together.

"I've no doubt," Duncan said, "this is a mad scheme to usurp my new estate. You've heard how grand it is and aim to conquer the land."

His brother laughed, as they all did. After all, no one knew what to expect from the hall aside from what the steward had described to Duncan. Was it in good condition? Did it need repairs? Was it a modest house, a small cottage, at least equal to Cois Greta Park? There was no way of knowing until they arrived. Duncan confessed to being as anxious as he was excited.

To look at him now, no one would assume anything could make him anxious. He wore his Light Dragoon regimentals, his sword at his side. With such garb, he could make a lady swoon and a gentleman cower — blue jacket with white facing and silver lace, edged with white cord and looped upon the breast, gold cuffs and collar, and white breeches, finished with a crimson silk sash worn over his left shoulder. Earlier, he had worn boots of jacked leather with turned down cuff at the knee, but now he wore striking dress shoes that allowed her to admire his muscled calves. More than once, she admired him with a head-to-toe perusal, then hoped no one noticed.

Good heavens. Tonight would be their wedding night. She could scarcely breathe each time she remembered. Was he thinking about it as much as she? It was fortunate she had all afternoon to build fortitude. As much as she wanted the wedding night now rather than later, her nerves were getting the better of her. Despite their open flirtation and the insinuations she had used to antagonize her mother, she and Duncan had never been intimate beyond stray kisses. They had been too busy during their once-upon-a-time trysts challenging each other on horseback or to swim the farthest in the lake to consider anything more, not to mention Duncan had always been a gentleman with her, she the one who stole kisses. Tonight was the night.

The butler walked over to Duncan and whispered a private word. All eyes turned to Duncan as he rose from his chair.

"If you'll all excuse me. My horse has been readied. Best stay in where it's warm. I shan't be long." With a wink to Mary, he followed the butler out of the room.

All eyes now turned to Mary.

"Don't look at me. I have no idea what he's doing."

Not long did they have to wait before the thunder of hoofs accompanied the squeals of delight from the children outside. The wee ones gathered together and stood still, watching as a white stallion cantered by the group and the dining room window. The seated guests stood to join those already standing, peering out the window in curiosity.

Duncan, poised majestically on the stallion, turned the horse to do another canter before walking Caesar to the children. They clapped and hopped from leg to leg.

"Who's first?" he trumpeted over the din.

Hands raised. Children clamored. The guests laughed.

Pointing to a shy girl who hid behind an older boy, Duncan asked, "Would my lady do me the honor of riding with me?"

The girl looked all around, eyes wide. When she seemed certain he meant her, she stepped forward. A groom Mary had not seen through the commotion walked over to pick up the girl and hoist her into Duncan's outstretched arms. They took a moment to situate themselves securely, Duncan fanning out her dress so it looked pretty and covered her ankles. In a moment's breath, they were off, walking at a snail's speed that might as well have been a full charge if the girl's exclamations were anything by which to judge. She giggled, shrieked, and bounced — much to the dismay of both Caesar and Duncan, Mary thought.

He went as far as the orchard, turning short of the vista, and returned, exchanging the girl for a skipping lad. This continued from one child to another until only two remained, eager for their turn around the park with the gallant officer on his white stallion, or perhaps from their perspective it was the dashing hero on the dapper steed.

"If you'll follow me, my lady," said a voice behind her.

Startled, she turned to see the butler, his expression blank, his demeanor expectant.

"Me?" she asked, a hand to her bosom.

"Yes, my lady. If you will." He bowed and walked to the door, pausing to wait for her.

Looking around at the guests, she gave a slight, though not entirely unladylike, shrug. Everyone looked to each other for answers. Mary's eyes met Drake's. He flashed her a sly grin.

There was nothing to do but follow the butler. A footman had her pelisse, bonnet, and gloves at the ready. She snuggled into the fur when the butler opened a side door that led into the yard and around to the children. At her approach, Duncan lifted the last child in front of him, Bernard. The boy waved enthusiastically at her. Duncan nodded, then steered to the copse of trees west of the orchard.

The children gathered around Mary, eager to share their excitement at riding the horse.

"Was it not grand?"

"Did I look a fine horseman?"

"Did you see me?"

"Did Mam see me?"

"I wanta horse!"

The voices converged in a babel of confusion.

All Mary could do was laugh and repeat to the wind-chilled, pink faces, "Yes, we all saw. You each looked marvelous."

Soon, Duncan and Bernard made their return round to the group, only they looked from a distance to be far more festive than when they had left. Mary tilted her head to one side, trying to discern the colors mingled with the figures. The closer they came, the more she squinted.

Not until they were some feet away did she realize what she was seeing. They were adorned with flowers. Around Caesar's neck was a wreath of blue and white. Bernard's arms cradled dusty pink clusters with silvery petals, piled so high he could not see over without careening his neck. In Duncan's arms was a bouquet. Clad in a mischievous smile, he stopped before her and gave a shallow bow, his movement restricted by his son and the ridiculously wonderful flowers.

Mary had not realized her hands were pressed to her mouth until the warmth of her breath heated her cheeks. With a laugh, she bounced and fanned her face.

Two grooms stepped forward to help Bernard with his flowers and to assist him off the horse. Little hands reached up to take the bouquet from his papa. Spinning in a circle of excitement, he rushed over to Mary.

"These are for you," he said with a hasty bow.

"Thank you. They're beautiful."

"Your turn." Bernard spun in another circle and ran to his cousins, already bored with the chivalry.

"My turn?" She looked about her, confused.

Turning, she stared back at the window of onlookers only to discover they were coming outside, each taking a rose or cluster of petals from the groom. Mary looked up at Duncan, questioning.

"Do me the honor, my lady?" he asked, holding out a hand.

"Whatever do you mean?" Alarmed, she stared, rooted in position.

A groom stepped over to her. "My lady." He sketched a bow then moved next to the horse, cupping his hands to serve as her foot lift.

Oh dear. They were quite serious about this.

Puffing her cheeks with a grand exhale, she tucked the bouquet into her left fist and propped her foot in the groom's hands. She slipped her free hand into Duncan's, and with a push off from the ground, she was hoisted by groom and gentleman onto the saddle before Duncan. Bouquet held firmly, she grinned at the onlookers.

A warm arm snaked about her waist and pulled her against the hard chest, holding her firmly.

As Caesar took his first steps, the crowd rushed at them to toss petals into the air. The rose shower rained pink, petals landing on hair, mane, and dress. She shrieked as Duncan traversed the storm of flowers. From her precarious position, all she could do was wave to the crowd as Duncan held her fast, though when the pace quickened, she latched onto his arm with a squeal.

"You're mad!" she said.

"You mean besotted." He kissed her temple.

When Caesar turned away from the park rather than returning, Mary braved a glance to Duncan. He chuckled but said nothing.

"You have to tell me at some point, you know. Where are we going?"

"To the bedchamber, my lady."

Her jaw dropped. "You *have* gone mad!"

"Between the wedding breakfast and the wedding bed, I choose the latter."

Caesar quickened his gait.

"But what about the guests? What about Bernard? It's barely afternoon! We can't retire *now*!"

"The guests are happy entertaining themselves alongside my parents and your relations. Bernard is to stay at Cois Greta Park for the evening. If I can't make love to my wife in the afternoon on our wedding day, all is lost. We can go to bed now, and we will. Any more protests?"

He was laughing at her! Crinkles formed in the corners of his eyes, and the cleft in his chin deepened. The rumble of his chuckle tickled her arm.

"But it's only afternoon! What will we do for the rest of the day?"

She ought not to have looked up then. His expression answered the question aptly.

"Oh," she mouthed.

The chilly air meant nothing to the flame her cheeks produced. Blushing so deeply, head to foot, she was all but perspiring in her bridal dress.

Oh, was all she thought for the ride to Lyonn Manor where they would stay in the State Rooms for the evening. Or the afternoon rather.

Sharp, the blade glided against Duncan's cheek. In the dressing room of the State Rooms, he sat still, enduring Peter's careful ministrations—a fresh shave, a thorough cleaning, a splash of cologne, a new robe. The shave had been a necessity. It was frustrating how quickly his stubble grew, bristles darkening his jaw only just passed noon on most days. Too often he had seen the evidence on Mary, the red around her lips where his stubble pricked her skin. Today she would meet with smooth cheeks. Not a bristle would she feel.

Task completed, Duncan stood for Peter to slip the dressing robe over his shoulder, securing it around the nightshirt. The valet stood back to inspect his handywork.

Fisting the rug with his toes, Duncan admired the reflection in the mirror. Perfect — no shadows on the chin, hair brushed into place, teeth clean. Ready, Duncan dismissed his valet and walked the length of the room to the chamber door.

It was not every day he stayed in a king's suite. Days earlier, when he had arranged today with meticulous care, he had a thorough look about the State Rooms at Lyonn Manor. In addition to the lord and lady's bedchambers, the suite had its own drawing room, dining room, and small library, ready at all times for a visit from the Royal Family should they travel north. The suite dated from the sixteenth century, the duke had explained. The bedchamber was adorned with a carved stone chimney piece, silk wall coverings, gilded ribbing and molded pendants on the ceiling, and a crowned four-poster bed. With the sweeping bedcurtains tied back, one could admire the exquisite plasterwork above the bed.

However chilly was the outside, it would not be so in the bedroom. All had been readied by his instructions. The fire would be roaring in the hearth, the bed warmed by a bed warmer, and soon the body heated by the consummation.

With a hand to the chamber door, he paused, closing his eyes. After all these years, they would be together. And after all these months, he would be able to feel divinity, no longer inhibited by a lack of sensation. He had lost sleep worrying if he would be able to perform. Even if he could, he worried he would not be able to feel. More than once he had wished they had made love at the lake before he joined the Army. Now, he was pleased they had not. Now, he had a newfound appreciation for what it was to feel pleasure.

Two deep breaths later, he knocked on the chamber door. He thought he heard a faint squeak, but he could not be sure. He opened the door.

Light spilled across the room from the fireplace, all curtains barring the grey outside. Never did his eyes have to roam the room to find her. She sat on her knees on the bed covers, hair cascading over her shoulders, adorned in a lacy nightdress that did little to conceal her silhouette.

He approached the bed without a word, just a slow smile that accompanied his disrobing into only the nightshirt.

She scrambled to the head of the bed and tugged at the covers until she could pull them about her. Then she smiled. A smile punctuated by two darkening red blotches on her cheeks.

"Nervous?" he teased, lifting the covers so he could climb in beside her.

"Ha ha. Not a bit. What would you give that idea? I'm not so naïve that I don't know what happens. Do I seem nervous? I'm not at all nervous." Her words ran together in a hasty jumble, her voice shaky.

All he could do was chuckle as he settled next to her and pulled the sheets over his legs.

"I do admit I was most embarrassed when I had to explain to my maid that the wedding night would begin this afternoon. She assured me she knew, but I don't see how that's possible; so clearly, she was trying to placate my embarrassment, but how mortifying to have her ready me, knowing full well what was about to happen! I think all future marital time should be away from the eyes of servants. In the forest where they can't see, perhaps. Or maybe if it's too cold we could send them all on holiday for a day, but then no, they'll know why. Will there be many servants at Sidwell Hall, do you think?" she rambled, her sentences running together.

Duncan studied her as she chattered on, talking nonsense. Was this the same woman who had climbed onto his lap in the drawing room? He could scarcely believe it.

Once upon a time, before he left for the campaign, she had made her interest known of wanting to kiss him uninhibited, though at the time all those stolen kisses had been on the grassy bank of their lake. They had never surpassed those kisses. He could not understand anyone's desire to spoil the marriage bed by anticipating vows. As much as he had loved her at the time, he never would have shamed her, forced her family's hand, or eloped, thus estranging her from the family. He had known the only way to ensure she was not ostracized by her family was to court her openly as a man deserving of her, as a decorated officer. Duncan had been determined to earn their respect and earn the right to court her.

He found it difficult to believe his bride was the same woman who had flirted so outrageously with him during their youth, who had always been the one to initiate physical affection, almost desperate to be hugged and held and loved. Mary, a skittish colt on her wedding day? Slipping an arm around her shoulders, he tugged her to him. Her chatter, which had not yet stopped, accelerated, increasing an octave.

They had all the time in the world. He leaned back against the headboard, his arm still around her. Drawing circles around her shoulder with his fingertips, he listened to her babble, a faint smile on his lips. The wedding had been a success, no one to halt the ceremony based on their incapability, and now they could begin their life together after all these years. What more could he ask for than to have her by his side?

With his free hand, he trailed his fingertips down the sleeve of her night-rail until his fingers reached her hand. He laced his fingers with hers. "I hope they changed the sheets since the King's last visit," he said, interrupting her.

Mary stopped talking. She turned her head to him, her brows drawn together. It took a moment, but at last she laughed.

"I should think," she said, "the concern would be in changing the sheets before his next visit." She giggled until she realized what she had said, then lapsed into a bashful silence.

Bashful would never have been a word Duncan would use to describe Mary. Never. Strong. Determined. Stubborn. Even coy. Never bashful.

This would be a day he would not soon forget if for no other reason than seeing this new dimension to his ladylove.

"Do you suppose we're the first newlyweds to make use of the room?" he asked, his fingertips playing a scale along her arm.

"Yes, I believe so. At least in my lifetime. To my knowledge, the King only stayed when my father was alive, before I was born. The prince, on the other hand, has stayed countless times. He and Drake are friends, you know."

And off she went again, talking about who-knew-what at galloping speed.

While she talked, he smoothed her hair behind her ear and leaned in, pressing his lips to her neck just below her earlobe.

Her words halting mid-sentence, she made a sound akin to *meep*. He heard her breathing sharpen and felt her pulse quicken beneath his lips. Her skin was torrid. Ah, yes, this was more what he had in mind. Inhaling her lavender scent, he puckered his lips to her fiery skin.

"How many times have you done this?" she blurted out.

His lips, poised inches from her skin for another pucker, dried.

Righting himself, he stared at her and frowned. "Not a conversation I want to have on my wedding night."

"Afternoon. Wedding afternoon. But I want to know. Are you experienced?"

Grinning, he returned to her neck, murmuring between nibbles, "Let's find out."

Hands to his chest, she pushed him away, however gently. "Are you avoiding the question for a reason?"

He sighed. "I wouldn't say I'm avoiding it so much as hoping we can skip the verbal serenade and begin the physical display of our undying love."

She giggled. He had not meant to make a joke.

Thumping his head against the headboard, he said, "Two women."

Her eyes widened. "On what basis will you be comparing me to them? I would hate to make a cake of myself. A few pointers would be appreciated. Are there things I should do or not do?"

What else could he do but laugh? "Mary, I will not be comparing you to anyone. You'll know what to do once we get started. I promise."

"What was it like?" she asked.

His laughter died a slow death. "It was a long time ago. It was what it was. Hasn't anyone taught you that ladies shouldn't ask such questions, certainly not on their wedding night?"

"Wedding afternoon," she scolded with a giggle. "Who were they? When?"

He heaved another sigh. Bending his leg, he draped his arm over his knee and ran a hand through his hair.

"My first time was hardly worth remembering. I was, I don't know, sixteen, maybe? The haber-dasher's niece came to town. We knew all about her, courtesy of the haberdasher's son, who regaled us with tales of his exotic and experienced cousin. No idea her age. Older. Nineteen maybe. I'm guessing here. If I recall, she took me to the stables for a roll in the hay. I'm sorry to disappoint you further, but I don't remember her name, much less what she looked like. I was so nervous, I can't even tell you if

I enjoyed it. I suppose I did. It was over embarrassingly fast, and I was picking hay out of my clothes for the rest of the day."

He looked back at her, still frowning, his eyebrows raised. What else was he supposed to say about it? Dashed uncomfortable to say as much as he did. Nothing could douse him with cold water faster than such a memory.

Really, any memory of a woman other than Mary would have such an effect, but most especially the memory of his first. He did have a vague recollection of her, at least more than he disclosed. Cynthia? Cindy? Sandy, maybe? Raven hair, not unlike Mary's. Voluptuous, also not unlike Mary, though she was far more curvaceous. What he recalled most was not the itch he suffered in his nethers for a solid month after bedding her, but that her attentions were not exclusive to him. Each of his mates had a turn with her. That had been quite the blow to his ego. Ah yes, the haberdasher's niece. Not one of his finer memories. At the time, though, he was pleased with himself for finally losing his virginity.

"That doesn't sound very exciting," Mary said, moving to face him, sitting on her knees again. "What about the other woman?"

Exhaling from his cheeks, he thumped his head against the headboard. "Cian's wife was soon to enter confinement. He invited the family to London for the spring and summer months to celebrate. I was, let's see, eighteen by then, I suppose, or thereabouts. I met a young widow in the park, and she fancied me. I fancied her, as well, as young lads do. I wouldn't have called her a mistress, but I suppose that's what she was, at least during that brief stay in London. Are you jealous?"

Mary shook her head. "Go on."

"What do you want to know?"

"Did you love her?" she pressed.

"Oh my goodness, Mary." He laughed self-consciously. "I enjoyed having a bed partner, but that's as far as the emotional attachment went. I don't recall us having much in the way of conversations to be honest. I'd like to think I learned a thing or two that year about what women enjoy, but what do I know? I was just a pup."

Again, he recalled more than he said, though his words were truthful. Lydia had been her name, the widow of a viscount. The peer had lost his life in a duel over another man's wife. Lydia favored Duncan because he was not a peer more than for any other reason. He could not even remember how he wound up at her townhouse the first time. He did remember visiting nearly every night for the length of his time in London. It was a far different experience than his first. Their parting had been amicable.

"And there was no one else?" Mary asked.

Why the devil were they having this conversation? One thing was certain, at least; she appeared to have lost her nervousness. She watched him in earnest, an avid listener.

"I was just about twenty and had my eye on a farmer's daughter. I was considering courting her, though I had not decided. I took a ride to the lake, fancying a swim and a think, and before my eyes, a goddess appeared on horseback. From that moment, my world changed."

"Oh, you mean you met me."

Laughing, he muttered, "Of course, I mean you."

"Did you always want to join the Army?"

For pity's sake.

Tapping his fingers against his knee, he said, "Yes and no. I romanticized it all during childhood. By the time I reached the point where I was tupping haberdasher nieces in barns, I had lost interest. If you must know, I was planning to become a farmer. It's how I met the farmer's daughter I mentioned. I was helping him, learning the trade and all that. But then I met you, and everything changed."

"Why didn't you want to be a farmer anymore after meeting me? You never mentioned it." Her words were defensive, her tone hurt.

"No, I never mentioned it because I knew if I were to court a duke's daughter, I needed a better plan. Your mother would have laughed me out of the house if I said I was a farmer. I thought as a high-ranking officer, I could earn a modicum of her respect. Then came the injury, and here we are now. I never did ask her permission, but it's probably for the best. I suspect I'll never earn her respect."

Ignoring his words of her mother, she asked, "You don't still want to be a farmer?"

"No." Realizing his tone was exasperated, he softened his next words. "I want to be your husband and run the estate I've been awarded. From there, we'll see. What else would you like to discuss? We have all afternoon and evening it would seem."

He folded his arms over his chest, ready to spend the afternoon talking. At some point before tomorrow's dawn, he would remove that night-rail of hers. He hoped.

"If you'd only been with those two women, and you favored me, why did you never accept my invitations?" Mary asked, remembering all her failed advances.

Duncan had been the consummate gentleman. Well, no, not quite. There had been some heated moments by the lake in her youth when she thought they were seconds from disrobing, but he never followed through. It was no end of frustration for her. She was certain her mother would allow them to marry if they had been intimate. How else were they to be together? Or so she had questioned at the time.

"Those women were different, and you know it." He cast her a knowing look, firelight dancing across his chiseled features. "I wouldn't mind one of those advances now, though. I promise to accept."

She laughed, looking at him from beneath her lashes.

Of all the times to be nervous, Mary was embarrassed to find it was her wedding day. For so long, she had wanted to feel his arms around her, to know what it was to be loved, and yet now that the moment had arrived, she was inordinately nervous. What if he found her too prudish? Conversely, what if he found her too wanton?

There, seated before her, looking for all the world like the strongest and most virile man alive, was her husband wearing nothing except a nightshirt. With the right word from her, he would be without even the nightshirt. She wanted this. She feared this. What if he found her wanting? The longer she delayed, the more anxious she became.

"Come here," he said.

She hesitated, running the tip of her tongue over her dry lips.

He held out an arm. "I only want to hold you. We can talk all day if you'd like. We've a lifetime together, remember? Let's talk."

She scooted to him, nestling to his side as his arm came about her. At the mere touch of him, her pulse raced. Finally, she would be loved. If only she could relax.

"Do you suppose the pendants on the ceiling are to hang one's hat?" He asked.

"Absurd! Everyone knows they're in place to remove the King's wig when he enters the room. One step in, and the first pendant would sweep the wig off his head."

"Must be a tall wig," Duncan said in complete seriousness.

"You've a good point, sir. They must be for the Queen's wig, then."

Duncan laughed, kissing her forehead. "I always loved this about you, Mary. We spent hours at that lake laughing over ridiculous things. Do you remember? I've never felt so comfortable with someone in my life." Lowering his mouth to her ear, he said, "It does help that you're the most beautiful woman I've ever known."

Mary buried her face against his chest. The rumble of his chuckle tickled her nose. With a deep inhale, she breathed in the heady aroma of his cologne, a scent mingled with freshly bathed man. A glimpse of the chest hair at the hollow of his throat recalled when she had last seen him shirtless—vulnerable, in a laudanum-induced dream, none the wiser that all in the room around him had feared death or loss of limbs. How differently that bare chest would look now once he removed the nightshirt, strong and muscular, the chest of a survivor rather than an invalid.

She looked up, replying to his patience with a coy smile. "Are you still ticklish on your sides?"

"Am I—I beg your pardon?" He stared at her, perplexed.

"You were always the most ticklish along your sides. Do officers lose that as they move up in ranks?"

His expression was one of such confusion, she could not help but laugh and test the theory. Flexing her tickling fingers, she raked gentle nails down his side then fluttered the fingers against his skin.

In a flash of movement, accompanied by a sharp intake of breath, Duncan grabbed her wrists and tossed her on her back, pinning her arms over her head. He hovered above her, his face lowering to hers.

Just when she thought he was going to kiss her, he said, "You brought this on yourself."

Releasing her wrists, he sought revenge, tickling her sides in retribution.

With a violent jerk away from his hands, she screeched, scrambling to escape as his hands raked her body in spasms of tickles. Still trying to angle away from his reach, she went in for a counterattack, fluttering her fingers over his flesh.

She was not sure who kissed whom first. One moment hands were at sides, the chamber filled with shrieks of glee, and the next, his mouth was on hers. She wrapped her arms around his neck to capture him as she kissed back with as much ferocity, if not more.

"Am I dreaming?" Duncan asked when their lips parted. His eyes searched hers. "You're so perfect. You can't possibly be my wife. Tell me I'm not dreaming, and I can keep you."

Duncan leaned back, propping himself on an elbow, and looked down at her. He studied her for long moments, running a finger down her cheek to trace the curve of her face.

Mary tugged at his arm. "If this is a dream, you had better hurry before you awake, and we both miss the best part."

Chuckling, unhurried, he rained kisses over her face. "Happy wedding day, Lady Starrett. Today is the beginning of our forever."

Chapter 19

Though dusk was still at least two hours away, the blue autumnal sky had begun to darken, the wind picking up speed and the chill worsening. Duncan burrowed into his greatcoat and spared a glance at the carriage beside him.

It was good that he rode Caesar to Sidwell Hall rather than travel in the carriage with the women and children. At each stop along the way, Mary's cheeks had glowed with a rosy sheen every time her eyes alighted on him. It was also good that his parents were an openly loving couple without prudish views, and that his brother and wife shared a similar outlook, for there could be no doubt in anyone's mind about what Mary blushed.

The journey to Durham had been long. With stops along the way to rest the horses, eat, and allow Bernard an opportunity to disperse pent up energy, it had taken them all day. His plans for exploring the grounds and stable block would have to wait until the morrow. All in the party would need to rest once they arrived. While he may be used to long distances riding a horse, neither his father nor his brother was accustomed to it, their fidgeting in the saddle a tell-tale sign. At least his brother had one of the finest horses he had ever ridden, namely Mary's beloved

Athena. In the carriage were his mother, his sister-in-law Miranda, his three nieces, Mary, and Bernard.

He knew the moment they drew near the hall; the land changed. Without riding the park with the steward, he did not know exactly what all belonged to him, but he knew it comprised of some three-hundred acres, much of which was farmland cultivated by tenant farmers. In the lingering light, Duncan could spy crop fields, open fields, grazing sheep, woodlands, and the occasional peek of a running stream. Exploring the grounds and home farm would be a delight. Did this all belong to him? He thought it might.

According to Mr. McLarren, the previous owner had spent a small fortune on landscaping the park with meandering streams, wandering and sinuous nature walks, bands of trees wrapping about the entire park, and small formal gardens surrounding the house.

He had teased Mary last night with tales of the morning room's terrace garden. Foxgloves, lavender, agapanthus, roses, sweeping bowling greens, and more, all as the centerpiece of a holly walk, and situated parallel to a kitchen garden with such herbs as thyme, peppermint, and chives. Duncan wondered if he would arrive to an overgrown disaster or if everything was pristine. If Mr. McLarren were to be believed, the family was in for a treat. What he had not teased Mary about was the stable block. That would be a surprise. The former owner had collected thoroughbreds for racing, and thus had tripled the fortune he spent on landscaping to build an impressive stable block visible from the hall, complete with clock tower and gentleman's lounge.

Duncan had wondered how the man had any money remaining for the upkeep of the estate when he saw the accounts of how much the deceased owner spent on his hobbies. The estate brought in a modest income, but nothing to match the expenses of the owner. Then, if the man had no heir or family, perhaps he had been right to spend his wealth on what he enjoyed, knowing there was no one to whom to leave it. Duncan glanced at the carriage. He could just make out Mary's silhouette and Bernard's wave through the window. What a fortunate man he was to have a family.

When they reached the stone gatehouse, Duncan's blood pumped with vigor. This was his. This was his home. And it was bound to be grander than anything he could have conceived in dreams. The long ago plan of becoming a farmer would have involved a humble cottage on someone else's land, a tenant to someone else, perhaps even a baronet. And now, this was *his*. *He* was the baronet.

The parade of horses, carriage, luggage carriage, and servants turned past the gates and through the gatehouse to follow a winding drive surrounded by trees on one side and open fields to the other. No signs of the hall yet, just a lengthy drive.

After what felt an eternity, Duncan's heart beating a tattoo against his ribcage in anticipation of the first glimpse, they came to a tree-lined portion of the drive. The mirroring row of trees, with red and yellow tipped branches canopying the gravel, queued like saluting soldiers. If he squinted, he could see their destination at the far end of the tree tunnel, a teasing peek of ashlar stone hidden by cleverly poised evergreens.

Both his father and brother stole glances to see Duncan's immediate reaction. He could not keep the grin from his lips.

They promenaded through the sabre arch of trees, drawing ever closer to the house. Whoever planned the trees to block the view except for the single glimpse of a vertical row of windows was either ingenious or cruel. Duncan sided with the latter.

Enough of this! He wanted to see his home. With a touch of Duncan's calves, Caesar trotted ahead of the group, bound for their destination.

And then, finally, there it stood.

Trees made way for an open lawn that would have been dramatic of its own beauty but made more so by the dotting of people gathered about the Palladian house. Duncan was not sure where to look first — the house or the people, or the stable block for that matter. He had time for only a quick glance to the house before the people descended on the party.

A three-story, five-bay block of ashlar stood in majesty against a backdrop of golden hued trees, broad lawns, and a stable block that rivaled in size. While no contest for the grandeur of Lyonn Manor and one-wing smaller in size to Cois Greta Park, Sidwell Hall was a beauty. He would not call it a stately home, but it was all too clearly well-maintained and a point of pride to the former owner, just as it now was to Duncan. And certainly, it was grander than anything he had ever dreamt of owning.

Grooms rushed ahead of the greeters to aid the arrivals. Duncan paid little mind. He dismounted, fleetingly hoping he did not stumble in front of strangers since it still took a good deal of effort to discern when his foot hit the ground.

The crowd approached, a disordered mixture of hall staff and what he assumed were villagers and neighbors. In the middle of the entourage was the steward.

Mr. McLarren scuttled forward, pushing his spectacles up his nose before accepting Duncan's outstretched hand.

The steward spoke first. "Welcome to Sidwell Hall, Sir Duncan! I trust your journey was well. As you can see, the message you sent at your last stop arrived in time for us to ready for your arrival."

"I can see that," Duncan said with a chuckle and a broad smile. "I admit I never expected such a warm welcome. I had hoped you would be available to meet us, but nothing more crossed my mind."

"Oh, no, Sir Duncan, we could not allow a war hero to arrive without fanfare! Your neighbors have all been eager to meet you since word first spread of your ownership."

The steward turned his attention to behind Duncan. Approaching were the horses and carriages that had fallen behind when Duncan trotted forward in haste. McLarren waved hands to grooms and foot-men. With finesse and expertise, the man directed a well-orchestrated ballet to see to the guests.

Duncan, meanwhile, began shaking hands with a sea of smiling people. Some bowed, some accepted his hand, and some embraced him as a long-lost relation, taking him quite by surprise. He had memorized so many names during the steward's stay at Cois Greta Park, but he knew none of their faces. Nevertheless, the whole experience was reminiscent of the village he had just left behind. In a strange way, he felt he was coming home. But then, he was.

Stealing a moment away from the crowd, he headed to the carriage just as Mary descended the steps. Casting a blushing glance his way, she turned to see the crowd, her eyes widening. Bernard saw no one except his papa. He rushed at Duncan with arms raised. Before his little feet could come to a stumbling halt, Duncan swung him into his arms. Only once in the journey had Bernard begged to ride with his papa, realizing after a short distance that it was terribly boring and far more fun to be in the carriage. And so, it had been a long time since he had seen Duncan, two hours at least.

Bernard on his hip, Duncan made the rounds to introduce the people and the staff to his family, his hand on the small of Mary's back, his parents, brother, and brother's family standing behind them.

The whole of Sidwell Hall could fit into one wing of Lyonn Manor, but she loved it. This was *hers*. No longer was she an unwanted daughter or spinster sister. She was the wife of a colonel and baronet, lady of her own manor.

Though they had not seen any of the gardens or park after arriving, they had toured inside before dining over a feast specially arranged by a cook who was eager to welcome the new master and his wife. The rooms were cozy in comparison to what she was used to. This was a place in which she was certain she could be happy.

The grandest aspect of the home was its decorative plasterwork; though not gilded, ribbed, or with pendants, every room had a painted mural or elaborate design. The drawing room's ceiling was a shimmering gold with intricate swirls that sparkled in the candlelight, centered with a blue medallion. Even the bedchambers, all of them, had some of the most fascinating plasterwork designs she had ever seen, not meant to impress with wealth so much as dazzle with artistic beauty.

However much she wanted to see the park, she spent the morning touring the servant wing with the housekeeper and discussing household matters, including meeting with the cook to plan the menu. Duncan and Mr. McLarren toured the park, alongside her father- and brother-in-law. She could see the park any time, she told herself. There was no sense in being disappointed on her first day just because she had not been invited for the ride.

The house was immaculate in cleanliness and furnishings. The only feature lacking was the nursery, all too clearly a suite of rooms on the second floor that had not been designated for children until recently. Duncan must have requested the steward prepare a nursery. Only, the dear man did not have an eye for children's needs. Did he not have children himself? Ah, but they were older, and Mary realized his wife must have taken care of such details. It was enough for now, but she would request more be done soon.

After a brief visit in said nursery to see the children and have a word with the nannies, and then a brief visit to the drawing room to talk with Mrs. Starrett and Miranda, she set off to explore the gardens. She had wanted to invite them to join her, as a good hostess should. Solitude, however, suddenly sounded like a grand idea. And besides, they were not guests; they were family.

Nuzzling into her fur, she set off to the formal gardens. There was no butler, a point that would need to be remedied soon, but a footman had helped her into her coat, bonnet, and gloves before guiding her to the gardens.

The air was turning from chilly to frosty sooner than any of them had expected. It was a good thing the family would only stay for a week before returning home. Being snowbound at an inn along the way would do no one any favors. Mary pulled her bonnet tighter around her ears and shivered.

How divine was this garden? Quaint, to be sure, but splendid in its own way.

A sitting room on the first floor overlooked the garden. The dining room on the ground floor faced it. Whoever designed this had an eye for beauty. A bowling green stretched before her, flowerbeds running parallel, and gravel paths to either side, framed by boxed hedges. It was far different from her mother's rose garden or the manor's parterre and knot gardens, but she liked it.

Though it did not have the bright array of spring and summer color Duncan had described to her from the steward's descriptions, it had its own autumn and early winter beauty, not without color. Yew hedges, hollies, and laurels held their green. Yellow flowers of a winter jasmine contrasted against the bare branches of the rose bushes and surrounding trees. If she was not mistaken in memory, she thought there were snowdrops and aconites awaiting winter's snow so they could bloom in early spring to herald the coming of next season.

She followed the path around the garden before circling back to explore the rear of the house. There she found a terraced morning room with its own garden. A courtyard stood to one side, connecting the house with the servant's wing. Skeletal branches of what she thought might be wisteria climbed the stone. It must look dramatically romantic in spring.

"Mary! There you are," a voice called out to her.

She turned to spy Duncan coming around the side of the house, his cheeks pink from a wind-blown ride, his shoulders broader than usual with a caped coat. Unable to control her reaction, she felt the flush of both desire and embarrassment to see him. Her cheeks warmed and her stomach fluttered. She could not look at him without remembering their wedding night. With familiarity of married life, the embarrassment would fade, she knew, but for now she relished in their intimate connection, in knowing she was his and he hers. Any worries she might have once had about their not being able to have children of their own were now supplanted with the hope that one day Bernard could have a sibling.

"I've scoured the house looking for you." He greeted her with a kiss to her temple. "I should have known I'd find you in the garden. You always did prefer the outside to in. Come. I've something to show you."

Without waiting for her reply, he tucked a hand at the small of her back and directed her to the front of the house.

Each time his shoulder brushed hers, she remembered the tenderness of his embrace. Each time his fingers pressed against her spine to guide her to their destination, she recalled the touch of his fingertips to her cheek as he adored her, Lady Mary now Lady Starrett.

So aware of him and so lost in the memory of their wedding, she did not realize they were heading to the stable block until halfway across the drive. When the realization struck her, she quickened her pace.

"Thank you, Duncan," she said as they approached the archway. "I've been wanting to see Athena all morning but have not had a chance to get away."

"You'll see her soon enough, but I have something else in mind for you," he said cryptically.

Mary knew there to be a lounge in the front of the block. They walked past it without a visit. Stables with a lounge sounded divine. If she had designed a stable block, she would have included such a luxury.

When they rounded the long row of stalls, she was first struck with just how enormous was the complex. The ducal stables had been impressive, but nothing to this. There could be no doubt this was designed by a connoisseur of horses. The block stood two stories, not including the clock tower, and formed a quadrangle with a central courtyard that had ample room for maneuvering a carriage and four.

Duncan steered her to the center of the courtyard.

"What do you think?" he asked, turning in a circle, arms outstretched.

She took it all in with a deep inhale of horse cologne, that familiar fragrance one could only find in a well-mucked and clean stable.

The windowed lounge she could identify easily, as it looked out to the courtyard with a perfect view of not only the dark timber loose boxes, but also the washing area and exercise grounds. She turned circles, impressed with all she saw. It was not difficult to tell where the carriage and cart horses were stalled versus the previous owner's thoroughbreds, all of which had gone to auction after his death—a pity, that, as she would have loved to have them now, even if it were not thoroughbreds she hoped to breed rather warhorses. The other horses were intended to be housed on the opposite end with the carriage, out of view of the lounge, with single, open stalls. The stalls were roomy as far as stalls went, but nothing to the loose boxes.

Alternating columns partitioned the boxes, one horse per box. Athena would have one to herself, of course. Mary did not doubt Caesar was tucked into a sizable stallion box.

"It houses upwards of eighty horses," Duncan said.

"Good Lord. Does it really?"

"I've already spoken to McLarren about making the needed alterations for foaling. This is designed to display thoroughbreds, not for breeding. We spoke to the stablemaster this morning, a fine fellow who helped design this very stable block. He believes the space can easily be altered for breeding, especially with so many loose boxes already in place. Had this been mostly stalls, he says it would have been a greater undertaking, not daunting, but not pleasant, either. As it is, he's inspirited by the task, eager to transform this to match our vision."

"What else is my dowry good for? Use it."

Duncan ran a gloved hand through his hair. "I'll take care of your needs, Mary. Let me worry about this."

She turned to argue but after seeing the hard set of his jaw decided against it.

"Come. I've more to show you." His hand returned to the small of her back to lead her to the loose boxes.

"More? There can't be much more to delight me than this. I can only take so much excitement in one day, you know."

He leaned close to her ear and whispered, "I beg to differ. You can take a great deal more excitement in a single day. Believe me when I say I aim to delight you."

Mary's pulse quickened, and she knew her neck was reddening.

In quick strides, they reached the first loose box. Duncan opened the door and stepped aside for her to enter. Expecting to see Athena, she stopped short to find a dappled grey stallion. It was neither Caesar, who was solid white, nor the horse her father-in-law rode. So startled was she, she almost failed to notice the flowers. When she saw them, her hand covered her mouth in surprise.

Yellow flowers were woven into the horse's mane, alternating with long braids tied by tiny blue ribbons. The horse looked at her and nodded.

"Oh my. Aren't you handsome," she exclaimed as she approached to stroke the stallion's neck.

She looked him over, sparing a questioning glance to Duncan.

"Meet Galileo. He'll be turning four in February, just before breeding season begins," Duncan said.

"We have a sense of his size now, and though he might grow yet this year, I'd wager this is what we can expect of his foals. Any sired by him would make fine warhorses, don't you think?" When she opened her mouth to speak, he stepped out of the box, ushering her with a hand. "There's more."

With whispered words to the stallion, Mary followed Duncan to the next three loose boxes, a two-year-old mare in each, all with braids and woven flowers.

Duncan leaned his shoulder against the columned partition while Mary admired the third mare. "It'll take time to breed horses for cavalry. The horses will need to be about five before they can start their career, but training should begin earlier than that. It'll take nearly two years to fully train them for war, eighteen months if in a pinch. Given this is a long-term investment, I thought we had better start right away."

She struggled to wrap her mind around the news. "These are for me?"

He grinned devilishly. "I hope it's a good wedding present. I've not overstepped, have I?"

Running her hands over the mare, she shook her head, speechless. Her dream was coming true before her eyes.

"However eager I was to share this gift, Mary, I admit I was apprehensive you'd not like my choices or be disappointed not to have purchased them yourself. In the end, my desire to surprise you won."

"They're perfect, Duncan. Truly perfect." She leaned in to whisper sweetness to the mare. "Are you hoping to train them?"

His startled look surprised her in turn. "Train them?"

"Isn't that what you're thinking? I breed them, and you train them? You must have remarked a dozen times in letters about the lack of training of both horses and soldiers. And you just said yourself, training should begin early. That's what you had in mind, yes? You'll train them as Army cavalry horses."

"Truth be told, Mary, I hadn't factored myself into the equation at all." He was frowning, his arms crossed. "I'll have to think on it. And for that matter, I'll have to send a few letters to see if our services would even be of interest to the Army."

"Will Caesar not be sired?"

"I believe he's looking forward to it." Duncan's frown turned to a smirk. "But I wanted you to have horses of your own for breeding. Your own stallion with your own mares. If you'd like, I'll have McLarren bring you the paperwork and research he's conducted, and you can work with him to arrange for more mares or whatever your heart desires. The stablemaster, as I mentioned, is excited about the prospects of your plans. He and McLarren have been plotting since I arranged for your wedding presents."

"I'd like to meet with the stablemaster myself."

Duncan raised his brows. "Would you?"

"Yes, I would." She lifted her chin and pulled back her shoulders, prepared for his argument.

He shrugged. "We'll make it happen, then. I took the liberty to choose the breed. I hope you don't mind."

Exhaling in relief that he had not tried to control the situation by demanding to be the decision maker and messenger to the steward and stablemaster, she stepped out of the loose box.

"Why Andalusians?" she asked.

"The Army favors Arabian stallions, and I hope to prove Andalusian geldings and mares would better serve for cavalry. If you're going to breed warhorses, why not make a statement? Arabians are beautiful but too high spirited and stubborn for the battlefield. With good training, yes, they can make fine cavalry horses, and they are a joy to ride — I've always wanted one, if you must know — but they're too hotblooded for war."

"But if you're training them, would it make such a difference?"

Duncan nodded, leading her across the courtyard to the lounge. "Andalusians, like Caesar, make perfect warhorses. Docile and gentle but brave. Adaptable, quick to learn. Though Caesar's a stallion, I hope to convince the Army to change over to geldings and mares. There's nothing more awkward than a stallion getting a whiff of a mare and deciding love is more important than battle, not to mention a stallion's typical temperament."

This was all so fascinating. How was it that she had not researched this on her own? It had been on a whim she thought of breeding warhorses, but from there she had not given it much thought. The letter she had sent to Mr. Edmund Tattersall had been her attempt to research. What a daft cow she was to have expected a man to tell her the answers, which had been the very reason she had avoided going to Drake. Somehow writing a letter was her way of doing this on her own.

Listening to Duncan explain horse breeds for war made it clear how little she knew about cavalry horses or breeding and how much she should already have learned from research. She resolved to take matters into her own hands, starting with a conversation with the stablemaster.

And speaking of taking things into her own hands, as soon as she entered the lounge and the door shut behind her, she found her hands ungloved and wrapped around Duncan's waist.

"Kiss me," she ordered.

He complied like a good husband, pulling her against him in a tight embrace, his hands cupping her shoulders.

There was something erotic about a tangled embrace while standing in a stable block. Though the lounge was enclosed, Mary found the lingering aromas of the stable strangely arousing to her sensibilities. Would he think her silly if she wanted to snuggle in the lounge while admiring the stable yard, perhaps exchanging words of endearment? Dash whatever he would think. She longed to nestle herself on his lap and nuzzle his neck, this wonderful husband of hers who had *heard* her vision for the future, truly listened to her and moved heaven and earth to take the necessary steps to make this vision happen. He had not laughed at her, ignored her, or otherwise. He had taken her wishes to heart. Mary was overcome with love for him and wanted nothing more than to rest her cheek on his shoulder and share a tender moment as they gazed out onto their future.

Feeling daring, she said, "Sit."

He chuckled, kissing her temple. "I hadn't realized I married such a commanding woman."

Taking her hand in his, he walked them to one of the chairs and sat. Before he could realize what she was about and protest, she hiked up the hem of her dress and sat side-saddle on his lap.

Brows knit, he said, "As much as I like where this is going, I think we should continue it in the lord's bedchamber."

Ignoring his assumption, she wrapped his arms around her waist, kissed the side of his neck, and sighed against his cravat, content.

"Mary, we're in the stables, lounge or no lounge. I've not told anyone to make themselves scarce, and as such, a groom could walk in at any moment. There's not even a fire in the hearth for Jupiter's sake."

"Hush. Can a wife not sit on her husband's lap while admiring the stables? Hold me while you tell me of your horse purchasing adventure. That's an order."

He obeyed with a contented sigh of his own, although she rather thought she felt the rumble of a chuckle in his chest. "If this is how you show gratitude," he said, "I'll give you a wedding gift every day of the year."

Mary leaned back to look at him with a noncommittal batting of eyelashes. "And here I was worried you'd think me an oversentimental female. Instead, you think I'm gifting you attention. I rather like where this is going. Tell me more about these daily gifts."

He laughed, unmistakable this time from the contented sigh. "Didn't you want me to tell you about the horses? Now we're to promises of daily gifts? You're awfully demanding for a bride. As your husband, I might have to take you in hand, teach you to obey me rather than the other way around."

Ever the mature woman, she pulled a face.

Duncan frowned. She returned his frown. When the corners of his mouth twitched, Mary started giggling, and soon they were both in peals of laughter. A groom entered the courtyard and paused to stare at the lounge windows, confused by the sound of laughter. This sent them into another wave of laughter until tears pooled in their eyes.

Yes, she was going to enjoy married life.

Duncan was thoroughly enjoying married life.

Granted, it had only been five days since the wedding, but a glorious five days it had been. Mary had an alarming habit of pulling him into darkened rooms with an amorous appetite. Who was he to complain? He must be the luckiest man alive. Granted, if she kept this up, his heart may give out at an early age. Each time he made to say something to curb her attentions, he reminded himself not only of how long they had to wait to marry, but that for a disturbing length of time he had feared they would never be together physically. He took nothing for granted when it came to his ability to walk or feel.

How could a man not enjoy marital bliss under such circumstances? He wore a smile to break his fast. He wore a smile to ride about the park with his father and brother. He wore a smile to take tea with the family. He wore a smile to dine in the evening. And he definitely wore a smile to bed.

Mary's expression was no less blissful. The poems he left for her every day helped. When he had an early meeting with the steward, he left one on his pillow for her to find when she awoke. Before heading to the nursery for reading time with Bernard, he left a poem in her dressing room. On the day he met with the tenant farmers, he left one tacked to Athena's door for her to find before her ride. He had already written enough poems to last him the remainder of the month, one per day.

The grandest scheme of the week that he could credit for her smile was his plan to build a small conservatory on the terrace of the morning room. He wanted Mary to have a freshly cut rose every day. With a conservatory, they would be able to grow roses year-round. After a quick talk with the head gardener, it was on the books to complete in early spring.

However good of an idea, this resulted in a meeting with McLarren wherein Duncan suffered a light scolding, for the conservatory was a stretch on the estate budget on top of the alterations to the stables. They could do it, but it would be stretching the account thinner than what the steward liked. Trusting the man's expertise, Duncan agreed to a monthly budget.

There was always the dowry. Yes, the dowry would set them up for life, but he was determined to do everything from the estate's funds and his own. If he could not take care of his wife by his own means, what sort of man was he?

He only hoped the horse breeding could generate enough income to pay for itself. A stud farm was something the estate could not afford to sustain on its own, but with an Army sponsorship, it would pay for itself and turn a tidy profit. He was even toying with the idea of studding more than warhorses. It was a pity the thoroughbreds had been auctioned, for they would have made ready horses for private breeding and sale.

He plotted and schemed all morning over the horse breeding potential. That was, after all, his forte: he organized; he planned; he led. Charles had been wrong when he said there was no place for Duncan except the battlefield. This was his new calling. He would train and breed horses alongside his wife.

That afternoon, following a ride with his father and brother, he took the stairs two at a time. With the men resting and the women shopping in the village, he would have at least an hour to spend with Bernard and his nieces in the nursery, assuming they were not down for a nap.

To his surprise, his sister-in-law Miranda was in the nursery, Olivia on her lap.

Bernard spotted him before Miranda, tossing aside the miniature horse he had been playing with to run to his papa. Duncan lifted him into his arms.

"We're playing castle," said the boy.

Duncan eyed his two nieces playing with their dolls behind a make-shift wall of blocks and pillows. "How exactly does one play castle?"

Bernard giggled. "I'm a knight."

"Ah, yes, I see. You lay siege to the castle walls with your trusty steed? What happens to the dolls and your cousins after you tear down the wall?"

Wriggling out of Duncan's arms, Bernard ran back to his horse. "They're damesols. I have to rescuted them."

Duncan nodded, his expression serious. "Rescuing damsels in distress is a serious business. I believe we have the right man for the job."

Bernard had already turned back to his game. A glance to the "damesols" proved they might not want his chivalry, for the dolls were having a tea party behind the castle wall.

He took a seat next to Miranda, who was reading to a sleeping Olivia.

"Have the nannies turned in their notices so soon?" he asked.

"I talked them into a brief rest. Though, if I know either of them, I'm willing to wager Eloise is decorating her new room and Sarah is packing for our return home."

"Sounds accurate. I thought you, Mama, and Mary were shopping in the village for the day?" Duncan had recommended the outing over dinner knowing how much Mary loved to shop.

Closing the book and shifting the drooling girl to her other knee, Miranda said, "We were. For all of an hour. Georgina and Mary are in the morning room, ensconced in the important business of choosing flowers for a hothouse. Your mother is determined to recreate her own here at the hall. Mary is going along with everything, as she insists she doesn't know a rhododendron from a holly. I'm not sure if she's serious or placating your mother."

Duncan chuckled.

Looking about the room, he realized it needed a woman's touch. The steward had done his best on somewhat short notice. Eloise would have ideas for what the nursery needed. He would invite her to a meeting with McLarren soon so they could do justice to the nursery, not only for Bernard's sake, but for any future wee ones. Dare he hope, before long,

Bernard could have a sibling. After all his worries of never being able to have natural children with Mary, he was of a sudden eager for that very thing.

Miranda interrupted his woolgathering. "Worried she'll turn the house into a giant conservatory full of plants?"

It took him a moment to trace his thoughts back to their conversation. "If she so wishes, we will live among the foliage as jungle natives. Today went well? You like her? Why was shopping limited to an hour? I expected not to see the three of you until this evening or late afternoon at the earliest."

"We had a lovely time, and she's a sweet girl. I admit to feeling dowdy around her. She's so polished and proper. But she's sweet and doesn't put on airs, not even when my nervous chatter gets the best of me. We only shopped for an hour, maybe less. Talked with the shopkeepers, met villagers, and called on two neighbors."

Duncan waved a hand. "She must have been under the impression neither of you wanted to shop. It's her favorite pastime. She could have been at it all day long if left unattended."

Miranda frowned, looking at him quizzically. "Actually, she said she didn't care for shopping and only went because she thought we did. All settled that none of us did, we took to meeting people instead."

"Don't you see? She was trying to please you. Shopping has always been something she's enjoyed. A new bonnet, hours with a modiste for fittings..." His sentence trailed off.

"I don't doubt she once enjoyed shopping, but now it would seem she doesn't. Wasn't she sixteen when you left for the continent? The pastimes of a sixteen-year-old are different from that of a lady of one and twenty, Duncan."

He huffed, crossing his arms. "I think I know my wife well enough."

For snippets of the day, he had imagined Mary's excitement at buying some frivolous thing. He had always found it endearing to hear her tales of shopping. There were letters even that detailed her adventures. Had it been so long ago?

"Of course you do," Miranda said, standing.

Duncan stood, as well, all eyes of the children on them in case the two adults tried to escape.

Turning to her girls, Miranda said, "I'm only going to put her down for a nap. Don't give me those long looks."

Reassured, the children returned to their play. Duncan watched his sister-in-law tuck Olivia into a child's bed, feeling extraneous.

"We leave in two days. Will you be well on your own?" She gave him a knowing look. "Quinn is worried about you not having anyone to help."

"Nonsense. I have Mary, and I am quite well."

"You know what I mean. Papa Sean wants to send both wheeled chairs in case something happens."

Duncan frowned. "Nothing will happen. I'm recovered, am I not? I have Mary, and she'll see to everything and anything. I welcome you all to stay as long as you would like, but I will not want to burden any of you out of fear. I must live my life, as must all of you."

"I don't doubt Mary is able, but.... Well, if anything does happen, promise you'll send word to

Quinn or Papa Sean right away." She knelt next to the bed and brushed the hair out of her daughter's eyes.

"I'm almost fully healed. To look at me, you'd never know aught was wrong. Tell me I'm mistaken." He waited, brows raised.

With a scowl of reproof, she said, "You're as stubborn as Quinn. Promise to send for us if something happens."

"I don't need a hall full of nursemaids, Miranda. I only wish to move forward with life. I'm perfectly well."

The evening before the family was set to leave, Mary sat in bed, embroidering. The candlelight was too dim by which to see well, but she was determined to keep busy while she waited for Duncan. It was far too early to retire, technically; nevertheless, they had retired early for the whole of the week, both eager for intimacy before slumber. Tonight, however, it would seem only one was eager for intimacy. He was nearly an hour late already.

She stabbed at the lace. Had he grown tired of her so soon? Did she not please him? Dropping the embroidery to her lap, she gasped—what if something had happened and he could not walk? *No, do not think like that.* He would be able to call for help if something happened.

She tied off her thread and set the tambour frame on the side table. She was cold, lonely, and feeling unloved.

The week had been grand, truly, but each day sent Duncan off to do things on his own without a single invitation to her. He met with the tenant farmers without her. He arose early to meet with the steward without her. He rode about the park without her. However much she enjoyed his poems, she would rather have him by her side, the two of them doing things in tandem, riding together, calling on neighbors and tenants together, meeting the steward together, running the estate together. So hungry for affection, she kept accosting him wherever she met him. How else was she to show she needed and wanted him?

Snuffing the candle, she pulled the covers over her and buried her head in the pillow.

It was not as though she did not have things to occupy her time. A household did not run itself. And there was the family to entertain. The anxiety stemmed from the family's impending departure, she was positive. She had fallen in love with the family, wanting them for her own, and soon they would be leaving her alone in the house with Duncan and Bernard. Such a moment ought to be thrilling. But if he stayed busy all day, every day, what was she to do? With whom was she to talk? A solitary life yawned before her, the very thing she had wished to escape at Lyonn Manor. At least there she had her sister-in-law Charlotte to keep her company at the manor. Was it too soon to miss Charlotte? They had been the dearest of friends since the moment her brother brought him a bride, the two ladies being near in age. Well, however soon it might be, she did miss Charlotte. Terribly.

The door opened.

Mary squeezed her eyes closed and lay still. The light of a candle brightened her eyelids.

"Mary?" Duncan whispered, padding across the floor.

She heard his candleholder tap against the side table. A rustle of fabric. The soft tumble of the banyan against the floor. The dip of the feathered mattress.

Feigning sleep was not so easy when she could hear, feel, and smell every movement of him climbing beneath the blanket. The waft of his cologne was so enticing she could not immediately remember why she was angry. Oh, blast. Why was she feigning sleep? Had she not been waiting for him so they could be together?

A hand enclosed her shoulder. She still wore her nightdress, but she could feel his warmth as he leaned his chest to her back as though readying to snuggle against her for an evening's slumber.

"Are you asleep?" he asked, tone hushed.

With faux grogginess, not willing to admit she had been waiting for him for an hour like a love-sick bride, she said, "Only just. What time is it?" She added a stretch for good measure, her chilly legs brushing against his warm ones.

"I'm glad I've not kept you waiting. I never expected to be so long."

Turning, she propped her head against her hand. She looked at him from beneath her lashes, hoping she appeared alluring in the candlelight. One look at him melted her annoyance.

"What kept you?" she asked with an exaggerated moue.

His arm snaked about her waist, tugging her to him. "I was reading to Bernard. I've not read to him since the wedding. He couldn't understand why not and asked if I was sick again. I think we both know the real reason." He waggled his eyebrows.

"Reading to Bernard?" She frowned.

Why had she not been invited? That was something she would have enjoyed. She would have invited herself if she had known, though it was possible the boy did not yet feel comfortable with her. Was it Bernard who did not want her to read to him, or was it Duncan not wanting her to intrude on time with his son? Either way, she felt the chill of exclusion. They were supposed to be a family.

Pushing herself upright, she sat on her knees to face him. "Is this something you intend to do every night?"

A crease formed between his brows. Raising onto his forearm, he said, "It is. Am I to infer from your tone that you disapprove? So help me, Mary, if you say the nursery is no place for a man—"

"Pardon? What are you implying?" She was taken aback by his accusation, hurt and defensive. "How dare you think me like my mother."

Duncan sat up in a swift movement, his hands on her arms. "I said no such thing. I only thought for a moment that—well, never mind what I thought. I know you're not like others of your station. I'm sorry I said that."

Studying him for long moments, she finally said, "I only wondered why you had not invited me. I should like to read to him too. If I'm not wanted—"

He interrupted with a soft laugh. "Our first misunderstanding as a married couple is over who will read to our son. You see the humor in this, yes?"

Our son.

Her lips inched into a returning smile.

Our son.

Duncan dropped his hands to her lap, taking her chilled hands into his and rubbing warmth into them. "I hadn't thought to mention it. It's a standing tradition between us two men. My only thought was for him. I'm sorry not to include you. I'll ask him tomorrow if he'd like you to join. You do want to join?"

Mary nodded, feeling a right proper ninny now. "Yes, I would like to join. I want a family, a real family. I've been on my own my entire life when all I've ever wanted was a family. Give me a chance, and I'll be the mother mine wasn't."

"We're already a family. I only need you to be *you*, not what you think your mother wasn't. She's not so terrible, is she? She only wanted what was best for you."

"She doesn't even know me, Duncan! She's never wanted what was best for me. Not once did she come to the nursery when I was a child. Most certainly, she never read to me. My childhood was spent with nurses and governesses, nary a mother in sight until I was old enough to be married off to the man of her choice. She's never wanted what was best for me."

Duncan continued to rub her hands between his, his frown deepening. "Now that you have a family of your own, I think it's time you forgave her, don't you?"

"Forgive her?" Mary said, pulling her hands from his. "Forgive her for what? Wishing she never had a daughter? Wishing I were the heir's spare instead?"

"There's no reason you can't make peace with her, Mary."

"I don't want to make peace. I never want to see her again." She folded her arms over her chest.

"You don't mean that. She's your mother. I saw how much her attending the wedding meant to you. I never wanted to come between you and your family, so don't put me in this position. My whole intention of entering the Army rather than eloping with you was to ensure you were not estranged from your family. I refused to steal you from them. Even now, I feel like a coward for asking permission of your brother. All my work to earn her respect with a worthy military rank is for nought if I hide behind your brother and you hide behind me. I'm determined to call on her before the new year. And I'd like you to make peace with her."

Mary laughed as though his words were the funniest she had ever heard. "Call on her? Earn her respect? Will you listen to yourself? You asked permission from my brother because he's head of the household now, not my mother. No matter what you do, you'll never be good enough for her."

His expression turned so menacing, her humor faded.

"What is that supposed to mean?" he asked.

"You know what I mean. You're the youngest son of a colonel. It doesn't matter what accolades the Crown gives or who your grandfather is, you'll remain nothing more than a youngest son."

Duncan turned from her, reaching to the floor for his banyan. As he slipped it over his shoulders in jerky motions, she panicked, reaching for his arm.

"What are you doing? Why are you dressing?"

"I'll sleep in the lady's chamber. At least there I won't be judged as a worthless youngest son." He tossed the bedcovers aside and swung his legs over the four-poster frame.

Mary threw herself against his back, wrapping her arms around his neck. "Don't you dare leave this bed. And don't you dare pretend for a minute to believe that's what I think of you. To me, you're everything. You're my greatest hero. It's my mother who thinks you're unworthy, not me. If you put words in my mouth, I'll put salt in your tea."

He sat still beneath her chokehold. Though he did not speak, he at least did not get out of bed or leave the room.

"Duncan, there's no point in seeking her approval. Neither of us is worthy of her."

"I don't accept that," he said, a hand wrapping around her wrist. "If you're not going to maintain a relationship with your mother, I left you for the Army for nothing."

"But you loved it. And look what all you achieved. We wouldn't be in this lovely home if you had not accomplished all you set out to do as an officer. It was more than valor to you, I know. it was the opportunity of a lifetime and one you wouldn't trade for anything. Your time at war was not for nothing. Rather than second guessing your decisions, understand that my mother isn't the type to build and maintain relationships. I know her. She doesn't want to make peace. She's glad to be rid of me."

Duncan turned to face her. Releasing the stranglehold, she sat back on her knees.

"At some point, we're both going to have to deal with her, Mary. She's a millstone about your neck whether you see it or not." Moving his legs back under the covers and pulling her to him, he said, "I'm sorry I upset you."

"I shouldn't have got upset. I apologize, as well. Is this the part where we forgive each other for the next hour? Preferably unclothed?"

He chuckled and kissed her cheek. "We should argue more often if it leads to this." Trailing fingers over her shoulder and down her arm, he tugged her closer.

"I would prefer if it leads to this without the argument. Could we agree to that?"

"Mmmm," he mumbled against the curve of her neck before he looked up as though remember something important. "I thought you liked shopping."

"Shopping?" She stared at him, perplexed. "Yes, I suppose so. As much as one can take pleasure in eyeing fabrics and baubles and ribbons, that is to say, not much at all unless it involves a new riding habit. I enjoyed it when I was a little girl."

"No, I distinctly recall you like shopping. You know, bonnets and frivolity." He danced fingers around his head in the shape of a bonnet.

Mary laughed as she leaned over him to snuff out his candle. "I grew out of that just after my come-out." When he grunted, she said, "Come here, foolish man, and kiss me like we're making up from an argument."

"Yes, my lady." His words muffled against her lips.

Chapter 20

The household awoke early to break their fast together before seeing the family off to Northumberland. They wanted to get an early start in hopes of arriving home before dusk.

Mary was anxious about their departure. She pushed food around her plate, unable to eat more than a few bites. Having the in-laws here had been wonderful. While Duncan busied himself, she at least had the family to keep her company. What would she do once they departed? She would not admit this, but she had in some part married Duncan for his family, having fallen in love with them as her ideal. A foolish thought when she loved Duncan to distraction, had married him to be with him, and had known they would not live with his family for eternity. Alas, the melancholy would not abate.

For the time they had remaining, she chatted with Miranda, as delighted by the woman as she knew she would be when they first met. Miranda was a compassionate woman and a nervous talker. Mary loved this about her. Such stories the woman could weave! More than once, Mary suggested Miranda ought to write a book. However much she had blushed at the recommendation and insisted there was enough to do as a mother of three and a vicar's wife, she all too clearly favored the suggestion. Mary decided to send her enough paper and writing supplies to write a dozen books. A Christmas gift, she would claim it.

The closer the hour drew for them to depart, the closer Mary came to weeping. *Oh, please don't leave. Stay forever!* But that was foolishness. They had lives and homes of their own. The village church would be missing their vicar.

As the family gathered in the entry, donning coats, bonnets, gloves, cloaks, boots, and sundries for a cold travel home, Bernard approached Mary, looking ever so sheepish and shy. One look at his teary eyes had her shedding the morning's anxiety. So selfish of her! She was not the only person who was overwhelmed by their departure. Bernard had never known life without them, not since he came to England with Duncan. His whole time as Duncan's son had been with Duncan's father in London first, and then with both he and Georgina at Cois Greta Park, complete with nigh daily visits from Quinn, Miranda, and their three children.

Here Mary was, nervous to be alone with her new family for the first time, but what of Bernard? He would not fully comprehend the departure of his grandparents, uncle, aunt, and cousins, and from this point forward, he would be in a strange house with a strange woman and his papa. This must be quite the ordeal for him. What a selfish ninny she was!

Mary picked up Bernard and balanced him on a hip. "Good morning, my sweet. Are you sad to see them go?"

He nodded then tucked his face against her shoulder.

"Think of all the fun we'll have! You'll have to help me explore the house. We must investigate every room for evidence."

One eye peeped up at her. Muffled words asked, "Esidance of what?"

"Why, evidence of who lived here before. We must discover the mystery of their past. Their favorite foods and hobbies. What they did each day. Which chairs were their favorite. Who their guests were. Do you think we'll find evidence of kingly visits?"

He shook his head but giggled.

"Will you help me investigate?" she asked, tugging his hat tighter around his ears so it would not blow away.

He nodded, turning his face to her. "I don't wanter sleep in the nursery."

"Oh, darling, Mrs. Eloise will be there, remember? She might be scared to sleep there alone, so she'll need you to keep her company. Will you be brave for Mrs. Eloise so she's not scared?"

Bernard made a noncommittal sound somewhere between a harrumph and a grunt.

"What if I joined you and Papa for reading?" she asked. "I could help tuck you in and check the room for fairies."

"Fairies?" he asked with more incredulity than curiosity.

"Yes, fairies. Pesky things that leave gifts for brave little boys. We can't have them leaving gifts, now can we? No one wants fairy gifts. Pish! I'll have to check the room to ensure there are no fairies."

He stared at her, his brows a worried weave of wrinkles. "But what if I want fairy gifts?"

"Oh, well, hmm. You'll have to convince me, so I don't chase them away. The best way to convince me is to be brave since that's the quality fairies like best. Rather than shoo them from the room, we can ask Cook to prepare a plate of fairy-sized biscuits to invite them. I can bring the plate, and we can all read together. How does that sound?"

A finger to his mouth, he said, "What sort of gifts? Do they bring horsies? I wanter horsey."

Mary laughed, glancing at the family who were gathering at the front door, ready to brave the cold air, the carriages waiting outside. "I think a horse would be far too large to fit in the nursery, don't you? Just imagine trying to get it up the stairs!"

Bernard giggled. His face turned solemn just as quickly as it had smiled. "My mummy's in heaven."

She was taken aback by the non sequitur. Unsure how to respond, she gave a slow, "Yes. Yes, she is. Do you miss her?"

He nodded, pulling at Mary's sleeve, not looking up. "Will you be my new mummy? I won't love you as much as my real mummy."

"Oh. Oh, Bernard." Her eyes burned and her throat tightened.

If she thought responding before was difficult, it was nothing to now.

A gust of cold whipped about them as the door opened, everyone in a cacophonous din of voices stepping out to face the chilly air that was feeling more like winter with each passing day. Before long, Mary and Bernard were standing alone in the entry save an invisible footman. Duncan cast a curious glance behind him as he stepped outside behind his brother.

"She will always be your mummy," she said. "I know she loves you very much. If you'd like me to be your new mummy, I would be deeply honored and never expect you to love me as much as her. Are you certain?"

Hiding his head against her arm again, he nodded.

"We'll celebrate tonight with a book and those fairy biscuits. Now, shall we follow the others and wave goodbye?"

Another nod. Mary set him down. Nearly before his feet touched the ground, he was racing out of the door and pushing past Duncan to throw himself at his grandpapa. They would all have to wait for her to join. Taking off her gloves, she swiped at damp cheeks.

A blurry Duncan stepped around the front door. "Is all well?"

With a sniff, Mary nodded and slipped on the gloves. "Your son, *our* son, rather, just asked me to be his mummy. On the understanding, of course, that he will not love me as much as his real mummy." She laughed after another sniffle.

In three strides, Duncan took her in his arms. His embrace was breath-stealing tight.

When they joined the others outside at last for hugs, Mary felt none of the anxiety of before. Everything would be well. Everything would be perfect. How had she ever been nervous to share a house with only Duncan and Bernard? They were her *family*.

The little family of three stood on the gravel drive to watch all depart, arms waving, lips smiling, each hopeful.

Had he known it was a dream, he would have awakened. That was the discomfort of dreams — one assumed it to be reality while suffering its effects, unable to break free of the horror.

Duncan sat immobile in the wicker, wheeled chair. He ought to be frightened. The legs were unresponsive. All sensation gone. Without someone to push the chair, he was trapped, a painting of a pebbled stream his only view. He ought to be frustrated, depressed, angry even. Instead, he was impassive.

A lethargic arm pulled Mary to him. Sensation and ability waned in his arm, as well. He knew he would soon lose all movement, knew it as certain as the sun rose and set each day, yet he could not muster enough emotion to care. Inevitability worn as a mantle about his shoulders.

Blocking his view of the pebbled stream, Mary stood, a coy smile playing at her lips. With a sway of voluptuous hips, she climbed into the chair with him, straddling his lap. He was aware of the kiss upon his lips but could not feel it. Felt nothing. Even as her back arched and her breasts bobbed in an attempt to entice him, he felt nothing. His body did not response, nor did his heart. *He felt nothing.* His only melancholy was for the lost view of the stream.

Duncan awoke with a groggy groan, a hand resting on the empty space next to him, a pillow tucked between his knees. His hand roamed Mary's side of the bed, feeling for evidence of her. Nothing. For a disorienting minute, he feared he was back at Cois Greta Park, an invalid, having awoken from a dream wherein he could walk and marry and physically love. Dare he try moving his legs? Dare he open his eyes to see which was dream and which reality?

The lingering scent of lavender on her pillow wafted happy reality. He smiled into the pillow, inhaling deeply.

It was not the first of such dreams. The nightmares haunted his evenings every few days, not visions of battlefields as he had once suffered but memories of the loss of limbs and sensations. As long as he awoke to this reality, he was not bothered; although, he would prefer to wake with her by his side. Not only did he long to see her face each morning, but he was ready to prove those nightmares false, ready for love.

After a quick wash and fresh shave, he found his way to the morning room, Mary halfway through a plate, a letter in her hand. She spared him a glance, her attention on the letter.

Oh, this would not do. Ignoring the sideboard of food for the moment, he circled around the table to grip the sides of her chair.

Lips inches from her ear, he whispered, "You. Me. A darkened room. Now."

A hand shooed him away. "Later. I'm reading a letter from Charlotte."

"Saucy minx," he replied.

His mouth to the side of her neck, he purred. She tittered, the sound light as air and filled with tinkling bells.

Swatting at him again, she said, "Eat, you beast. I want to finish my letter."

He brushed his lips to her neck. Teasing her earlobe between his teeth. When she moaned, he knew victory.

Tossing the letter to one side of her plate, she made to rise from the chair.

Two hands on her shoulders, he said, "I'm raven-ous." As soon as she moaned again, he released her to head to the sideboard for food. "We'll have to find that darkened room later."

Behind him, she scoffed. "You're a foul beast, Duncan. You shall pay for this teasing."

"I look forward to it."

He filled his plate with a meaty selection. Before he returned to the table, an unseen footman delivered his coffee. Splendid.

Neither Mary nor Duncan spoke for several minutes, Mary engrossed in her reading, Duncan savoring the meat. All meat and dairy at the hall was supplied by one of the tenant farmers. A convivial chap. Duncan had met him on several occasions, twice in the company of his father and brother and once with the steward. The fellow had five children, all too old to be playmates for Bernard, but the wife could be on friendly terms with Mary given the opportunity.

Then Duncan wondered if Mary would call on a farmer's wife, granted she was a gentleman farmer's wife, not a farm laborer's wife, but still, the thought gave him pause. Duncan saw nothing wrong with inviting them for dinner, but would Mary? A tiny voice in the back of his mind reminded him she dined with dukes and duchesses on a regular basis, not with farmers and their wives. Who would be more uncomfortable at such a table?

"You're awake early," he said, veering his thoughts from the myriad prejudices.

Nodding, her eyes trained on the letter, she said, "Earlier. I've already visited with Bernard, met with the housekeeper, met with McLarren, and taken a turn about the park with Athena."

His cutlery paused mid-air. He made to speak, but she looked at him from over the edge of the paper and raised her brows.

"You, sir, are not the only one who can wake early or meet with the steward."

The corners of his lips twitched upwards. "Are you mocking me?"

"Me? Never. I'm far too busy and important to mock you."

"I see how it's going to be. And just what was so important this morning that required a meeting with the steward?"

Folding her letter and tucking it next to her plate, she took her time to taste her tea, skewer a cut of bacon, pop it in her mouth in a sinfully seductive way, and chew with agonizing slowness. He leaned back, drumming his fingers on the table.

She swallowed and took another sip of tea before saying, "Butlers."

"Butlers?" he echoed.

"Yes, butlers. Or a butler, rather. I can't do without one. McLarren sent enquires the day after your family departed. It's now been a week's wait. He's optimistic we should receive a character reference or five any day. I've asked Charlotte for recommendations on what I should look for in a good butler, but her advice, however helpful, leaned more towards sending me her first footman. I would much rather McLarren look into this. He best knows the staff and house. Don't you agree?"

Duncan had not realized he was chuckling until she scowled at him. "And here I thought I would do all the work while you shopped. You're a new surprise each day."

"Shows what you know." She harrumphed. "Despite your prejudice against my sex and station, I am a woman of independent mind and means." Mary looked down her nose at him until they both laughed.

All week he had been getting used to her not being sixteen anymore. That may sound unusual if said aloud, but he had fallen in love with her during the span of fifteen and sixteen, and that was the Mary he knew best. She was no less Mary now. She was, simply, different. He had realized this the moment of his return, but now that he shared his days and nights with her, it had become astonishingly obvious. In so many ways, she was a stranger he was only now becoming acquainted with, a stranger who resembled his first and only love but was an altogether different person. Did she feel the same of him?

Not on every topic did she agree with him. In fact, on most topics, she disagreed. Their conversations were not contentious, at least, not all of them, though all were lively. There was a poise about her with which he was unfamiliar, a haughty gaze she never used to have, an enjoyment of things both domestic and lordly — hiring a butler being a prime example; should that not be his task? Even her expressions he did not know. Each day presented a new discovery.

"How's your family?" he asked, nodding to her letter.

"They've been waring over baby names, Charlotte and Drake, that is. Theo asks about me every day, Charlotte says. I still get teary eyed when I remember his chin wobble the day we left. Oh, my sweet

Theo." She ducked her head into her cup of tea before continuing. "Drake mentioned paying us a call in a month or two. He has a tentative engagement in Durham, though he's not yet heard word if it's before Christmas or after. There's a little hospital for which he hopes to raise money."

He stared at her, expression blank.

"His concerts raise money for charity," she said. "You didn't know? Well, no matter. According to Charlotte, he's been working himself ragged on a new opera for the occasion."

Tapping the side of his coffee cup, he thought how to say this delicately. "I know he's a composer, though I admit it came as a shock to learn since I had heard no mention of that before I went to war. But raising money for charity? That must be your sister-in-law's doing. Your brother, if you'll pardon my saying, is too frivolous for that sort of thing."

"Nonsense. He has a heart of gold."

He opened his mouth to respond then thought better of it, resisting the urge to argue.

What he could recall about her brother was an entitled noble who did nothing but play. The Duke of Annick's love affairs were infamous, especially the long-term affair with a notorious marchioness. Duncan could even recall word of a duel or two. Perhaps the duke had settled down to married life, especially now that he had a son. A redeemed rake. It had certainly come as a surprise to learn the duke had taken responsibility as head of the household. Before Duncan left for the Army, the Dowager Duchess of Annick ran the household with an iron fist while her son enjoyed his freedom.

Changing tactics to avoid a morning argument, he asked, "Do you miss them?"

"It's only been two weeks," she said with a laugh. "One of those weeks was kept busy with your family. I've hardly had time to miss anyone." She looked into her teacup, her smile slipping at the corners. "Yes, yes I do."

Duncan felt a stab of guilt for taking her away from them. At least Durham was not terribly far. It was not as though they had moved to London.

"Will your nephew and mother be joining for the journey south?"

Mary grimaced. "Theo is always welcome, and I hope he does come, but my brother would not dare invite *her*. He knows better."

"You should invite her."

She looked at him sharply. "We've been through this." Her tone was edged in warning.

He shrugged and finished his breakfast.

All too clearly changing the topic, she asked, "How long until we have a response about the horses?"

"Everything takes forever in the Army. Turtle slow. We might hear something by the end of five years." He winked when she looked up, startled. "I wrote to a fellow who is most likely to have a ready response. At least from him we'll have an indication if this is a plausible plan. A more definite answer may take longer. We can work with plausible, at least for a short while."

"And if they say no?"

"Warhorses are always in need. I'll look elsewhere if the Army isn't interested. For obvious reasons, it is my first choice. If it comes to it, we don't have to breed warhorses. Andalusians are fine horses for many means."

"I promise not to be too disappointed, then." She smiled.

Not until he felt her foot on his thigh did he realize why she smiled. Good heavens. She must have been inching those toes up his shin for some time. He had not felt it, of course. But now that her foot rubbed his thigh, he most certainly could feel it. Her smile became more devilish as he nursed his coffee, eyeing her over the rim.

"Didn't you promise me a darkened room?" she asked with a bat of her eyelashes.

Oh, yes. He did enjoy married life.

These were the moments when Mary knew love. Duncan's shoulder pillowed her head, her fingers trailing across his chest. It was an evening like most others. The snuggling was her favorite part.

Every night, they read to Bernard together, Duncan's hand finding its way to hers to lace fingers or brush strands of her hair while she read. She relished his touch. This was what she had longed for during the course of her life—human touch. Once Bernard's breathing slowed, they closed the book, bade Mrs. Eloise goodnight, and slipped off to Duncan's bedchamber. Sharing a bedchamber with her husband had been unexpected for Mary. To be held every night. To reach a hand and feel him next to her. To wake to his arm draped over her waist. Oh, what glory!

In the darkness of night, she often wondered if her mother had ever been held like this. Was that why Mother was so cold? Was that why Mother never touched her children? As soon as such thoughts crept in, unwanted, she banished them with all the passion she could give to Duncan, filling her world with the touch of all-consuming love. She did *not* want to think of her mother and certainly did not want to rationalize or justify her mother's refusal to love Mary.

Some nights, the couple fell asleep soon after retiring. Most nights, such as this night, they talked, getting to know each other as two strangers who married youthful fantasies.

Inhaling the musk of his cologne and sweat, Mary nuzzled closer. Duncan's fingertips brushed circles on her shoulder.

"What do you suppose our life would have been like if we had eloped?" she asked.

Her pillow lifted and lowered as he took a deep breath.

"We wouldn't have had a butler," he said, chuckling, the sound reverberating against her ear.

"How silly. That's not what I meant."

"Isn't it? I rather think it is. The only money to my name was what my father had set aside for me, enough to get a start in life, but not sustainable. There would have been no servants. You would have needed to learn to cook. I would have needed a profession to support you. I might have become a farmer yet, though I had little experience, only what I had gleaned from Mr. Bauer."

Mary propped herself on her elbow. "Mr. Bauer? Is that the farmer whose daughter you wanted to court? You fancied Miss Poppy? She has terribly bucked teeth." She wrinkled her nose.

"Aw, yes, Poppy," he said dreamily. "Ye horse teeth I do love. Ye words of wit shat like a dove. Ye breath of odious perfume I adore. Ye whiskered chin longs for amour."

Throwing her head back and laughing, she pinched his arm. "You are no poet, sir, and she was not *that* bad. I can, however, see why you fell in love with me at first sight if she was my competition."

"You think me so vain? I'll have you know she was kind and clever."

"She married the butcher's son two years ago." Mary ran her fingers down his nose, over his lips, and along his jaw.

"Did she? I didn't know. Pimple-faced boy, last I recall, though I suppose he's not a boy anymore." He studied her, his eyes dark in the dying light of the fire. "I shouldn't think you would have liked life if we had eloped. My grandfather might have been able to secure me a position. Someone who served with my father might have, perhaps a fellow officer with land could have offered me work. Though it's possible we could have had your dowry, I highly doubt it."

"Our love would have sustained us." She dashed a kiss to his nose.

With a hollow laugh, he said, "Love doesn't put food on the table, Mary."

"Who needs food on the table when *we* can be on the table, our bodies joined in holy matrimony."

Duncan's laugh was rich this time, full of humor. "I see. It's that sort of conversation, then. Not at all the serious kind."

His knuckle under her chin, he tugged her to him until their lips met. He moaned his approval of the lingering kiss.

"What if you met me now?" she asked. "Let's say we bump into each other at the hat shop. Would you fall in love with me as you did before?"

"But I thought you don't like shopping? And if I'm in a hat shop, wouldn't it be assumed I'm buying a bonnet for a special lady?"

She pinched him again, smirking.

"Ouch! I'm going to be bruised before morning." Lacing his fingers with hers, he said, "Have it your way. If I saw you now in a hat shop, while I'm purchasing a present for my mother, I would think you far too grand a lady for me and hide behind the plumes on display."

"Too grand for you? What nonsense. You didn't think me too grand before."

"You were different then. You were young and carefree. If I remember correctly, your hair was flying about your shoulders, your head bonnetless. I would never have known you a lady, much less a duke's daughter. It wasn't until you drew closer that I finally recognized you as Lady Mary, but by then I was too besotted to care. Now? You're a woman, Mary. You wear your station on your sleeve whether or not you realize it. One look at you, and anyone would know your blood is blue."

She might have taken offense had his hand not been rubbing her back, his lips smiling.

"Your turn," he said before she could respond. "Am I all you imagined me to be while I was away losing a campaign?"

"And so much more," she teased, freeing her hand from his so she could poke the tip of nose with her fingernail — she was tempted to pinch it, just to antagonize him. "One look at you would have told me you were a man who could give unlimited pleasure. It's the muscles, you know."

His chuckle was soft and throaty. "I see my honesty is returned with jest."

"You don't believe me?" she questioned in mock disbelief. "I'll have you know, I would have lured you behind the shop and had my wicked way with you."

Growling, he pulled her to him. His lips met hers in a deep and lasting kiss. The teasing man did not follow through with all his kiss promised, as he rested her head against his shoulder to resume their cuddle.

Settling in, her leg slipped over his, her foot finding his foot. She brushed her sole against the top of his then stopped. He could not feel that, could he? Testing, she pinched the side of his foot between her toes. No response. His fingertips continued drawing circles around her shoulder blades, his breathing steady. She gripped his toes with hers. No response. How curious not to feel one's feet. He could not know, then, that her feet were chilled, stealing the warmth of his.

With a giggle, she said, "Evenings wouldn't be half as fun if you had not recovered. I'm so pleased you're as good as healed. Come to think of it, those darkened corners wouldn't be much fun either."

She had meant it as a jest, something to make him laugh and be cause to toss her on her back for a wrestle or tickle or more. Instead, the hand on her back stilled. His breathing shallowed.

Backtracking with a laugh that was just a tad too forced, she said, "You know what I mean. I would feel no differently about you if you were still in the wheeled chair, but we can both admit the intimacy is one of the best parts of marriage." Another laugh, also too loud.

She rained kisses across his chest. When she hugged him to her, resting her head again, she waited for his response. His hand remained still. He remained silent.

The silence thickened, a weighted blanket that smothered her, pooling sweat where she had only recently been chilled.

Just when she thought she might suffocate, he spoke.

"I'm not altogether certain we would have married if I had not regained movement."

She held her breath and bit her lower lip.

"I could be wrong," he said. "Though we would never have shared a bed. You cannot begin to understand the difficulties or the humiliation."

Raising to her forearm again, she tried to brush off his words with humor, not wanting this to turn into what it was becoming. "There you go again with nonsense. There are other ways to enjoy each other physically, as we've both discovered."

Though the room was darkening with the dying fire, she smiled her seduction. Whether he could see it, she was uncertain.

"You assume I would want to be touched," he muttered, his voice a low croak.

Her humor defeated, her smile gone, she said, "I couldn't live without your touch. I need it. Do you understand? I need it as I need air to breathe."

Before she took her next breath, Duncan flipped her onto her back, pinning her to the bed. His mouth came hard against hers, angry, frightened, desperate, filled with words unspoken. She gave herself over to the fury of passion, banishing all thoughts of a world without his touch.

Snow crunched beneath Duncan's boots. Despite the visible puffs of breath about cold lips, he grinned, making his way across the drive to the stables.

It had taken until the first week of December to receive a response, a month since moving to Sidwell Hall, a little over three weeks since he had written to his lieutenant colonel, now a colonel in his own right. Duncan had hoped the man would respond quickly; he had not been disappointed. In fact, he was more than pleased since the response carried the news of the promotion, as well, happy tidings indeed for there could not be a finer fellow for the rank.

Letter grasped between gloved fingers, Duncan strode through the stables in search of his wife. Not in the lounge. Not in the loose boxes. Not with Athena. Dash it all. Where was she when he needed her?

Her laugh called him to attention. The sound led him up the stairs by the hayloft. A gentleman's chuckle joined her merriment. Following the commotion, he came to the stablemaster's private rooms. One of the myriad horrors that had plagued him during his paralysis was that if he could not be the man Mary needed, she would seek affection elsewhere, a reason among the thousands why he had refused to wed. At the sounds of shared laughter beyond the door, he knew a surge of fury and fear.

Throwing open the door, he was startled to find the stablemaster leaning against a desk, brandy in his paw, the steward behind the desk with his finger on the rim of his spectacles, the coachman at the fire with hands fanned for warmth, and Mary in a chair by the window, her posture pristine, her smile and glass of brandy alluring.

"Duncan!" she exclaimed, setting the brandy aside and coming to him with hands outstretched. "You have perfect timing. We've set the date for the first studding. Not until March, but we thought it cause for celebration. Persephone is to be the lucky lady. Come. Drink."

She took his hand in hers and dragged him into the room. He gave a nod to all in the room and watched the stablemaster pour a drink for him. Chagrined to have thought foul of the situation, he now sniggered. Mary had to be the only lady of his acquaintance who would be sequestered in a room off a hayloft with servants and brandy, celebrating the date two horses would mate.

Waving the letter, Duncan said, "I bring you more reason to celebrate. Lieuten — that is, Colonel Archer has responded to my enquiry!"

Blank stares met his gaze.

"My contact in the Army, of course. The very letter we've been waiting for." Voices clamored around him. "He wants to spearhead this himself. Says they've spent a small fortune importing horses from the continent for cavalry officers. The volunteered horses are used for transport, and the purchased horses from here in England are too well-bred for cavalry, typically hunters spoiled with quality foods and accustomed to life in the stables. He sees promise in my proposal. Archer has tentatively agreed to fund the breeding program on the promise I begin training right away."

Everyone spoke at once. Duncan let them talk, enjoying their excitement, before raising a hand.

"We need stalls readied for four horses. Since it'll be three to five years before our foals will be of any use, Archer is arranging for four horses to be brought here. We're to train them—or I am, rather. In April, they want to see what I've done. We'll take the horses to London. If Archer and his contacts like what they see of my training, they'll fully fund both training and breeding."

Duncan looked to Mary, unable to keep from smiling. Their plans were coming to fruition!

He did not mention that the officer's ball would be around the same time. With luck, she had forgotten about it. Although they would be in London with the horses, he had not decided if he wanted to attend the ball. Walking was challenging enough without feeling his feet, so he doubted he could dance. And the idea of being celebrated as some great war hero made him feel nauseated.

Mary looked back at him, the only one in the room frowning. "Why can't you show Caesar? Why do they want you to train these other horses? I thought you said it takes up to two years to train a horse for cavalry. April is four months away. Are the horses even Andalusian geldings? He's setting this up for failure."

"No, he believes in this and in me. He's behind this all the way. The horses won't be fully ready, but it'll be enough to show them my techniques. They need to see the techniques, and not on a horse that's like an extension of myself, which is quite different from how I would be training horses for their officers."

"But *four* horses?" Mary protested. "I don't like this, Duncan. Four horses in four months. It's snowing for heaven's sake."

The men in the room looked everywhere but at him.

"What do you think of Starrett & Starrett's Cavalry Program?" he asked, ignoring her concerns. "Or Starrett & Starrett's Cavalry Breeding & Training Program? Too much? I thought so. Starrett & Starrett's Cavalry Program then. For the breeding and training of heavy cavalry horses for British Army officers. I'll begin the training immediately, as soon as they arrive. This is our only chance."

Mary folded her arms over her chest, her displeasure obvious for all to see. The stablemaster, on the other hand, refilled drinks.

Duncan was already planning the training to accustom the horses to commands and to campaign life, which had unique diet, sleeping, and riding requirements, including riding in inclement weather. Although Mary was concerned with the snow, among other things, Duncan found it an ideal condition to prepare horses for what they might face in the field.

The four-month limit, however, which would be cut short with the travel time they would need to get to London, concerned him more than it did Mary. He dared not voice the concern. What the devil was he going to do in four months that would showcase his training techniques?

Chapter 21

Despite the deep snow, Duncan persevered.

He pressed a leg to the horse to initiate a left turn. Together, they trotted ten paces with an exacting rhythm before Duncan pressed the opposite leg to initiate a right turn.

Pulling his coat more tightly about him, he shivered. In the silence, a crack shattered the air, accumulated snow heaving a distant tree branch to the ground.

The grooms who gathered in the yard to help break-in the horses looked as cold as Duncan felt, but a warm fire would have to wait. Already two weeks had passed, several of those days lost to the horses traveling from a fellow in Yorkshire who volunteered the two pairs. The days were lost in terms of training but not planning. Duncan had spent long hours devising a training plan to fit their time limit. Much depended on the horses' temperament. Thus far, they were docile, brave, and obedient, praise be. With the help of the grooms, Duncan managed to accomplish the lunge work, mounting and dismounting, circling, turning, and walking, all within a week's time, working each horse every day except Sunday.

For the next week and a half, he and the grooms would work on trotting at various speeds and instructing leg-only direction. The horses needed to learn the same movements with exacting precision from left-hand-only commands, right-hand-only commands, both hands, and leg-only commands. Though they would not yet be ready for field tactics when there was barely enough time to master commands, Duncan would need to incorporate gear, sword brandishing, and loud noises to help prepare the horses for the battlefield. A horse's agility and obedience were one thing, the battlefield another. Being able to turn as quickly as a man on foot while simultaneously seeing the glint of a sword, hearing gunshots and the clang of steel, smelling blood, and avoiding trampling prone figures were quite challenging for a horse.

"Colonel!" a groom called out. "Approaching."

Duncan circled the horse around with a leg nudge. The horse obeyed, an adept pupil.

Mrs. Eloise trekked her way from the gentleman's lounge, Bernard hoisted on her hip. The boy was bundled so well, he was likely sweating beneath the layers, never mind the chill. Signaling a groom, Duncan dismounted, giving the horse a pat and stroke.

"Mrs. Eloise," Duncan said, approaching the pair.

Bernard's arms were already reaching out for his papa. Unable to resist the request, Duncan took Bernard from the nanny.

Mrs. Eloise curtsied and said, "Pardon my bringing him, sir. He wouldn't sit still. Said he wanted to be here with you. I told him it was too cold, but—"

"No need to explain. I understand. We've a future horseman in our midst!" Duncan laughed and walked back to the horse with Bernard in tow, leaving Mrs.

Eloise to return to the warmth of the lounge. Nodding to a groom, he ordered, "A chair for my son."

In minutes, a chair was readied for Bernard to sit in the yard with them, a groom at his side for safety. Duncan walked the horse over to the boy, maintaining a safe distance.

"Shall we teach the horse a new skill, son?"

With a rapid nod, Bernard exclaimed, "I wanter do it!"

"Watch me first. We're going to teach the horse to rein-back. The first lesson is done on the ground. Once accomplished, a groom will mount for the second lesson, and we'll help from the ground. The final lesson will be a legs-only command. Ready for the first lesson?"

Bernard scrunched his features. "Whasa rainy beck?"

"Ah. Good question. I see you're an astute horseman. Rein-back is when the horse walks backward on command. Let's suppose an enemy is charging at me, and I want to back away. The horse will need to walk backward with even steps in a straight line so we don't break formation with the other cavalry. The trick is not to angle the haunches, turn, sidestep, or have uneven steps. The horse will be prepared to lunge forward at any moment of the rein-back. I give the signal with my legs by pushing as far back with my calves as I can, and the horse will walk back, and then when ready to leap or charge, I'll squeeze my calves. Leaping and galloping aren't for several more weeks, but it's never too early to learn rein-back. Ready?"

The boy stared wide-eyed, studious and fascinated. Bernard's expression made Duncan smile.

Ensuring his son could see what he was doing, he faced the horse and pressed a hand to the horse's chest, pushing gently. The horse sidestepped.

"Did you see that?" Duncan asked. "That was a sidestep. What do we want him to do instead?"

Bernard worried his lips.

"Walk backward in a straight, even line," Duncan said.

Bernard nodded, as though he understood perfectly and had been just about to say that.

Duncan worked with the horse for a good bit longer, instructing his son just as much as the horse. Once the horse accomplished the task in confident and even steps, Duncan signaled for a groom to mount.

"Would you like to do it?" he asked Bernard.

Rarely had he seen a brighter smile. The boy leapt out of the chair and stumbled through the snow to reach his papa's side. Duncan lifted him onto his shoulders. Snow-packed shoes rained white clumps onto Duncan's coat.

"When I say 'back,' we're going to press the horse right *here* on his chest. I'll do it this time, and you watch. Next time, you'll do it. At the same time we act, the groom is going to signal the horse with his ankles and calves. Ready?"

A happy rhythm was thumped onto Duncan's head.

"Back," he commanded.

On cue, Bernard pressed the air, mirroring Duncan's hand to the horse. Ever obedient, the horse stepped backward.

Lowering Bernard off his shoulders so the boy could reach the horse, they gave it a second attempt. When the horse stepped back at Bernard's touch, Duncan stroked the horse's neck with praise and kissed his son's forehead, rewarding both for their accomplishment. Bernard was overcome with glee. He squealed and wriggled, ready to help with more training.

"Jamie's going to work with the horse now to rein-back with leg-only commands. While he does that, shall we train another of the horses? We have three more horses to train the same technique."

Delighted, Bernard wormed his way out of Duncan's arms, ready to be a big boy in the training scheme.

For over an hour Bernard stayed with Duncan. The boy's nose and cheeks were red by the end, and he had a distinct sniffle, but both father and son had a grand time of it. Duncan promised to allow him to help train every day. Showing the boy how to do lunge work would be a good place to start. At some point, he would need to learn to ride, the sooner the better, as far as Duncan was concerned, though he would have Caesar be the mount for that task.

Training the horses, however accelerated was the schedule, was the most fun Duncan had had since joining the Army. When he first started the training, he thought little could top his enjoyment—until Bernard joined him. Being able to work in tandem and teach his son his methodologies for building a horse's confidence and trust in the rider was beyond what words could describe. Fatherhood may have come about unexpectedly, but it suited him.

The next day brought another surprise—Mary.

He was mounted on one of the stallions, working through a lesson on shoulder-in. This horse was the most temperamental of the four. They'd been at this for well over an hour, but the horse continued to try to neck-in.

As horse and rider turned into a circle, Duncan moved his inside leg before the horse's girth to prompt him to trot the front legs with shoulder-in and the hindlegs straight. However responsive the horse was when doing this to the left, he was stubborn about doing it to the right. Both sides had to be mastered before the lesson could end. Duncan was not frustrated. There must be endless patience with such training and plenty of confidence, for the horse would sense the rider's emotional state.

As they circled back around, Duncan spotted one of the other horses trotting his direction, the snowfall giving the black stallion a majestic bearing. Curious why a groom was bringing over one of the horses that had already learned this lesson, he halted and waited. Only when the pair moved closer did Duncan realize it was not a groom.

Mary rode the horse with skill and sensuality. A smile broadened Duncan's lips. He waited for her to come alongside him, admiring her crimson riding habit. How the devil he ever thought a groom rode towards him, he would never know. The snow was falling steadily but not enough to blind him, and she was a stunning vision in red and black against the white backdrop.

"Is this to be the only way I see you for the next few months?" she chided.

"Am I preoccupied? Sorry, my love. Duty calls." His gaze swept over her in dramatized appreciation. "After all my hard work to break-in that horse, you're going to ruin him for male riders. He *is* to be a war-horse, you realize."

"Show me what to do, and I'll assist."

Duncan laughed heartily. "A noble gesture, but what I'm teaching can't be done with a side-saddle."

Mary raised her crop. "And this isn't a sufficient substitute? I can do anything you can do. And if you say it can't be done, I'll take that as a challenge and request to be saddled astride."

Duncan raised his brows. That was a sight he was not at all prepared to witness. No, on second thought, that was a sight he was not prepared for anyone else to witness. He, however, would love most dearly to witness that sight, just so long as he was the only one to see it.

"I don't doubt you, my dear," he said. "My concern is the horse would learn riding techniques in a way he'll not see on the battlefield. Leave the training to me. You could, though, aid in other ways. What about riding out with Athena and providing a distraction for these horses? That would help with the battlefield training."

Her eyes narrowed and her lips pursed. "Not what I had in mind. You doubt my prowess?"

"Mary, love, I do not doubt anything when it comes to you and horsemanship, but these horses are being trained for war, not the hunt."

"Challenge accepted," she said before turning the horse back to the stables.

The fluidity with which the horse responded to her was impressive, to say the least. So impressive, it stole his attention from the so-called challenge.

Shrugging at her retreating back, he returned to his task with a pat to Tristan's neck and a swipe of the snow from the stallion's mane. Success was swift, as though the horse had been motivated by Mary's presence. They worked the maneuver several times before changing tactics to haunches-in, a movement Tristan took to easier than shoulder-in, never mind it was a more difficult task. And then Duncan's attention was distracted again.

He never should have doubted her.

On his final round of working the horse haunches-in, Mary rode towards him once more. That she returned did not shock him so much as the fact that she was all too clearly riding astride.

The sight of her riding habit's skirt hiked up to mid-shin, revealing some sort of legged petticoat for propriety and warmth, her hips undulating to the gait of the horse, and both legs spread wide about the horse's girth, caused a single reaction in Duncan.

Desire pulsed through him.

He shifted in the saddle from discomfort by the time she reached him.

She greeted him with a smirk. "Now you cannot tell me I can't perform your maneuvers. Instruct, sirrah! Let us train together before my nose freezes."

She expected him to concentrate while staring at her mounted astride? By Jove. No woman should ever ride astride, and no man should witness it if it ever did happen. Never would he be able to forget the sight of her thusly.

Running a gloved hand along the back of his neck, he grimaced. "One lesson only."

"You think me incapable of doing more?" Her tone formed icicles.

"Not you, darling. Me. I'll last one lesson before I'll have to carry you to the hall for a tête-à-tête."

"Ah," she said, her cheeks rosy, though not from the wind chill.

The next day, Mary woke early enough to take care of the household tasks, dress, and be at the stables before Duncan arrived for another day of training.

Poised atop one of the horses, seated astride, she looked down her nose at her husband, a single brow arched, baiting him to argue. It did not take a telepath to know he was displeased. His lips set in a grim line, a crease forming between his brows. He humored her for less than an hour before instructing her to return to the hall. Blood was almost shed as she kneaded her talons on the reins.

Thinking it best not to argue against him in front of the staff, she huffed and returned as ordered. Not until supper did she see him again, by which time he was too exhausted to argue with her.

Two days followed similarly, Mary hoping to wear down his reserve to allow her to assist. Both days resulted in the same outcome. She did not care one bit for being shooed from the stables. While he insisted it was not because she was a woman or lacked the skill, being a woman *was* the problem, for he would not allow her to train side-saddle, nor would he allow her to ride astride in front of the grooms. However pleased she should be to have had the hour-long opportunities he granted her, she did not find it flattering to be *humored*.

Sunday, at least, was a day Mary cherished, for there was no talk of training or horses, just a day of visiting the village church, seeing the people with whom she was becoming more familiar with each passing week, and a day together as a family, building snowmen and enjoying snowball wars. His hand held hers throughout the day, and he sneaked kisses every chance he could get. A perfect day.

Training resumed the next day. Though she stayed busy with household tasks, she did not see Duncan until supper. As with the previous week, he was too exhausted to do more than listen to her talk about her day and answer her questions in monosyllables. He was, in fact, too tired to do more than fall asleep upon reaching the bed.

Tuesday brought more frustration. Try as she might to assist with the training, he brushed her aside. As exhausted as the day before, he fell asleep after only a quick kiss.

Wednesday, Mary pointedly avoided him, taking her supper elsewhere and joining him in bed well after he retired. To her chagrin, he was snoring rather than awaiting her arrival.

And that brought them to Thursday. Today.

Mary sat in the parlor, arms crossed, legs crossed, foot swinging. Fingers drummed against her arm.

Nearly three weeks after the horses had arrived, she had seen her husband so few times during the day she could count the cumulative total on one hand. Nights did not count. No, on second thought, they did count. This week, specifically, they counted. For two weeks, they had shared the nights together, a blessed reminder of their mutual affection, even if by day he was little more than a ghost. For the past week, he had been too exhausted for more than a few chaste kisses.

This would not do.

To top off her annoyance, Bernard had taken ill with sniffles and a chill. Every day he had gone out with his papa for at least an hour, sometimes far longer, working the horses in the snow. Three years old and he was not only lunging the new horses but riding Caesar — in the freezing cold.

This would not do.

The door opened. Duncan swaggered in, closing the door behind him. He shook snow from his hair and patted it from his coat.

For crying in a horse trough, he was still wearing his coat! Her foot swung faster.

"I hope this is important," he said. "We're on a tight schedule."

"Am I interrupting your schedule? Oh, dear me, well, I do apologize. Carry on, then," she said through gritted teeth.

With a quizzical stare, he made for the door to leave.

"Don't you dare leave this room, Duncan," she said when his hand reached for the handle.

"But I thought you — never mind." He ran his hands through his hair and took the chair nearest her. "Has something happened to the new butler? He was snowbound last I heard. Is he delayed again?"

"This has nought to do with Mr. Sherman. This is to do with you."

His eyes wide and brows raised, he looked genuinely surprised. "Me?"

"Yes. You. This is not working. It's supposed to be *our* program, and yet you won't allow me to help. On top of that, you're out there all day, every day, and always exhausted by end of day, leaving no time for us to talk or share time together. Even Bernard is so desperate for your attention he's made himself ill from the weather."

Duncan propped his elbows on the arm of the chair and laced his fingers. His expression remained surprised. "Heavy charges you lay at my feet, Mary. Where do I begin?"

It might have been a rhetorical question, but Mary took it literally. "Bernard is a fine place to start. What are you thinking by allowing him out in this weather for hours? And he's far too young to be working with horses."

"I learned my way around horses at his age. It's never too early, and he's fast becoming a skilled horseman. I'll not coddle him."

"I'm not suggesting you coddle him, simply be aware of his age."

"And would you have me leave him in the nursery all day to be raised by his nanny?" There was an edge to his voice.

"I'm not my mother, and I resent the insinuation." She glared in response, her foot swinging again.

Duncan heaved a sigh. "I'm not insinuating anything. My point is, I will not have my son spending his days by the fire, unable to work a horse. I don't know what his future may hold, but maybe he will want to take over as trainer one day, should this program be successful. Or maybe he would want a profession with horses, such as joining the cavalry like his papa."

Mary gave a mirthless laugh. "Absurd. A tutor will see he's prepared for Eton and Oxford."

"A tutor?" Duncan leaned forward. "What's wrong with his being educated in the village?"

"Oh, really, Duncan. It's not like he's going to be a blacksmith. A village education is as good as no education at all. My nephew is a year younger and already learning penmanship. I want the same for Bernard. He'll have only the best."

Duncan ran a hand over his face. "I have a village education."

"Oh." Mary blanched.

"My father taught me until I was ten. At that time, the vicar took it upon himself to open a village school in the church. We met every Sunday after service."

"Well, that might have been good enough for you, but it's not good enough for a son of mine. I'll not have him reaching the age of ten without knowing his letters."

"I repeat: my father taught me. What do you suppose I've been doing with Bernard? I've been teaching him myself these past few months and intend to continue. As it is, his professions will be limited. Perhaps you've forgotten, but he is an illegitimate boy who lucked into guardians. He can't even inherit the baronetcy. Before you insult me again, you should think on those points."

Mary sat up straighter, uncrossing her arms to clench her fists in her lap. "I did not intend to insult you. I only want what's best for him. I believe that to be a tutor. When the time comes, he can choose for himself if he wishes to go to Eton or not. You should want the best for him, as well, and not resign him to some low fate. Let him decide."

Duncan narrowed his eyes. "Some low fate, eh? And should he wish to join the Army?"

Mary wrung her hands. "No. I'll not allow it."

"What happened to letting him decide?"

"I meant let him decide his education, not allow him to wake up one morning and decide he wants to face the pointy end of a sword. I spent enough years worrying about you. I'll not do it all over again with my son."

Frowning, Duncan studied her. He did not respond for some time, leaving a heavy silence between them. Mary hoped she had not overstepped. She did not mean to imply his choice to enter the Army had been a bad one or that it was a low profession. But not again could she suffer the waiting and not knowing. Though he looked well now, he had not come back unscathed, and the wound could have been far worse. There was no guarantee his condition would not return. Even now, she knew he had not regained sensation below his knees. How could he wish this fate for his son should Bernard decide war sounded romantic?

"Your other charges?" he asked at last, side-stepping further discussion of Bernard, or perhaps conceding to her point of view.

"I want to help. I'm a skilled horsewoman, and this ought to be a joint effort. Simply because I'm a woman does not mean I should deal only with plans and successes. I want a hand in the process."

He leaned back against the chair and rested an ankle on his opposite knee. "I understand, but no. Not now at least. When we train in the future, we'll work something out. For now, I'm under a tight schedule and can't have you as a distraction."

"I am not an ornament hanging about the stables! I am a skilled horsewoman and can—"

Duncan held up a hand to interrupt her. "You are a distraction to *me*. Riding astride is strictly off limits. When I see you astride, all I think about is—well, I'll not have it. And I'll not have the grooms seeing you on a horse like that. Besides, I don't want you to take a chill. Please, let me handle the training this time. After London, should all go well, we will have our own schedule to work with and can work together."

Mary gave a curt nod. She was not at all pleased, but he had his points.

Chin raised, she said, "If I'm not to participate, then neither are you. Every day, all day, you're out there doing the work of a groom. I did not marry you to spend my days alone."

Duncan propped his temple on a fist. "Right. Shall I notify Archer we forfeit the program?"

"Don't be silly. Instruct the grooms on what to do, and let them do it. There's no reason you should be out there doing all the work. That's what servants are for."

"Leave our entire livelihood to a handful of grooms who have never seen the battlefield or handled a warhorse? I think not, Mary. I'm up against an impossible task of breaking-in horses *and* training them for the field within only four months. Just getting a horse to leap from a gallop is a ten-week long training, and I'm going to have to do it in two weeks. Let's not forget there are four horses, not one."

"But you needn't do it on your own. We have the grooms. Use them."

"They're already helping with what they can," he said. "When it comes to it, I'm the only one with field experience and technique. If a groom makes on error in training, all our plans are ruined. Too much is at stake. These horses need to be perfect for what I plan to demonstrate in London. I don't have time to correct habits that inexperience may create."

Mary sighed, frustrated. "Wouldn't it be better to take a day or so to train the grooms than to spend all your time doing the work? You can supervise for a few short hours each day. I'm tired of an empty house. We've not even called on anyone in a month. What must the neighbors think?"

"I'm trying to fulfill your dream and secure us financially, and you're worried about what the neighbors think?"

"Keeping good relations is important. We're new here. It's vital we establish ourselves and build a reputation. I appreciate all you're doing, but we needn't worry about finances. We have my dowry, of course. If seeing my dream come true means never seeing you, I would far rather live off the dowry. I did not marry to see this dream fulfilled. I could have done it on my own, need I remind you. I married to be with you."

Duncan sat up and reached a hand to take hers. Her heart fluttered at his touch. Oh, he did care! He did understand.

"My pride will not allow me to use your dowry. Set it aside for whatever daughters we may have, or use it for pin money. Before you argue, know it's not all to do with the dowry. I need some occupation, Mary. I can't sit idle, twiddling my thumbs and calling on people all day. I need a purpose, a mission. I am a leader and a horseman. What would you have me do all day without some occupation?"

"You don't have to spend *all* day training. If you don't trust the grooms, couldn't you hire someone? Our stablemaster should know someone perfect for the task. What if you had an officer do it? You could even have soldiers come to work the horses. You train the officer to supervise the enlisted or recruited, and together the horses and privates could learn. Isn't that part of the problem, both unskilled soldiers and horses, not just the horses?" Looking at her hand in his, she asked, "Why do you have to do everything yourself? If you're a leader, then lead."

He squeezed her hand, running his thumb over her knuckles. "It would take too much time to arrange. Not to mention I couldn't leave them unsupervised until I was certain. But you have a point."

She looked up, shocked to see his brown eyes smiling. "I do?"

Duncan nodded. "Yes. It's a shame we can't somehow train the officers alongside the horses. Don't you think? A well-trained warhorse is wasted on an officer arrogant enough to think foxhunt dressage is sufficient preparation for military equitation. I'm not in a position to train both, though. It's something I could take up with Archer for the future, assuming this goes well."

"Yes, for the future," she muttered, disappointed.

The corners of his eyes crinkled. "In the meantime, will you be satisfied if I agreed to instruct the stablemaster in my techniques so that he might then train and supervise the grooms?"

Mary bounced and clasped his other hand. "Yes! Oh, yes. Anything so that you can be here with me rather than out in the snow."

"If this fails, it's on your head. We'll have no recourse other than to take up as highwaymen to support your dreams of horse breeding."

"We shall be the very best highwaymen. No one will outrun us."

Duncan laughed and pulled her into his lap. Home, Mary wrapped her arms around his neck and nuzzled her temple to his.

Chapter 22

A world of white looked back at Mary from the carriage window. Bare branches flexed against fallen snow, the treetops naked in the wind. It had not snowed since Friday, but neither had the sun shone to melt the flakes.

"Mr. and Mrs. Childress were amiable," Duncan said, seated across from her.

She turned her attention to her husband. He looked stunning in blue. The ensemble was not new, but there was something about him in blue that made Mary's heart pound. Perhaps it was the memory of his dragoon regimentals on their wedding day. She did like how the intricate knot of his cravat gave him a distinguished air, which was a curious sentiment since she had always favored him for his devil may care attitude of youth.

His attire and presentation had never been disheveled. Such was not Duncan's style. But there had always been a careless air about him. No longer, though. Lost were such sensibilities on a battlefield. Now, his attitude was more serious than carefree, somber more than comical. His clothing reflected care. There could be no doubt he took pride in his appearance. With each passing day, Mary found it more to her liking, enjoying her own sense of pride at having him on her arm when calling on neighbors or attending church. Never had she found a distinguished gentleman attractive. Until now.

Leaving the warmth of the muff, her hand squeezed his thigh, her lips accompanying with a teasing smile. "Yes, perfectly amiable," she said. "Thank you for paying calls with me these past few days."

"I've enjoyed myself. We've needed to do it, but I was too preoccupied to see beyond the stables. This is what living with me is like, if you must know. Once I focus on something, I see little else beyond it. I focus on the mission until it's completed. One task at a time. Tick, tick, tick, until it's finished."

"I'm good for you, then. No one needs to be so focused all the time." With a flirty smile, she massaged his thigh.

Smirking, he swatted at her hand. "Eh, eh, eh. Wait your turn, my lady. We still have one more call to make, and I'll not greet them standing at attention."

Mary replied with a moue.

"Saucy minx."

The carriage came to a halt not long after.

Mr. and Mrs. Swanson were their closest neighbors, wealthy gentry with a home that nearly rivaled Lyonn Manor in grandeur. Mary and Duncan were shown into the parlor where a congenial Mr. Swanson and a haughty Mrs. Swanson awaited them. Mrs. Swanson's plumes were tall enough to reach the ceiling. Judging from her jewelry, the woman had wanted to impress the daughter of a duke. Mary could not read the assessing look she gave Duncan — curiosity? Approval? Disdain? There was no way to know, not that Mary cared. They were here to do their duty of calling on their closest neighbor, nothing more.

Mr. Swanson bowed. He was a short gentleman, slight of build. Despite a bald spot, he powdered his natural hair rather than wore a wig. Mary disliked both wigs and powder, but she knew they were still popular with the older crowd, not that the Swansons were terribly older.

"Allow me to introduce my son and daughter," Mr. Swanson said, waving at the bashful pair. "My son Mr. Laurel Swanson."

Mary nodded to the young boy, perhaps all of fifteen and with a terrible case of pimples.

"My daughter Miss Lucy Swanson."

A pretty girl with dimples and ringlets curtsied, her eyes lingering on Duncan.

Mrs. Swanson invited all to sit. "Lucy is to have her come-out this year. The most important year of a woman's life, as you know, Lady Mary."

Ah, yes, and so it began. Mrs. Swanson was already angling for an invitation to one of the Duchess of Annick's parties. Such invitations were coveted, and attendance would launch the girl into the best of Society. It was not lost on Mary that Mrs. Swanson chose the honorific of a duke's daughter by which to refer to Mary rather than her married name of Lady Starrett. This told her everything she needed to know about Mrs. Swanson.

Turning to Miss Lucy Swanson, Mary said, "While I'm certain you've readied your wardrobe well in advance, allow me to recommend a London modiste. She'll ensure you have a dress fit for a duchess' ball."

On cue, Mrs. Swanson and her daughter simpered and tittered. Had Mary been of low breeding, she would have rolled her eyes. Instead, she spoke at length about the shades and hues that would best suit Miss Lucy's hair and eye color and the invitations they should accept above all others. Implied but not spoken was Mary's intention to ensure Miss Lucy received an invitation to the annual ball. She would, of course. Not because she liked the Swansons, but because they were neighbors, and Mary knew the way of the world.

Duncan carried on his own conversation with the gentlemen, having a grand time from Mary's estimation. Also not lost on her, but certainly lost on Duncan, was Miss Lucy's more than obvious overtures with her eyelashes, paying more attention to him than to her mama or Mary. Smug was an understatement for how Mary felt about that.

The drawing room door opened, stealing everyone's attention.

A shabbily dressed fellow stepped into the room. He looked to be about Mary's age, tall and slender with stubble on his cheek, long, straggly hair, and a nervous shake of the hand. Mary disliked him on sight.

How discourteous, she scolded herself.

Mr. Swanson stood and waved a hand to the man. Mary could not help but notice Mrs. Swanson's wrinkled nose. Miss Lucy grimaced. Only Mr. Swanson and his son seemed pleased with the newcomer's appearance in the drawing room.

"Please, join us, Robin." Mr. Swanson turned to Mary and Duncan, his arm around the young man's shoulders. "May I introduce my nephew to you? This is Mr. Robert Preston, my sister's boy. He's staying with us. Robin, these are our neighbors, Colonel Sir Duncan Starrett and Lady Mary Starrett."

"Colonel?" Mr. Preston asked. "Of the Army?"

"Yes, for the length of the Flanders Campaign," Duncan said.

"Ensign Preston at yer service, sir." He saluted Duncan, making a grand show of it.

"Well, well!" Duncan exclaimed, shaking Mr. Preston's hand with vigor. "An honor, Preston. Which regiment?"

In less than a minute, the two were engaged in an enthralling discussion of their military histories, enamored with the acquaintance. Mary cringed. The man was appalling.

A Bristolian, his accent gave him away. The voice was nasal, as though he had a chill, the words catching at the back of his throat. With an extra *l* added to words that ended in a vowel, an exaggerated *r* to words ending in *r*, and a missing *l* on words that ended in *l*, everything he said grated Mary's ears. Not that she held his voice against him. *Everything* about him annoyed her.

His demeanor was no more appealing. He was blunt to the point of abrasive and wore an expression so flat and reserved that Mary could not read him. Nephew of Mr. Swanson or not, Mary would wager he hailed from less than savory origins. She hated to begrudge Duncan a newfound friend, but did the man have to be so low?

Duncan appeared to notice none of the man's lesser qualities. The two carried on until it was well beyond the polite time to depart. Mary made conversation with the Swansons as best she could, hoping they did not realize the passage of time but knowing they did. How mortifying. For an additional fifteen minutes, she attempted to get Duncan's attention. Only when she stood and said louder than necessary that it had been a lovely visit, but they must depart, did Duncan finally notice.

All stood and bade farewell. All except Mr. Preston. He had the audacity to follow them to the drawing room door.

"It's been a pleasure, Robin," Duncan said with a familiarity he had not expressed half an hour ago. "I'll send a card. You must join us for dinner soon."

Mary bit her tongue.

Duncan admired Mary's profile against the buff carriage seat. She watched the scenery as they trekked home, unaware that the view across from Duncan was far superior to whatever snowy mess was outside.

Although the Swansons were neighbors, it was still a fair distance from Sidwell Hall given the unsavory road conditions. The coachman would have to go back through the village for a more accessible route.

While part of Duncan's attention remained at the stables, fretting over how the stablemaster was handling the training, he had managed to enjoy the past few days. It felt good to socialize. And nothing would beat the pride he felt with Mary on his arm.

What a fortunate day it had been! Not only to have spent it with Mary in good company but to meet a fellow soldier. Duncan did question if the chap had not sampled too much of the laudanum before joining them in the drawing room, but regardless, it was a pleasure to speak with someone who shared the kinship of war. From what Duncan gathered, Robin was convalescing with his uncle's family, a quieter and more comfortable setting than his own home.

The first thing Duncan would do upon returning home would be to send an invitation to dinner. Would tomorrow's dinner be too soon? Surely not.

"Mary, love, would tomorrow be too soon?" he asked.

"Too soon for what?" She untied her bonnet strings, setting the hat on the seat next to her.

"Inviting Robin to dinner."

She frowned. "Ought we?"

Duncan met her frown with his own. "Why would we not? It's been a long while since I've had the opportunity to talk to someone of my ilk, Lord Altonwey not included."

"Yes, well, Mr. Preston is not really of your ilk, is he? There's something shabby about him. I don't mean to be rude. He's probably a kind man. But I don't think he's quite the type we ought to invite to dinner."

Folding his arms over his chest, he said, "He's only just returned from war. I looked no less shabby when I came home. In fact, I'd wager I looked far worse."

"But that's you, and this is him. I don't trust the look of him."

He was positive he wore a ferocious scowl. He felt ferocious. Granted, he did not know the young ensign personally, but he would never judge someone from a single look. She had not even conversed with him.

Duncan's irritation was too pronounced to attempt an explanation for why the man may not look his best. What would she have thought to see Duncan after his father brought him from one hospital to the next, an unpleasant ship voyage in between? He had been living on gruel for over a month, bedridden from the surgery to remove the ball from his lower back. He had looked frightful. Would she not have trusted him upon seeing such a sight?

"I'd like to invite him to dinner. If you spoke to him, perhaps your opinion would change."

Mary pursed her lips and lifted her chin, her gaze returning to the scenery.

The remaining drive was silent. The chill in the air had once enticed him to warm her in at least ten different ways upon returning home. Now, it settled as ice in his veins. However ridiculous it was to be irritated over an ensign he did not know, he felt justified in his annoyance. The Mary he knew would never judge a man based on one meeting.

By the time they arrived at the hall, Duncan had not decided if he should bring up dinner again or invite the ensign without Mary's approval. He did not have long to dwell on the answer. Mr. Sherman, the new butler, greeted them with a letter arrived by royal messenger.

Mary followed Duncan into the parlor. Breaking the wax seal, he opened and read the contents. Had he been alone, he might have tucked it away so she could not read it, but as it happened, she waited with expectant brows raised.

"It's from the prince." He folded the letter and handed it to her.

"The Prince of Wales? He wrote to you?" Taking it from him, she opened it and scanned the contents. "It's another invitation to the officer's ball. I'd forgotten about it, with all that's happened. He's questioning why you've not accepted the invitation. Duncan, I do believe this is being held in your honor, or at least partially so. Now that you're well again, we can go. Oh, this is delightful! Send a note of acceptance right away."

Taking the letter from her, he folded it and slipped it into his waistcoat pocket. She watched him, her eyes bright with excitement.

"You want to attend?" he asked.

"Of course! Aren't you looking forward to it?"

He grimaced. "Not especially. It's a ball to honor the great heroes of war — the officers. What of the men who served under them? What of soldiers without rank? What have any of us done to warrant celebration? It'll be an evening for people like Altonwey to preen their peacock feathers, deserving or not."

His definition of heroism and that of his fellow officers differed. He believed in a lasting effect, something that influenced well beyond the immediate and the self. A field maneuver was a far cry from heroism in his eyes. Though Crown and country felt otherwise, he was not a hero.

If he could realize success with the training and create a program that would affect the whole of the cavalry, that could be heroic. How many lives would he save with better bred and trained horses? If he could somehow tie in officer training, all the better. There was so much potential in the plan. So much to make him worthy of the accolades.

Mary eyed his waistcoat pocket, as though re-reading the letter through the fabric. "Can you not accept the honor on behalf of your men? Represent your regiment by attending."

"Pretty words, Mary. You just want an excuse to attend a ball at Carlton House."

It took her a moment to realize he was teasing. His wink did the trick.

Once she realized his intention, she laughed. "Hardly. I've been there. Prinny and Drake are friends, you forget. But I do want to dance with you. Think how dazzling that will be. We've never danced together. I want to. Let's. Please? Will you accept?"

Sweeping the back of his fingers down her cheek, he said, "If it'll make you happy, we'll go. I can't promise dancing, however. I do good to walk convincingly. You may not see my struggle, but it's there."

"What fun we shall have in London!"

"I'll accept the invitation on one condition. You agree to accompany me to Tattersall's."

She made a sour face. "I'm not fond of the new owner. He doesn't like women."

Duncan arched a brow. "Sounds like you owe me a story. Lucky for you, I've no interest in meeting with the owner. I merely want to purchase an Arabian."

"Well, that's a surprise. I thought you said they were temperamental."

"They don't make good warhorses, despite their popularity with officers, but I've always wanted one for my own personal enjoyment. You don't think Caesar would be jealous, would he?"

Mary laughed.

The event he had been dreading changed shape, forming itself into an evening of promised pleasure. Archer would be there. As would other officers he knew and liked. Above all, Mary would be with him.

His directive was clear. This ball would mark his success, his worthiness of a duke's daughter and the baronetcy. Rather than enter the ball as the fallen officer, the injured who could not return to service, he would enter as a conquering man, the colonel who would make an influence beyond his call of duty. The meeting with Archer and company would be in April, the ball in May. By the time they went to the ball, all would know if the training demonstration was a success and if a program contract had been signed.

So much was at stake. Their financial security, his pride, his worthiness.

He could not afford to be distracted again. Several days had been lost calling on neighbors. He never should have left the training yard. The stablemaster, though he meant well, did not know the intricacies of cavalry formation and commands. The little bit Duncan showed him would have helped, but Duncan had no doubt this time away slowed the training. He could not rely on others to complete the task as efficiently as he could.

From this point forward, he would train harder, faster, and better. In the end, it would be worth the effort, for he would be the hero Mary and Bernard needed.

Chapter 23

Mary awoke the next day to an empty bed. She broke her fast alone. She met with the steward, housekeeper, and butler alone. She visited the nursery alone.

The past several days had been blissful. Four days. Four days of them spending time together, being a partnership wherein they raised their son together, met with neighbors together, ate together, rode together, conversed together. Four days. Her words had fallen on deaf ears if he thought that was enough.

She wanted this program as much as he did, perhaps more so since it had always been her dream to breed horses, but it was not something she wanted someone else to do for her. This was something she wanted to share with Duncan, the two working in tandem, both with the training and breeding. She had said as much. He had heard nothing, or so it appeared to her.

The second Mary completed her morning tasks, she donned her riding habit and headed for the training yard. If he was determined to do this himself rather than lead instructors to use his techniques, then so help her, she would convince him she was capable of training alongside him. It was not as though she had never trained a horse. Athena was a product of her training. Mary had no way of knowing how a warhorse needed to be trained, though, nor what Duncan's technique was, but she was a quick study. They would do this together or not at all.

Swatting the riding crop against her palm, she marched through the stable block past curious grooms, ignoring the calls of the stablemaster, and proceeded to her husband. He was leading one of the horses over a low bar. Excellent. The first stages of teaching a horse to leap. Her specialty. She had always been superior at leaps.

"Good form," she said as she approached.

Duncan looked away from the horse, his brows furrowed, his lips pursed. "What are you doing here? I gave them strict orders not to allow you in the yard."

"Did you? That was foolish." She thwacked the crop against her skirt.

"I can't afford to be distracted. I still have the other three horses to introduce to the bar. The clock's ticking, Mary. I'll join you later today. Go back." He turned to the horse.

"I'll work on the next horse while you finish with this one."

"No," he snapped. "It'll be faster and more efficient if I do this myself. You're costing me precious time."

Mary barked a laugh. "Because training one horse at a time versus two or even four is an efficient use of time? I may not be familiar with your technique or how a warhorse's leap differs from a traditional horse's, but I do know how to train a horse to leap. Far better than you, I would wager. I'll fetch Pegasus while you finish with Trident."

Waving a groom to take his reins, he stepped over to her. "Mary. No. We can sort out how you can help once this training is completed, once we have the contract. Until then, let me do this. I've wasted too much time as it is. I can't afford to lose more days ensuring you're doing everything correctly. I certainly can't be distracted by your presence in the yard. Go back inside. We can ride together in a few days. Will that suffice?"

Though it quivered, Mary raised her chin. "The past four days were wasted time?"

"Fire and brimstone. You know what I mean."

"Perfectly."

With a curt about-face, she left him to his training. Schooling her features so the staff would not see how upset she was, she returned to the inner courtyard and past the stables. She could not know if he doubted her prowess as a horsewoman, did not want to be with her, was prejudice against her sex, or otherwise. What she did know was this program was not more important than her marriage.

If she accepted what he said about his solo training being only for this short stretch, then she supposed she could harness patience, but she knew once the contract was secure, future training would be much the same. Duncan was too proud and too stubborn not to insist on being the head trainer. Even with the contract, he would still make the same argument, never mind the pressure of time would not be upon them. All speculation, she supposed, but she felt assured she was right. If she did not set boundaries now, she would lose him to the stable yard and be blocked from their collaboration in the cavalry program.

Lost in thought as she was, she nearly missed the man coming up the drive on foot.

Halting, she stared dumbly as he approached. Who was thick enough to walk here on foot in this weather? The sun had risen with her this morning, the first sight of it in days, but it had not stayed long enough to melt the now dingy snow. The temperature alone should discourage a lengthy walk.

The figure loomed closer, face burrowed in a coat that had seen too many winters, hat tilted forward to block the wind.

"May I help you?" she asked, her tone more accusatory than cordial.

He missed a step, startled by her voice. It would seem she was not the only one so lost in thought she did not pay attention to her surroundings.

Recovering with a foot shuffle, he looked up. "Milady! A proper welcome for me, yer bein' here, innit? I never expec'ed such fanfare."

Of all the people she could see today, Mr. Robert Preston would be the last.

"Our meeting is purely coincidental, I assure you, Mr. Preston. Have you come to call on my husband?

"I were surprised by the missive, but as luck wou'ave it, I'm available. Where's the good colonel?"

"Missive?" she asked, not liking being at a disadvantage to this shabby creature.

His glassy eyes met hers, accompanied by a smile that inched too slowly across his face. If ladies gambled, she would wager he was in his cups. Laudanum? Gin? She could not say, but he teetered ever so slightly on his feet, his movements lethargic, his expression far too serene.

"The good colonel's le'er. About trainin' warhorses. Said were time sensitive. Here I am! Not been
on a horse since summer, mind. Itchin' t'ride. Nothin'
like ridin' in the cavalry. Nothin' like it." His glossed
eyes looked away, as though he drifted into a memory
or dream.

"My husband invited you to train the horses?"

Politeness was ingrained. She could make a rat
feel welcomed and comfortable in a drawing room.
And yet her tone and words to this young ensign
spoke volumes about her feelings and mood.

It was not fair for her to dislike him, but she did.
He was grubby, low, and inebriated. What really irritated her was that Duncan had invited *him* to help
with the training but barred her.

Mr. Preston rubbed his nose with a gloved hand.
"Show me the way. Eager t'train some warhorses."

"You should know, he has a special technique. The
horses are only to be trained his way."

The man stared at her as though she were daft.
"He's t'teach me, mind. Not that I need teachin'. I'm
a fine cavalry officer in me own right. But if he wants
it done proper, I'll do it. Make the colonel proud."

"You'll find him in the stable block. Good day, Mr.
Preston." She dismissed the man with a nod and proceeded to the hall.

Heavy footed, she climbed the stairs to her bedchamber and rang for her maid to change her into a
warm day dress. Had she not been so angered, she
would have taken Athena for a ride. It was for the
best she did not. One ought not ride angry.

Once changed, she made her way to the nursery. Bernard's chill was improving with far fewer

sneezes and sniffles, but he remained in the nursery until Mrs. Eloise gave her consent. Until that happened, Mary made a point to visit throughout each day. She was determined to be the mother her own was not. For hours each day, she played and read, hugging Bernard and kissing the top of his head as often as she could, never wanting him to know a day without love.

Easing the door open, she poked her head in. Bernard was sitting on his bed, rolling the wheeled horse she had given him at their first meeting. Mary tugged at her bottom lip with her teeth. What a dear boy. She caught Mrs. Eloise's attention before Bernard could spot her. The nanny, seated by the window, a book in her hand, waved Mary into the room.

The *clunk* of the door drew Bernard's attention.

"Mummy!" he squealed, holding out his arms.

In quick strides, she crossed the room and pulled him into a hug. She buried her face in his hair, not wanting him to see her tears. He had never called her mummy before. And today was a day she needed it most. Dear boy!

Blinking wet eyelashes, she said, "You must be feeling better to be playing with your horse."

She leaned back and made herself comfortable at the end of his bed. Bernard nodded and pushed the horse to her with an accompanying neigh and snort.

"Where's Papa?" he asked. "He said we could go riding."

"Papa is working today. He's dreadfully busy, so we must entertain ourselves and wish him all the best."

He gave a little pout. "He said I must learnter ride if I wanter horse. I wanter rayben. May I have one?"

Mary wheeled the horse between them, making it rear on hind wheels until Bernard giggled. "A rayben?" Mary questioned. "I've met a great many horses, but I'm uncertain I've met a rayben."

"You know. A raaaayben. Papa says they're temportle."

"Oh!" she said with a laugh. "An Arabian! Yes, he says they can be temperamental to train. I wouldn't know, for I've never tried. We'll have to take his word for it, won't we? If I tell you a secret, will you promise to hold it dear and not say a word?"

A rapid nod followed widening eyes.

"Right," she said, lowering her voice to a whisper. "I'm going to write to my brother to secure an Arabian for Papa. It'll be a grand surprise and our little secret. Promise not to tell?"

Bernard's jaw slackened. "Promise." Taking the wheeled horse from Mary, he said, "A real rayben. Do I get one too?"

"Oh, darling." She ruffled his hair. "Not yet. As Papa said, not until you learn to ride. Although, I did see you atop Caesar looking mighty dashing."

Now that she had said her plan aloud, she could not change her mind. Bernard would be expecting to see an Arabian arrive with his uncle when Drake and Charlotte visited.

As poorly as the day had gone, she wanted to change her mind. One day ought not affect her. Although, as focused as Duncan was on the training, he may not have time for a pleasure horse, at least not until they returned from London. Nevertheless, she wanted to do this for him, just as he had surprised her with the stallion and mares.

Had she known supper would be so disastrous, she never would have written her brother that afternoon.

So late training was Duncan that supper had to be postponed two hours, much to the consternation of the cook and Mary. After a long day with the only opportunity to see her husband being the barring from the stable yard, Mary was in a foul mood. She sat in the drawing room embroidering, her foot tapping a tattoo into the rug.

When the drawing room door opened, she nearly dropped her embroidery. Her concentration had been on what she would say to him rather than the needlework or her surroundings.

Duncan stepped inside, dressed for supper in a handsome ensemble that almost made Mary forget she was annoyed with him. Almost. Until Mr. Preston entered. The man wore the same attire in which he had arrived this morning and smelled so much like a poorly mucked stable stall, she had to wrinkle her nose to keep from sneezing.

Tossing her embroidery onto the table in careless abandon, she stood, her hands folded at her waist.

"Mr. Preston. I hadn't realized you would be joining us." Another rude comment she never would have made under normal circumstances.

But then, these were not normal circumstances. In any other situation, she would have welcomed the person as though she had not only expected them but been looking forward to their company. This man, however, was not the company she desired. She had not been consulted. In fact, her opinion had been dismissed, as she recalled sharing with Duncan only yesterday her thoughts on the ensign joining them for dinner.

Duncan stepped forward, a smile on his lips, though the dark underside of his eyes revealed how exhausted he was from the day.

"Mary, love, I've invited Robin to join us. I knew you would understand. He's been an irreplaceable help today. I've asked him to come as often as he can to continue to help. As useful as the stablemaster is, he's unfamiliar with the needs of cavalry. Robin and I spent much of today discussing my techniques."

"Yer husband's a right smart man, milady," Mr. Preston said.

Mary did not respond to either of them. She nodded and proceeded into the dining room, leaving them to follow.

Cook would be up in arms downstairs. Not only two hours late, but now an unexpected guest. Should she wish to serve Duncan cold coffee in the morning, Mary would defend her.

Mr. Preston sat at the far end of the table with Duncan, away from Mary, a blessing since he could not insult her olfaction. The dining room table was not large, not like that of Lyonn Manor. Of course, Lyonn Manor also had two dining rooms, a lesser and a formal. Neither of them was as small as the one at Sidwell Hall. She preferred it this way. Well, except for when there was an unpleasant guest. As isolated as she felt at the far end of the table, the proximity with Mr. Preston was still too near.

By the end of the first course, the two gentlemen had all but forgotten her presence. They talked of the training mostly and Duncan's vision for the remaining time. From what she could glean, she had a fairly accurate visual of what he planned for the London demonstration, although without knowing the methods, she could not recreate the training.

When her patience wore thin at being ignored, she cleared her throat in dramatic overture. "Mr. Preston. What brings you to the Swanson's, and how long do you plan to stay?"

He wiped his mouth with the linen. *Wiped*. Mary shuddered at his table manners. A heathen if ever she saw one.

"Robin, milady. Mr. Preston's me father. I'm just Robin."

"Yes, well, 'just Robin,' what brings you to Durham?" Her posture adjusted to oppose his, her spine straighter than normal, her chin higher than ever, her lips pressed tightly.

How her mother could shake a man in his boots with a single stare, she could not say, but she wished in this moment she could summon such powers of persuasion. Finding her inner Catherine was not something she had ever before wished.

Eyes narrowed, she glared at him as he spoke.

"Convalescin, milady. Home's too small'n'noisy. Me mum's family may be well t'do, but me mum run off with her true love, a miner, as t'were. She's me uncle's favorite sister. He's what bought me commission, me uncle. I were proper grateful."

"And…" Mary's voice trailed off, hoping he would answer her questions. When he did not, she asked, "That brings you to Durham why, exactly? And for how long? You don't appear to be injured."

"It's in me head, innit."

"I see." She did not see.

Her eyes flicked from Duncan to "just Robin." Duncan's head bobbed as he listened. From his expression, however tired, she gathered he saw what the man meant. She did not.

The man added, "Me uncle's house is quiet. Gives a man a chance to think. Gotta' quiet the noise in the old noggin."

"Quite." She returned her attention to her meal.

Mr. Preston was not finished. It seemed once the man began, he could not stop.

"Me aunt wants me out. But it weren't her house. If me uncle says I stay, I stay. I don't wa'a be where I'm not wan'ed. Don't suppose you have room for a guest?"

"No," she said before Duncan could feel hospitable. "I'm afraid not, Mr. Preston. My family arrives within the week."

That brought the conversation around to the family visit, which, given it was her family, should have included her. Alas, their guest turned to Duncan to ask about the family, leaving her out of the conversation once more.

She listened to the conversations that followed, bored and excluded. Neither tried to include her. In some cases, she could understand, such as the stories of soldiers they both knew. Once supper concluded, she was shocked to find they planned to stay behind with port and cigars. Without her.

That may be the life to which most women were accustomed, but not Mary. Mary had always been one of the men, so to speak, unless other ladies were present, and then she would entertain them while the men shared private conversation. There were no other ladies present this time. And yet it was made clear the men would join her in the drawing room after port and cigars. *Join her*. She was ousted from the room.

In a sulk, she returned to the drawing room and wrenched her embroidery off the table. Had there been a pianoforte, she would have played the most obnoxious tune of her repertoire to annoy them from the other room. To that end, she needed to purchase a pianoforte for the hall. How were they to teach Bernard to play? Or entertain guests? Or annoy husbands and ensigns? She would use dowry money if she had to. McLarren would know what was best.

For ten whole minutes, she stabbed at her woman's work, taking out her frustration on the unsuspecting muslin. When she dropped her needle the third time, she huffed. Tossing the tambour back on the table, she returned to the dining room door, pressing her ear against the wood. Not the most ladylike of behaviors, but no one had ever accused her of possessing ladylike qualities.

"And I said to him," Duncan was explaining, "'Your knapsack will be lighter.'"

Mr. Preston howled with laughter at whatever the joke had been. "That's why you made it, sir. You've a sense of humor."

"What are your plans, Robin? Are you returning or selling out?"

"Don't know. Nothin' else to do. What's a man like me t'do? I've nothin' but the Army. If I had somethin', I would sell out. Can't close my eyes without seeing it all. How do you do it?"

Mary could hear the creak of a chair, someone shifting position.

"It's all about having a mission. When my attention is focused, I'm too preoccupied to remember."

The clink of glass, a bout of silence, another clink.

"Laudanum helps, I've found," Mr. Preston said. "One drop and the dreams stop. Don't suppose you have any? Feelin' the old cramp. Shoulda brought me bottle. Could use a drop in me wine."

"Afraid not, Robin. I had enough of it under physician orders. When I first arrived, I instructed the steward remove all bottles from the hall, assuming there were any. Have you tried focusing your attention elsewhere? The horse training may help."

"You've the grand life, sir. A wife and family and all. How old's the boy? Memory's not what it used to be."

"Three. He turned three in July. Mary wants to hire a tutor soon."

"I woulda' liked a tutor. Couldn't afford one, not on a miner's salary, not with twelve kids to feed."

She could hear Duncan's chuckle from the other side of the door.

"I told her a village education would do."

"Cor. Wha' you do that for?"

"To antagonize her. I had a village education, you know. Wasn't because my parents couldn't afford a tutor but because they thought it would humble me. I want the best for my boy, Robin. He'll have the finest tutor I can afford. Don't let on to Mary, though. I want to tease her about it some more before I consent."

"You're a lucky man, sir. If I had a family, wouldn't go back."

Another creak of a chair.

"I enjoyed it," Duncan replied. "It wasn't roses and sunshine, but I was good at what I did. I would have returned had it not been for the injury. I hadn't planned on leaving when I did, still had a few more years in me."

Mary stepped back from the door, not wanting to hear more. She studied the wood grain. It took all her might not to weep in the doorframe. He had not planned on leaving the Army. He was to leave her waiting several more years. He would have returned to war. Never had Mary felt so small, so insignificant, so unwanted.

Picking up her embroidery, she took it upstairs, leaving the men to entertain themselves for the remainder of the evening.

Sunlight reflected in the puddles of melted snow. From the look of the turn in weather, there would be no snow for the twelve days of Christmas, merely the leftover sludge from the snow of earlier in the month.

Duncan hated that her family would be seeing the park at its worst, covered in frosted mud and remnants of dirty snow. They were due to arrive two days after Christmas Day, wanting to celebrate the day of with their family, the Earl and Countess of Roddam. They would then spend the remaining days of Christmas at Sidwell Hall before arriving at their ultimate destination in Durham for the charity concert on Twelfth Night.

Had it not been for the demands of the training, he would have packed up his little family to spend Christmas Eve with his parents and brother's family, and then Christmas Day with her family and cousin. As it was, he could not afford to lose the time.

The training was the most important. He had to prove to the Army his technique was superior. Once they contracted him to breed and train warhorses, all would be well. He could relax and work at his own pace. Mary's ideas for training instructors were nothing short of brilliant, and he would be able to do that once this contract was signed. If he botched this opportunity, they would lose the chance. He would not allow her dream to wither because of his own negligence.

He worked hard that day from sunrise to sunset. Robin helped. The man may be a laudanum addict—for reasons only a fellow soldier could understand—but he was a dashed fine cavalryman. He knew the moves and necessary training. Further to his credit, though he arrived both mornings in a laudanum daze, he did not drink a drop all through training, remaining focused on his task.

It did not take long for Duncan to explain and demonstrate his technique to the young ensign, the light touches that would make all the difference in the horses understanding the commands and moving as agile as a dancer. It was good, especially, to have someone who understood the battlefield to help ready the horses for the noises, sights, and smells, something Duncan alone could not recreate with authenticity.

So long was the day, Duncan missed supper. To his dismay, he even missed reading to Bernard. The boy was fast asleep when he arrived in the nursery. Even Mary was breathing deeply, her inhales punctuated with soft ladylike snores.

The night before had been far more enjoyable with Robin joining them for supper. It was good to talk to someone who understood. There was a kinship between soldiers, sentiments understood that never need be spoken. There were those like Charles Brumley, now Lord Altonwey, and then there were those like Robin. Duncan bemoaned the system, for advancements were nothing more than purchasing a higher commission, leaving those with wealth, like, Altonwey, to advance through the ranks, while the good ones, like Robin, to remain junior officers. True, the higher ranks were promotion based, but not the field officers. Too many of those field officers were like Altonwey, pompous, arrogant fools. They flexed their muscles and preened their feathers but let the enlisted do the work. The few, the good, were like Robin. They kept their muscles and feathers to themselves and rode in formation, sacrificing themselves to protect their men. Duncan could relate to Robin. He could not relate to Altonwey. It was the good men who paid the dearest price in the end, of course.

He wondered if Mary could understand. Altonwey was from her world. Robin was not. Could she understand that some friendships broke social barriers? When he had come to bed the night before, she had been angry, though she had not explained why. He suspected it was because she did not like Robin, proving she did not understand what Robin had been through or why Duncan valued his newfound friendship.

Tonight he dared not wake her. His body was beyond the point of exhaustion. Once the contract was signed, he would make it up to her. Only a couple more months.

Duncan nestled next to her, wrapping his arm around her and tucking his hand between her side and the sheet. Inhaling that lovely lavender scent that was home to him, he tugged her close.

The next day, he woke before Mary. Her head rested on his chest, her legs twined with his. He extricated himself as gently and silently as he could, not wanting to wake her. It would be another grueling day. He needed to work on the leaps, an eighteen-day training schedule that would move from leaping over bars and narrow trenches to leaping at a gallop over hedgerows and wide ditches. They had only just begun training to leap over a bar.

He worried he was pushing the horses too quickly. Ideally, they should be spending a month on each training block, not a week. As it was, he was doubling up the training to teaching each month's worth of skills per week. Thank heavens for studious and tame horses, even if they were stallions.

But how much time would he lose with her family here? He could not spend all day, every day, training horses with them present. In a small way, he resented their coming. The timing was terrible.

Once dressed in his riding gear, he trudged to the stables. He would start the morning with a ride on Caesar, then take out the breeding stallion Galileo. The mares and Athena could wait for Mary or the grooms. As soon as Robin arrived, they would begin training in earnest. The young man was set to

arrive at sunrise, plenty of time for Duncan to take
out their stallions by pre-dawn light.

For the whole of the morning, he bemoaned his
exhaustion. It had been a good night's sleep, but his
body disagreed. It felt as worn as the night before. To
his embarrassment, he stumbled twice in the stables.
His feet dragged. Acutely, he was aware of the disadvantage not to feel his feet, something he had not
worried about in some time since he was now well-ac-
customed to walking by the feel of his hip's gait. The
stumbles were nothing to concern him, products of
exhaustion, nothing more. He would feel spry with
a few good nights' worth of sleep, once the training ended.

The sooner the London trip, and the sooner this
contract was signed, the better. If he could hand
over the training to someone competent, he would,
but no one could do this as efficiently as he, and
he would not risk it until he knew for certain the
instructors were competent enough to replace him
as trainer.

He worked through nuncheon, worked through
tea, and though he was starving, missed supper yet
again. As with the day before, Bernard was asleep
when he slipped into the nursery. At least Cook had
left him a covered plate in the kitchen, which he
devoured with relish before heading to his dressing room to wash off the stench of horse sweat and
dress in a nightshirt and robe. Throughout his dressing, he rubbed dry eyes, vision blurring from the
need to sleep. Soon. Just get through the training.
Then he could sleep until noon if he wanted. Once
washed and dressed, he stumbled groggily into the

lord's chamber, a hand on the door frame for added support.

This time, when he arrived in the bedchamber, Mary was not asleep in bed.

Duncan's wife sat at the table by the hearth, drumming her fingers.

"Mary, love, why are you still awake?"

One look told him she did not have a migraine. Her foot tapped the same irritation as her fingers, her lips pressed together. She glowered at him from across the room.

"I could ask you the same question," she countered.

Running a hand through his hair, he said, "You know what I've been doing. I hadn't meant to keep you awake. As kind as it is, you needn't lose sleep to wait for me."

She bit back a laugh, her lips twisting in anger. "I needn't wait for you for anything, for you're nothing more than a ghost. You've given me four days in two weeks. Those four days were hard won. Your son hasn't seen you once in two days, and before that, he could only see you if he braved the snow. Do you even know if he's well or still sniffling? Rather than spend time with us, you're with that dreadful man all day. Is his company so much better?"

Duncan crossed his arms over his chest and leaned against the bedpost. "He's not dreadful. He's helpful. And you know very well I'd rather spend time with you and Bernard than outside in the cold or with someone I've only just met."

"Prove it. Let the stablemaster do his job. We've already been through this conversation. Do I need to explain the problem all over again?"

"This isn't my choice, Mary, but something I must do to make our dreams a reality. Those four days stalled the training. The grooms did their best, but their best wasn't good enough. I've had to spend precious time retraining what they were supposed to have done. And now I wonder what's to happen when your family arrives. I'll lose more time. My only hope is that Robin can fill my role for the time I'm not there."

"You trust him more than me? You won't allow us to train together, but you'll allow him to train in your absence?"

"He knows warhorses. You don't."

"Yes, I'm quite the dunce when it comes to horses. And such a great trainer is he that he needs to join us for dinner, as well?"

"Once. I've invited him once. Our acquaintance may be brief, but there's a kind of bond men share over war. You can't understand what that means. I appreciate and value him as a fellow soldier."

With a laugh, she said, "I appreciate and value the chambermaid, but I don't invite her to dinner."

"Can't you hear yourself, Mary? You sound like your mother. You hold his station in life over his head just as your mother would. Is this how you would have seen me had we not been neighbors? Robin is a fellow officer, and though his upbringing may be common, he comes from gentry, not unlike my own family. He understands me and what I've been through in ways no one else can."

In hushed tones, every few words cracking, Mary said, "Why can't I be the person who understands? Why won't you let me in?"

He rested his forehead against the bedpost. "There are things I can't and won't explain. What Robin understands is the same any devoted soldier would, things we understand without saying."

The hearth fire crackled in the silence that stretched. Despite the warmth, Duncan felt chilled. He wanted nothing more than to take Mary to bed.

Not until she touched his arm did he realize she had moved from the chair.

Squeezing his forearm, she said, "We're supposed to be partners. In everything. The program, raising Bernard, our marriage. I chose you because you always treated me as an equal. Now, you're treating me as some vapid woman. You can't keep doing everything on your own, not only because we should be doing them together, but because you're exhausting yourself. You may not see the dark circles beneath your eyes, but I do. You're working yourself too hard. I don't mean to speak so harshly, but it rips me apart to see you taking all of this on yourself and pushing beyond the point of sanity. Even now, your hand is trembling. You can scarce stand. The training is important, yes, but not more important than your well-being or our marriage. Will you allow the grooms to finish the training? Will you do this for me?"

He wrapped an arm about her waist and pulled her to him. "Let me get through this training, and we'll sort it all out then."

She pushed away from him. "You're not listening." With a stifled sob, she asked, "Are you doing this to pretend you're still in the Army? To forget you've married me? I overheard you, you know. I overheard you tell that man you wouldn't have left the Army had it not been for the injury. You would have returned. You would have left me *again*."

"Oh, Mary, no, no, no. Whatever you overheard isn't the whole of it. No, I didn't want to leave the Army, but neither did I want to be without you. I thank the injury for forcing my hand. If given the chance, I wouldn't go back, not now, not ever. You're my world now."

Stepping to him again, she rested her cheek on his shoulder. "Then desist all this foolishness. I would rather have you than this program. I wish I had never told you I wanted anything to do with horses. Had I known then, I would never have breathed a word."

Why did she not understand how important this was? If he could focus, if he could think straight, he could explain the importance to her, how vital it was this training succeed and how crucial he be the one to complete the training his round. If only he could focus.

Duncan rubbed her back before saying, "Once this is over, you'll think differently. I'm going to make this a program you're proud of. We've only a couple more months."

Throwing her hands in the air, she walked away from him.

Chapter 24

The Duke and Duchess of Annick arrived two days after Christmas Day. They did not come alone. Accompanying them were Theo and Catherine.

Mary nearly swooned when she saw her mother descend from the carriage. Her saving grace was Theodore wrapping arms around her leg and wanting to be picked up, a novel occasion since he typically did not like being carried. She focused her attention on him, avoiding confronting her mother who eyed every frozen ornament, plant, and stone outside the hall. Though Catherine's features remained as icy as the weather, Mary detected a sneer beneath the haughty veneer.

Despite the presence of her mother, Mary looked forward to her family's visit. The past two days had been difficult. Other than attending church on Christmas Day, she and Duncan had not spent more than their evenings together since the argument. Their interactions were tense, each believing themselves in the right. She saw his perspective. Really, she did. But she did not think he saw hers. What was this contract worth if by the end of it he was worn too thin? What was it worth if their relationship unraveled before the London trip? And who was to say he would relinquish control of the training even after the contract?

With her family present, she could put all such thoughts away and enjoy company. Bernard had been beyond excited at the prospects of playing with his cousin Theo. Mary had not the heart to mention Theo was all work and no play. Maybe Bernard would be good for him.

Oh dear. She had never breathed a word of Bernard to her mother. Did Catherine know? Surely, she must. Mary was surprised the dowager duchess even deigned to stay at the hall with an illegitimate child under the same roof. Catherine had at one time refused to visit her nephew's new baby because her illegitimate niece would be in residence as midwife. People did not change, least of all her mother. And yet the woman was here.

With Bernard at Mary's side and Theo on her hip, she eyed her mother as the dowager duchess walked about to peer through the garden gate, the gold-handled cane crunching against the gravel as she explored.

Drake and Duncan spoke as Charlotte approached to kiss Mary on the cheek.

Charlotte looked radiant. Her cheeks were pink and round. Impending motherhood became her. With the high-waisted, fur-lined pelisse, her pregnancy was noticeable, a sizable mound outlined in fashionable wool. Mary was uncertain when the baby was due, but she wondered if her sister-in-law would make it to London for the Season.

"You look wonderful!" Charlotte exclaimed. "There's a rosiness to your cheeks that's most becoming. Married life suits you as well as it does me."

Mary hoped Charlotte did not think her with child. She most certainly was not. Her courses had begun that morning, late but arrived, nevertheless. She also hoped Charlotte would not take too long of a look at Duncan for the dark half-moons under his eyes did him no justice. Though he slept deeply each night, it was not for long enough to recover, and he was not eating as he should. Instead, he worked sunrise to sunset in the cold. It was any wonder he had not yet collapsed. That was what worried her the most, and Mr. Preston's presence did not help matters since Mary believed he spurred Duncan's insanity to do this without the help of the grooms. Mr. Preston certainly would not be able to tell that Duncan's hands had developed a tremor, that he misstepped more than he should, that he could not concentrate as he ought. She could not see how Duncan could continue for another two months and two weeks. Somehow, she had to convince him to lead rather than do all the work. Somehow.

A hand resting on her belly, Charlotte leaned in to whisper. "The *you know what* is arriving with the luggage carriage. Though we stayed at the village inn, they managed to fall behind us. They should be along shortly. Let's get everyone inside so he doesn't see until we're ready."

Mary nodded, setting Theo down. Bernard wasted no time in taking his cousin's hand and dragging the boy inside with him.

"Come, everyone," Mary said. "We have tea in the drawing room."

Catherine was the first to accept the invitation, though she cast Duncan a long and assessing look before entering Sidwell Hall.

Spirits were high as the family took tea. Duncan's expression brightened with each passing minute, appearing to enjoy the camaraderie with his brother-in-law and the questions Charlotte volleyed about Starrett & Starrett's Cavalry Program. Catherine kept her mouth busy by nursing her teacup, listening to every word but saying nothing. Mary could feel her judgement as a looming cloud.

Bernard and Theodore spent most of the time in the nursery with Mrs. Eloise. Thrice, they made brave escapes to race into the room and antagonize the adults, much to the chagrin of the nanny, who was unaccustomed to keeping up with a hyper Bernard, usually quiet and well-behaved, much less two hyper boys.

Charlotte tittered each time Theo ran into the room, his hand in Bernard's, inseparable from his new best friend. "He's normally a strict follower of rules," she said as he raced back out of the room to follow the nanny and Bernard back to the nursery.

Mary had to agree with Charlotte. Never had she seen Theo so active or so wild, and yet here he was, racing in and out of a forbidden room as though he were a London street urchin.

"I don't know what's got into him," Charlotte said.

Mary's eyes flitted to Catherine, thinking she could read the woman's mind. *It's the company he's currently keeping*, she would be thinking. Bernard, the bad influence, for all illegitimate children were born of bad blood.

Drake laughed, "Denial, wife. Denial. You can deny it all you like, but he's mischievous when your back is turned. And I know just where he gets his antics." He winked, sending the duchess into a deep blush.

Mary refilled teacups and added new sandwiches and biscuits to each plate. "How are Sebastian and Lizbeth? How's Mr. Trethow? I would have dearly loved to join you for Christmas, but we've been busy with the program. With the trip to London so soon at hand, we daren't leave the training to servants."

Her eyes met Duncan's. He had not the courtesy to look abashed.

Did she resent that they had not celebrated Christmas Day? She supposed a little. Such a day had meant nothing at Lyonn Manor during her youth. Now that she had her own family, she wanted Bernard and any future children to know what it was to have family and good spirits.

"Splendid!" Drake said, his ringed fingers rubbing together with *clinks* of gold. "Our cousin, Lord Grumpy, didn't dare rain on the festivities. I believe I even saw him smile when he thought no one was looking. Lizbeth kept the children entertained. Mr. Trethow is the most devoted grandpapa a child could ask for. He kept them playing pantomime well past their bedtime."

"How are the children?" Mary asked.

"Good. They're children. What more is there to say?" Drake laughed.

Charlotte scoffed. "Men are terrible at this sort of thing. Freya has taken over the castle as lady of the manor since Lizbeth is in a delicate way. She bossed around the staff, ordered about the guests, and was as superior as a four-year-old could be. Her brother Cuthbert followed her everywhere to undermine her authority and undo all her actions. If she brought Lizbeth an herbal tea, he put one of her dolls into the teacup before Lizzie could drink it. If she brought Lizbeth a book from the library, he swapped it with a hairbrush."

Mary enjoyed the visual far more than anyone. Long hours she had spent in the nursery each time the family had visited Lyonn Manor.

Duncan turned to Drake. "What's this concert that brings you to Durham?"

"While my cousin invests his wealth, I can't give mine away fast enough," he said with a laugh. "All of my operas are written for charity. This one's for a little lying-in hospital not far from here. They've opened their doors thanks to some old man's trust—" He winced and laughed when Charlotte poked him in the side. "I mean, a notably generous benefactor, by way of a viscount, entrusted his money to open the hospital. I'm here to celebrate with a charity concert. All proceeds go to the hospital. If my fame as a composer is anything to judge by, they should be set for years to come."

Charlotte rolled her eyes at her husband's arrogance.

The drawing room door swung open to two stomping boys, the wheeled horse on a string bouncing behind them. Theodore ran past everyone and clambered onto his grandmama's lap.

Mary froze, the rim of her teacup touching her lips.

Catherine frowned at the boy.

In a voice of disdain, the dowager duchess said, "This is not how the Marquess of Sutton behaves, and certainly not the heir to the dukedom."

Theo ignored her, burying his head against her bosom. "Want one, Grandmama. Best toy ever. Want. Want. Want." He tugged at the wheeled horse.

Bernard walked up to them and picked up the horse. "Please, can he? It *is* the best toy ever. Mummy gave it to me."

He pointed at Mary. All eyes turned her direction. Her teacup remained poised.

Bernard set down the horse, moved the rope into Catherine's hand in case she might want to give it a tug, and then tried to climb on her lap next to Theo.

"What's the meaning of this?" Catherine asked. "I'm not a chair. Do I in any fashion resemble a drawing room chair? Young men sit properly in chairs of their own. I'll not be sat upon."

The boys stared up at her with wide, worshipful eyes, then climbed down, promptly finding chairs of their own. Theo struggled to climb into his, but with Bernard's help to hoist him, it was not an unsurmountable task. They both then sat as straight backed as Mary had ever seen them. Bernard trained his gaze on Catherine, who stared back at him.

Rubbing a finger under his nose, he said, "Are you my grandmama?"

The room itself seemed to hold its breath.

Mary set aside her teacup and saucer and stood. The gentlemen stood with her out of politeness. She would not allow her mother to bully her son. Running her palms down her dress, she readied to whisk him out of the room before Catherine could reply. She was moments too late.

"If you are my daughter's son, then logically, you are my grandson. However," she began with a long pause, "I will not have any grandson of mine *wipe* his nose, and certainly not with his *finger*. Disgraceful. If

you wish for me to play with this *thing* on a string,
you will have your nurse take care of that runny nose
before I can finish counting from ten. You do know
your numbers, don't you?"

Bernard nodded, made to rub his nose again, then
stopped.

"Ten. Nine. Eight." The dowager duchess began
to count down.

Bernard and Theo both scrambled out of their
chairs and raced to the door before she reached seven.

Looking up at everyone, Catherine appeared startled that they all stared at her. Mary held her breath.
The dowager duchess made to say something, but
the drawing room door opened yet again.

The butler stepped into the room and bowed.
"You are all summoned to the front drive," said Mr.
Sherman.

Mary tore her gaze from the woman mas-
querading as her mother and eyed a giggling
Charlotte and a winking Drake before looking to a
furrow-browed Duncan.

"The front drive?" Duncan echoed. "Whatever
could Mr. Sherman mean by sending us outside?"

They followed him, the dowager duchess included,
though she left the wheeled horse behind.

When Duncan stepped onto the drive, he was not
expecting the sight before him. An Arabian stallion,
black except for one white sock, stood majestic and
noble. Several grooms and the stablemaster surrounded the horse, reins in hand.

A glance to Mary told him all he needed to know. Her cheeks flushed. She looked away, as though embarrassed by her gift in the wake of their quarrel. Before all, even her mother, especially her mother, he strode to Mary. Snaking an arm around her waist, he tugged her to him, smacking his lips to her surprised ones.

The duke whistled. The duchess giggled. The dowager duchess harrumphed.

Releasing Mary, he approached the Arabian. He had always wanted one. Not that he would neglect Caesar or think any less of him, for Caesar and he shared an inseverable bond. Caesar was an extension of himself. That did not stop him from wanting an Arabian. They had no business being warhorses, but they made the finest personal horses.

This one was glorious. The coat glistened, reflecting the dull light of the sun with a fine sheen. The mane waved in the cold, winter wind. A proud beast. The horse knew he was grand. He knew he was superior. A fine stallion.

Duncan ran a hand over the haunches.

"He wants a kiss," the duke said.

Looking over, perplexed, Duncan wrinkled his brow.

The duke nodded to the stallion.

Looking back, Duncan realized there was a sprig of mistletoe perched on the saddle. He laughed, glancing back to the crowd.

"Go on! Kiss him!" the duke encouraged.

"Pucker up, colonel," the duchess teased.

With an exaggerated shrug, he walked around to face the stallion. "I know we've only just met, and this may be too soon, but what do you say we give the crowd what they want? It'll be our way of breaking the ice in our acquaintance."

As though on cue, the Arabian curled its lips and leaned to him, nipping at his face. Their audience howled with laughter. Duncan dashed a quick kiss to the stallion's muzzle.

Mary clapped her hands, a broad smile lighting her face. He had missed that smile. So focused he had been, he had missed a great many things, but that smile most of all.

"What's his name?" she asked.

He thought for a moment, running a hand down the horse's forehead. "Bucephalus."

A smattering of applause.

"Well, old boy," His Grace said, "take him for a ride. Let's see you on this champion."

There was little else he wanted from this day but to ride him. It was too soon, though, and he was not feeling his best. All morning, he had been stumbling over his feet. He was just so bloody exhausted. His muscles ached. His head ached. His eyes strained. Even in the drawing room, he experienced the peculiar sensation of skipping seconds, as though his mind and body were dozing to sleep while he remained erect and wide-eyed. At this rate, he would not last the two more months needed for the training. But he had to try.

Patting the horse, he was torn as to what to do. The crowd teased and cajoled. His inner voice begged to ride. He had no way of knowing the horse's prior experience or training. Riding was the last thing he needed to do straight away. And yet…

To the devil with doubts.

"I'll ride!" he shouted to the family.

More applause.

"Pardon me while I change first. Silk shoes and horses do not make a good combination."

And off he went, racing back into the hall and up the stairs to ring for Peter. His blood pumped in anticipation. His own Arabian! This never could have happened if he had become a farmer.

After only one misstep on the stairs, and one frustrating moment when he forgot why had entered the dressing room, he was back with the family, ready to ride. Admittedly, he was surprised his mother-in-law was still present. He had been certain she would return inside while he changed. His own cowardice had wanted her to return inside — the woman intimidated him as no Army general could.

With a broad smile to his audience, he approached Bucephalus.

For a few minutes, he stood with the horse, rubbing the neck, introducing himself, promising this would be their only ride until they could become better acquainted. His mind was already working out a training schedule that should not interfere with the warhorses. He needed to spend time with Bucephalus, not riding, but observing, being present, talking, allowing the horse to get to know him and become comfortable in his presence.

Handing the mistletoe to one of the grooms, Duncan hoisted himself into the saddle. The stallion was none too sure about such a movement. His ears went back, and he pawed the ground. Duncan rubbed the horse's neck, talking softly to him until he settled down. Bucephalus shook his head as Duncan situated himself on the saddle.

"Just a quick ride, eh boy?" he said to the stallion. "A quick ride, and then my man will spoil you. I do believe there's a loose box waiting for you, as well as new friends to meet."

Another shake of his head, the stallion pranced. Had the family not been looking on, Duncan would have dismounted. The stallion was not keen on being ridden today. Duncan ignored his voice of reason, wanting the family to be proud. His wife had purchased an Arabian for him, after all. He could not disappoint her. In some small way, he also wanted to prove to his mother-in-law he was a great horseman, someone who could provide for her daughter through the cavalry program.

With a squeeze of Duncan's calves, Bucephalus walked forward. All looked on.

The horse's gait was smooth. A grand ride indeed. Duncan whispered compliments to the stallion as they moved into a trot. After a wide circle about the front courtyard, he took off at a canter down the long drive.

The wind stung his cheeks. The skeletal trees saluted his passage. For the stretch to the gatehouse, he was back on the planes of the continent, riding reconnaissance, working out a strategy of approach. He drank in gulps of fresh air, feeling freedom at his fingertips. With an agile turn, he circled back. A sweet tempered and responsive horse beneath him, he cantered back to camp, ready to share with his men the plan of action. They would want to take the hill rather than the circuitous route. The view would be advantageous, and it would shorten their arrival, giving them the element of surprise. He looked about him, admiring the landscape.

The sight of the hall with the family gathered at front brought a moment of confusion. How had he arrived here? Was he dreaming of what could be because he did not want to return to camp? He would much rather explore this wondrous dream wherein he was married to his true love with a house of their own, a large home he could never afford, riding a horse he could never own. Such was the nature of dreams, allowing the impossible to be. The trouble of enjoying the dream was he could not tell if this was actually a dream or a hallucination. Was he on his way back to camp, or was he in his tent deep asleep? Unsure, he continued further into the dreamlike vision. A dread tightened his chest—what if he was still at Cois Greta Park, trapped in a laudanum dream?

Shaking the confusion from his mind, he settled back into reality—he was returning to camp and allowing his furtive imagination to play tricks on him. As he cantered forward, replaying what he would tell his men about the route, the front door of the illusionary hall opened. Bernard came running down the steps.

Blinking, Duncan shook his head again. What the devil was Eleanor's little boy doing away from the camp and participating in his fantasy? He slowed the horse to a trot, brows drawn.

"Grandmama!" the boy shouted. "Mrs. Eloise wipeded my nose!"

All turned to look at the boy just as he spotted Duncan.

"Papa! A rayben! I wanter ride!"

With those words, the boy raced towards Duncan, arms flailing, words squealing and tumbling together.

Bernard's name was shouted from the lips of those standing before the hall. Mary took off at a run after him. Duncan tilted his head, watching the scene, not understanding what he was seeing.

In a flash of sunshine reflecting on the steel of the garden gate, Duncan veered to the left to dodge the Frenchman's sword. His horse sidestepped and cantered forward. Why was Bernard on the battlefield? Good God, who let the boy onto the battlefield?

Duncan surged forward to protect the boy from the French soldiers. They were everywhere, swords drawn, bodies strewn, a sea of red and pain and fear. He had to get to the boy.

Bernard drew closer, Duncan driving the horse faster, the soldiers on the boy's heels.

As the soldier chasing the boy screamed, Duncan saw an ethereal Mary push past and grab Bernard. Something shifted in the world, and Duncan saw his in-laws watching in terror. Panicked, he squeezed his legs to stop the horse. The horse sidestepped but kept going, straight for Mary and Bernard. Afraid, confused, lost in a combination of realities, one superimposing over the other, he pulled the reins, hard.

The horse shuffled to a stop and reared on hind legs, coming back to the ground with a stomp of hoofs. As Duncan reached to grab the horse's neck, it reared again, tipping backwards and taking Duncan with him.

Arms wrapped around Bernard, Mary watched in horror as Duncan landed on his back, Bucephalus falling backwards with him and rolling over her husband's supine body before climbing to its feet.

Grooms surrounded the Arabian in seconds, calming him and ensuring he was uninjured. The stablemaster ran over to Duncan, who lay still on the ground. Mary could not move. Her legs were rooted. Her arms trembled about Bernard whose face was buried in her dress. Through the buzz in her ears, she heard someone approach behind her.

In the voice of a commanding officer, the dowager duchess said, "Go to your husband."

Spurred to action, she released Bernard and ran to Duncan.

The stablemaster knelt over his body. When he looked up at her, shaking his head, she knew she had seen the face of death. The world blurred, her palms making desperate swipes at her eyes. She raced forward and flung herself to his side.

"He's not breathing, my lady," said the stablemaster.

"Then make him breathe," she screeched.

The useless man only stared back to Duncan, as helpless as she.

Mary knelt at her husband's side, hands folded in prayer. They looked on for an eternity, her world crumbling before her.

With a shuddering gasp, Duncan's eyes flew open. He grabbed at the stablemaster's arm, struggling for breath. After several failed attempts, he sucked in air, gasping and panting.

He looked about him, wild-eyed and dazed. "Lieutenant Colonel," he said to the stablemaster. "Archer, they've taken my legs. I can't feel my legs. The sawbones took my legs. Go on without me. Lead the troops. Crest one more hill and you're there. Tell Mary I love her."

Taking his hand in hers, she said, "I'm here, Duncan. I'm with you."

He turned his head and stared at her, disoriented. "I'm sorry I couldn't come home to you. I'm so sorry. I only wanted to make you proud. I'm so sorry."

"But you are home," she insisted, squeezing his hand.

Men surrounded them, orchestrated by her brother.

Drake's strong arms pulled her away from Duncan. "We need to get him inside, Mary. Your butler's sending for the physician. Follow Charlotte. She'll take you into the drawing room."

"No. I'll stay with him." She fought off his grasp.

"Follow Charlotte, Mary. We'll send for you, but we need to get him inside."

An arm enveloped her shoulders. When she turned, it was to find Charlotte standing next to her. Nodding encouragement, Charlotte turned Mary back to the hall.

Chapter 25

Shadows danced on the canopy, partnering the reflected light of the hearth fire. Duncan stared at the four-poster canopy above him. Only a short while had he been awake, regaining consciousness from a blackness worse than death. Try as he might, he could not reach the bell pull. And so, he stared at the scene above him, waiting.

Through the pounding headache, through the throbbing pain in his back, through the dead weight of his legs, he recalled the events clearly.

Several times, he almost cried out, panicked about his son and the horse, about Mary. Each time, he stopped himself. In this moment, he lay in limbo, not knowing if they were well or injured. The fear of them being injured, of him having been the cause, was too great. He preferred the limbo. In limbo, he could pretend all was well. He could dash the image of them trampled beneath horse hoofs. With every ounce of willpower, he clung to one version of reality. He dared not call out and have it shattered. So help him, if he had injured them…

The bedchamber door opened and closed.

Duncan was afraid to sit up. Everything ached. Turning his head, a motion he regretted when it sent a stab along his spine and through his skull, he saw the duke approach and pull over a chair.

"How do you feel, old boy?"

"Like death," Duncan croaked, his voice hoarse.

"You gave us a scare. It's good to see you alive." His Grace rested elbows on thighs, steepling his fingers. "The physician is on his way."

"Where's my boy? Is he safe?"

"He's well and unharmed. He's in the nursery with my son."

Duncan exhaled, squeezing his eyes closed for a moment. "And Bucephalus? Did I harm him? It was my fault, not his. See that Roland, the stablemaster, looks after him. So help me, if I injured that horse…"

"He's fine. All is well. No one's injured but you, old chap. Before you ask, Mary is well, also, though she's pacing a hole in your drawing room rug. I take it you won't be joining us this evening for supper?" His Grace chuckled.

Grimacing, Duncan said, "Not unless you can bring the dining table in here and have the cook spoon feed me." He did his best to smile. "Will you do something for me, Your Grace?"

"Come, we're passed formalities. You're my brother. Drake, please."

"Will you take Mary with you?"

"Ho, ho," said the duke. "Wait one moment. What are you asking of me?"

"Take her with you. And Bernard. They'll be better off with family. I've failed them. I can't even ride a horse, much less train one. What do I have to offer them? Too many times this year I've seen the underside of a canopy. This is no life for them."

His brother-in-law cleared his throat, rubbing the back of his neck. "I can't tell you how to think or feel, but I can tell you my sister won't leave your side."

Duncan shook his head, a terrible move given how it made the room spin. "Try to convince her. She'll be better off. I'm not worthy of her. I can't even ride a bloody horse."

A knock on the door interrupted them, sending His Grace to answer.

After a few whispered words, the duke turned into the room and said, "I'll leave you to your thoughts. The physician has arrived from the village. I'll just have a word with the man before he comes in."

When Duncan did not answer, the door closed with a soft *thunk*.

Never had he been so humiliated. What sort of life was this for her to live with a man like him, bedridden yet again, a failure? He could not complete the training from bed. After all his work, he may never walk again. His injuries could be permanent this time. The training would not be completed. All her dreams, all their dreams, gone. What sort of horseman was he if he could not stay mounted? To endanger the horse as he did…to endanger his son…in front of the Dowager Duchess of Annick, no less. He wanted to weep, but his chest hurt too much for the effort. What a worthless pile of horse dung he was.

Mary paced, rubbing her arms with vigor though she was not cold. The physician had been with Duncan for over half an hour. She tried not to think of the ramifications of such a tumble. It had all happened so fast that she could not say how much of the horse had rolled onto him or what parts of him had been affected. What she could say was that it was a miracle the impact had not been fatal. As long as he was alive, any other injury did not matter. They could deal with anything. They had dealt with wheeled chairs before, had they not? She would need to write to his parents, of course.

The drawing room door opened. The butler showed in the physician. For the life of her, she could not even recall the man's name.

Drake stood and offered him a seat. Mary reached her hand to the window casing, holding herself upright. Her legs trembled.

"He is relatively uninjured, Your Grace," the physician said. "There's bruising and swelling on the right leg, most pronounced along the shin and foot, some bruising along his back, but I could ascertain no breaks or sprains. The worst injury is, what we call in my profession, a concussion. This is when the brain is, shall we say, shaken. Such a commotion in the skull results in lethargy, confusion, memory loss, among other problems."

Drake nodded. "Is it serious? Will he recover? Is there anything we can do for him to ease the pain?"

"No, no, it's not serious. In my experience, the brain rights itself within a fortnight. Encourage him to sleep as much as possible. The vibrations of the brain from the impact will still in their own time. He needs to sleep."

Mary gripped the window casing, worried she might collapse. He was well! He would be well! Two weeks, and he would be back on his feet.

She could not get into Duncan's bedchamber fast enough. Before she could race from the room, she had to play the polite hostess. She invited the physician to stay for dinner. He declined, to her relief. After idle conversation, they were able to send him on his merry way. For a quarter of an hour, she had worried he would never leave.

As soon as the butler showed him out, she cast her family a pleading look then mounted the stairs.

The door closed behind her with a creak. She stared, eyes riveted on the bed. Hesitation lingered, a moment's indecision. Should she run to him in glee? Should she let him rest?

Her decision was somewhere in the middle of her two choices—go to him but let him rest. Thinking he may be asleep from exhaustion or from the concussion the physician had mentioned, she crept to the chair next to the bed, careful not to make a sound.

Duncan lay with an arm slung over his eyes. She recalled the last time she had seen him like this, only at that time he had been unconscious and shirtless, bedbound at Cois Greta Park. Now he wore a shirt, the covers pulled to his waist, and though he did not move to acknowledge her, she knew he was well and not bedbound, not this time.

Moving the chair closer, she sat. It was not yet noon, but the curtains were drawn, the room lit only by the fire. The whole of the occasion mirrored the first time. Subtle differences marred the reflection. When she first went to him after receiving word from his father, the room had been sweltering hot. His parents had looked on as she took his hand. He had smelled of unwashed body, his cheeks rough with an early beard's growth. Now, he smelled heavenly, a mixture of cologne and horse. She inhaled and smiled. Her fingers ached to touch his close-shaven cheeks. No one looked on this time to see if she did.

Mary reached for his hand and began lacing her fingers with his.

He wrenched his hand away, folding it over his chest. She flinched at the unexpected rejection.

Without moving his other arm from over his eyes, he said, "Leave me."

Shifting in her chair, she tucked her hands under her legs. Despite the fire, the room was chilly. If she had been warmed by his presence and their fortune with his good health when entering the room, she was feeling an icy coolness now.

"I most certainly will not leave," she responded. "Did the physician explain everything to you?"

"Yes."

The answer was more of a grunt than a word.

"Good. Then you know all is well. He recommended rest for the next week or two, which I daresay you need regardless. And that's that. We couldn't have asked for happier tidings."

He did not respond. He did not look at her. For long minutes, he lay still and silent. The physician had listed the effects of the concussion, so she was in some way prepared for his behavior. That did not make it pleasant or acceptable. Her vision of the moment had been one of elation, one where they could share in celebration that he was well. She had even convinced herself halfway up the stairs that he could join them for dinner a time or two during his rest period, should he be feeling spry.

"Go home with your brother," he said.

Tears stung her eyes at yet another rejection. "Have I done something wrong?" Her voice was nought but a whisper.

"Go home, Mary. This will never work."

"I am home. What are talking about?" She swallowed, a lump in her throat. When he did not answer, she took a deep breath and said, "You're perfectly well. The physician said so himself. He said your head took a little shake and your leg and back are bruised, but nothing to cause concern."

Throwing his arm to his side in exasperation, he expressed with words of venom, "Don't you understand? It's over. I don't care what that leech says. I can't feel or move my legs. Just like before. I may never walk again. This time it could be permanent. No miracle surgery. Even if I do return to normal, it's no use. I can't even ride a horse without endangering you or Bernard. My mind is too addled. I'm of no use to either of you."

"You're exhausted is all. You could never harm us. The new horse was merely startled by Bernard."

He shook his head, then winced. "You said yourself, I made Bernard sick by encouraging him to stay at length in the cold weather, and now I've nearly trampled him, you along with him. I can't trust myself to protect either of you. I can't even provide for you, not without training those horses, not if bedridden. It's all lost. I can't train them in time, not now. I can't do anything except lie here, an invalid."

"They're trained well enough as it is. With what you've taught them already, we'll have something grand to show in London. They'll be impressed by all you've done."

"And who's to demonstrate if I can't walk? It's no use. They're not far enough along in the training." He moved his arm back over his eyes. "Even if they were, what does it matter if this is to be my lot in life? I told you before I didn't want a nursemaid, didn't want to be a burden."

"I know you want this, and I do, as well, but not at the risk of our happiness," she pleaded. "We can write to your contacts and tell them we're no longer interested. We don't need this. We always have my dowry."

"Stop. I'll not hear of it again." His tone was brusque. "A real man would provide for his family. With nothing to offer you, I don't qualify."

She stared at her lap, uncertain what to say. There was such despair behind his words, a man who had lost faith in himself. In her eyes, it had been only a tumble. Could one little tumble be the cause of this, or had he been feeling this all along, throughout their marriage, perhaps before their marriage? He had made it clear on several occasions he would not marry her unless he was able bodied, so had all his work since, all his training been his way to prove to her he was fit as a man, fit to provide for her? She wanted to rail against him for all of that being utter hogwash, but she believed this was deeper engrained. All she knew to do was face him with practicalities. If she could not convince him he was not unmanned, her only hope was to prove to him none of it mattered. He was a leader, after all, and could just as well lead from a chair.

Resolved, she said, "Then provide me with your technique, and I'll complete the training. If this is so important to you, let me do it."

"No," he said. "I'll not have you out there laboring long hours, not in the cold, not with horses. I'll not have you parading in front of the grooms riding astride. I'll not have it, Mary. This is not woman's work."

"I've trained before. Don't underestimate me. If you tell me your techniques, I can do it. The training can continue while you rest, and once you recover, we can continue the training together with the help of the grooms."

"It's not only the training. It's everything. There's something in me that's broken, Mary. I'm broken. My body doesn't want to work. My mind doesn't want to work. It was selfishness that drove me to marry you. I never should have. You deserve someone who can provide for you and protect you, not some broken man. Go home to your family. Leave me be."

Her lower lip trembled, but she raised her head high. "You are my family. And you're right about being selfish. How dare you give up on us, and our son, all because you overworked yourself to the point of exhaustion. What are you so desperate to prove? You're the most selfish, most stubborn man I know. Hardheaded and, at the moment, juvenile."

She waited for him to answer, watching the rise and fall of his chest as he breathed in and exhaled a frustrated breath.

Realizing he was not going to respond, she said, "I don't know why you've lost feeling in your legs again, and I don't care. Why? Because it doesn't matter. We've been through this before. I'm at your side regardless. We'll make it work."

He scoffed a laugh. "You're not listening. I don't want to make it work. I'm worthless. I'm helpless. I'm useless. I have a pounding migraine and just want you to leave."

"You, sir, are a horse's arse. It'd serve you right if I did leave you."

She stood, smoothed her dress with cold palms, and walked out.

Leaning against the window casing, Mary looked out to the front drive. She stared at the scene of the tumble only hours prior. He had been so excited about the Arabian. Not in a long time had Mary seen such elation, such wonder on Duncan's face, the enthusiasm with which he rode. How had it all gone so wrong and so quickly?

There had been a time or two in her youth when she had fallen from a horse, namely when she tried to sneak a ride on her brother's stallion before he gave her Athena. Though she had never had a horse roll onto her, she had not found falling off all that troubling. Her bum had been sore, but that had passed in a day. Why Duncan should be so despondent, she could not say. The physician was not concerned with the loss of mobility, as it was all to do with the impact of the fall and nothing more.

Was it all to do with the training? This was supposed to be a fun partnership with the breeding and training program, not a matter of upset.

She hugged her arms, the chill more than skin deep.

"Hiding, I see," said a haughty voice from behind her.

Mary closed her eyes. Her mother had found her. She rested her forehead against the window, the cold sending a shiver down her spine. With a sigh, she squeezed her upper arms with chilled fingers and turned to face Catherine.

"I'm surprised you're still here," Mary said. "After meeting Bernard, I was certain you would leave."

Catherine arched a brow. "He's a boy."

Mary snorted. "He's still illegitimate. His being a boy makes a difference?"

"Yes."

All she could do was gape at her mother as though the woman had sprouted two heads. Neither spoke, each glaring down the other.

Using the cane as a prop, Catherine navigated to a parlor chair. Once seated, she studied her daughter.

"It is different for a man than it is for a woman," Catherine said. "An illegitimate man can be accepted by Society should he wish, with the right family. A woman would never be given the opportunity. If the boy is intelligent and courageous, and if he desires acceptance, he shall have it, though some doors will remain closed. Mr. Bernard Starrett has gumption, something I value."

"And you accept him? Because he's a boy? Never mind that he's illegitimate?"

"Do we *know* he's illegitimate?" Catherine questioned. "From what I understand, he was born on the continent during a time of war. Who is to say his mother and father did not marry in secret? It's not uncommon."

Mary frowned, not following.

Her mother continued. "For all Society knows, he's the legitimate son of a soldier and his bride, both deceased. It's your husband who insists on the narrative of raising some low woman's bastard. I had thought you cleverer than this. Raise this boy however you wish, but think on the consequences of your choices."

Mary mulled over her mother's words.

Not being Duncan's son, he could not inherit the baronetcy, but being legitimate could certainly change his fate. She had never thought to lie about his birth. But who would know the truth? No one would dare question them. She could imagine Duncan's resistance to a lie, but there was nothing to keep them from it. Bernard need never know. Had Duncan not told her, even she would not have known. Warming to the idea, she made to speak, but her mother spoke first.

"I've not come to speak of the boy," she said.

"I suppose you've come to rub in my face what a wretched choice I made with my marriage. Here to tell me I've made a mistake and should return to Lyonn Manor?"

Catherine sneered. "You've made your choice. You must live with it. I'm here to question your intentions with an injured husband."

"Not that it's any of your concern, Mother, but I shall stand by my husband through his recovery. Once he's improved, we'll resume the training and breeding program. Are you here to discourage my supporting him? Or are you planning to discourage our plans with the horses? If you say my husband is weak, I will cast you out of this house. It is my house, you recall."

"You have always been a willful girl, but I've never thought you ignorant," Catherine said, narrowing her eyes. "Why do you always paint me a villain? I am not. You have accused me of not knowing you. It is you who misunderstands me. All I have ever wanted is what is best for you, but you remain obstinate. Do you not think it would have been better to accept one of my proposed suitors? While your lover played soldier, you could have found prestige and wealth. You could have forged your place in society. By the time he returned, you would have been a widow with all the right connections. Neither of you would have needed to labor with horses like common servants. You could have accomplished your plans without needing to prove mettle to some officer in London. If you had only married a duke first, as I had intended."

"Yes, Mother, well, I didn't. And we *want* to labor with the horses. It's what we enjoy."

Catherine smirked. "And yet *you* are doing no such thing. What you must learn is that if you want something, you must do it yourself. You can depend on no one. Would it shock you to learn I proposed to your father, the Duke of Annick? I was not yet sixteen. I proposed, and I became his first and only duchess. What I want, I get. Your choices, however, are haphazard at best, always made in defiance of me. Stop villainizing me. I'm merely wiser, not a force with which to be reckoned. My advice is to decide what you want, then do it."

The next morning, well before visiting hours and with tired eyes after a sleepless night alone in the lady's chamber, Mary sat in the Swanson's drawing room, waiting. She had been waiting for nearly ten minutes. This was quite preposterous.

Staring at her hands folded in her lap, she questioned if she should leave. This was a foolish idea. She had no business being here. All evening and through the tossing and turning of the night, her mother's words had circled above her head, taunting her. There was no way to know her mother's intentions with such words, but Mary interpreted them how she wanted to hear them—permission to be a disobedient wife.

The drawing room door opened, sending Mary to her feet. She felt anxious and hoped it did not show.

Mr. Robert Preston, wearing a rumpled ensemble topped with hair flattened on one side, entered, a quizzical expression aimed her direction. Had he been sleeping? This late into the morning? He stepped into the room, his eyes glassy, his eyelids drooped. Ah. Not sleeping. Well, perhaps that, as well, but he had all too clearly spent the morning hugging a laudanum bottle. Mary was tempted again to leave. What had she been thinking to come here?

"Lady Starrett," he said, his speech ever so slightly slurred. "Never expected you to call on me."

"Neither did I," she said, clasping her hands at her waist. "You aren't training the horses today. Why not?"

He rubbed the side of his nose. "The colonel said he needn't me help 'til the family were gone. Were he expectin' me after all?"

"No. I hadn't realized you would be absent." She cleared her throat, clenching her hands. "My husband has suffered a tumble."

Mr. Preston's expression tightened. He looked away towards one of the windows, as though studying the landscape, before turning back to her.

"By tumble, do you mean—"

"He has fallen and injured himself. Mr. Preston, I'd rather not stand about exchanging dialogue. My family is awaiting my return. I'm here because you're a cavalry officer and know my husband's training technique. I will be taking over training from this point until my husband is recovered. I do not, however, know his technique. I need your help. Would you consider resuming the training, starting tomorrow morning?"

His brows rose high on his forehead, almost disappearing into his hairline. "You wan' me to train the horses?"

"Yes. On a full-time basis until either my husband recovers, or the horses are ready for London, whichever occurs first."

Scratching his chin, his brows still raised, he grinned. "I can go wi' you now if you'd like."

"That won't be necessary. Tomorrow will suffice. I must make one thing clear, though. If you dare arrive to my stables under the influence of anything aside from strong coffee and a good night's sleep, I will turn you away and never allow you onto my property again. I would appreciate your cooperation."

The grin stretched wider. "Yes, milady. Clear as crystal."

Chapter 26

T ristan cantered towards the bar, steady and sure-footed. In swift steps, he vaulted into the air and over the bar with ease and grace.

Mary held onto her wits, for there were no reins. Laughing, she trotted over to Robin, who was working Pegasus.

"How did we look?" she asked, all smiles and good spirits.

"Like cavalry. How'd he respond?"

"No hesitation except after the jump. He was none too keen to slow."

Robin nodded. "Relax into the seat. Sit back rather than squeeze with the calves."

Tutting, Mary said, "I'll not have you talking of my calves, sirrah. Such talk will lead to beheading."

"Too right, milady." Robin grinned before nudging Pegasus to follow the path to the jump bar.

A light lean, and she and Tristan were off at a walk to follow behind Robin. For nearly a week, she and the Bristolian had been training together. For three to four hours in the early morning, Robin guided her through Duncan's techniques, much of which was done without the aid of reins or bridle. Commands were more to do with body and posture than legs or hands. Never had riding been so freeing for her.

For the first day, she had ridden astride, thinking the training was all to do with leg commands. Once she realized that was only a minor part, she switched back to the more comfortable side-saddle, which the horses did not seem to mind as they were just as responsive to her commands as to Robin's. She would, admittedly, never ride the same again. Athena would have quite the surprise coming when Mary showed off her new skills. The training was, of course, for the horses to learn commands and maneuvers, but Mary learned right alongside them.

Robin, clear eyed, freshly shaven, and looking altogether youthful and dashing, circled back to the yard to wait for Mary and Tristan to complete another jump. She made quick but steady work of it, using her body to relax into a trot after hoofs met earth. Patting Tristan's neck, she steered him around to the yard with a tilt of her pelvis.

"Well done today," Robin said when she arrived. He dismounted, handing over the horse to a waiting groom.

"Thank you. I believe those words are deserved. Now that I'm off to entertain the family, what are your plans?"

With the help of a groom, she dismounted and peeled off the riding gloves, her palms sweaty despite the cold temperature.

"Roland and I are going to work the other two over the bar and show five of the grooms the moves. He's handpicked the grooms himself, the hardest workers, he says. Going to leave about two o'clock, mind. Me uncle wants me there in case anyone calls. Think he's hopin' I'll fancy a girl and settle down. Sell my commission."

Mary began walking to the stable entrance, Robin at her side. "Tell me on the morrow if anyone steals your heart. I'm keen on you staying in Durham."

He leaned back with exaggerated shock.

She laughed. "Who else will be our head trainer?" she asked. "We'll need one, you know. If all is to work out how I've planned, that is. Let's talk more on that later, shall we?"

Shaking hands as equals, Mary left Robin to his work.

Not once had he shown up looking dazed. Not once had she smelled alcohol or suspected he had sampled the laudanum before arriving to Sidwell Hall. The change in him was shocking and obvious. While his accent could not be helped, he was otherwise a changed man. Oft she wondered if this was the Robin the Army had known. By ruled measure, he had earned her respect this week.

Just as she reached the servant's entrance, not wanting to traipse through the main entry in disarray or smelling of horse with all the family at home, she heard boots crunching gravel behind her. She turned to find Robin jogging to her.

She tilted her head to one side.

"Milady," he said, stopping mere feet away. "I don't mean to presume or take liberties, but I've been meanin' to say and I've not. So here goes. The colonel's not yet well?"

Mary pursed her lips. She had not seen Duncan since their argument five days ago. The few times she had tried to go in, the butler or one of the footmen said he did not wish to be seen. As much as she wanted to barge in, what was there to say?

"I do not believe so, no," she said with hesitancy.

"I thought not. Tell me if I overstep, milady. 'Tis not me intention. I don't presume to know your husband well, but I do know soldiers, and I know meself. A man like the colonel needs a mission, some purpose. You can't let him be idle. The mind wanders."

"Thank you, Robin. I'll keep that in mind." She nodded and made to turn back to the doorway.

"Check for laudanum, will you? A man like him needs to keep occupied or he becomes a man like me."

Looking back to him over her shoulder, she said, "You're a strong man, Robin, and I couldn't do this without you. Remember that."

Propped against the headboard of the four-poster bed, Duncan stared at his legs beneath the covers. It had been a long five days. Each day, he regained more feeling and more range of motion, though his head still pounded. He could not yet feel past his pelvis, but he could stand and walk a short way before dizziness overtook him and the pain in his right leg ached him back to the mattress.

His family was here. Not the whole family, but his parents, Quinn, and Quinn's family. Mary had sent for them, curse her. They had bustled into the room the day before yesterday, disturbing his peace. Part of him was happy to see them. The part that saw their presence as a reminder of his failure was not happy. And now, both families were together, dining each night, entertaining each other throughout the day, all the children having a grand time. Such a grand time everyone was having, they did not need him around.

Not only could he not protect and provide for his wife and son, but it would seem they did not want him for those purposes. McLarren had brought the news of Lady Starrett wanting to hire a full-time head trainer. Curse the man, but he had already worked the budget to make it happen! Oh, but that was not the worst of the horror. His *wife* had disobeyed his orders and taken the training of the horses into her own hands. Although he could not see the progress for himself, the steward raved about the success he had heard from the staff, including from Roland the stablemaster.

Duncan was extraneous. They did not need him.

In the darkness of each night, his mind wandered. With his inability to do his duties has husband in this state, and possibly never if he did not regain further feeling, would she stray? Had she already strayed? With all this time spent in the stable block, could she be tempted by a real man? Duncan ground his teeth at the memory of hearing her laughter coming from the stablemaster's private rooms. The laugh and the sight of the door haunted his dreams.

Two days before her family planned to leave for the charity concert on Twelfth Night, Mary put her foot down. She banished the footman who stood guard at the lord's chamber and saw herself into the room, much to Duncan's astonishment and Bernard's delight.

Their son was perched on the bed, pretending to read a story to Duncan, the words he spoke in lyrical narration a far cry from the words on the page. She had only a moment to take in the scene before Bernard spotted her. He tossed the book aside, narrowly missing Duncan's right leg, and clambered off the bed.

"Mummy!" he said, arms raised wide.

"My darling," Mary said, scooping him into her arms.

"I readed to Papa."

"Yes, I see that. How thoughtful of you." She brushed hair from his forehead to ready for a well-placed kiss.

"Down," he commanded. "I wanter go play."

As soon as feet touched rug, he was out the door with a heavy-handed door close. Just as quickly as he left, he circled back.

"You readed to me tonight?" he asked, his head poking through the doorway.

"Of course. Have everyone gathered so they can enjoy the story, as well," she said.

He nodded, then closed the door again with another near slam. She winced.

And now to face the grouch. She turned into the room to pin him with a glare.

Duncan's arms were crossed, his expression fierce. "My son doesn't appear to need me either."

Mary wrinkled her nose. "What on earth are you talking about?"

He grunted but said no more.

She pulled a chair next to his bed, feeling his eyes follow her as she moved. There was no rush. She took her time. In exaggerated and slow movements, she made herself comfortable in the chair, arranging her dress just so, tucking a curl behind her ear, taking a deep breath.

Once settled, she took him in, expecting to find him unbathed and scruffy after five days of recovering. To her surprise, his cheeks were bare, and he smelled of soap. As she studied him, he slid his left foot until he could prop an elbow on his knee. His right leg remained stretched. So, it would seem he was not bedridden. For how long had he regained mobility? Why had he not joined the family?

"Have you come to stare at me, or is there something you wish to say?" he asked. "My head is throbbing, so please, don't take long."

Scowling, she said, "You've not seen me in five days, and that's what you have to say to me?"

He shrugged. Irritating man.

"I've come," she said, "to ascertain your health and put an end to whatever your foolishness is."

Duncan closed his eyes and leaned his head against the headboard. "What do you wish to know? I can walk, but it makes me dizzy. My right leg is blotchy purple from where Bucephalus fell. My back is no less bruised. I can't feel below my pelvis. I'm humiliated by what happened. And most importantly, I'm not worthy enough to dine with your family. All my efforts to prove myself have been for nought. I've made a proper fool of myself instead. And now, for what do you need me? You can run the program yourself, raise Bernard yourself, do everything without me."

Of all the reactions he probably did not expect, it was for Mary to laugh. She could not help herself. It

was a pretty enough speech full of woebegone sentiment and genuine pain and heartache. And yet she
laughed. It began as a giggle, her hand covering her
mouth to hide the mirth, but then it evolved to something far heartier. Before long, she was clutching her
side from a cramp.

When she recovered herself, the laugh lingering
on her lips, she was none too surprised to find him
staring at her as though she had gone mad.

"I'm happy to amuse you, I'm sure," he said.

"I do apologize. I don't know what came over me.
Relief that you can walk, perhaps."

He grunted.

"No, I believe that it was your comments of proving yourself that tickled my laughter. What are you
trying to prove, Duncan?"

Flicking his fingers with his thumb, he stared at
the book Bernard left on the bed. "Everything I've
done has been to prove myself worthy of your hand.
I won't have people look at me and think you married
below your station. I want them to look at me and
think I'm accomplished and strong, someone who
has earned the right to eat at the table with a duke's
family. All my efforts, and I humiliated myself in front
of everyone, including your mother."

"Oh, Duncan." She laughed again, but this time
only a soft chuckle. "There is so much more to you
than whatever it is you're trying to prove. You write
me poetry for crying in a saddle blanket. I've saved
every note you've ever written to me. I don't think
those lines were written to prove anything. Those
came from the heart. That's what makes you worthy
of my hand, nothing more. *You*, just as yourself, with

your wit and charm, are worthy. There's nothing you need to prove. Training all the warhorses in the world would not change how I feel about you or how my family feels. You're my hero and have been since I first met you. What did you have to offer then? Nothing except yourself."

His elbow resting on his knee, he covered his face with his hand.

Reaching out, she clasped his free hand, gripping it when he tried to pull away. She held tight, pressing her palm to his palm and lacing their fingers.

"We're a team, you and I," she said. "My dream is to be with you, no matter what that looks like, be it with you in a wheeled chair, on a horse, or in a bed as you make love to my sensibilities with another penned verse."

"But you don't need me. For what would you need me? You can do it all yourself. I don't want to be a burden, not as broken as I am."

"I need *you*, not because I need you to do something for me, but because I need *you*. I'll say it as many times as I need to for you to understand. The dream I had of breeding horses, which has evolved to training them, as well, was a vision I had for us to do together. It's not something I need, rather something I see us doing in tandem. I never even envisioned us *doing* the work rather overseeing it, hiring the staff together, spending time with the horses, an hour or so every day, simply being together. A way for us to spend time together doing what we enjoy."

Letting his hand fall from his face, he looked at her with red-rimmed eyes. "Has it truly taken a concussion and a bruised body for me to hear you?"

"I'm afraid so." She nodded.

"What do we do?"

Squeezing his hand, she said, "We get you out of this bed for starters. You must join your family for dinner before they leave, and yes, I do mean my family, also, when I say *your* family. Afterwards, I can bring Bernard here for story time. Just because I can read to him doesn't mean he wants to do it without you. He needs you as much as I do. Tonight, I want to sleep with my husband if he's not too bruised to have me beside him. And finally, let's see, ah yes, the horse program. Think on it, will you? You're meant to be a leader, not a laborer. Leading instructors is a grand mission for you to undertake. *Lead*, Colonel Starrett."

He cast her a soft smile. "Yes, my lady, as you wish. I say this next part not with unkindness, but because my head is hurting so much that my eyesight is blurring. Would you mind terribly if you left me to close my eyes? Not *leave* me, but you know what I mean."

"Of course." Removing from the chair, she kissed his forehead, ran a hand down his cheek, and left him to rest.

Quill scratched paper. This was not a poem. He had already finished the poem. This was a letter to Colonel Archer. Through the throbbing of his head, he worked, too excited about his idea not to capture it now.

Maneuvers and discipline. Dressage and tactic.
These are nothing in the thick of battle. Soldiers
must be disciplined, must know maneuvers on the

field, must apply the training directly. Too many officers, specifically, think themselves skilled cavalry because they are skilled at the hunt. How often have we berated this mentality? The difficulty is maneuvering in large bodies as a single unit, riding and fighting in tight formation, something they are not prepared to do. Both horse and soldier must learn one-handed and no hand equitation. Soldiers must be practiced in tight formation while wielding weaponry. What is a well-trained warhorse beneath an arrogant foxhunter inexperienced in warfare? Whereas a well-trained officer will lead his men by example and technique. The training of officers alongside horses is imperative, but I propose a more radical approach: the training of all cavalry soldiers alongside the horses.

He tickled his chin with the quill feather, lost in thought as to how to describe his vision. The migraine did not help. His plan was not to convince Archer but to tease him into wanting to discuss the plan in London. This letter would whet Archer's appetite and give Duncan more time to plan. He hoped to more fully develop a cavalry training academy that would allow him to lead but not spend hours in a training yard. Should future injury occur, his leadership would not be affected.

Rewetting the quill, he continued, his letter almost complete, which was a relief since he was nearly out of paper, at three sheets as it was.

The Starrett & Starrett Cavalry Program will include a training academy, allowing recruits to train alongside horses. There's no greater bond. Instructors, namely pensioners, will guide soldiers in breaking in their assigned horse using the Starrett principles of warhorse training. Training manuals, lesson plans, and field maneuvers will be prepared and delivered into your hands in London at time of demonstration. In addition, I propose the warhorses graduated from the program be registered to serve as reserves. After successful completion of each campaign, they will be returned to the program for continued training until needed. One caveat: should a soldier bond with said horse and wish to retain for personal uses, he may with minimal fee.

Finishing the letter with a brief itinerary of what he would demonstrate in London, he signed it, sanded it, folded it, and sealed it. Done. It would be an expensive letter to post but worth every coin. Now for a more formidable task.

This task was six years overdue. Every attempt he had made to impress the Dowager Duchess of Annick had ended with injury. That could not be mere coincidence. Too afraid of her to face her, he had circumvented a discussion by doing everything else he could to earn honor and prestige and be a worthy suitor and husband for her daughter. Not much good it had done him.

His definition of what it meant to be a husband and father had been warped by the efforts. All this time, his family needed him for himself, not because he could labor or fight, or prove perfection or sexual prowess. They simply needed *him*. Had he realized

this as a young man, would it have made a difference? Would he have gone to war or courted Mary
in more traditional ways? There was no way to know.
He did know he may have underestimated her had
he gone a more traditional route. The sixteen-year-old
version of Mary was a vast reach from the one-and-
twenty version of herself. She was stronger than he
in uncountable ways.

If she could find the courage to train warhorses,
could he not find bravery within himself? He could
not avoid a confrontation with his mother-in-law forever. He had this one chance, for they would leave
in the morning.

Hand on the cane Mr. Sherman had secured for
him, Duncan pushed to his feet. His right leg throbbed.
His bruises smarted. His head ached. There was not
a step that did not cause him to wince. With each
wince, he was reminded of two things. Feeling was
fast returning to both legs, all the way to his knees,
for which he was grateful and would not take for
granted. And he would never again try to prove himself worthy, for he alone was worthy.

Chapter 27

E ven as he took the stairs to the parlor one step at a time, one cane-thump at a time, he loathed that Her Grace might think him weak to need a cane. With a gentle reprimand and subsequent reminder to himself, he thought, *I am worthy*.

The thought dissolved on his tongue as soon as he opened the parlor door. The dowager duchess was already there, seated and waiting. Her expression, carved of marble, was menacing.

"You call me here, and yet you keep me waiting. Not an impressive impression," she said.

As he limped into the room, the mantel clock chimed his punctuality.

He did not take a seat. She did not invite him to sit. Her Grace sat straight-backed, tall and intimidating even from a chair. One look at her churned his stomach and quelled his confidence. Between an army of Frenchmen and Her Grace, he would take his chances with the Frenchmen.

The one humanizing factor was her cane. It posed in her hands, one hand on top of the other, gripping the gold handle. It might have been another intimidating factor, a weapon in the hands of a tyrant, but it humanized her in his estimation. He looked down at his own cane as he favored his right leg. Surely her cane was no

more an ornament than his. She was not old enough
to need a crutch. Had she, too, been injured?

"Have you taken my measure? Sized the opposition?" she asked with an arch of a slender, black brow.

"Are you my opposition?" Feet hip width apart,
he affected ease in his posture, limited only by the
cane and the bruising of the leg.

"You tell me, young man. You are the one who
has summoned me. Come to declare war? Peace?
Your undying affection for my daughter? Your devo-
tion and admiration to the Annick dukedom? Your
apologies for bringing my daughter from a manor
to a hovel?"

Smoothing his bristles, he swallowed his pride.
Gulped may be more accurate.

"Your Grace, I've come to ask for your daughter's
hand in holy matrimony."

The woman's frown deepened, the creases around
her mouth becoming more pronounced until she
looked severe. "Is it because you injured your head
or because you are a simpleton that you ask for my
daughter's hand when you have already wed her?
Without my permission, I might add."

"Neither, I assure you. I wish to correct my
mistakes. I should have come to you first to ask permission. I lacked the courage."

"And now you have the courage? How reassuring." She sneered.

"I hope it is reassuring." He clenched his cane until
his knuckles whitened. "I've allowed fear of you to
control my actions. Rather than court your daughter, I
met her in secret. Rather than ask for her hand, I went
to war. Rather than come to you once I had returned, I

sought her brother for permission. Rather than listen to her sage advice, I ran myself ragged. Rather than listen to my own conscience, I rode a horse who was not yet ready to be ridden. So many other choices I've made have been to prove to you — before I could face you — that I was worthy of your daughter. Even after marriage, I was unworthy. I knew it. I knew you knew it. And I feared your censure."

Her eyes narrowed as she looked him up and down. "You no longer fear my censure?"

"On the contrary, I'm terrified. The difference is I realize my worth is not determined by you. I come to you as a man humbled by my choices. Despite the baronetcy, despite my military rank, despite the program I'm setting up alongside my wife, I have only myself to offer, and that must be enough."

If she could not hear his knees knocking, it would be a miracle. A bead of sweat trickled down his forehead. In the middle of winter! He dared not dab at it for fear he would call attention to his nervousness.

"Strength compels you," she said. "As does a sense of honor. I am pleased to see my daughter has not become a nursemaid nor have you lived up to the expectation of dishonorable cad. I knew your character well enough. No man of honor arranges trysts with a duke's daughter unless for nefarious purposes. I'll have you know that had you compromised her, not only would I not have allowed the marriage, but I would have had your head on a platter for my dinner party. I say now that you have not lived up to my expectations."

He gawked, hoping he did not appear to gawk. Was she insulting him or complimenting him? He believed she was complimenting him in her own way.

"Thank you, Your Grace," he said, feeling another bead of sweat form on his brow.

"You are inferior to my daughter. As such, I expect you to prove yourself every day for the rest of her life. You must earn the right to stand by her side. I don't mean by riding a silly horse or facing foes with a sword. I mean by loving her in all the ways I could not."

His jaw ticked. He knew not what to say.

"You are my son-in-law, regardless if I find you favorable. I do, however, recognize valor in your bravery to face me. I do not value cowards. The world is full of them, and they will be the death of great nations. You, it would seem, are not a coward. Stand tall. You have my permission."

She nodded in reverence.

Was she in earnest? By Jove, he hoped so.

A smile tugging at his lips, he asked, "If I had come to you before I went to war, and I had asked permission for Mary's hand, would you have granted it?"

Her sneer returned. "Of course not. I would have expected no less than you to ask for her hand every day for a year, at the least. Then, and only then, might I have believed you wanted my daughter and not her dowry."

He chuckled, the humor not lost on him that he was chuckling in the presence of the Dowager Duchess of Annick. "And then, would you have consented?"

"No," she said. "But I would have known you to be sincere."

"You should know that I was, and remain, sincere. I've not touched her dowry and have no plans to do so."

"It's unfortunate. I was beginning to believe you intelligent, but when you confess such foolhardy sentiments, I find myself corrected. Is it stubbornness or stupidity not to use it? Are you proving something? I assume the marriage contract details all her assets? The estate in Scotland, the trust funds, and so forth?"

Duncan nodded.

"I take back my compliments. I do not give you my approval if you're too thick to enjoy the spoils of marriage."

She turned away from him, her chin high.

Duncan could only chuckle.

When they parted, he felt a sense of rightness with the world, along with a desire for a late honeymoon in Scotland.

That evening, Duncan lay on his back, staring at the canopy, an arm tucked behind his head. Mary's cheek rested on his shoulder.

"Fifteen," she said.

"Is that all?"

"Hush. I'm still counting and don't want to lose my place."

A chuckle rumbled in his chest. While his fingers drew figure eights along Mary's arm, her fingers traced every bruise on his torso. He dreaded her braving a look at his leg. It was not a pretty sight and any wonder how it had not fractured.

"Nineteen. Still counting."

"You'll be at this all night."

"Not all night. I have far better plans for the next half hour." She circled a fingertip around one of the bruises over a rib, a particularly ticklish spot, no less.

"I hope your plans aren't what I think they are. You underestimate the tenderness of my bruises. I beg for another week to recover."

She pouted and propped herself onto her forearm so he could see her moue.

"Not convincing, my love. The bruises hurt. Don't think I don't want to share a loving evening with you, for you would find me a most willing participant, but I would rather not anger my aches any more than I have to. I beg for a few more days."

Batting her eyelashes to no avail, she huffed and returned her cheek to his shoulder. "You'll be pleased to know that Bucephalus and Caesar have become fast friends. I must warn you, though; by the time you return to the stables, you may find a corpulent Arabian waiting for you. The stablemaster has spoiled him."

"I've not yet thanked you for the gift. It's always been my dream to own an Arabian. Now that I do, I owe him apologies."

He was itching to return to the stables, not to train, just to ride. Much time with Caesar and now Bucephalus had been lost because of his shortsightedness and reckless behavior. One more week he would give himself to heal, and then nothing could keep him from the stables.

"About what did you speak with my mother today?" Mary asked, interrupting his thoughts. "Mr. Sherman said you were both in the parlor."

"Traitor," he mumbled, stroking her hair. "If you could have picked any topic to dissuade me from a tumble, it would be this one. There's no hope for you now."

Rather than laugh, she waited for his answer.

He exhaled deeply. "We talked about you. Us. Our marriage. My cowardice."

"Your cowardice? You've never done anything cowardly in your life."

"No? I beg to differ. But that's not the point. The point is we had a good conversation, as good as one can be had with her, I suppose. You said she's close to your cousin Lady Collingwood and to your other cousin's wife Lady Roddam?"

He felt her head nod against his chest.

"I don't understand it," she said. "They're both such kind women. How can they stand her?"

"Perhaps they value her forthright nature."

Mary scoffed. "Tyranny, you mean. Did I tell you she proposed to my father?"

"Did she? Hmm. I would have liked to see that." So tickled by the visual, he laughed, sending Mary's head bouncing against him.

She moved to stretch out her arm and prop her head in her hand. He angled to admire her. Long lashes framed her dark eyes. There was a softness to her features that her mother lacked. The two shared a remarkable likeness, but the dowager duchess had none of the softness of Mary's expressions. Being a duchess, and at so young an age, she could not have had a difficult life, and yet she wore the lines he had seen only in the most hardened soldiers.

"Lord in heaven, you're a beautiful woman," he said.

Matching roses blushed her cheeks. "You're changing the subject."

"Am I? It connects in my concussion damaged brain. Mary, your mother leaves tomorrow. I want you to talk to her."

Her pink cheeks paled as she pursed her lips. "Why? I'll be happy when she leaves."

"Have you ever talked to her about how you feel? Let her know how much she's hurt you over the years?"

"You think she doesn't know? Oh, she knows. No qualms about it, she knows. Her hatred is intentional." Mary stared over Duncan's shoulder, deep in thought. "Nothing good would come from me confronting her other than more heartache. There's only so much rejection one can take from their own mother."

"I understand, love. I do. But she said something today that struck me as odd. I think you should talk to her. If the two of you can't make peace, at least you'll have tried. Life's too short not to try. Three times in a year, I've faced death. There are no words in this world worth taking to the grave. Let them be said. If she hurts you again, then you'll know you've done all in your power to salvage the relationship, and the problem lies with her, not you. But have you ever tried to confront her about it?"

"No," she admitted. "I've avoided her as much as I could over the years. Every year becomes more difficult, each encounter more strained. I fear at some point, we'll both burst or strangle each other. I can't forgive her for how she's treated me all my life, but if it came down to it, a life-or-death situation, I could accept her for who she is — a heartless woman incapable of love. If I accept that about her, then I suppose

I really must forgive her, for how can I expect love from someone without a heart?"

"Mary, Mary, Mary," Duncan repeated, crossing an arm over his chest to cup her cheek. "I believe, though I could be wrong, she acknowledges her treatment. I believe she wants to make amends."

Mary frowned, staring at the bedlinen. When he realized she had no more to say on the matter, he pulled her to him and tucked her head on his shoulder.

In a chair before the hearth, Mary waited. This early in the morning no one was awake except her, Duncan, the servants, and her mother. She had sent a missive to her mother to meet her in the drawing room. Though not as grand as a single room in Lyonn Manor, it was still the most ornate and the largest, the only room that would do for meeting her mother.

This was not a meeting she wanted to have. Somewhere in the night, she found it in her heart to forgive her mother for never loving her. All too likely, her mother had wanted a spare heir and resented Mary's birth. Could she fault her mother for that?

Catherine was due to arrive in a quarter of an hour. Mary was early, steeling herself. For over half an hour, she had been poised in the chair, her spine straight, her hands folded, her ankles parallel, and her mind racing through all the possible scenarios of their conversation.

When the drawing room door opened, Mary nearly leapt out of the chair, not expecting her mother so soon. She tensed.

Countless times, Mary had been summoned by her mother, never the other way around. How was she to go about this? What was there to gain? There was far too much to lose. She did not like making herself this vulnerable. Jaw clenched, she watched her mother make her way to a chair.

Much as Mary had done the other day, Catherine took her time to reach a level of comfort, in no apparent hurry to begin the conversation.

Her mother fixed her with a stare. "Is it a habit in this household to summon me at odd hours for interviews?"

Mary took a deep breath, exhaling slowly. "I forgive you for everything," she said without preamble. "Your coming to my home tells me you want me as part of the family. Or I hope it does. You have surpassed my expectations by accepting Bernard. Thank you. Above all, Mother, I forgive you for not loving me."

Catherine leaned back, her eyes widening.

"But," Mary continued, "this is my household, and I will not have you speak disparagingly to me or any person or object in the house. For too long I've suffered your tyranny, fighting against you with rebellion and misbehavior. No more. I am my own person. I choose not to be goaded by you any longer. I forgive you and free myself of your judgement."

Although each word had been spoken with precision, nothing rushed, nothing colored with anger, it had been a tumble of thoughts void of cohesion. She would not be cowed despite the ineloquence. Looking to her mother, she saw an arrested expression, one mixed with shock and incredulity.

"You forgive me for never loving you?" Catherine asked.

Mary nodded. "All I ever wanted was your affection. Think worse of me if you will for admitting I misbehaved in my youth to get your attention. You ignored me for the entirety of my childhood. Only when critical did you notice me. All I wanted was some indication of care. I know I'm the greatest disappointment of your life, first born a girl, then wayward and insolent, then disobedient, and now married to someone of my own choosing. It would be too much to ask for you to acknowledge your mistreatment, beg for forgiveness, and remedy your ways. You've not the heart for it. And so, I absolve you of all sins, if not for your sake, then for mine."

Catherine stared, looking bewildered.

Not often had her mother been speechless. The few times she had were in moments when words failed to express her disapproval and disdain. Mary recalled the time, at age nine, she had sneaked fresh horse dung onto her mother's dining chair. Words had failed her then. Or the time, at age sixteen, Mary had stomped on a suitor's foot. Words had failed her then, as well.

Catherine's black eyes studied her daughter. Mary sat still, accepting the assessment for what it was — her mother finding fault in all Mary was and had said.

"Everything I've done," Catherine said, "has been out of love. Not the recklessness you young people call love; I've loved both my children in the only way I know how. You know nothing of the harshness of the world, of what life without love is truly like."

Catherine's expression glazed as she stared at the cane resting against the side of her chair.

Continuing, the dowager duchess said, "Do you know why I use a cane? Let me enlighten you. My father crushed my ankle when I was twelve years of age. It was my punishment for running through the gallery. This was not an isolated incident. My father knew nothing but violence. He showed his children love by beating the bible into them for even the most minor infraction."

Mary bowed her head, eyes trained on her hands.

"Do you know why I proposed to your father? I was sixteen at the time. Your father was two and forty and in need of an heir. I met him at the annual shooting party. The duke was to stay for the week. I saw him as my chance to escape. So intent was I to snare him, I became careless, dismissive of a weak ankle that had never properly healed. I ran down the stairs hoping to catch his attention when the men returned from a day of shooting. My ankle gave way. I tumbled, landing in the vestibule for all to see."

Catherine paused to look about her as though to search for her next words.

"Within an inch of my life, my father beat me for humiliating him, the severest beating of my life. I could not walk for weeks, could not breathe without wheezing, could not see out of one eye from the swelling. I dictated to my lady's maid a marriage proposal to the duke. She wrote it and had a trusted footman, now my butler Mr. Taylor, might I add, hand deliver it. The duke arrived the following day. For all His Grace's vices, I never looked back."

Mary wiped tears from her eyes. She would never have wished such a life on anyone. Why had her mother never divulged such a secret? Why had she never talked about her past?

"This is the love I've given you, Mary, a life free of violence. I have loved my children by spoiling them and never laying a hand on them. This is the only way I know how to love."

Dabbing her nose with her handkerchief, Mary said, "I'm sorry you suffered, Mother. I am. I wish you would have told me sooner, talked to me about it. I know nothing about you, just as you know nothing of me. No, you've never laid a hand on me, for which I'm grateful, but that's the point. You've *never laid a hand on me*. A hug would be nice. A kiss on the cheek. Something. Some words of affection. You may not be violent, but your words can cut as deeply as any hand. I don't equate you to your father; please, don't misunderstand. But of all the ways to love me, you chose an extreme that left no room for perceived love."

"I would not have a weak daughter," Catherine replied. "I would rather have a daughter of independent, strong will, who can defend herself and rule a county than one weakened by emotion."

"Would it have been too much to hug me? Do you even recognize how your treatment affected me, even if it was meant well?"

Catherine harrumphed. "Only we can choose how we react. We cannot control how other people react. It was never my intention to harm or hurt you. Quite the opposite. I do regret if I caused you pain, but I would not alter my choices. You must understand my intentions. I was motivated by far greater fears than the consequences of my daughter not being hugged."

"I suppose that's as close to an apology as I can expect. Where does it leave us? Do we return to bickering, or do we hug?"

"Neither, I should think," Catherine said, pushing herself to her feet with her cane. "We shall live our lives with a keener understanding of each other and, I should hope, mutual respect. I should like to know my daughter if she would speak with me rather than rebelling and lashing out as she's done these many years. That choice is yours. For now, I am for the morning room in hopes of tea. Are you to join me, or shall you continue to blubber into the linen until your face is unbecomingly puffy?"

With an unladylike snort, a sound somewhere between a laugh and a sob, Mary tucked away her handkerchief and accepted her mother's outstretched hand.

Chapter 28

April 1796
London

Mary stood with a group of officers, all watching Duncan and Robin perform remarkable feats, given the horses only had a few months' worth of training. The horses showcased a routine specially designed for today, a series of movements for dressage exhibition, each move coordinated to exemplify the horse's agility and maneuverability in combat, and most importantly, their ability to respond to corporal commands rather than reins.

Duncan had decided to invite the young ensign to London to show each horse's ease in tight formation with another rider performing alongside him. He had confessed to Mary in private that he also wanted someone present who knew the routine should anything happen. She did not dare protest that she knew the moves as well as Robin knew them, for she understood the officers to whom they would be demonstrating would not appreciate a woman rider, especially if on side-saddle.

From the sidelines, she observed, cheering on the two in silence.

Through each change in routine, she eyed the officers for a flicker of expression. Their faces were unreadable, a stone visage. For twenty minutes per horse, the two men performed. It seemed such a short amount of time for all those hours, days, and weeks of practice.

As Duncan poised Trident for the standing leap, Mary held her breath.

When Mary and Duncan walked into the townhouse two hours later, they were greeted by eager faces. Sean and Georgina sat by the front window, a grandchild on each knee. Cian, Duncan's brother, who Mary had not met until arriving in London, lounged on a settee.

"Yes?" Sean asked, eyes darting from Duncan to Mary and back.

"Yes." Duncan spoke with somber tone, his eyes downcast.

He waited for the word to sink in, then looked up to wink at everyone, his face cracking a broad smile.

Mary gave a little bounce. "We have the contract! And they loved the academy plans. What did they say?" She turned to Duncan. "Oh, yes, I remember. They said that this academy would start a new chapter in cavalry training and could change the face of military training."

Opening his arms wide, Duncan swung Bernard into the air and onto his shoulders. "They were stunned by the performance. Archer admitted they had only expected the horses to be broken-in enough for me to demonstrate my training technique. They never

anticipated fully trained horses. Stop smirking, Mary."
He eyed her. "So impressed, not only did they sign the
contract, but they've agreed to fully fund per annum
the breeding, training, *and* the opening of the academy.
We're officially on contract with the British Army."

"Son, that's grand!" Sean said, alternating a bouncing knee to entertain the grandchildren.

"Mary, dear," Georgina said, moving the children
off her lap to stand. "I don't mean to interrupt happy
tidings, but a message came for you. The boy said to
give it to you right away."

Pulling a folded bit of paper from her dress pocket,
she handed it to Mary, who took it into the entry hall
to read in private. Distantly, Mary heard Cian say
that Quinn and Miranda were upstairs in the nursery
with his own wife and children. She would have to
bring them the good news. Or so she thought until
she read the message.

In swift steps, she dashed into the drawing room.
"Can't stay. Must go. Bernard, down. Duncan, come!"
She rushed over to the awaiting footman to take
bonnet and gloves.

"Good heavens. Is it bad news?" Georgina asked,
still standing, her face lined with worry.

"My sister-in-law is having a baby! As is my cousin's wife. At the same time!"

Without waiting for their replies, she dragged
Duncan behind her.

It proved to be a long evening. Charlotte gave birth first,
within an hour of Mary and Duncan's arrival. Mary

was delighted to meet her second nephew, Thomas Mowbrah, a wailing and wrinkly boy who sent his older brother running from the room with hands clasped over his ears. Not until two in the morning did Lizbeth give birth to a little girl, Colette Lancaster. It was fortunate there was a good deal of time between births, for Mary's cousin Lilith had presided over both. Since neither new mother had anticipated going into labor today, or yesterday rather, they had both been at the ducal London house, another convenience for the dear midwife and baroness.

Seeing each baby made Mary feel the ache for a child of her own. Since her monthly courses had come regularly, there was no hope for a baby yet, which was just as well, she supposed, given how much time they devoted to raising Bernard. If a baby never came, Bernard would be quite enough. If one did, Bernard would be a superior brother. He longed for playmates, and Mary longed for a house filled with the laughter of children.

Given the late night, Mary and Duncan remained at the ducal house until late morning, breaking their fast with her family first. By the time they returned to their own townhouse, the home was empty, with everyone out calling on neighbors and friends, even Bernard having gone with his grandparents to meet their friends in town and tour about London.

Mary sank into the settee with Duncan and propped her feet on his thighs. "Do you like the house?"

"I do. I think McLarren made a good recommendation." He slipped off her shoes and tossed them to the floor. "And you don't mind that it's not in one of the fashionable squares?"

Mary scoffed. "Where would we put the horses? Our contract will have us bringing horses to London every year. The mews behind those so-called fashionable houses are embarrassingly small. We need the stables that come with this house, even if it's a distance from the City. It's close to my cousin's London house, so that's something. You don't mind that it's rather…large?"

He smirked as he rolled down one stocking after another. "Impossible. We must christen every room, which I daresay means we'll need to double our efforts if we're to make it to each room by the time we leave London this summer—two rooms per day?" Tossing the stockings, he reached for her hand and kissed her palm, then her wrist, then worked his lips upwards one inch at a time.

"Oh, come now," she said in a haughty tone. "It's not that big."

"Isn't it?" Duncan waggled his eyebrows.

Mary snorted. "And you're positive you don't mind that we used dowry money to purchase it?"

He moved her arm over his shoulder and leaned towards her on the settee. "Only if you don't mind that we're using even more of it to expand the stable block and training yard at Sidwell Hall."

When he puckered a kiss to the side of her neck, she giggled. "Wicked man. Don't distract me. It was *my* idea to expand the stables, so don't you dare take credit. Now, what are you trying to accomplish with all this leaning and kissing you're doing while I'm trying to carry on a casual conversation?" She eyed him with arched brow.

Rather than reply, he grinned mischievously and possessed her mouth in a lascivious kiss.

The officer's ball was a far grander event than Duncan expected. He had assumed it would rival in small ways the balls he had attended on the continent, but the prince had wanted to celebrate in royal style, sparing no expense. If Duncan had been nervous about attending, it was nothing to standing in the Great Hall of Carlton House, surrounded by the prince and military leaders. There were plenty of officers far humbler than he in attendance, Robin, for example, but that did nothing to ease his nausea.

To say the event was a squeeze would be an understatement. Not everyone in attendance was of military affiliation, as he had expected. The prince had doubled the evening as his showcase of the Carlton House renovations, a massive undertaking of over a decade. For the brief time they spoke after Duncan and Mary's arrival, their host had sniffed at the renovations, dissatisfied still even after all the work, wanting to extend the lower levels and include a Gothic conservatory of epic proportions—would this affair not have been remarkable in such a locale, the Prince of Wales had asked those around him. Duncan was under the impression the man would not be satisfied until he had created a palace.

The guests were encouraged to mill about the place at their leisure, something Duncan planned to take advantage of as soon as the dancing began.

Mary stood at his side, her hand on his arm, imbuing him with strength. Without her, he never would have considered himself heroic. But she was right. It was not just about war. He had battled against the odds, fought the demons that would have held him back, and found the will not just to survive but to strive and thrive. He was courageous at *life* and a hero to his family.

"Look," Mary said, squeezing his forearm. "There's Robin. Why's he standing alone?"

Duncan followed her gaze. Robin stood behind a yellow pillar, staring about him in bewilderment.

"He looks smart in the regimentals. Don't you think?" she asked.

"Are you trying to make me jealous?" He walked them in Robin's direction.

"Over Robin?" she laughed. "How droll, darling."

"I suspect, to answer your question, he's standing alone because of the very reason you first disliked him. We're surrounded by peers of the realm and heirs to peers, many parading as military heroes, although few have earned their valor. Officer or not, Robin is the son of a miner. He does not feel he belongs and knows those around him agree. I would argue I don't belong either, but I have the benefit of a father with a rich military history and a grandfather who's a viscount. Robin has nothing more than a wealthy uncle."

"They've seriously misjudged him if they don't include him. And is this not supposed to be a military ball to celebrate heroes, not peers?" Mary seethed the last words through her teeth as they approached the pillar.

Hands outstretched, Mary greeted Robin. The man looked relieved to see familiar faces, his shoulders relaxing and his jaw slackening.

Mary kissed each cheek and said, "I may not know many in attendance, nor do I know their military ranks, but I do know a few of the nobles. Come with me. Let's make some introductions, shall we?"

Robin's eyes widened, looking altogether like a cornered fox.

"No one would dare cut you if I make the introduction. I'm the daughter of a duke, remember?" She waved off Duncan. "Go. Converse. I'm going to play my role as your dutiful wife." With those words, she led Robin over to a nearby group in red regimentals.

Duncan smiled, the dramatic change in Robin since they first met not lost on him. For the next half hour, he explored room after room, all filled with people admiring artwork, talking, judging, laughing. More than a few people he knew. He lost himself in several conversations, remembering the camaraderie of old.

Only when he heard the orchestra strike up for the dancing did he go in search of his wife, who he found in the Crimson Drawing Room, sharing whispered words with a pretty redhead who was ogling Robin from across the room. The man was none the wiser, carrying on his own conversation with a group of blue regimentals, all cavalry. From the sound of the laughter, Duncan wagered they were laughing with Robin rather than at him.

Duncan approached the ladies, bowing to both. "If you'll excuse us, I've come to collect my wife. The first dance is about to begin."

The young lady curtsied herself over to another group.

Mary stared at him with a half-smile. "Are we to dance?"

"Not exactly." Tucking her hand in the crook of his arm, he led her through the rambling maze of rooms and down the Grand Staircase, his destination the garden.

The garden was an oasis hidden in the middle of a bustling city. In such a haven, one would never know they were in London. Couples and groups milled about, exploring the multitude of winding walks. Finding privacy was not easy. With dancing inside, Duncan had not anticipated so many guests to venture outdoors. The couple covered a sizable portion of the garden, nodding to those they passed, until they found a hidden alcove with a bench and fountain.

Duncan steered his wife to the bench, but she dug in her heels when she saw his destination.

"I had hoped to dance with you, Sir Duncan."

Had they been home, he mused, he would have seen her bathed in moonlight. The London sky was not so accommodating. Instead, he smiled at her upturned face in the soft lighting of a single nearby lantern.

Snaking an arm around her waist, he pulled her to him. "Stand on my feet."

Mary laughed. "Has it been so long, you've forgotten how to dance?"

"I'm not altogether sure I can dance when I can't feel my feet, my love. I have something different in mind. Now, stand on my shoes so I don't accidentally crush your toes with a misstep."

Eyeing him askance, she took a tentative step forward onto his dress shoes.

"Ow! Good Lord, woman!" He screeched, doubling over to reach for his foot.

When she covered her mouth with her hands, Duncan laughed. "Only jesting. Come back here."

He tugged her to him, wrapping her arms around his neck and his own around her waist. With a tight hold, he twirled her around the center fountain. It did not matter that they could not hear the music. In serene silence, oblivious of the city beyond the garden walls and the partygoers elsewhere in the greenery, they danced, eyes trained on each other.

"You've enchanted me," he said.

She smiled coyly. "Have I? I didn't know I possessed such a talent."

"I'm walking, aren't I? And dancing. And in love. All because of you."

"In love? Are you? After all these years, you still feel the same?" Her brows drew together.

"Not the same, no. Not even close. I was infatuated with a pretty girl and thought myself in love. I know that now only because there's no comparison between how I felt then and what I feel for you now."

"Oh, those are pretty words, colonel," Mary said, blushing in the pale light, or he assumed she was. "Are you certain we made the right choice by marrying? You haven't realized we're horribly suited for each other?"

"We are as suited as the moon and stars in the sky."

Mary threw her head back and laughed. "I believe you said the same line when we first kissed."

"I did." He chuckled. "In truth, we're not the same people we once were, Mary. And this could have been a disaster. But it's not. You give me the will to persevere, the courage to face my weaknesses. You've grown into this enchanting woman I never could have dreamed would care for me, someone who trains horses, who ignores her husband's wishes because she knows a better way, who recognizes prejudices and overcomes them, who accepts and loves those in need. Your strengths are many. Never had I imagined you would become this woman, and I love you with every beat of my heart."

Freeing herself from his hold, she stepped onto the lawn. The palms of her hands dabbed at her cheeks. Duncan pulled free his handkerchief for her to use.

"You really love me?" She asked. "Not the memory of how we used to be, but me as I am now?"

Not caring that she was sniffling into the handkerchief, he enfolded her in his arms, leaning his cheek to her temple. "I love you as the woman you've become, the woman you are now, yes. For all the traces of the young girl I fell in love with, you're someone altogether more wonderful, strong, and independent. And I think we can both agree, I'd be lost without your brilliance."

Stifling a sob, she laughed into his shoulder. "I can't tell you how much this means to me. I've loved you since you first rose from the bed in Cois Greta Park, determined to make the most of your situation for the sake of Bernard. From the moment you confessed that in the darkness of night, I knew I loved you, not the boy from my childhood who indulged my rebellions and cast me sultry smiles on the bank of the lake, but you, the grown man you've become, the devoted father, determined leader, and passionate lover. You're the strongest and bravest man I know, Duncan."

Angling back, he sneaked a finger beneath her chin and lifted her face to meet his. Duncan pressed his lips to hers, relishing the feel of her soft flesh and inhaling her lavender scent. When he leaned back, he paused, taking in every sense around him.

"Mary. Brace yourself." His eyes meeting those of his loves, he stretched out one leg and wriggled his toes. "I can feel my right foot."

She framed his face with her hands.

"Come here, enchantress," Duncan said.

In a whirl, he scooped her into his arms and twirled her once more around the fountain.

Epilogue

December 1806
Ten Years Later

The Red Drawing Room of Lyonn Manor was in chaos. Children raced about the room, screeching in delight. Parents chattered, their voices raised above the din. From time to time, a dog barked, and a bird squawked.

The Duke and Duchess of Annick hosted their annual holiday party — family only, of course. Frost coated the lawn outside, but inside, the hearth fire roared and crackled.

Mary stood at the window with her sister-in-law Miranda, watching Duncan and Bernard with an Arabian, the youngest foal of Bucephalus, and Bernard's gift for surviving his first term at Eton. At fourteen, the boy was already nearly as tall as Duncan with promises of being taller. His limbs were as gangly as ever, but his curls would win the ladies one day, or so Mary teased him. As they watched, Theo, now thirteen, ran across the lawn to see the horse. Although not a horse lover like his cousin, Theo was inseparable from Bernard, the two being best friends.

Miranda turned to Mary, talking over the noise in the room. "At least your girls are all under ten. My

Emma is already begging for a come-out. Wants to go to London, she says. Only fifteen and already has a head for boys and balls. 'Don't grow so fast!' I tell her. Alas, to no avail. Her heart is set on romance." She shook her head, then glanced over her shoulder at her girls, Sophie, Emma, and Olivia, all gossiping by the pianoforte across the room.

"The trip into Scotland will do her good," Mary said.

"I agree. She can't possibly get into trouble with her grandparents as chaperones. They'll spend six months in the highlands visiting Georgina's family. I'll feel at ease with her away from the village boys."

"Already has her eye on someone?"

"Five of them, more like," Miranda said with a laugh.

The two turned from the window just as Sebastian and Lizbeth's son Cuthbert and their daughter Colette dumped a bucket of wet snow on their fifteen-year-old sister Freya. Shrieking, her hair matted to her face and the shoulders of her dress ruined, Freya ran after them, Charlotte in hot pursuit, shouting about ruining a Persian rug.

"Now *there's* someone with a head for boys," Mary said. "My cousin tells me that Freya has her eye on a boy in Yorkshire, a neighbor of Lord Pickering."

"Yorkshire?" Miranda questioned. "What would she be doing in Yorkshire?"

"They have an estate there, one of Sebastian's earldoms. My cousin also has a business deal with the Marquess of Pickering, some sort of canal that travels from Northumberland through the Pickering march in the moors to ship the coal from Sebastian's mine.

They frequent Yorkshire every few months." Mary eyed her children. "I'm so thankful my girls are too young for boys."

Mary's eldest daughter Kitty was nine and followed Cousin Olivia everywhere. Mary spied her trying to sneak into the trio of Miranda's girls at the pianoforte. Grace, eight, and Penelope, seven, Mary's two youngest daughters, were playing a game with Sebastian and Lizbeth's twin girls, eight-year-olds Ishtar and Isis. Lizbeth and Charlotte's father, Mr. Cuthbert Trethow, was overseeing the game, apparently losing from what Mary could tell by the squeals of the girls. Mary's son, Edmund, only five and the youngest in the room, was attempting to talk his grandmama into letting him sit on her lap. Catherine was in turn attempting to teach him to sit like a proper young man and heir to a baronetcy.

Charlotte and Drake's other two boys, Thomas and Hayden, were showing Lilith and Walter's two children, Benjamin and Jane, how to call the cockatoo named Captain Henry to them. They were having rotten luck if Mary could judge from Ben and Jane's unimpressed expressions.

Having given up on his grandmama, Edmund headed for the fireplace where Lilith's dog Jasper was curled on the rug, attempting to rest his aged bones. The dog was ancient and being tormented by Duncan's wolfhound Fergus, who was determined to have a fellow playmate. Mary was about to walk over to stop Edmund from turning Jasper's ears into bird wings when she saw Jasper's tail thumping on the rug.

Bernard and Theo rushed into the room, sending the door *thunking* into the wall behind it. Duncan swaggered in behind them, an apologetic expression after hearing the door make contact. After all these years and four naturally born children, Mary's heart still fluttered to see her husband. His coffee-brown hair was grey at the temples, though he was only six and thirty. It made him look distinguished, Mary thought.

"Did you see me?" Bernard asked in his baritone voice. His question was asked to the room at large. "Theron is a beauty! And he's mine!"

"The horse is grand," Theodore said, taking long strides to his father. "I want an Arabian. Will Uncle Duncan's horse sire one for me, too?"

"That's something you'll need to ask Uncle Duncan. But need I remind you, you don't like horses?" Drake howled with laughter.

"I do now." Theo waved over Bernard to help convince his father. "Did you see the horse, Grandmama? I want one!"

Duncan made his way to Mary. Miranda excused herself to join Quinn and Sean in their conversation with Lizbeth and Lizbeth's aunt Hazel.

Sneaking a kiss to Mary's cheek, Duncan leaned his shoulder against the wall and wrapped an arm around Mary's shoulders. She sidled closer to him, tucking her side against his hard frame.

"I take it he enjoyed his surprise," Mary said.

"Understatement of the year. I believe we have an enterprising horseman on our hands. He's already making training plans."

"Like father, like son." Mary pinched Duncan's side until he laughed and dodged her. "You missed poor Freya being doused in snow by her siblings."

"Ah. That would explain the shouting match I heard coming from the stairs. And speaking of the devil…" He nodded to the open door as a newly changed Freya marched into the room, head held high.

Hazel said loudly enough for all to hear, "Be sure to tell young Samuel about being iced."

Freya's cheeks turned a rosy pink. Mary covered her mouth to hide her laughter. The teasing began, all started by Hazel. The children — little devils, the lot of them — started singing songs of wedding bells between Freya and Lord Pickering's neighbor, the young Samuel. If it were not all so funny, Mary would feel sorry for Freya, who was a shy girl, even if a bit stubborn.

"Shall we join them?" Duncan asked, tugging Mary forward.

With a nod, she walked arm in arm with her husband to join the family. As they arrived to the sitting area by the hearth, Hazel stood to embrace Freya, who was red-faced and close to tears.

"Come now, sweetie," Hazel said, winking at Lizbeth and Sebastian. "Auntie Hazel meant no harm. I'll have you marry for love and no other reason. And not until you're five and thirty, at least."

Freya laughed at that remark and asked, "Like you? You married for love."

"Of course, my dear. There was no love greater than that between myself and Lord Collingwood, God rest his soul."

Mr. Cuthbert Trethow cleared his throat. "Oi! I beg to differ. The love between myself and my Elizabeth knew no bounds. No love greater — harrumph!" He smiled at his sister in good humor. "In fact," he said, looking around to make sure all heard, "I loved her so much, I was disinherited for it. Top that, sister!"

"Disinher — what is this nonsense?" Hazel said, returning to her seat. "Is *that* what Papa told you? Is *that* why the two of you had a falling out? Oh, dear boy, you were disinherited the moment Papa decided Lord Collingwood's son should be my betrothed. He must have told you that tale to cover his own embarrassment for disinheriting his fourteen-year-old son."

Cuthbert crossed his arms. "Poppycock. I was threatened disinheritance if I married Lizzie. The entailment was a threat."

Hazel shook her head. "Have we never spoken about this?"

"I never did because I thought it would embarrass you."

"And now who's embarrassed, hmm? Papa lied, Cuthbert. It was part of the bribery he used to ensnare Baron Collingwood."

Mary's cousin, Lilith, took a seat, her eyes flitting from her husband Walter to her mother-in-law Hazel. "Bribery? And here I thought you and Harold married for true love."

Hazel winked at everyone gathered around. "If you believed everything you heard, you'd be too gullible for your own good. Harold was my true love, all right. If souls have mates, he was mine. But not at first."

Freya kneeled on the floor before Hazel. Mary and Duncan took seats next to Charlotte and Drake. While the children continued their games and gossip, the adults gathered around Hazel and Cuthbert.

"Tell us, Aunt Hazel," Freya pleaded.

"Yes, do," Charlotte said. "You've said for years it was a love match."

"And it was," said Hazel. "Only I was the last to know. My father and my future father-in-law had been friends since childhood with plans to unite their children. Baron Collingwood had other plans when the time came, his eye on another girl for his son. My father wasn't bothered until I was nearly embroiled in scandal concerning another young gentleman who shall not be named." She pressed her hand to her chest. "Oh, yes. Shocking, I know. *Me* involved in scandal? Never, you say! 'Tis true! Or almost. Until Papa became desperate to marry me off in haste before scandal could spread. Papa had to sweeten the deal for the unrelenting Baron Collingwood to marry his son to me, much to both Harold's and my protests, for we did not get on."

As the family leaned in to hear Hazel and Cuthbert's tales of true love, scandal, and disinheritance, Mary smiled at Duncan who winked back at her. Looking around the room, Mary knew the deepest happiness of her life. This was, after all, what she had always wanted—a home filled with family and the laughter of children.

A Note from the Author

Dear Reader,

Thank you for reading this book. Supporting indie writers who brave self-publishing is important and appreciated. I hope you'll continue reading my novels, as I have many more titles to come. To learn more about the era, traditions, etiquette, and more, consider visiting my research blog, a new post added every one to three months: www.paullettgolden.com/bookresearch.

I humbly request you review this book with an honest opinion in as many venues as possible, be it Goodreads, Amazon, or otherwise.

One way to support writers you've enjoyed reading, indie or otherwise, is to share their work with friends, family, book clubs, etc. Lend books, share books, exchange books, recommend books, and gift books, be it personally, to a library, in a Free Little Library, or to a secondhand bookshop. If you especially enjoyed a writer's book, lend it to someone to read in case they might find a new favorite author in the book you've shared.

Connect with me online:
www.paullettgolden.com
www.facebook.com/paullettgolden
www.instagram.com/paullettgolden
www.twitter.com/paullettgolden

You'll also find me at such places as Goodreads, Bookbub, Amazon's Author Central, and LibraryThing.

All the best,
Paullett Golden

If you enjoyed *The Colonel and The Enchantress*, read on for a sneak peek of the next book in The Enchantresses.

The Heir and The Enchantress

Teaser from 2020 edition

August 1754
Cornwall

The coup of the year was the party at the Longfirth estate. Miss Hazel Trethow pinched her cheeks in the foyer mirror. This would be *her* coup if she had her way. And she would have her way.

Her curls assessed, her bosom primped, her rouge heightened, she headed for the drawing room. As soon as the door opened, a babble of voices cut the foyer's silence. The hostess, Miss Agnes Longfirth, sat near the double doors with her friends, all tittering and fanning themselves. A quick look around the room revealed a gaggle of girls but no gentlemen. Hazel's heart sank. Had they declined the invitation?

"Hazel!" Agnes rose from her chair in greeting.

"Oh, Hazel, they've *all* agreed to come" said one of the women.

"Even *him*," said Agnes.

Kissing her friend's cheek, Hazel took her seat in the circle. With deft hands, she fluffed the skirt of her *robe à l'anglaise* to ensure the outline of her hoops showed to advantage.

The party was no ordinary party. Agnes' overbearing parents were traveling the continent, having left her in the capable hands of the governess who, as luck would have it, was in love with the gardener and willing to make a deal with her charge that Agnes could host a party in her parents' absence on the condition the governess could spend the week undisturbed in the gardener's cottage.

Agnes looked about her. "While none of our esteemed guests have arrived, I'm positive they will. The butler will escort the gentlemen here as they arrive, and we will greet each with all the delight our fair bosoms have in store."

The ladies looked one to the other, giggling with accelerated fanning.

"Once we've claimed our gentleman for the party," Agnes continued, "we may spend the remainder of the week in his company, uninhibited by guardians or parents. At last, we can all *live*. Whoever thought up this ridiculousness of chaperones should perish in a duel."

"But what of the butler?" voiced one of the girls.

Agnes waved a hand. "Don't worry about him. I caught him in the pantry with a scullery maid this summer. He won't breathe a word of our transgressions and will do all our bidding."

The honored guests of the occasion so happened to be gentlemen, rakes to be precise. One such gentleman was the love of Hazel's life. Granted, she had never met him. But everyone knew of him. And she was determined to have him, one way or another. Anthony Faldo, Viscount Brooks.

Her lips ached to know the pleasure of Lord Brooks. Should all proceed as planned, Hazel would long at last have her first kiss.

About the Author

Celebrated for her complex characters, realistic con-
flicts, and sensual portrayal of love, Paullett Golden
writes historical romance for intellectuals. Her novels,
set primarily in Georgian England, challenge the
genre's norm by starring characters loved for their
imperfections and idiosyncrasies. The writing aims
for historical immersion into the social mores and
nuances of Georgian England. Her plots explore
human psyche, mental and physical trauma, and personal convictions. Her stories show love overcoming
adversity. Whatever our self-doubts, *love will out*.

Paullett Golden completed her post-graduate
work at King's College London, studying Classic
British Literature. Her Ph.D. is in Composition and
Rhetoric, her M.A. in British Literature from the

Enlightenment through the Victorian era, and her B.A. in English. Her specializations include creative writing and professional writing. She has served as a University Professor for nearly three decades and is a seasoned keynote speaker, commencement speaker, conference presenter, workshop facilitator, and writing retreat facilitator.

As an ovarian cancer survivor, she makes each day count, enjoying an active lifestyle of Spartan racing, powerlifting, hiking, antique car restoration, drag racing, butterfly gardening, competitive shooting, and gaming. Her greatest writing inspirations, and the reasons she chose to write in the clean historical romance genre, are Jane Austen and Charlotte Brontë.

Connect online
paullettgolden.com
Facebook.com/paullettgolden
Twitter.com/paullettgolden
Instagram.com/paullettgolden